MORE PRAISE FOR *LAKE BURNTSHORE*

"*Lake Burntshore* is a summer camp story like no other. Ambitious in theme and impressively effective in narrative, this novel brilliantly unpacks the extensive harmful impacts of colonialism with nuance and care. From Palestine to Ontario cottage country, Aaron Kreuter deftly gives agency to and celebrates the humanity of the people of the land. To anyone in a diaspora that's struggled under oppression for generations, this story hits very close to home. By honouring the land and the people fighting for recognition and justice, *Lake Burntshore* is both timely and timeless.

—WAUBGESHIG RICE, author of *Moon of the Crusted Snow*

"Funny, frank, and sexy, *Lake Burntshore* is a richly felt examination of the Jewish diaspora. Aaron Kreuter's storytelling will transport you to your coziest, most carefree memories while also holding up a mirror to the adult you've become. This story really is a summer to remember."

—GABE LIEDMAN, writer and comedian

"*Lake Burntshore* hooks you from the beginning. Aaron Kreuter is unafraid to examine our views of displacement and genocide and our relationship with the land. A must-read!"

—CHRISTINA WONG, author of *Denison Avenue*

OTHER PRAISE

"What if the worldview you were raised in turns out to be monstrous? In the stories that form *Rubble Children*, Aaron Kreuter examines a Jewish community in flux, caught between its historical fealty to Israel and a growing awakening and resistance to it. *Rubble Children* is a book of great range: at once political, communitarian, empathetic, funny, revolutionary, touching, and hopeful. This is a work that is essential for our moment.

—SAEED TEEBI, author of *Her First Palestinian*

"Although *Rubble Children* is an important book given the current climate, it's Kreuter's characterization and storytelling abilities that make it a must-read. These are stories of growing, healing and understanding, powerfully told and skillfully wrought. History, culture, religion and politics play a part in each of these stories, but at the end of the day, it's the humanity of the characters, and the vagaries of their nature that makes Rubble Children such a compelling read.

—JEFF DUPUIS, *The Miramichi Reader*, August 10, 2024

"*You and Me, Belonging* is a dazzling debut. Sexy, biting, and sharp. Kreuter's prose is swift and clean. These stories are slyly funny while delivering a sucker punch to the heart. They are full of adventures and dashed dreams, art, sex, desire, and brawn. Brilliant."

—LISA MOORE, author of *Caught*

"In *You and Me, Belonging*, Aaron Kreuter captures our universal quest for belonging and meaning with great compassion and nuance. Told from a range of viewpoints, and spanning continents and decades, these beautifully conceived stories are at once boldly political and fiercely personal, and explore what it means to be young, Jewish, and North American in a messy, complex, and conflicted world."

—AYELET TSABARI, author of *The Best Place on Earth*

LAKE BURNTSHORE

ALSO BY AARON KREUTER

Fiction

Rubble Children: Seven and a Half Stories

You and Me, Belonging

Poetry

Shifting Baseline Syndrome

Arguments for Lawn Chairs

Non-Fiction

Leaving Other People Alone: Diaspora, Zionism, and Palestine in Contemporary Jewish Fiction

LAKE BURNTSHORE

A NOVEL

AARON KREUTER

Published by ECW Press
665 Gerrard Street East
Toronto, Ontario, Canada M4M 1Y2
416-694-3348 / info@ecwpress.com

Editor for the Press: Jen Sookfong Lee
Cover design and artwork: Ian Sullivan Cant
Map illustrations: Alysha Dawn

LIBRARY AND ARCHIVES CANADA CATALOGUING IN PUBLICATION

Title: Lake Burntshore : a novel / Aaron Kreuter.

Names: Kreuter, Aaron, author.

Identifiers: Canadiana (print) 20240516311 | Canadiana (ebook) 20240516338

ISBN 978-1-77041-763-2 (softcover)
ISBN 978-1-77852-369-4 (ePub)
ISBN 978-1-77852-370-0 (PDF)

Subjects: LCGFT: Novels.

Classification: LCC PS8621.R485 L35 2025 | DDC C813/.6—dc23

This book is funded in part by the Government of Canada. *Ce livre est financé en partie par le gouvernement du Canada.* We acknowledge the support of the Canada Council for the Arts. *Nous remercions le Conseil des arts du Canada de son soutien.* We would like to acknowledge the funding support of the Ontario Arts Council (OAC) and the Government of Ontario for their support. We also acknowledge the support of the Government of Ontario through the Ontario Book Publishing Tax Credit, and through Ontario Creates.

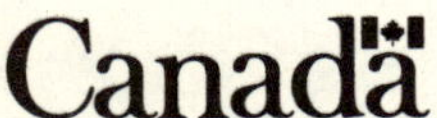

Canada Council for the Arts
Conseil des arts du Canada

PRINTED AND BOUND IN CANADA

PRINTING: MARQUIS 5 4 3 2 1

For Steph,

Always

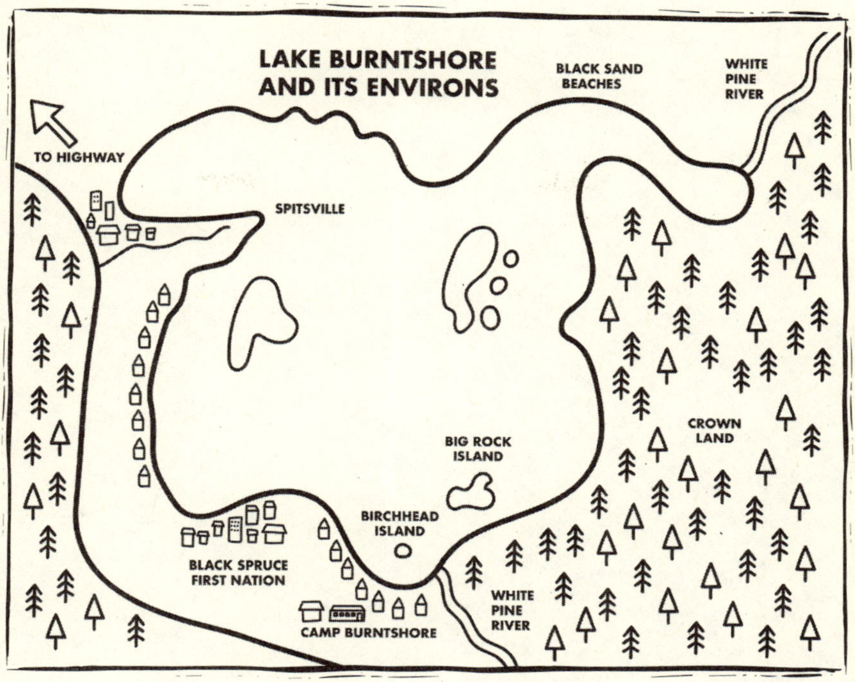

LAKE BURNTSHORE AND ITS ENVIRONS

BLACK SAND BEACHES
WHITE PINE RIVER
TO HIGHWAY
SPITSVILLE
BIG ROCK ISLAND
CROWN LAND
BIRCHHEAD ISLAND
BLACK SPRUCE FIRST NATION
WHITE PINE RIVER
CAMP BURNTSHORE

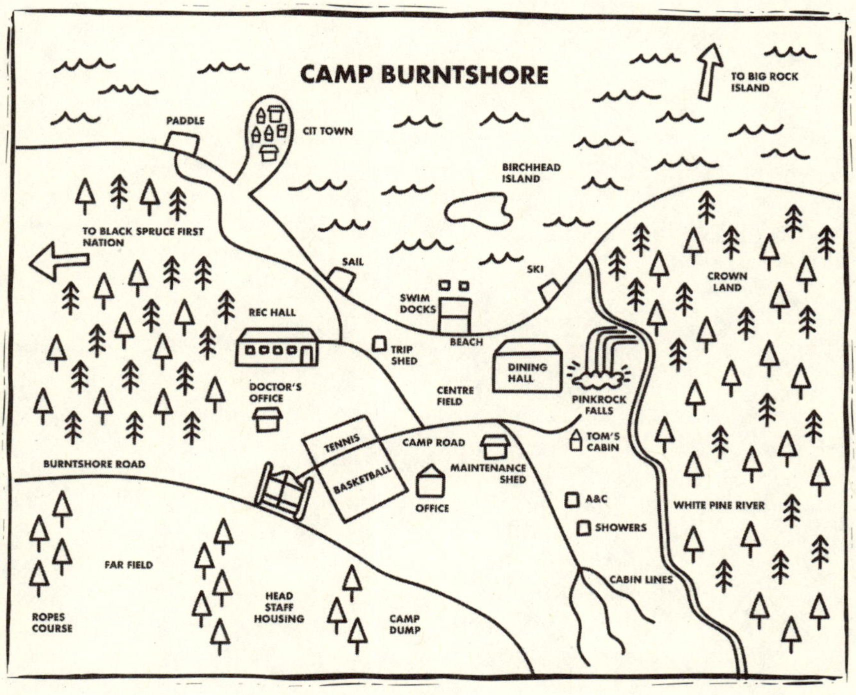

CAMP BURNTSHORE

TO BIG ROCK ISLAND
PADDLE
CIT TOWN
BIRCHHEAD ISLAND
TO BLACK SPRUCE FIRST NATION
SAIL
SKI
SWIM DOCKS
CROWN LAND
REC HALL
BEACH
TRIP SHED
DINING HALL
DOCTOR'S OFFICE
CENTRE FIELD
PINKROCK FALLS
TENNIS
BASKETBALL
CAMP ROAD
TOM'S CABIN
BURNTSHORE ROAD
MAINTENANCE SHED
OFFICE
A&C
WHITE PINE RIVER
SHOWERS
FAR FIELD
CABIN LINES
HEAD STAFF HOUSING
ROPES COURSE
CAMP DUMP

CONTENTS

PART 2

PROLOGUE

Leaving Brett's cabin and crossing the road back to camp, the night sky charged with stars, Ruby couldn't believe what had just happened. Could Brett seriously be trying to buy all the Crown land across the river? Brett's gall, his greed, his arrogance, his smirking face as he'd told her, left her shocked, shook, wounded. The other things he had said, the other things he admitted to, would, as the hours passed, also sneak up on her, but for now, Ruby fixated on the land. She was walking through centre field, almost at the dining hall, the lake marmoreal in rising moonlight. Ruby could already picture the disgusted expression on Etai's face as she told him. Etai's big, beaming face. A cloud passed over the moon. The lake rippled. Ruby went up the dining hall stairs.

What a summer it was turning out to be.

PART 1

SPRING 2013

By the time Yonatan pulled into camp, it was late evening. He turned off the gravel road and drove right up to the cabin that had been his summer home for the past six years. He dropped the gate of his truck, but after a moment of staring at the bed's contents, he lit a cigarette and walked across the road, through the camp, and towards the lake. He sat at the shore. Early May and the sun was destroying itself on the pine trees, orange and yellow solar yolk splaying through the combed clouds. There were zero bugs. For the next few weeks, he would be alone. He took a drag. The lake lapped the rocks at his feet, silver and black, moving and static, alive and hypnotic. What secrets hid in its watery world? Yonatan stubbed the cigarette out on the rocks, pocketed the butt. The sun was gone; soon it would be dark.

There was a lot of work to do.

The next morning, he did a walkthrough of all the buildings, cranking on the electricity, checking for dead animals or living ones, making a checklist of everything that needed to be done. At night he put his cabin together, plugging in his stereo, unpacking his clothes, unrolling the worn rug he brought up every summer over the cold wooden floor. He cooked most of his meals on the charcoal barbecue he set up on his porch. He mowed centre field. He mowed new field. He recaulked two windows in the dining hall. He painted a wall in the infirmary that had been water-damaged over the winter, replaced a window. He oiled the lawn mower. He laid many ant traps. On the third evening, having not seen another human being since he left Toronto, he drove his truck to The Patio and drank a pitcher of beer on the eponymous patio with the locals before driving back to camp slowly, his brights on, the windows down, a cigarette tipped out of his mouth. The stars were out, the piney air was near ice, he was utterly aware of how utterly alone he was. Well, that would change soon, he thought, laughing.

A week later the black flies arrived. He was standing on centre field trying to get the stalled lawn mower to start when they seemed to rise up from the ground like smoke.

David Margolis joined Yonatan in early June. Even with Yonatan working non-stop through most of May, there was still plenty to do. Together, they lugged the water fountains out of the dining hall's basement, installed them, turned on the water. They set up the tennis courts, the basketball courts. They sawed off dangerous-looking tree limbs on the oaks lining main road. Yonatan enlisted Margolis's help in weeding the garden he kept behind his cabin (started five years ago, Yonatan loved seeing what he could coax out of the ground each season). They mopped and scrubbed the kitchen, where they would now go most mornings to make pancakes and eggs, to toss a football or a Frisbee over the shiny workstations and boat-sized mixers. At night they methodically smoked weed in every cabin, building, field, firepit, road, and shore of the camp. The loons arrived from Florida, flapping their wings on the water in ecstasies of return. Walking across the road to Yonatan's cabin one night, they discovered three dead snakes in a pile, their necks bloodied. Tom came up for a weekend with Jenna and the dogs to see how everything was shaping up, if anything needed serious repair or replacement. Brett was still off backpacking in South America; Yonatan did not miss his presence.

The afternoon after Tom and Jenna left, Yonatan and Margolis took the twenty-foot ladder and the Shop-Vac to the rec hall to clean the spiderwebs from the rafters. They took turns climbing to the top of the ladder, Shop-Vac in one hand, nozzle of the vacuum in the other, the forty-foot orange extension cord angled from the wall outlet to the swinging, sucking belly of the vacuum. "Tom really doesn't have to pay you for that extra month before I get here. We could easily handle all of this work," Margolis said as Yonatan, arm outstretched, nozzled the wooden beams of the roof. He was yelling to be heard over the whir of the engine. Dust floated languidly through the large, empty space of the rec hall, the bare, lifeless stage, the old piano, the beat-up drum kit.

Yonatan kept vacuuming. Margolis, at twenty, was a decade younger than Yonatan, still with all his hair and lacking a beer gut; Yonatan was already head of maintenance when Margolis had been a rambunctious camper. But this was his third summer joining Yonatan at pre-pre-camp, and they had a loose, affable relationship. They never talked about anything serious, though, and Yonatan hoped they never would.

"He knows that," Yonatan said eventually. "He mostly does it as a favour. Six months at the warehouse, six up here. It's the perfect arrangement." Yonatan was well aware that there was no "mostly" about it: his place at Camp Burntshore, his role, was entirely due to Tom's largesse. And what *was* his role? It was to keep camp running, to keep the facilities maintained, to stay out of trouble. That last one was no longer a problem; as far as Yonatan was concerned, his days of trouble, especially camp trouble, were over, something he had aged out of. It was up to others to make trouble now, like Margolis, stocky and cocky Margolis—who, with his face-first attitude, impenetrable confidence, and dash of subversive intelligence (just a dash!), kept trouble around him at all times. For five summers now, Yonatan merely observed, lived vicariously, kept the toilets plumbed and the windows airtight. This summer, he imagined, would be no different.

Not that he was going to explain any of that to Margolis. He kept vacuuming: it was immensely satisfying to suck in the thick, dusty cobwebs. It was like creation in reverse, making clean what was unclean. Yonatan felt like he could do this forever, even with the weight of the gently swinging vacuum pulling on his arm.

"Man, you live the life," Margolis said from below. "Building furniture in that warehouse all winter, up at camp for the rest of the year. It's the fucking dream! Okay, dude, come down, it's my turn!"

The days were getting longer; soon they would be at their longest. The spring wildflowers were raucous along the roadside: black-eyed Susan, Queen Anne's lace, buttercup, purple cress; they were eating strawberries right from the stem. Summer was hurtling towards them. Soon the head staff would arrive, followed days later by the rest of the counselors and speciality staff. And days after that, the kids, the cause and the reason for this place carved out of the woods fifty years ago by Tom Balter's father on the south side of Lake Burntshore, a medium-sized lake decently built up on its west side with cottages, the town, the Black Spruce First Nation reserve, and the camp, undeveloped Crown land on the rest, the black sand beaches that gave the lake its name along the northeastern shore, accessible only by boat and trail. For now, Yonatan and David played tennis, grilled steaks, dropped bug bombs in the woods, made roaring fires spent passing bottles and joints and talking about the glory of past summers. Mornings, Yonatan would smoke his first cigarette on his porch, think about the precarious alchemy of camp: you put these buildings like this, the swim dock like that, bring together these particular people in these particular cabins, arrange their day thusly, feed them specific food and tell them specific stories, condense time and space to within a hundred metres of the lake, and from that, camp is born. Every summer the ingredients differed slightly, and every summer it worked. Would it be possible to throw something into the mix that would toss the whole complicated balance off-kilter? Yonatan supposed it was, though in his fifteen-plus years at Burntshore he had yet to see it.

The morning the head staff were due to arrive, Yonatan and Margolis went for a naked swim. The swim docks were still piled beside the swim shed; it would take more than four hands and four legs to put those beasts in. They swam fast and loud for Birchhead Island, scampered out onto the hard, hot rocks. They were tan, fit, relaxed, almost entirely out of weed. They lay back on their elbows, breathing deep, looking back at the shore, the buildings beyond.

The camp was nearly ready.

CHAPTER 1

THE BUSES ARRIVE; DEBS KEEPS EVERYTHING RUNNING SMOOTHLY; TOM GIVES A SPEECH; GLAZER SMOKES A JOINT

Deborah Glassman stood by the side of main road, clipboard in hand, keys flashing on her wide hips, orange curls fighting against a hopeless hair tie. Behind her were the tennis courts, in front of her the basketball courts. Main gate, fifty feet to her right, was wide open, a mouth awaiting its meal. Any minute now a line of chartered yellow school buses was going to stop in front of her and 316 children would be disgorged: 316 scared, excited, funny, horrifying, mean, talented, not-so-talented, introverted, extroverted, homesick, horny, short, tall, thin, fat, Jewish, not-Jewish (a tiny, dedicated minority), white, Black, Asian, surprising children. And it was up to Deborah—Debbie to her friends, Deb to her parents, Debs to everybody who knew her as Camp Burntshore's program director—to orchestrate their arrival. It was a part of her job, that, like all parts, she took extremely seriously.

The whole year led to this moment; Debs knew that the first day of camp sets the tone for the entire summer. As she put it today at the post-breakfast staff meeting, she wanted a very successful, very organized first day. Most of her staff were lined up behind her along the dirt road that continued on to their left, severing centre field and the lakefront from the rest of the camp before terminating at the kitchen's loading doors, wearing their staff shirts—green for cabin staff, grey for speciality, black for head staff. It was easy for Debs to spot the first years, nervous for their inauguration on the receiving ends of the buses. The head staff, calm and relaxed, joking around, their own clipboards in hand, ready to corral the kids into their units and then into their cabins. And all the staff in-between. Some of the guys feigned boredom; the girls chatted quietly. These were the people through whom Debs would make the Camp Burntshore summer of 2013 one of the most memorable times of the campers' lives.

Debs saw the first bus make the turn into main gate, dust pluming in its wake.

"Okay! Here they come!"

After the organized chaos of the unloading, the kids were led to the basketball courts by unit, where their knapsacks and toolboxes would be searched by the assigned staff. Ostensibly for peanut butter—Camp Burntshore: proudly peanut free since 1998!—but for the older kids it was also the first screen for pot or alcohol or contraband cellphones. Debs was helping some forlorn little eight-year-olds, one of whom was crying big juicy tears, when she saw out of the corner of her eye that something was going on with Daniel Glazer—second-year staff, real smartass, almost didn't get hired back—and Scharfy—counselor in training, a good kid, excellent sailor, younger brother to Eve (staff for four years); since last summer he had grown a head of ratty dreadlocks. Daniel was talking harshly. Scharfy looked terrified. Debs should find out what that's about. She was about to write a reminder down on her clipboard when someone tugged her sleeve.

It was Yonatan. "Raskin called. He's with the kids from Ottawa. The van got a flat outside Petawawa. They're waiting for CAA."

"Okay, keep me posted." Debs looked at the pen in her hand, hovering over her clipboard, jotted down *Raskin—Petawawa—flat*. "Can you help out with the duffels in the rec hall?" she asked Yonatan. She didn't hear his response though—one of the buses was backing up, beeping shrilly, much too close to some ten-year-olds who were watching another kid flick a yo-yo. She ran off.

For the next two hours, the usual first-day stuff, nothing too serious, nothing Debs hadn't encountered before. A missing knapsack. A little girl looking for her older brother. The Farberman twins were unhappy with their cabin. In the rec hall the Tripping, Ski, and Sail staff were helping campers locate their duffel bags, which had arrived the day before and were loosely organized by cabin. Older campers walked out of the rec hall like a row of ants, duffel bags on their bent backs, the staff lugging the younger kids' bags. Debs's walkie was squawking—they needed her in the kitchen. One of the oven racks' wheels had popped. Leaving the kitchen, Debs saw Martin Gold and Ayelet Cho standing at the river in the woods. Both CITs. Martin lived in Montreal, Ayelet in Toronto; they had been together last year, but Debs was mildly surprised they had remained together through the year. They might be one of the camp relationships that makes it all the way; was a camp wedding in the offing? Casey Mustard was with his cabin, having them do calisthenics, the kids laughing and grunting with effort; now, there was a great counselor, already engaged, already making memories. Stephen Stolow was sitting with his guitar on the steps of his cabin. Tom's two dogs, Piper and Daisy, were running and playing, feeding off the first-day excitement.

Debs was on her way to dinner when Polina—one of the CIT staff, at Burntshore on-and-off since she was eight, her parents met here in the '70s, her short hair dyed blonde—ran up to her. "Tom caught Glazer smoking a joint behind the trip shed."

"What? Oh, fuck." She pushed her clipboard into Polina's hands, ran towards head office. As she ran, she noted that that was the first *fuck* of the summer. She'd have to mark it in her notebook.

As she ran, she also planned. The first day and already a casualty. Okey dokey. Glazer was the junior staff in cabin 12; could David Margolis run the cabin without him? Maybe she could switch a speciality staff into 12 as an extra sleep-in, try to hire somebody for second session.

Debs was almost at the head office. She could already hear Tom yelling.

After dinner—meatloaf and mashed potatoes, the same every first night—Tom stood up. It was time for his annual welcome speech. Tom was wearing his standard camp outfit: jeans, work boots, a flannel shirt that had a little extra first-day crispness. His full head of black hair newly cut, his handsomely weathered face calm, stern yet gentle, obviously used to being in control (not even Debs could tell that half an hour ago he'd been furious, firing Glazer barely twelve hours into the start of camp). Seasoned campers and staff knew the beats of the coming speech by heart; it was the same every year.

"I'm going to tell you two stories. Like all stories, they are deeply connected," Tom began, a professor introducing his lecture, radiating assuredness, knowledge, warmth. "The first story is about where we are right now, within a stone's throw of Lake Burntshore. The land we are sitting on is over three billion years old." The staff had been listening to Tom's speeches for all of pre-camp, so most tuned him out. The younger and new campers hung on his every word, entranced by this adult who was unlike any other adult they knew. "For thousands of years, above us right now would have been two kilometres of solid ice. The lake we all enjoy so much every summer started off life as a large crack in the hard basement rock formed by mountains hundreds and hundreds of millions of years ago. A shallow sea deposited sediment into the crack, and, much more recently, the glaciers scoured it out, leaving us not only this lake but thousands of others throughout Ontario. Where we sit right now, where we will sleep and eat and swim and play and learn and make lifelong connections over the next eight weeks, was, believe it or not, once near the equator, covered by volcanic ash. It once was a mountain range rivalling the Himalayas. It was once a shallow sea of long-extinct animals, fish with enormous eyes, crabs with pincers the size of Dobermans. It has been part of four different continents. Every rock, stone, and pebble of Burntshore carries this deep history of the planet within it. The rocks don't forget. As a famous geologist once said, 'The mind grows giddy gazing so far back into the abyss of time.'"

Debs scanned the long tables of children and teenagers. Every few summers, Tom's talk of ancient ice and bug-eyed fish caused a younger kid to cry, precipitated nightmares. The kitchen staff—Anishinaabeg from the Black Spruce First Nation reserve down the road—had come to the kitchen doorway to listen to Tom's speech. Cindy Georgetown, the head chef, was standing behind her staff with a massive ladle in her hand, her black and grey hair in a tight bun, the same smirk on her big, expressive face whenever she listened to Tom lecture, pontificate, or excoriate. Big and competent and boisterous, Cindy gave Tom a hard time, especially in front of her staff, but they were good friends.

Tom rolled up the sleeves of his flannel, revealing sturdy forearms covered in black hair. "Now, for the second story. A long time ago, I was a pharmacist. Hard to believe, I know. Well, mixing pills grew thin very quickly, but at least I had my summers here. In my early forties, I was on a post-camp canoeing trip in the Peel Watershed with my oldest friends. Do you know the Peel Watershed? It's a massive, undeveloped, complete ecosystem of mountains and valleys and rivers in the Yukon. And rocks. Oh, the rocks. Well, I'm here to tell you that it was there, in the Peel Watershed, that I fell in love with those rocks. As we were paddling past monolithic outcrops, I started repeating to myself: 'I will never take another rock for granted again. I will never be flippant towards rocks again.'" The entirety of the camp repeated this line with Tom a second time, the disaffected, the bored, those who claimed dislike for Tom and his dictatorial, zero-tolerance ways. It was a line that would be repeated throughout the summer, as it had been every summer since Tom returned from the Peel a changed man. "Well," Tom continued, smiling for the first time since taking the mic, "what did I do with my newfound appreciation for the older things on the planet? I went back to school. I got a PhD in geology. The rest, as they say, is deep history." Yes, Tom was now a practising geologist, an assistant professor at the University of Guelph. A practising geologist who spent his summers at Burntshore, as Debs's boss. As everybody's boss. "And that's what I want to tell you about camp. The land we are on is exceedingly old, yet here we can be new. We can make new decisions, face new challenges, decide who we want to be."

Debs, who was standing beside the head staff table, her clipboard to her chest, absent-mindedly nodding along to Tom, heard it before anybody else did: the sound of a van pulling up in front of the dining hall. Raskin. The kids from Ottawa had arrived. Debs slipped out. Tom was still talking, describing the geological processes that led to Burntshore's famous black sand beaches.

Raskin was standing beside the van, helping the Ottawa kids pile out. The kids looked excited, nervous, exhausted, elated, a little dirty, ready with a story for their friends and cabinmates during the forthcoming bonanzic first-night splurge of candy and laughter. The sun was low and large over the choppy lake, the world brilliant amber.

"Don't worry about your bags for now," Debs said. "Go on into the dining hall. Go on. Tom's nearly finished his welcome speech, but you can grab some meatloaf while it's still hot."

When the kids' backs were turned, she gave Raskin a big, open-mouth kiss.

"I'm ovulating," she breathed into his ear.

Raskin pulled back. He had two days of stubble on his normally clean face. His brown eyes gleamed. "Yes, boss," he said.

Debs turned to head back into the dining hall. It was nearly time for her to take the mic, to give the usual first-day warnings, to be serious and practical after Tom's flights-of-fancy: always listen to your counselors;

meals are at eight o'clock, twelve-thirty, and six-thirty; don't leave your cabin after lights out; remember that this is bear country; never go to the river unsupervised.

"Turn that engine off," she said over her shoulder.

"Hey, Debs." Debs was making her night rounds, visiting cabins, making sure everybody was settling in, starting to put faces to names for the new kids. She had a meeting with her head staff in twenty minutes in the staff lounge. The air was warm and sweet. She turned. It was Ruby Shacter. Fifth-year staff, in unit 2, her kids—who have had her as counselor for three years, since they were nine—adored her, her mother was a camper in the early '80s, she was very political, could have been unit head this year if she wanted but preferred to remain regular staff. Ah. Glazer was her cousin.

"What happened with Daniel?" she asked.

Debs clicked through the possible answers. She could lie, say something came up at home. But, no, that wouldn't fly, and what would be the point? She could tell her she'll hear at the weekly staff meeting. No, probably not the best choice. As usual, honesty was the clear course.

"He got caught smoking a joint."

Ruby laughed. "What a fucking idiot. His dad is going to kill him!"

Debs shrugged. "Tom also caught him with a bag of about thirty pre-rolled joints."

Ruby blinked. "Where is he?"

"In Tom's office. He'll be gone by lights out."

"What a fucking idiot," Ruby repeated. Debs could see that Ruby's diagnosis of Glazer wasn't exactly a new thought for her.

With that, Debs wholeheartedly agreed.

The sun was gone. The kids were safely in their cabins; bunk nights were commencing. The first day was officially over. If Debs concentrated, she could feel the nervousness, excitement, joy that was threaded complexly between bunk beds, cabins, trees, trails. She stood in the middle of cabin line 1, took it in. Her own first day of camp was almost thirty years ago, but it was easy enough to bring it sluicing back: the newness, the smell of the woods, the fear and desire, the startlingly fast, startlingly efficacious sensation that this was the best place on Earth, and it was hers. After that first day, there had been seven years as a camper, one as a CIT, four as staff, five as head staff (during which time she got her joint degree in Jewish programming and sociology from Brandeis), three years without Burntshore, and then two years as assistant program director and four as program director, and now here she was, at the beginning of another summer. If anybody could understand what the first night of camp meant to these kids—children who, like all children, want something to believe in, to belong to, to give their all for—it was Debs; for most of the children under her care, camp was that thing. She took a deep breath. She could hear the wind going through the pines. It was forecasted to be a hot week. What kind of summer it would be, only time would tell. Time, and her role as program director.

One day down.

CHAPTER 2

THE FIRST NIGHT; RUBY TELLS HER GIRLS A STORY; BUTTER LAKE; THE DOCKS; STOLOW GOES FOR A RUN

Ruby watched Debs walk away. Why would Glazer—that idiot—have a bag of pre-rolled joints on him? It made no sense! He and Ruby had split a half ounce for the summer, and it was safe in Ruby's toolbox. It made no sense. Guess it's my half ounce now, she thought. He must have confiscated the joints from a camper during the PB search or something . . . What a fucking idiot. She pictured him during pre-camp, those four bacchanalian days of boring workshops and debauched nights, standing knee deep in the river, completely naked, fucked out of his mind, his head back, a lit sparkler fireworking sharp and golden out of his pursed mouth. What'll he do with his summer now? His dad will definitely make him get a job. If he ever lets him leave his room. Ruby laughed. Uncle Joe was *not* going to take this well.

Ruby entered her cabin. The girls were all on their beds, taking a break from setting up their bunks, putting their clothes away, organizing their shelves. Empty duffel bags lay on the floor like shed skins from huge, fat snakes; by tomorrow they'd be stuffed under bunks, forgotten and ignored until it was time to go home. The cabin perked up when Ruby entered, reshuffled. Danielle Brown and Dawn Simons, Ruby's co-counselor and sleep-in, came out of the staff area. Ruby checked her watch; she hadn't realized it was so late. "Everybody brushed and ready for bed?" she said in greeting. The three staff members led the cabin through the first bedtime routine of the summer: roses and thorns, song of the night, lights out. The girls, however, were too excited to go to sleep.

"Ruby! Ruby! Are you and Phil still together?!"

"Ruby, your hair is so short!"

"Dawn, what do you think of Casey Mustard?"

"Danielle, can I show you my fancy stationery?"

"Ruby, can you tell us a story?"

"Sure!" Ruby sat on one of the girls' beds, Danielle on another. Dawn went back into the staff area. The cabin smelled like cedar, fresh laundry, shampoo, the tiniest hint of fear.

"Now, this story takes place a long time ago. A long time ago, there was a group of girls called the cabin 9 kick-asses—"

"That's our cabin!"

"June, shut up!"

"Anyways, the cabin 9 kick-asses had been wandering in the woods for forty years. They ate bugs, boiled plants for teas and soups, caught crayfish with their bare hands. They were looking for a place they could call home. They walked and walked and walked. They walked up a mountain. They walked across a valley. They walked through a forest of towering white pines, oak trees the size of the CN Tower. They walked until they couldn't walk anymore, and then they cut down some trees and built canoes with their own hands, and also paddles, and they paddled across a lake and down a river. Finally, after forty years of walking and paddling, walking and paddling, walking and paddling, they found the perfect spot. 'This, from now on, will be our home,' they said together. That spot was right here, on the shores of Lake Burntshore."

Ruby and Danielle stood up quietly. At least three of the girls were asleep. Ruby touched each bed as she made her way to the staff area at the back of the main cabin, in its own alcove. Dawn was already asleep, curled up in her Hudson's Bay Blanket. Danielle got into her bed, picked up her journal; her hair was still wet from the shower, the flowery smell of her shampoo filling the small space. Her tennis racquet wasn't hanging on the hook Ruby and Danielle had put in during pre-camp but was on Danielle's bed with her—in the craze of the first day she had still managed to fit in a game. Ruby went to her own bed, with its scratchy grey blankets and faded yellow sheets (the same yellow sheets she had brought to her very first summer at camp). On the shelf above her bed, beside her sweatshirts and sweatpants, she had four books: *Always Coming Home*, *The Apprenticeship of Duddy Kravitz*, a selected writings of Frantz Fanon, and *The Collected Stories* of Grace Paley. In the toolbox under her bed was the weed, a grinder, rolling papers, a small ceramic pipe, lighters, matches, hair ties, tampons, lip gloss, Vaseline, envelopes, and stamps. Even though there was nothing but a hanging sheet separating the staff quarters from the rest of the cabin, it felt private, adult, theirs. Ruby lay on her bed for ten minutes, her sandals still on, let her exhaustion swim on the back of her eyelids like deep-sea monsters, pushing herself up just before she fell into unconsciousness.

"Who'd you find to have a game with on the first day?" she said.

"Yonatan didn't have much going on." Danielle didn't look up from her journal.

"Who won?"

"I did. He has a great forehand, but I got him on the backhand returns. Phil came by looking for you."

Ruby scoffed. "I have nothing to say to him." A surge of angry energy lifted Ruby into itchy life. She jumped off her bed. "I'm going to the dining hall, want to come?"

"No thanks," Danielle said, biting her pen. "I'm in for the night. Oh. Fallon was here just before you came back."

Fallon, their unit head. Shit. Fallon and Ruby already barely got along. Fallon was only a year older but might as well be from another generation; where Ruby never accepted the status quo and loved camp for its difference from city life, Fallon was all about rules and boundaries and using camp as a springboard into her future career. Ruby not being in her cabin on the first night was definitely not going to inure Fallon to her this summer.

Ruby grabbed a hoodie off her shelf and left the cabin, walked down the well-worn path of cabin line 2, in and out of the aura of the lamp posts, crossed centre field, the grass crunching under her sandals, the lake black and bottomless, and went up the stairs and into the dining hall, which at night was a very different place than it was during the camper-focused day. Most of the older staff who weren't on cabin or night duty were there, drinking out of water bottles, playing guitar. There was a platter of grilled cheese on one of the tables—the staff snack, courtesy of Cindy.

They turned to Ruby, called her name, welcomed her.

She joined them.

An hour later, Cindy's voice cut through the din of thirty or so staff catching up, reminiscing, laughing. "Ha ha, here's hoping, Tom!" It sounded like Cindy was standing right next to the kitchen door.

Everybody reacted immediately to Cindy's warning, stuffing water bottles under sweatshirts, readjusting, decoupling.

The kitchen door swung open, and through it came Tom, a plate in his hand, Piper and Daisy excitedly running around him. The dogs weren't usually allowed in the dining hall, adding to the shock of Tom being there.

"Mind if I join you?" he asked. Ruby noticed the bottoms of his jeans were wet; the top two buttons of his green flannel were unbuttoned. His compact frame resounded with the accumulated assuredness of a lifetime of being the only adult in rooms full of teenagers.

He sat down on the same bench as Ruby. On his melamine plate was a grilled fish, whole, its one visible eye staring vacantly, a pile of grilled cheese stacked beside it.

"Catch of the day?" Stephen Stolow asked, his guitar in his lap.

"Just reeled her in this evening," Tom responded, deftly cracking open the fish. He ate silently, wielding his fork and knife with expert flourishes as he pulled the white flakey meat clear of the bones. Tom never came to the dining hall for staff snack; it was as unexpected as it was anxiety-inducing. The staff watched him eat. Barry Blum stopped dealing cards to Raskin and Phil (Ruby and Phil studiously ignoring each other all night). Ruby saw that Fischer was visibly drunk, swaying on a bench perpendicular to Tom's (Ruby also registered that Casey Mustard, who was the senior counselor in their cabin, must have taken cabin duty to let his second-year party for the first night). Fischer was still holding a water bottle of dark rum in his lap, his gel-slathered hair in uniform spikes. Fucking idiot. Did he want to get kicked out? Including Glazer, that would have to be a first night Burntshore record.

"Have I ever told you about Butter Lake?" Tom asked finally, wiping his mouth with a napkin as he surveyed his young employees. Nobody answered. Tom folded the napkin in half, in half again, sat back. Here comes a story, Ruby thought.

"This was about twenty years ago, when I was still in my PhD. A bunch of us would fly into a fishing lodge in Northern Ontario every spring for the trout fishing. One spring, we paddled two lakes over from the lodge and portaged—more like bushwhacked, the trail was so overgrown—into a third lake, Butter Lake it was called, that nobody had fished in decades. That first spring, we were pulling fifty-, sixty-pound trout out of the lake as if our lines were magnetic." Tom stopped, leaned forward, forked a piece of fish. Ruby saw that when Tom's head was down, Fischer took a swig from his water bottle. "Anyways, we loaded our canoes with fish, laughing with joy, and that night we ate til we were sick, drank a little too much wine." Tom sighed. "Butter Lake. It was like paradise. A deep, clear lake surrounded by high cliffs of beautifully banded gneiss. The next spring, as soon as we landed, what did we do? We paddled over to Butter. The same the next spring, and the next."

"Aren't there laws about how much fish you can pull out of a lake per day?" Phil asked. Ruby, involuntarily, thought of Phil's dad, the weekend warrior fisherman.

"There certainly are, Phil. This is, after all, a cautionary tale. These trout, they were like the fish of Eden. I dreamed about them all year. It was the fourth spring at Butter Lake that we noticed the fish were not quite as big, not quite as plentiful. The fifth spring, the fish were half the size. The next spring, the lake was empty."

"What happened?" Ruby asked, genuinely curious.

Tom sat, thoughtful, his napkin now folded into a tight square in his hand. There was not a speck of meat left on the fish skeleton. Tom took his last half of grilled cheese, ripped it in two pieces, and dropped them for the waiting dogs, who swallowed them in synchronous gulps.

"What happened. Well, we probably pulled out too many breeding females those first few seasons, threw the whole ecology of the lake off. You know, a lake is a complicated place. Anyways, that's the story of Butter Lake. I think of it often during the first days of camp." He looked around at the gathered staff, lingered on Fischer, who held Tom's inscrutable eyes before looking down.

"Great story, Tom!" Fischer exclaimed, looking back up. Tom continued to look at him, before pushing the bench back and standing up.

"Yes, well, definitely something to ponder. Thanks for the company. Sorry for disturbing the homecoming. Don't stay up too late!" Tom took his plate and went into the kitchen, the dogs following behind, black tails wagging. They heard Cindy laughing.

There was a quiet moment in the dining hall. "To Butter Lake!" Fischer called out, raising his water bottle high in the air, taking a long pull. Other water bottles resurfaced. Ruby grabbed one out of Barry Blum's large hand, took a swig. Tequila. Ew. She took another, longer pull on the bottle.

Stolow strummed his guitar, conversations started up again, Raskin shuffled the cards, and before long the rhythm of the dining hall was restored.

Two hours later, they're at the docks, drunk as skunks.

Tova's out on the dock, yelling at the twinkling cottage lights on the shore across the lake and on the two inhabited islands. "Fuck you and your golf course! Fuck you and your two-acre dance floor in the forest! Fuck you and your fly-in fishing lodge! Fuck you and the virgin stand of white pine you cut down for your heart-shaped swimming pool!"

In the midst of everybody laughing, Phil comes up to Ruby. His pleading eyes are wet, his hair mussed, his mouth a tight, tentative smile.

"Get away from me!" Ruby shouts, pushing him.

"Rube—I'm sorry! It was an accident!"

"You *accidentally* put your dick in Talia's mouth?! There's nothing you can say. I saw you! Just fuck off!"

Phil looks really hurt, his eyebrows collapsing into themselves. He leaves the docks. Everybody's watching. Ruby stands there, blinking, angry, drunk, her bottom lip under her front teeth. "I'll race you to Birchhead Island," Fischer yells, already stripping off his clothes. Naked, penis swinging, hair still perfectly spiked, he runs towards the water. The only one who follows is Tova. It takes her a little longer to unlace her hiking boots, yank off her jeans—revealing the tattoo of an otter-tail canoe paddle on one calf, a windswept white pine on the other—but Fischer waits at the water's edge, dancing from foot to foot. Together they splash into the dark lake and front crawl to the island.

On Ruby's way back to her cabin, sometime after 4:00 a.m., she almost crashed into a bunch of CITs. They were standing beside A&C, five boys, stinking like whiskey and pot and pizza, their sweatshirt hoods obscuring their faces in shadow.

"Geez, boys, it's only the first night. Go back to your cabins before you get in trouble!"

"Yes, Ruby."

"Sorry, Ruby." She could see their faces under their hoods now. They looked ashen, petrified. One of them was moving his mouth, but no words were coming out. Ah, youth!

Ruby opened the cabin door as slowly as she could. As she tiptoed towards the staff area, a tiny, sleepy voice called her name. She padded over to the top bunk where the sound emanated.

"Yes?" she asked, stroking her camper's hair.

"I missed you, Ruby."

"I missed you too. We're going to have a great summer. Now go back to sleep."

". . . okay."

Ruby stood in the middle of her cabin. It felt great to be back with her girls. Her silly, sassy, sensitive girls. She truly loved them. She was going to give them an amazing summer, just like her favourite and beloved counselors had given her.

Ruby made it to her bed, lay down still dressed. Danielle was snoring. It looked like Dawn hadn't moved all night. Ruby could get not quite three hours of sleep before it was time to wake up again.

The camp was quiet. There were no lights on, no flashlights, no phone screens, no headlamps. A small fuzz of brightness bristled over the lake, turned the cabins, the tennis courts, the buildings, and the docks black and blue. Over in CIT Town, a small peninsula on the west side of camp, the door of the CIT girls' cabin squeaked open. A furtive head poked out, looked into the new morning, went out sideways through the door, sandals in hand, and ran back to his cabin, his heart bleating. Further away, a mother bear and her cubs tromped through the woods. A moose bent down to drink. At six-thirty, Stephen Stolow woke up. In the chilly dark of his cabin, he pulled on his shorts, socks, and shoes, leaving the cabin on soft feet. He stood on the porch, stretched his arms and his legs, and started to jog. In minutes he was off camp property and running on gravel roads among the sumac, rushes, and asters.

He had started waking up early to run three summers ago, his fourth year as staff. The trees, the cottage turn-offs, the sun coming up, the early rising heat—this part of the day was his and his alone. He was planning on stopping by the ropes course on his way back; in the dark floating hours of night a new idea for an obstacle course had come to him—perfect for the older kids—and he wanted to see if it was feasible.

By the time he got back, the rest of camp was starting to stir.

CHAPTER 3

BAGELS! SOLDIERS! (AND LATER, A CANOE RIDE)

The second day of camp, a Monday, and the bones of the daily routine that would form the skeleton of the next eight weeks were already starting to ossify. It was a process that started the first day, the first night, the first morning you woke up as a cabin, stood as a camp at morning song before filing into the dining hall, and continued until the end, when you'd board the final bus, when being apart from your cabin-mates seems a fate worse than death. Like death, though, that was all a long way off: during these first days—each of which were the length of three city days—the summer was endless, an ocean beside the highway, unfathomable. Down at the docks, the swim tests were underway, a controlled chaos of whistles, shouts of encouragement, whines of complaint, bodies slicing through water, treading for three minutes. During lunch announcements, before the usual cheering and table banging, the specialty staff introduced themselves and their specialties: Arts & Crafts, Landsports, Tennis, Paddle, Ski, Sail, S'Nature, Ropes, Drama. They each performed a little skit, ranging from the half-assed to the half-brilliant; a necessary, but exceedingly boring, element of the first days. Dinner was spaghetti with meat sauce, garlic bread, Caesar salad. For Evening

Program, each unit did their own thing; Ruby's unit played Plane Crash! The game went like this: a plane had crashed, leaving wreckage and survivors scattered throughout the camp. The campers, in teams of five, had to scour the camp, find the survivors (a.k.a. the staff), listen to their elaborate, melodramatic stories, and solve the mystery of what happened to them. It was an easy program that the kids loved. Ruby and Danielle were up on the dining hall roof, bloody wounds painted onto their arms, legs, and faces. This was their third year as co-staff, and their third year with the same girls. They had the kids screaming with laughter as they acted out their lovers' spat; Fallon came by in a fake cast, and they chatted and laughed for a while. Fallon, as usual when leading a program or wielding her authority, was in a good mood (Ruby relieved that Fallon had seemed to let her absence the first night slide). Ruby continued avoiding Phil, who was thankfully off with his own unit.

The next morning, the camp woke up to a surprise. Phil, David Margolis, Jeremy Kraftchuk, and Aimee Goldstein were gone. At first, campers and staff alike were confused, but at breakfast the rumours started, amid the passing of pancakes and the scratchy sound of cereal hitting melamine bowls. Tom showed up halfway through the meal, his face tense and unreadable, the sleeves of his plaid shirt rolled up. After morning cleanup, everybody gathered in centre field, and Tom announced, with Debs standing beside him, her thick curly orange hair flowing over her shoulders, her clipboard hugged to her chest, that four staff members were caught leaving camp without permission and had been sent home. "Behaviour like that is not permissible at Camp Burntshore, especially from our staff," Tom intoned. He was having trouble keeping the anger out of his normally highly controlled voice. Most of Aimee's campers were bawling inconsolably. Ruby wasn't at the meeting.

It was the period before lunch on the fourth day. A bunch of counselors were sitting at the bench beside the volleyball court, their campers at swim lessons on the docks. The sun was high and hot. The kids splashed and yelled from the lake. It was a perfect summer day; the machine of camp was well oiled, moving smoothly. As most of the talk when campers were not in earshot the past two days, they were discussing the booted counselors, who, contra to Tom's announcement, were not caught leaving camp without permission but smoking pot in the swim shed, and, as rumour had it, caught by Tom himself. What a scene that must have been, Ruby thought, sitting on the end of the bench, wearing her heavily tinted movie-star sunglasses, painting her toenails a pre-dawn blue.

"Kraftchuk is such a nut," Danielle said, Andre Agassi's *Open* sitting on her lap. *Was* such a nut, Ruby almost corrected. "Remember that time for his birthday, when he went to all ten What A Bagels in the city, got his free birthday dozen, shaved his beard, then went back to all of them and got another dozen?"

"The birthday bagel bonanza! Who could forget it? Entrance was a tub of cream cheese or a tomato or a cucumber, and then it was all you can eat!"

"And all you can bagel!"

"Fuck, what do you mean who could forget—I was constipated for a month."

"Sounds like a shitty party," Casey Mustard exclaimed. "Toronto bagels suck. Like, what even are they? Subpar New York knockoffs, that's what." Ruby looked up—did he purposefully overpronounce the second *t* in Toronto, or was that honestly how people from Montreal said it?

Most heads nodded in agreement. "It's Montreal or New York in the final bracket," Casey continued, flashing his heart-melting grin, "and the winner is undoubtedly Montreal."

"Nope. Nuh-uh. You'll never change my mind," Barry Blum said emphatically, shaking his big scruffy head. "New York bagels are the best bagels."

"Are you out of your freaking mind?" Danielle exclaimed, slamming the Agassi memoir shut. "It's Montreal all the way! How can you beat the chewy, nutty, golden dough joy that is a fresh Montreal bagel?"

"I'll tell you how: by eating a heavy, mountainous onion NYC bagel loaded with a full pound of whitefish salad!"

Ruby, who had moved on to painting her fingernails the same dark blue, hadn't gotten involved in the discussion yet, though she was tempted to accuse Danielle of being a traitor for favouring Montreal over Toronto. Ruby had been quiet since Phil and the others got fired, and not only because she hadn't smoked any weed in nearly two days—she was seriously thinking of abstaining for the rest of the summer—and was in the grumpy stages of withdrawal. She had been smoking with the ex-counselors in the swim shed when an uncustomary nighttime need to shit soured her stomach, so she'd passed the joint to Aimee without a word and hustled to the Monolith. Tom must have caught them just as she was wiping. Now, she was spooked, mad at herself for being so careless, feeling guilty she didn't ask Aimee to go with her to the Monolith (which she very nearly did), pissed at Phil for what she assumed he was already up to back in Thornhill, even though they were most certainly broken up.

"Toronto has its own bagel, and it's pretty good," Ruby declared, blowing on her fingers. If nobody else was going to, she'd have to stand up (as always) for the unfairly maligned, for the dispossessed, the forgotten.

Looking up from her nails, she caught sight of Debs, run-walking across centre field, clipboard in hand, her walkie-talkie swinging on her cargo-panted hip, her unkempt orange curls frizzed, frazzled, floating.

In Tom's office, Tom, Jenna, Brett, and Tova were waiting impatiently. The sounds of kids playing baseball, splashing in the lake, laughing and shouting, wafted in through the open screen door. Tom had his arms crossed, was focused on a big chunk of shale sitting on his desk. Brett was looking down, his head in his hands. The mood was tense. Finally, Debs rushed into the office.

"Well," Tom said once Debs was sitting and everybody had readjusted. "This is an unfortunate situation. We've never lost this many staff in an *entire* summer, let alone in the first week." Tom's expression, composed, sagacious, was familiar to everybody in the room: Tom undertaking the serious work of dealing with a camp crisis. "This marijuana epidemic is out of control. It would seem our out-of-sight-out-of-mind policy when it comes to the . . . activities of the staff at night is no longer sufficient. But it's the staff shortage we need to resolve, and soon."

"We're pretty strained," Jenna said, agreeing with her husband. "We expect to lose a few CITs over the course of the summer due to drugs or alcohol, but five staff members in the first three days?" She shook her head emphatically. "No good."

"There was that summer we had to fire the entire swim staff," Debs said, correcting Tom. What she didn't say, partly because it didn't need to be said, partly because it would just be a distraction, was that the entire swim staff had to be fired because Brett, who was then head of swim, had got them all drunk during a social the second last week of the summer. Tom kept them to finish the Bronze Cross swim tests the next day and then fired them all, even his son, heir to the camp. It was one of Tom's few sore spots. After the firing, Brett cut off his ponytail—which consisted of the same lustrous black hair that Tom still had a full head of—and disappeared for a couple of summers before his illustrious return. (Depending who you believed, he spent his time away backpacking through Israel, living in an Ashram in India, visiting the death camps of Europe, or learning Spanish in Bolivia. All Debs knew was that for two blissful years he was absent from both camp itself as well as the camp's Toronto offices, where he normally would hang out during the fall and winter.) Now, Brett was quite clearly being groomed, once again, to take over Burntshore. Debs thought Tom could announce it as early as next year.

There was an uncomfortable silence. Brett stared intently out the windows at the row of oak trees that lined the office road. Tova coughed.

"Well, that was at the end of the summer," Tom said, ending the awkwardness, "and this is the beginning." He turned to Debs. "How are we managing?"

Debs looked down at her chart. "Right now, we have Ari covering Margolis's and Glazer's old cabin instead of running Landsports, I have two staff floating between cabins 4 and 6. Aimee's cabin has fifteen girls, Talia is pretty strained. Until Stolow gets his CIT placement, he's all alone on Ropes. They're all being stoic about it, but it's an untenable situation."

Nods all around.

"Have we thought about hiring more staff?" Debs asked. This was the obvious, though difficult solution. "There must be somebody in the city who'd be willing to come up on short notice."

Tom glanced at Brett, and then his wife, before settling his gaze on Debs. "Brett has a, shall we say, rather unusual solution."

Brett was passing around pamphlets.

"Israeli soldiers?" Debs exclaimed, looking at the image of a smiling Israeli in full fatigues paddling in a canoe with a young girl, the sun beaming down on them.

"Not only do lots of camps have representatives from the IDF for the summer," Brett said, launching in like it was a shpiel he had been practising for days, "it'll substantially save on costs. I spoke to somebody at that office," he pushed his finger onto the contact section of the pamphlet, "and, though it's highly short notice, the lady there thinks they should be able to gather six or so soldiers to ship over. Possibly by the end of the week."

"Yeah, but . . . soldiers? It doesn't really seem in keeping with the Burntshore experience . . . does it? Won't it send the wrong message to the kids, and to the parents? Not to mention future potential campers?"

"What message is that?" Brett asked, feigning politeness.

Debs paused. She wasn't exactly political—or apolitical, depending how you looked at it—but she generally shied away from guns or uniforms or anything like that, even when they were Jewish guns or Jewish uniforms. It was something she had always avoided, at Brandies, in all the Jewish organizational spaces she had moved through, and especially at camp. She didn't want to explain that. "Just, that . . . well, c'mon, we all know what it would mean!"

Tom looked at Brett. Debs remembered years ago when Brett tried to be Orthodox for a couple of summers, wore a kippah, started a prayer club in the dining hall basement; she also recalled, the summer before Brett got fired, constant talk about making aliyah, moving to Israel. For Brett, always forcefully manifesting his Jewishness in one way or another, this newest plan wasn't a surprise. Debs did a quick calculation of which Jewish camps had visiting Israeli staff: Camp George, yes. Camp Biluim, yes. Northland, no. Gesher, yes. White Pine, Tamarack, New Moon, Manitou, Sumac, no, no, no, no, and no. There was that one summer Camp Tzedek, in the Catskills, hired fifty Israeli shlichim for one season—but that was preplanned, under different circumstances, the kind of thing that became legend. Debs didn't want that for Burntshore; Burntshore should not be a case study in the next academic monograph on Jewish summer camps, that was not Burntshore's style.

"Frankly, I think this is bullshit," Tova said, speaking for the first time. Debs was glad Tova was there. Head of trip, she was one of Tom's most trusted staff members. Tova had been Tom's student in a graduate geology seminar; he had poached her from her summer job at Outward Bound to build up Burntshore's tripping program, which she had done with characteristic excellence. Tova was every camp program director's dream. In meetings she was usually quiet; the fact that she was speaking up at all was momentous in and of itself. "Why bring in soldiers from a faraway land?" Tova continued, almost coming out of her seat, "Why not hire some teenagers from the reserve? They'd love the experience, not to mention the money."

"Calling them soldiers isn't exactly accurate, is it?" Brett answered quickly, his butt raised out of his chair as well. Brett's disdain for Tova had never gotten past Debs, but the jealousy written all over his face was a new discovery. "They're Israeli. They're our Israeli cousins. It's not like they're going to show up with their Uzis and automatics! Though that *would* be cool. Anyways, technically they'd be 'Israeli emissaries.'" Debs looked at the pamphlet, skimmed the middle panel. The phrase

"Israeli emissaries" did come up multiple times, but Debs quickly noticed that the "emissaries" would also all be enlisted soldiers. Brett was still talking: "We've been saying we've been wanting to up our Jewish cultural activities here, haven't we, Pa? What better, more economical, way than this? Think about how proud Grandpa would be—real Jews from the real Jewish homeland. And it won't cost us a dime!"

Tova scoffed. Tom looked at Jenna. Jenna gave Brett an encouraging smile. Debs closed her eyes, tried to picture it.

It would be a change, that's for sure.

They were still arguing about bagels. Ruby had found herself quite involved by this point, was talking in her yelling-into-a-microphone-at-a-protest voice. "What you're missing about Toronto is that there isn't just *one* kind of Toronto bagel. You can get anything you want in Toronto. A regular Toronto bagel from What A Bagel or Bagel World, a flat, a twister. C'mon, Toronto must be the only city with a true twister bagel—the Toronto Twister!" Ruby knew it was an uphill battle; she was vastly outnumbered by Montreal- and New York–bagel diehards. Bagel ideologues. Bagel turncoats.

"All pale imitations!" Casey enthused, his baseball cap recently flipped backwards, his Oakleys—which were never far from his face or hands—perched on top. "There's literally nothing like going into the original St-Viateur at dawn, that smell of the wood-burning oven, the seeds, the raw dough, freshly born circular miracles popping off those long wooden paddles right in front of your eyes, buying a half dozen, eating them right there on the sidewalk in Mile End while the sun comes up."

"I'm not denying that Montreal bagels are fantastic, I'm just saying that Toronto has bagels too, and that I happen to prefer them."

"Listen. I enjoy Toronto bagels, and, yes, I acknowledge they exist. But it's impossible to deny that Montreal bagels are simply the best. They are simply unique, simply perfect. The end. Period. The end."

"What about New York bagels?" Barry Blum asked.

"New York bagels are trash," Ruby pronounced. This sent everybody into an uproar. The argument started over again, in a yet higher key.

In Tom's office, no decisions had been reached.

Finally, Tom spoke. "When my father bought this land and started this camp, he wanted it to be imbued with the same Jewish warmth he grew up with in his parents' house. There were Shabbat dinners, Saturday morning prayers, blessings at every meal, lessons on Jewish history and tradition, even a Torah for a few summers in a makeshift arc in the dining hall basement. When he handed the camp to me and Jenna, we let that stuff slide; to keep up with the other private Jewish camps, we needed to embrace the secular, cultural parts of our heritage. Which I feel we succeeded at. More than succeeded at. Burntshore is, of course, still Jewish, but only nominally religious. This is how it's been for twenty years now. It works."

"This is the future, Pa."

Tom sat back. For centuries natural scientists were adamant that the geological world was static, created according to God's plan. But, as it turns out, they couldn't have been more wrong. The planet was constantly changing. The plate tectonic revolution was in the '60s, for Christ's sake! Endless dynamism, long periods of shifting calm followed by rocking cataclysm, is the name of the game. Shouldn't he, as an owner of a mid-sized Jewish sleepover camp in Central Ontario, harness the same principles as the globe? As Jenna had reminded him last night, the camp was going to be handed off to Brett soon enough. He understood Tova's anger, appreciated Debs's ambivalence—he felt it himself!—but didn't he owe it to Brett to take a chance?

"I think it's worth giving it a try," he said. "What do you think, Debs?"

Debs looked down at the shiny pamphlet again. The soldier's face was chiselled, his eyes proud and knowing. The girl was radiating strength, comradery, joy. Now that Tom had given it his approval, she'd have to have a legitimate reason to not be okay with it. Which, in the moment, she did not. Debs's allegiance was to Tom, was to camp. To Burntshore.

Brett, watching all this closely, smiled: he had them.

"I guess it wouldn't hurt to have a couple trained tacticians to round out the Ropes staff," Debs said, laughing at her own bad joke.

"Fuck this. Sorry, Tom, I'm out," Tova said, already standing. She left through the screen door, closing it halfway. Debs watched her walk off the porch: nobody at this camp, excepting his immediate family, would have gotten away with talking to Tom like that.

A slow minute passed.

"Okay, then." Tom nodded, the decision reached. "Brett, will you call this outreach office and see what you can arrange?"

Brett was standing, already opening the door that led into the front office. "Sure thing, Pa! You'll see, we'll turn this camp around in no time!"

Tom turned to Jenna, raised an eyebrow.

The future generation, remaking the world as they saw fit.

The bagels discussion had devolved into chaos. Casey and Ruby were yelling at each other, Danielle and Barry were play-fighting, the others were staring daggers.

Tova walked by, heading towards the lake, her legs pumping, her face set, her dark cherry canoe paddle in her hands. "Hey," Casey called out, "hey, T, what's your favourite bagel, Montreal or New York?"

"Or Toronto?!"

"Booooo!" Casey and Barry.

Tova stopped short, put her paddle blade on the ground, leaned on the shaft. She smiled wickedly. "Did our ancestors really travel across the shark-infested oceans with nothing but a dream and a recipe in their pockets for us to argue about what is the one true bagel? Fuck that univocal bullshit! I'm a bagel pluralist. Every bagel has something to say, to offer. To give."

Ruby stood up. Her nails were done, dried in the day's brittle heat. "Guys, I think that's it. Tova has spoken." She left the bench and walked towards the docks. A stalemate; fine, she'd take it. At least she didn't have to concede.

Besides, it was almost lunch. Time to collect her girls.

There's Tova at the canoe docks. She pulls her favourite canoe—a beat-up fifteen-foot canvas Chestnut, one of the only surviving boats from the camp's original fleet—down from the rack, portages it the thirty feet to the dock, flips it off her shoulders directly into the water. She gets in. She pushes off. She paddles gracefully, steadily, hard. She paddles past where the river empties into the lake, along the Crown land, her canoe getting smaller as she moves beside the vast tracts of undeveloped forest that the government supposedly kept in trust but really did with as it chose. She paddles past the black sand beaches opposite the camp's shore, the beaches that gave the lake its current name and which lent its sand to souvenir jars on windowsills across the world. There she is, rounding the northwest corner, paddling past the Town of Spitsville, named after the town's founder, Holleander Spitz, a Dutch settler who bought over ten thousand acres here in the mid-1800s. Tova's getting bigger now, coming closer. She glides past the Black Spruce First Nation reserve, the cottagers renting the reserve's cottages splashing in the water. On the first Friday of the first summer of camp, in 1963, Tom's father personally brought over trays and trays of Jewish food to the reserve, deli and chicken soup and kreplach: a story the people of the Spruce tell to this day. Now Cindy and her staff come from the reserve every morning to cook the camp's food. This one lake, one among hundreds of thousands, carries enough history to spend a lifetime unravelling.

Tova will pull back up to the camp docks just in time for dinner. She will have worked up a powerful appetite.

CHAPTER 4

WE FIND OUT WHAT SOME OF THE PARENTS DO; THE STAFF OF CABIN 9 PLAY CARDS

After EP—a raucous game of Family Feud—Ruby sat with her girls on the cabin's porch. The hour and a half between Evening Program and lights out was a low-key, social time: girls and boys visiting each other's porches, final basketball games of the day, the collective slide along the warm citrusy evening into the dark underworld of night. The girls on the porch were talking about one of their favourite topics: what their parents did.

"My parents run a small business out of our basement."

"My mom's a lawyer."

"Lawyer."

"Lawyer."

"Same."

"My dad owns a factory that makes the perfume they put on dog poop bags and garbage bags."

"Ew, gross!"

"My parents own a factory too!"

"What do your parents do, Ruby?"

Ruby looked up. She had been half-listening, picking her nails, biting her lower lip, enjoying the cool evening breeze. "My mom's a professor, and my dad's a dentist."

"Is that why you have perfect teeth?"

"No, you idiot, but it is why she's so smart!"

The girls moved on to one of their other favourite topics: the richest people they knew, what their houses looked like, how they, themselves, would one day become stinking filthy rich.

"Girls, don't forget that money isn't everything," Ruby said teasingly, though she deeply meant it. "What have I always taught you? FTR. Fuck the rich!"

FTR was just one of many acronyms Ruby had made up for her cabin's edification over the past three summers. There was BMT (bad morning thoughts). There was HBTB (hot boys, terrible brains). And, Ruby's personal favourite, which came to her in a dream the night before camp last summer: JAP. Journeys, awareness, possibilities. (A few of her acronyms—such as PMF, post-masturbatory fuzz—were only for staff ears . . .)

"But Ruby, we want to live in big houses!"

"Wouldn't you rather live in a place like this, where everybody has more or less the same?"

Ruby was reminding herself of her own long ago counselor and young-girl-role-model Chrissy Sugarman. Ah, Chrissy Sugarman. Ruby often wondered if she would ever again be as enamoured with another human being as she was with Chrissy Sugarman. Chrissy, who introduced Ruby to the Hip, who took her to her first protest, hundreds of thousands of bodies screaming and dancing against the Iraq War in downtown Toronto, forever filling Ruby's veins with the nectar of people power, Chrissy who modelled what it meant to be a cool, engaged teenager committed equally to their responsibilities and to having fun, Chrissy who now lives in Vancouver with a young family of her own and works with Syrian refugees.

"Of course!" June responded.

"Wouldn't it be cold in the winter?"

"There'd be heaters, dumbass!"

There's Fallon, coming up cabin line, in her black *Head Staff* sweatshirt, beelining towards the cabin. "Hi, girls. How's everybody settling in? Can I have a quick word with you, Ruby?"

Ruby jumped off the porch and walked with Fallon a little ways into the woods behind the cabin.

Fallon, as usual, was all business. Ruby stared up at her thin, severe face, her brown eyes framed by wire-rimmed glasses, her light blonde hair ruler-straight, as she talked, glancing at her clipboard every few words to make sure she wasn't missing anything. "Arielle's parents have been calling. They want to make sure she's acclimatizing okay to the new summer. They're also worried about the other kids not understanding. Can you shoot them an email? I already spoke to the doctor. He's going to call them tomorrow to talk about her new medicines."

"Yeah, for sure, Fal." Arielle was diabetic, with a slew of related—and, from summer to summer, constantly changing—health problems, and her parents were what you could generously call *very* hands-on. Arielle loved camp, and Ruby sometimes wished her folks would give her a little more space. "Nobody will give her a hard time about the insulin. They're all used to it from last year."

"That's what I figured. How's everything else going?" Fallon asked, half closing her eyes behind the thick lenses of her glasses in an over-serious approximation of fellow feeling.

Ruby bit her lip. Was Fallon asking about Phil? Or possibly about her cousin Glazer? Either way, it was odd for her to care. "Everything's great, Fal!" Ruby felt a rare, fleeting sense of comradery with Fallon. "Will you come say goodnight to the girls?" she asked.

After a boisterous bedtime—a drawn-out roses and thorns, a giggly song of the night, a relatively pain-free lights out—Ruby stayed in with Danielle and Dawn. She hadn't felt like partying since the swim shed, was still trying to avoid the pot smokers. Even though her withdrawal symptoms had somewhat mellowed, she was seriously craving a puff or two; she missed being stoned. But besides all that, what better way to bond with her cabinmates than a night alone with them? They crowded onto Ruby's bed in the staff alcove, played cards and gossiped, the Tragically Hip playing tinny and quiet out of Ruby's phone.

"Are you and Phil really done?" Danielle asked, squinting at her cards.

"I hope so," Ruby said, picking up a three of hearts.

"So, who're you going to hook up with this summer then?" Dawn asked. Dawn was the cabin's sleep-in, was third year Drama. She had a boyfriend in the city, was one of the few non-Jewish staff.

"Casey Mustard, obviously," Ruby said, discarding a nine of clubs.

The idea of Ruby and Casey Mustard fooling around was objectively hilarious, and the three young women were objectively losing it. "Shh, shh, we'll wake the girls."

"That's what Casey will say!" Danielle got out between breaths, bringing on a second wave of hilarity.

"I always thought you and Geoff would be a nice couple," Dawn said, the laughter subsiding. Geoff was kitchen staff, hailed from the reserve. He was a few years younger than Ruby, had just finished his first year at U of T.

"Ooohhh," Danielle agreed.

Ruby made a face. "Geoff? No way! He's a good friend, he's like a sibling." Ruby, in fact, had gone by the kitchen that day to talk to Geoff. They had seen each other a few times in the city, Ruby had helped Geoff pick his courses for second semester, and she wanted to know how they'd gone. Geoff commiserated about Phil getting booted, was surprised when Ruby told him they had broken up (and the reason for it), wished her luck when he learned of Ruby's plan to stay sober. Catch-up out of the way, they dug right into their preferred topic of discussion: the ravishes and soul-crimping stupidity of capitalism, the disappointment of Obama's first term, the limited hope for his second, Harper's non-sensical grip on the Canadian government. In a word, politics. The conversation was fast, witty, quick. The only other person Ruby could talk to like that was Seema, her best friend back in Toronto.

"If Seema didn't have a boyfriend, I would totally set Geoff up with her," Ruby said. Nearly as short as Seema, affable, quiet, hyper-intelligent but not the least bit show-offy, he and Seema would be the perfect couple.

"Oh my god, how *is* Seema?" Danielle asked.

"She's great!" Ruby said. "I should write her a letter soon. We promised to be pen pals this summer, old fashioned."

"I haven't seen her since we went to that Gaza protest back in the fall," Danielle said. Ruby remembered that protest well. Seema was wearing her keffiyeh, Ruby got between her and some Jewish Defense League assholes who were harassing her. She'd been at camp just over a week and already missed Seema terribly. It was politics that brought Ruby and Seema together, but it was their love of weed, their dark sense of humour, the powerful compatibility of their inner beings, that made them best friends.

The world of protests, of fanatical Zionist fascists calling her a terrorist-sympathizer and spitting on her, of Ruby and Seema smoking a joint in the woods on the edge of York's sprawling mall-like campus after a student council meeting, laughing about the heated arguments, walking arm-in-arm to York Lanes to eat heaping plates of Indian food, seemed very far away. Camp had its problems, sure, but it was a place Ruby could relax, a place she loved deeply. As she told Seema before she left, she knew how lucky she was to have somewhere like Burntshore to get away from the struggle, to recharge, regroup, come back to the school year more committed and passionate than ever. "Take advantage of that for as long as you can," Seema had said. She planned on it.

Ruby pulled a three of clubs from the discard pile.

"Gin," she said, laying down her winning cards.

CHAPTER 5

RUBY/STOLOW

Ruby woke up freezing, her blanket bunched at her feet. She pulled it back up and shivered. It was the first real night's sleep she'd had since pre-camp. At home, five hours of sleep would barely qualify as a nap, but here, five hours is a sustained REM bonanza. Ruby laughed to herself. She had passed out reading her Paley, a short story about a woman having an affair with a famous Yiddish theatre actor; the book was still lying on her chest. She rolled over, took her phone from the shelf. Seven-fifteen. Time to get up. She roused herself, peed, brushed her teeth before getting to work with Danielle and Dawn waking the girls. Half an hour of moaning, pleading, bargaining, blanket-kicking, rising, toilet-flushing, water-running, hair-brushing, dressing, and they were ready for breakfast.

The cabin, sixteen girls, two counselors, and one sleep-in, walked towards the dining hall in the early morning chill. The light had not yet focused, the heat had not yet burned off the dew, the night had not yet been fully banished. Everything felt still and slow, the girls' feet trudging through wet grass, other cabins approaching the dining hall from all three cabin lines, the head staff from across the road. White mist sat on the still lake. The sky was the thinnest gauze of blue. The whole camp standing at the flagpole for morning song. And then up the wooden stairs and through the wooden doors into the large open building that smelled of burnt hot chocolate and ketchup.

In the dining hall they sat at their cabin table—in the back corner, near the swinging kitchen doors—with Ruby and Danielle at one end, Dawn at the other. Nineteen melamine bowls on nineteen melamine plates. Forks, spoons, and knives. Napkin holders. Three boxes of cereal on the table—two Corn Flakes, one Rice Krispies. Two pitchers of milk. A pitcher of juice. A pitcher of hot chocolate. Ruby went up to get the breakfast's hot offering: egg log. She brought two portions of the oblong, spongey eggs on their melamine platters to the table to grunts and sighs of disappointment. Ruby took a healthy slice of the egg log, doused it in ketchup, and dug in. Something else she had learned from Chrissy Sugarman, crystallized during her first summer as staff: if she did not eat the meal, no matter what it was, some of her campers would not eat either (she knew all too well the dangers of the Westmount Diet—nothing but gummy bears and Diet Coke—and did not want it to take root in her kids). In the city Ruby would rarely eat breakfast, but here, keeping everybody fed and hydrated was among her most important daily tasks. At least Cindy's food was edible, unlike the prior head chef's. After she finished the eggs, she moved on to a bowl of Corn Flakes, the blueish-white skim milk poured right to the tipping point of the faded yellow bowl. The sounds of three hundred humans, most under the age of seventeen, nearly all under the age of twenty-two, eating, talking, coughing, laughing. Some boys were going table to table, trying to trade their box of plain Cheerios for Frosted Flakes. Ruby watched Dawn pour an hourglass's worth of white sugar into her bowl of Corn Flakes, the tiniest splish of milk.

David Stein came to the table, sat beside Ruby. "Did you hear?" he asked, all excited.

"Hear what?" Ruby asked, crunching on her cereal. Stein was the oldest non-administrative staff at Burntshore, wore nothing but camp or band shirts and sweatpants, which he always had his hands down, even while driving the ski boat, was an incorrigible flirt, gossip, prankster. He was the sole remaining Burntshorer of the CITs of 2003, one of the last truly wild CIT years—their sexual escapades, their drug use, their untouchable hotness, was the stuff of camp legend.

"Tom's bringing in some Israeli soldiers to replace everyone who got booted." Stein smiled with the novelty of it. "Brett's idea!"

Ruby spat out her mouthful of cereal, her girls closest to her bursting into giggles. Stein was the kind of person who you could never tell if he was bullshitting or not, but this, for some reason, had the ring of horrible truth to it.

"What? You're fucking kidding me," she whisper-yelled, not wanting her campers to hear.

"That's the word." David smiled again, took the spoon out of Ruby's hand, stuffed a heaping spoonful of her cereal into his mouth, gulped it down, stood up.

Ruby looked at Danielle, who raised her eyebrows. Ruby pushed her chair back, went to get a cup of coffee. Stirring cream into the thin brown liquid, she surveyed the dining hall. Counselors were standing, going from table to table, leaning in, whispering, looking around. Ruby felt like she was watching the rumour spread in real time—because that's all it was, right? A rumour? Casey Mustard sat like a king at the end of his cabin's table, his hands behind his head, Fischer beside him chugging orange juice, his hair perfectly spiked even this early in the morning, both of their plates a shallow sea of Tabasco, ketchup, and spilled juice, a big smile on Casey's beautiful idiot face. Did he start the rumour?

It can't be true.

Israeli soldiers, at Burntshore?

It can't be true.

Can it?

When Ruby's cabin exited the dining hall, it was into a different world than the one they left behind an hour earlier. It didn't only look different, it felt different. The sky was blue. The air was hot. The grass was dry. The lake lapped gently against the shore. The pines hugging the lake were vividly green in the clear, sharp light. The coming day was a big bright openness, a virescence. And out of that openness, there was Brett, quickly coming towards them, his hair a cold shock of black. Great, what does he want? He handed Ruby a folded-up piece of paper. "Phil wanted me to give this to you," he said. Ruby took it.

"Okay, girls, I'll race you back to the cabin!" she called out, already taking off at a run, leaving Brett standing there, his arm still outstretched, her girls calling and shrieking as they followed behind her. After putting on the Michael Jackson mix and haranguing the cabin into making their beds and tidying up before first period, Ruby opened the letter. It was written on Tom's Camp Burntshore stationery, the camp's logo—the sun rising over the black sand beaches—heading the top of the page.

Ruby:

I can't fucking believe this! Kicked out on the second night. Fuck fuck fuck. And before we were able to really talk about what happened at pre-camp. What am I going to do with my summer now?! My whole life is here. Do you think Tom will let me back next year? Oh Rubes, you should have seen him, he was pissed. *Yelling about camp values and responsibility and doing the right thing. Don't tell anybody this, but Margolis started* crying *while Tom was reaming us. Kraftchuk thinks somebody ratted us out, but who the fuck would do that? We shouldn't have been smoking in the swim shed so soon after Glazer got booted. Fuck. At least you weren't there—lucky timing, eh? We're trapped in Tom's office while he and Debs pack our stuff. Margolis has a car, so looks like we're heading back to the city tonight. (Aimee's dad is already on his way from Montreal to pick her up.) Fucking Toronto. A shitty summer in shitty-ass Toronto. Can't fucking believe. Rubes, I'm sorry about what happened with Talia, okay? It was a mistake. A big fucking mistake. I was drunk, I couldn't find you. After all we've been through, can you find it in your heart to forgive me? I'll wait for you in Toronto. Please, Rubes, don't throw away everything we have. I love you. I fucking love you. I'll wait if you'll wait. I'll write you every day.*

Phil

Each *f* in the triplet of *fucks* was in a different ornate calligraphy; Phil always had decent penmanship, though by the end of the letter it had devolved into messy boy-scrawl. Ruby read the letter a second time, her girls tucking in their sheets as they belted out the chorus of "Billie Jean," before folding it and putting it in her shorts' pocket.

For the rest of the morning, Ruby dwelt on the letter. Her first response was a single all-encompassing thought: he just doesn't want me to fool around with anybody while he's not here. Well, joke's on him, I'm going to fool around with as many boys as'll have me! (Her second response, fleeting in comparison, easily shrugged off: why did Brett take two whole days to give her Phil's letter?)

First period, they had Sail. The cabin were adept sailors, and the conditions were primo, so they got right out on the water, Ruby riding in a Laser with Barnie Ratner, the head of Sail, and this summer's only Black staff member. They moved out into the lake, riding the wind before tacking against it, the sun and wind spinning around them as they zigzagged across the water. She should thank Talia: it was about time Ruby had broken up with Phil, but she had been stuck, inert, luffing too close to the wind, but not close enough. She had loved him, yeah, but he had barely changed since his teenage years. The more politically active Ruby became, the more meetings she chaired and campus groups she joined, the more protests she organized—to divest, to freeze tuition, to free Palestine—the more

Phil seemed like, well, a loser, uninterested in the wider world, what at camp they called the Big Wide, basically anything past main gate. While Ruby took courses with names like "A History of British Colonialism" and "Radical Jewish Thought," Phil signed up for bird courses. He got along well enough with Seema, who had been Ruby's best friend since first year undergrad when they met at a protest in Vari Hall and discovered they were in almost all of the same classes. Both Ruby and Seema had a profound hatred of Zionism and the Jewish state—Ruby because of its ethnonationalism and twisting of Jewish history, Seema because, as a Palestinian, her whole family was pushed out of their village which was subsequently destroyed—and both loved smoking weed. Phil got along with Seema and her boyfriend, Jamil, especially when they were partying, which was, let's face it, often enough, but whenever politics came up, Phil would tune right out.

The wind was blowing against her face; she hadn't even noticed that Barnie had tacked them towards the dock. They were almost back on land.

Second period was A&C. They were making bracelets, spools of fishing wire and an assortment of glass and plastic beads in varying colours and sizes spread out on the wide tables. *Tel Aviv!*, the recent hit Broadway musical based on Theodor Herzl's sole novel, was playing on the stereo, the cabin loudly singing along. Ruby continued her post-mortem on her relationship with Phil as she strung a necklace of white crow beads, trying, and failing, to not be rankled by the inane lyrics that her girls seemed to know by heart. Two nights ago, when Ruby got back to the swim shed and found nobody there, she had panicked. She had been in the bathroom for what, five minutes? They wouldn't have ended the session before she got back, not without a reason. The small shed still reeked of pot (thinking of the smell now thickened Ruby's throat with desire). She had run to Tom's office, saw the light on, heard Tom's voice, controlled but raised. She stopped ten metres away. She could see the shadow of Aimee's high ponytail on the office wall. So her gut was right: they were busted. Fuck. She could wait until Tom left, go see them, say goodbye. For an instant this was what she was going to do, but then it passed, and Ruby went back to her cabin. Fuck Phil. They were over. What was there to say to him? The only reason they were smoking together anyways was because Margolis brought him along to the session; Ruby had thought of leaving, but she had already pitched on the joint. It's not like she couldn't, right now, get up from the A&C table, walk to the pay phone at the main office, and call him, yell at him for assuming he had any right to tell her what to do or not do. But she had no interest in speaking to him. Was she glad he was gone? she wondered, looking at her almost finished necklace. Yes. Yes, and no.

At lunch—grilled cheese and french fries, a camp favourite—Ruby was in a more sympathetic mood. She and Phil did have some good times. That first summer they hooked up, where all they could think about was finding time and space to be even a little bit alone. Those autumn, winter, and spring nights in Thornhill, smoking and fucking and doing homework and watching TV and laughing. But, even before he hooked up with Talia, they were moving in different directions. It was true. There was no need to stay mad at him forever. Poor Phil. What was he going to do in Toronto all alone for seven-and-a-half weeks?

By Rest Hour, Ruby had moved on from Phil and his letter and was focused on a more pressing crisis: the Israeli soldiers. Since breakfast, the rumour had solidified into near fact in Ruby's mind. What were Tom and Debs thinking? This was fucked. The camp would forever be changed. As she and Seema regularly discussed, often parroting lines from Professor Zipperstein, their favourite poli-sci prof, soldiers were nothing but the most violent tentacle of the state. Just last winter she had participated in a protest on campus against a talk by visiting Israeli soldiers on how to maintain "morality" while serving in the Occupied Territories. Morality—in the West Bank! What a joke! She could already feel her hatred of the faceless soldiers red hot in her gut. Burntshore's collective politics was confused at best, the camp the kind of place where a male staff member would wear a Rage Against the Machine T-shirt one day, an IDF shirt the next, and then sleep in a worn Che Guevara shirt. Ruby had plenty of

Free Palestine shirts at home, but she had not brought any to camp; a huge mistake, she was realizing now. She still got furious when one of the staff members wore anything with the IDF logo and would often say something, usually starting a huge argument—probably one of the reasons Ruby had won "biggest bitch" at the staff banquet two years running, just inching past Fallon—and now members of the actual IDF were going to actually be *here*, at Burntshore, corrupting the minds of campers and staff alike, teaching them that all Palestinians were their enemy and deserved to be oppressed? Ruby had been looking forward to taking a break from the political world of university, to sinking into the apolitical world of camp, but apparently that was too much to ask. Wait until she told Seema; she was going to flip. She'd write her a letter tonight.

Third period was Ropes. On the way over they ran into Debs. "Is it true what everybody is saying?" Ruby asked.

Debs smiled, never good at keeping a camp-related secret. "You'll know more by tonight," she said, as good as confirming it. Ruby's disbelief and anger flared up again, sour and hot in her esophagus. She needed to let off some steam. She needed a spliff.

They left camp proper and crossed the road to the ropes course, emerging into the small clearing to the west of new field and the head staff housing. Stolow's domain in the forest.

"How's it going, Stolow?" Ruby asked as they harnessed up June, Ruby's most outgoing camper, who was going to climb the wall first.

Stolow shrugged. Jewish-Korean Stolow, thin and wiry from a lifetime of climbing anything vertical, was wearing a blue tank top, red climbing shorts, and black fingerless gloves. "Ya know. It's not easy without any staff at all."

"I heard that Brett is bringing in some Israeli soldiers or some shit."

Stolow smiled. He knew something Ruby didn't. "Ah, yes, the emissaries. I hear they're all commandos." They laughed. Stolow, while usually staying out of it whenever Zionism came up, still loved Ruby for her combativeness. Ruby had come to Stolow's defense more than once when drunken staff had brought up his Korean heritage in connection with China or Japan. "How much shit are you going to give them, Rubes?"

"All the shit, Stolow. All the shit."

"Ruby, do I have to go up?" It was Clara. A good kid, she often didn't want to do anything that involved a little bit of fear or adrenaline, but she usually just needed some light prodding.

"Do you have to go up? Hmm. That depends. Do you *want* to go up? I think you should." Ruby knew that Stolow's most important policy on the ropes course—besides safety—was "challenge by choice." The kids should push themselves, but only as far as they were willing to go.

Clara smiled nervously, nodded. "Okay. I'll do it."

"Come on over here, and we'll get the harness on you," Stolow said, gently.

Ruby watched her girls up in the clouds. Seeing them up there, challenging themselves, reaching their small hands for the next hold, keeping the fear down as they slowly rose, she made a decision: that was the kind of summer she was going to have. She was going to soar in the sky, she was going to see the forest from above, she was going to live to her fullest, to her most passionate, to her absolute limit of love and hunger and fury.

Stolow helped the last of Ruby's girls down from the climbing wall, waved goodbye as they left to cross back over the road to camp proper.

Once he was alone, he walked twenty feet into the woods to rendezvous with Elijah. The trusted glass bong was sitting on a huge bole of a big white pine, along with an Altoids tin and a lighter. Stolow sat against the tree and took a hit, exhaling skywards, the smoke momentarily obscuring the crowns of the trees, the blueness beyond. He kept his head back, watching the higher branches shimmy and sway, feeling his usual affinity for the higher places. Stolow had been climbing since he could grasp with his hands, propel with his feet. Since he first laid eyes on the ropes course at eleven years of age, this was his realm, this playground in the pines.

Now, he spent his summers rappelling kids fifty feet into the air, coaxing the more earthbound to flights of fancy and joy. Stolow designed the new course, begged Tom for the money to get it built. He knew every inch of it backwards and forwards, could run the high ropes with his eyes closed. During pre-camp he had been running the course before breakfast—after a sleepless night of whiskey and pot and guitar—when he looked up from the tire bridge and saw two owls staring at him, heads cocked in amused owl wonder. "Hello, little friends," he had said. At night (at least, the nights he did sleep), Stolow dreamed of the treetops.

For fourth period he had the pre-CIT boys' cabin, which happened to be the cabin he was sleep-in for. A blur of fart jokes, teasing, egging each other on to climb higher and higher. Afterwards, Stolow took his time closing up, went for an end-of-work-day bong hit at the white pine, put Elijah and the assorted paraphernalia away in the knapsack he kept buried under leaves (an extra precaution with the kind of summer they were having . . .), walked by the docks for a quick swim on the way to his cabin, dove off the high jump tower. By the time he got to the cabin there was forty-five minutes til dinner. Stolow sat on his bed in the staff alcove, took out his guitar, started tuning it. Might as well warm up for the jams that were sure to take place tonight. He was working on a new chord progression he was excited to show Tyler, his best friend and stalwart jam partner; it had an unexpected diminished chord, which Stolow couldn't get enough of. He played a few times through the progression. By day, the ropes course, the climbing walls; by night, the guitar. This was how Stolow stayed connected to the high places all summer long. Though Elijah did his part too.

The boys, outside of the alcove, on their own beds, were talking sex stuff: surprise, surprise. Stolow stopped playing to listen.

"If a hand job is a hundred times greater than jacking off, and a blow job is a thousand times greater than jacking off, how much greater is sex than jacking off?"

"Ten thousand!"

"A million!"

Stolow sat back on his bunk, laughing. They weren't wrong, were they? He played "Let's Get It On" on his guitar, the boys erupting into laughter.

The cabin walked over to the dining hall together, the air still humid. Dinner was pasta, salad, and garlic bread. Stolow was ravenous, and he and the cabin's two counselors easily finished off the first platters of food before the campers got any. He stuffed himself with the saucy spaghetti, the buttery garlic bread, and the creamy Caesar salad, drank four cups of purple bug juice and two cups of water.

During announcements Tom asked to see all of the unit heads and head staff after the meal. It didn't mean anything to the campers, but there was a noticeable reaction among the staff, a ripple of dawning understanding. Stolow smiled: so it was true.

As everybody was leaving the dining hall into the early evening, bottlenecking at the front doors, Stolow caught Ruby's eye over the heads of some ten-year-olds. "Go easy on them, eh?" he said laughing.

Ruby laughed, smiled. "I'll think about it," she said.

Within an hour the news had trickled down from the head staff to the staff and from there to the entire camp. It was official: Tom was bringing in five Israeli soldiers to make up for the staff shortage. They'd be arriving in four days.

"Now, this will be a change for everybody, that's for sure," Tom had said at the head staff meeting, Brett sitting beside him, freshly showered, looking triumphant, Debs looking neutral, a facial expression that was not part of her natural repertoire, her hair corralled into a giant butterfly clip. "As always, though, the thing of prime importance is the campers. The smoother this shift is, the better for everybody. The best outcome would be if the campers barely noticed. Jarring change is not permissible. Now, from what I've been told, most of the Israelis picked out to join us have had experience with North American camps before, so there shouldn't be too much of a learning curve on that front. As always, if any of your staff have a problem that you can't solve, please come to Debs, Jenna, or me. Or Brett," Tom said, glancing over at his son. "In general, Debs will be in charge of making the new staff comfortable, so I expect you to report to her, especially those of you who will have one of the Israelis in your cabin or on your speciality."

After Fallon had gathered her staff and excitedly delivered the news—one of those rare times Fallon's face betrayed her feelings—Ruby and Danielle told their cabin. The girls were getting ready for EP, and there was a frenzy of excitement, questions, giggling.

"How many guys will there be?"

"Will they speak English?"

"My cousin lives in Netanya, do you think they'll know her?"

"What are their names? What are their names?!"

Ruby and Danielle answered the questions as best they could. Ruby didn't tell her girls how she really felt about the new additions; unless directly asked, Ruby tried to keep her anti-Zionist politics to herself when it came to her campers (though she wished she had said something earlier to puncture Fallon's giddy anticipation). She could already see that this policy was going to be hard to adhere to this summer. I wonder what Seema would say, she thought as she put on her sandals and walked her girls down to the dining hall. Some CITs were playing a game of Ultimate Frisbee on centre field. As they walked by one of the CITs—tall, good-looking, loose-limbed, one of two dreadlocked CITs this summer (this one white with chunky mismatched dreads, the other kid Black with neat, even locs)—hucked the disc down the field; Ruby watched it climb high and true through the air, thousands of lightning-fast rotations propelling it to soar above the camp. It was a big, beautiful throw. One of her campers called her name, and Ruby turned away before the disc started its descent.

Stolow, meanwhile, had helped out with his unit's EP. His campers' response to the news was similar to that of Ruby's cabin, except with more questions about guns and kill counts. Though Stolow's co-counselors did a good job, Stolow was happy he didn't have to handle it; one of the many perks of being speciality staff. For the most part, he could just sit back and let the cabin's counselors deal with any problems—it must be what being an uncle is like, he thought as he tuned his guitar and got ready to meet up with Tyler and the others at the ski docks. Leaving the cabin, lumber jacket on, toque in back jean pocket, spliff in front jean pocket, the smell of campfire already in the air, he thought briefly about what his new staff would be like.

As Stolow walked the dirt path towards the docks, Debs was just finishing up her rounds. She had gone to each cabin, to see how the news was being digested, to answer any questions the staff or campers had. So far it was much as she had expected. She let cabin 8 put a single braid in her hair; it was already subsumed in the orange conflagration. She was exhausted, but there were still many hours until sleep. She had not yet sworn today.

Night descended over the camp. The moon was the tiniest sliver of waning silver, a toenail thrown from a great height, wheeling through the pitched sky.

A LETTER FROM SEEMA

June 28, 2013

Ruby!

Hello, hello. Here it is: my first letter to you. I'm excited for this. I've never had a pen pal before. Well, not a paper-*and-pen pal. How have your first days of camp been? Is Phil behaving himself? I've been living in Canada for ten years, I* feel *Canadian in many ways (more than I feel Jordanian, but not more than I feel Palestinian :)), but still the concept of Jewish sleepover camp is foreign to me. (And yes, I know you've explained it to me* many *times, and yes of course I understand what it is, but do I* understand *understand? Nope. Not really.) What a word camp is:* camp. *For me, camp always meant refugee camp, where my cousins, aunts, and uncles live. Then I come to Toronto, start university, meet you, fall in deepest friend-love with you, learn that camp is this utopic paradise you spend eight weeks at every summer, where kids of all ages willingly give up their cellphones, video games, and computer screens to be in* nature *(and I guess more importantly to be away from their parents!), and that there's dozens, if not hundreds of them, all over the continent! And then, of course, there's those other camps, those camps you and I still live in the long shadow of. Oh my! Why this one word for so many disparate things? Tell me, Ruby!*

You missed a doozy of a union meeting yesterday. Mohammed and T.Y. got into a huge debate about the union's stance on closing the university for non-Christian holidays. Mostly, we were still debriefing from the last strike, going over our tactics; things are pretty much stalled til Jamil's trial finishes up. Writing it out, the meeting seems more like a snoozy than a doozy. Guess you had to be there. Oh—you're never going to believe this! The York "powers-that-be" have built a big "welcome" centre right in the middle of Vari Hall. It's like a huge octagonal desk. They think they can stop our protests by fucking up our common spaces—how wrong they are.

Speaking of Jamil's trial, it has been delayed yet again. He thinks the school is afraid, as they should be. Does the administration really think they'll scare the union from holding another strike? (Or are they just trying to suck us dry of money through lawyer fees?) Anyways, Jamil and the other defendants think they have a strong case. Going to the offices of the board of governors and demanding a meeting is perfectly within the bounds of a lawful strike, even if things did get a little "heated." Besides, as Prof. Zipperstein would put it, what better place than university to flex our activist muscles, demand justice now*? Anyways, it's all Jamil will talk about. He's studying case law to look for precedent! He says he wants to go to law school after he finishes his master's. Which just means: more student loans. Le sigh.*

The union, getting high on campus, sleeping in the library, getting all jittery on four cups of coffee isn't the same without you, Ruby. The first summer semester is almost over, and I'm going to be getting more hours at the restaurant, so I won't be up there as much for the next little while.

I await your letter. Send me the hot goss!

Yours in Struggle,
Seema

CHAPTER 6

NOT TO GET ALL DIURNAL ABOUT IT

— DAY —

The light starts as a faint scratch on the east side of the lake, spreads into a dark blue wound oozing through the pines. When the kitchen staff arrive from the Spruce on their bikes and ATVs the world is still dark, yet objects are beginning to resemble their daytime forms: pre-dawn. After turning on the ovens, Geoff sneaks out onto the porch, watches the sun come up over the chilly lake, fiery and golden in its windless repose, songbirds trilling in welcome all around him. Since taking an art history class last semester Geoff had been painting, had lately been obsessed with colour theory; how could he capture such vibrancy on the canvas? Hearing Cindy calling from the kitchen in Anishinaabemowin with the day's assignments, Geoff takes one more look at the peach-and-nectarine inferno and heads back to work. Shortly after, it's wake-up time for the rest of the camp. The sounds of bathroom doors swinging open and shut, grumbling campers, staff shaking them awake. Unit 1 is on morning song; they choose "Party Rock Anthem," flail and jump around the flagpole.

For breakfast, it's French toast, gallons upon gallons of corn syrup, the daily offering of cereal, bug juice, hot drink. During morning announcements, after all the singing and cheering and table-stomping, Tom reminds everybody to drink sunscreen and wear lots of water, it's going to be a hot one, a joke he'll repeat ad infinitum all summer.

Since it's Friday there will only be three activity periods, two before lunch and one after, the rest of the day spent doing a big cabin clean to get ready for Friday night. Tova and her trippers are prepping the gear for the first trip of the season, the lawn in front of the trip shed a sea of tents, packsacks, food barrels, life jackets, tarps. Ruby stops to look at the big map Tova drew and nailed to the trip shed door as her cabin makes their way to their swim lessons. The inaugural trip of the summer is the same every year: fourteen-year-old boys and girls, a three-night loop in Algonquin Park. Tova's careful, detailed drawing has the lakes outlined in blue, the portages in red, the line of the trip in black. Ruby remembers her own unit 3 trip well, feels a slight pang for no longer being a camper.

They'll miss the arrival of the Israelis. Ruby wonders what kind of camp they'll return to.

Ah, the first Friday of camp. From the end of third period until dinner, every cabin is busy making beds, sweeping floors, cleaning toilets and sinks, avoiding cleaning by hiding under the covers, playing cards, gossiping on beds, joking on porches, listening to their Friday cleaning music—if you were to walk down any of the three cabin lines you'd hear snippets of The Offspring, Wyclef Jean, Queen, Michael Jackson, Phish, the Dead, Grizzly, Ani DiFranco, Jefferson Airplane, Justin Bieber, Nicki Minaj—standing in line to shower, showering, scrubbing as much of the dirt and sunscreen off as possible, leaving the showers into that expectant warm Friday air, trading clothes, standing in front of mirrors, sharing cologne and perfume, hair gel and mousse, popping pimples, talking about girlfriends, boyfriends, potential partners for next week's social. Even though the whole camp gathers three times a day to eat together, Friday nights at Burntshore—as at Jewish camps throughout cottage country, from the most secular to the most orthodox—still conjure some of that traditional Jewish difference. Tom might have toned down most of the religious aspects of his father's heyday, but Friday night is nevertheless a special time at Camp Burntshore, even a sacred time: the end of the week, a celebration of the camp, of the summer, of being alive, of being in a tightknit Jewish collective on the side of a small lake in a vast country.

Everyone gathers in centre field before dinner to socialize, show off Friday finery of dresses, skirts, dark jeans, collared shirts, gelled hair, take pictures with disposable and digital cameras in endless formations, make silly faces, make serious faces, make happy faces, eyes caught mid-blink, illicit looks, arms around shoulders, the lake a dish of olive oil that the sun poured brilliant balsamic into as it tipped over the trees. Inside the dining hall, the tables are rearranged into a big horseshoe, with the campers sitting on the outside benches, the staff and CITs sitting on the inside, an innovation of Debs's, to help foster connections among units, cross-age community. Friday dinner is always the same: chicken soup, challah, chicken, roasted potatoes, boiled vegetables. For dessert, chocolate cake, the fudgy icing thick and sugary. One of Cindy's favourite meals to make, she often brings a couple of roasted chickens back to the Spruce, especially if her sons are visiting.

Friday night EP, a.k.a. FEP: the first official fire of the summer. The younger two units meet at the paddle dock firepit, the older two at the rec hall pit, and the CITs at the CIT Pit in CIT Town. Camp songs are sung, stories are told, unit heads make treacly speeches, campers perform skits, rituals are repeated, tweaked, created, glances are stolen, bonds are made, flames are gazed into. A few of the younger kids cry, overwhelmed with the bittersweet end of that incredibly finite mineral, a summer week.

Before lights out, Ruby and Danielle play their nightly round of roses and thorns with their cabin, walking up and down the newly swept wooden floor, using their flashlights as spotlights on their campers sitting on their bunks.

"Thorn," June says, lying on her stomach on her top bunk, her legs swinging behind her. "I forgot my second bathing suit at home. Rose: being back with all my stanky bitches!"

"Thorn: tonight's sweaty chicken. Rose: Stolow smiling at me while strapping me into the harness!"

"Thorn: Mikey farted at the fire, and it stunk. Rose: I don't think I'm in love with Mikey anymore."

After every camper has their turn, Ruby walks to the door. "Okay girls, lights out. See everybody tomorrow. Our first Saturday sleep-in. Yay!"

Ruby flicks off the lights.

— NIGHT —

Darkness descends in a burst of grapefruit pinks, blood-orange reds, and lemon yellows. Once the kids are asleep, staff who are not on cabin or night duty slip into their hoodies, into their light jackets, into their sweats, their sandals. Joints and pipes and lighters and water bottles of rum are slipped into pockets. Cabin doors swing open, swing shut. The discrete patterns of camp at night take over from their daytime variants: from kid-oriented to getting-fucked-up-oriented; from regimented, supervised activities to laughter and music and sex. From one world, another. Staff congregate at the swim docks, at the dining hall, at the staff lounge, at various firepits, at head staff cabins across the road, in the woods. Older staff yell at first years for having flashlights on as they cross each other in centre field: "Hey, dude, get that out of my eyes." The first years, unpracticed at traversing camp in the dark, lower their beams, embarrassed; yet another thing to get used to on the other side of the camper-staff divide. And though there are goings-on every night of the week, Friday nights are still Friday nights. The weekend is still the weekend. In a strange way, even more so than in the city.

Stolow finds Tyler at the ski docks, jamming with some of the first years under the meagre dock lights. He sits down, his guitar between his legs, takes in the jam. A few of the first years are good. Real good. Unusually for a camp jam session, one of the players is a girl. She's playing the chords of the progression with real flair. Who *is* that?

They're playing "St. Stephen," a regular jam at the camp, each player having a turn soloing. When it's the girl's turn to lead, she falls into her E Mixolydian solo with patience and control, behind which, Stolow thrills to hear, a vast ocean of music churns. Stolow unconsciously slides his guitar into his lap, plays a single strum for each chord in the progression: E, D, A, E. Tyler, without looking up, noticing the addition of Stolow's guitar, switches to playing a pared-down bassline on his acoustic, his long hair covering his rectangular, expressive face, his Cowichan sweater zipped up to his neck. Sure enough, the new girl's solo starts to build, taking its time, and then—Stolow digging into each chord, everybody else chugging along, Tyler pounding the root notes of the chords—takes off into glorious multi-note runs.

When the jam finishes, there's a pause in the music, a lake of dissipated sound holding them all together. Stolow and the girl stare at each other.

"I'm Stolow."

"Vlada."

"She's a first year," Tyler says, combing his hair back with his fingers.

"First year at Burntshore?"

"Nope, I've been here since I was nine."

"Fuck! Can't believe I didn't recognize you."

Vlada smiles, her eyes creasing.

"It's okay, Stolow. I recognized you."

Everybody laughs. The lake laps underneath the dock. Bugs buzz around the lights. Bodies adjust.

"Hey, Tyler, any new tunes?" Stolow asks, embarrassed from not remembering Vlada.

Tyler picks his guitar up, never one to miss an opportunity to perform. The camp's resident troubadour. His hair once again in his face, he pushes it back, unzips his sweater. "Always."

He strums an open E chord; while the chord rings out, Tyler retunes three of the strings by ear, putting it into open D add 9 tuning. "This one is called 'Ode to Intermarriage.'" Everybody laughs. "I'll dedicate it to Stolow, to his Korean mother and Ashkenazi father, and to all of us who are the blessed offspring of marriage outside of the Jewish faith. Some say intermarriage is the second Holocaust, but what do we say? We say phooey!"

Tyler starts to play. Stolow knew the song already of course, had heard it many times over the school year; his left hand is poised on the fretboard, hovering over the seventh fret. He knows just where to come in for his improvised solo, which he hopes will be a fiery one. Tyler's almost finished the verse. Even though his eyes are closed, Stolow can feel Vlada watching him, can see the creases on her face when she smiles like he's visualizing a chord progression. Stolow takes a breath. Tyler switches to the chorus.

Stolow starts to play.

— DAY —

On Stolow's early-morning jog, the low sun throwing near-horizontal beams of cool light, he can't get Vlada out of his head. It isn't just her looks, the shadows on her round, sweet face from the dock lights, the lake shimmering behind her. It's her musicality, her presence, her intelligence and feeling and being filtered through the strings and frets of her Yamaha acoustic. He runs past the entrance to the reserve, stops in town at the Kissing Oak, turns around, heads back to camp, his head now filling with the coming day: tire swings and high ropes, the wall and timed sprints up the rope ladder.

Later in the morning, Ruby's cabin is at S'Nature. Marula Margolis, wearing a yellow sundress, both arms stacked with bracelets, a crystal around her neck, no shoes, runs the speciality herself, with no support staff. Ruby and Marula are best camp friends while in the city, but at camp they're good city friends. An odd dynamic, but it works for them. In any case, this is the first time they have seen each other since they went for a midnight paddle sesh during pre-camp.

"Shitty about Phil," Marula says to Ruby before the period starts, the two of them alone in the S'Nature hut.

"Him cheating on me, or him getting booted along with your idiot brother?"

"Both, bitch!" Marula says, kissing Ruby on the cheek, grabbing her clipboard, and going out to Ruby's girls, who are waiting on the hard clay beside the hut.

Marula spends the period leading the cabin through what she calls a "guided tree meditation." They all lie down, and Marula walks among their bodies, depositing acorns, leaves, pine needles, branches, pieces of bark on the campers, talking the whole time in a soothing, lilting yoga-instructor voice. "Hemlock, pine, spruce. Elm, birch, maple, oak. Okay, everybody. I want you to think like a tree. Imagine yourself on this earth, rooted, grounded. Imagine drinking water up through your trunks, pushing it out to the very tippy-tips of each of your sprawling, reaching branches. Imagine sprouting from a seed, making it through your first season, growing taller and stronger, until a storm knocks you over, you're cut down for firewood for FEP. Oh, don't be sad, this is as natural as rainfall. But now, now imagine that this is only one part of your existence, your treesistence. Imagine every tree, while on Earth, also exists in a realm of undying trees." Danielle laughs beside Ruby, covers it up with a cough. Marula continues on, her voice softer now, quieter, you have to strain to catch it. "Imagine these trees living simultaneously in two dimensions. One here, susceptible to the blade, age, bugs, and wind, the other there, without death, timeless, pure shemesh, pure soul. The energy and safety we feel from trees is just the manifestation of them being two places at once."

"Marula's kookier than ever, eh?" Danielle says as they leave S'Nature.

Ruby shrugs. "Once a kook, always a kook. The girls seemed to like it though." It was true: most of their campers were skipping ahead of them, still holding onto their tree talismans.

At Rest Hour Tom, Debs, Brett, and the head staff meet to discuss how best to integrate the Israelis into camp. There are too many people for this meeting to comfortably take place at Tom's office, so they're in Tom's cabin, which is really an expansive A-frame cottage, the White Pine River gurgling outside the open back windows. From the front windows, the sounds of Yonatan cutting wood with a chainsaw. Tom's sitting in his brown easy chair next to the stone fireplace, the sleeves of his flannel rolled up, everybody else arranged around him on the couches and chairs. Since the decision had been made, Debs had busied herself doing research, reaching out to other camp directors, doing her best to find a workable situation for the new staff members. It was quite eye-opening how varied the approaches the different camps took to their Israeli staff members. Debs felt like she was back in school—had she ever done so much reading at camp before?

"There are two main attitudes Jewish camps seem to take to their shlichim," Debs says, using the Hebrew word for visiting Israeli staff. "Either the camp keeps the Israelis 'separate,' as representatives of Israel, staying in their own cabin, planning Israel-centred programs only, going on their own day offs, etcetera. *Or* the camps integrate them fully, they sleep in camper cabins, help in planning daily events, and so on. It's a spectrum, and the Israelis themselves have agency in how they fit into the camp, of course, not just the director and the administrative staff. Now, since we're bringing in the new staff members not for, ahem, ideological, reasons or anything like that, but simply because we need the staff, and the opportunity . . . presented itself, we should obviously—well, we have to—obviously—go with the full integration method. All of which to say, the five new staff members will be both counselors and speciality staff." Debs points to the chart she made detailing where the new staff would be placed.

"Well, it's not like we didn't *not* bring them in for ideological reasons," Brett says, Ari Dressler—head of Landsports, nearly bald, a handsome face with a nose that had been broken in any number of hockey fights, wearing a Leafs jersey—nodding in agreement.

"Yeah, once they are here, we might as well bring some Zionist content into play. Why not!" Ari enthuses. "They can teach us what it's like to be in the one Jewish army in the world."

"I know that the kids in my unit are very interested in learning what it's like to be in the IDF," Fallon adds, adjusting her glasses. "It's a great opportunity Brett and Tom have given us." Debs nods. Fallon's a terrific unit head, organized, efficient, tireless, willing to give everything she has for the kids, though Debs knows a lot of staff don't like her, consider her both a kiss-ass and a hard-ass.

"Not just that," Brett says. "It's not all about the army, you know. They can show us how different things are in the Jewish state. Culture, music, language, politics, history, the fight against the Arab states and the Palestinians. They can bring it all!"

Debs looks at Ari and Brett. She knew something like this was coming. She had decided to, for now, push off any talk of Zionism. She wishes Tova were here, not leading the thirteen-year-olds through the Algonquin Park backcountry. But Tom had decided to go with Brett's plan, so Debs was going to go along with it too, as best she could. "Good points Ari, Fallon, Brett," she says. "I suggest we wait for the new staff to arrive and get settled before we talk about how we will bring Israel-centred content into our programming agenda. If the Israeli emissaries are game, then maybe we will do a few low-key Israeli-Canadian cultural exchange Evening Programs or something like that."

"Sure," Ari says, shrugging it off, "whatever." Brett remains impassive. There is definitely trouble brewing there. Fallon's writing something on her clipboard. Debs looks at Tom, who nods in response.

"Okay," Tom says, "moving right along."

— NIGHT —

The sun sets behind a weighted blanket of clouds; no colour manages to slip out from underneath. Once it is fully dark, staff venture out into the nighttime world. Elijah gets passed around in the white pines, head staff lodge gets hotboxed, night duty catch kids bunk-hopping, a glow-in-the-dark Frisbee is thrown under the inert, starless sky.

A half dozen staff are in A&C, making Shrinky Dinks to an interminable, tension-laden Grizzly jam. Ruby's making a Palestinian flag keychain she plans to mail to Seema with her next letter. When Fischer notices what Ruby is filling in with her pencil crayons, he guffaws loudly.

"C'mon Rubes, that's a fucked up thing to be making right now."

"How so?" Ruby has yet to get into it with anybody about the soldiers, has been waiting for a moment just like this. Fischer's the perfect sparring partner: a self-avowed Zionist, he spent the year after high school on Year Course, living in Tel Aviv; he and Ruby often argue about Israeli/Palestinian history, much to everyone else's annoyance. "Pass the green, please," she says to Danielle, trying to sound calm, collected, nonchalant, though she's bristling in anticipation, in the sweet, rolling agitation of pre-anger.

Fischer scoffs, takes a swig from his pop can, which, Ruby can smell, is full of whiskey. "Well, for starters, Palestinians want us all dead."

Ruby glances at what Fischer's drawing: a porcelain toilet, the tank sporting a pair of massive breasts. Ruby has to admit that Fischer's not a bad drawer.

"Dude, read a fucking book," Danielle says, Ruby's heart fluttering to have a comrade with her.

Fischer glances at Danielle, returns to Ruby. "Israel keeps us safe. Ruby, you know this. How is that flag any different from a swastika?"

Now it's Ruby's turn to guffaw.

"You have it exactly backwards, my friend. Zionism happened to the Palestinians; not the other way around. The Jews who founded the state founded it on Jewish supremacy. How is that not abundantly clear? Oh, right, you either don't read or just don't care! This flag is a symbol of hope and struggle against oppression. Unlike that other one."

"Guys, guys," Marula says, coming in as peacemaker. Her Shrinky Dink, of a towering white pine in a halo of yellow light, is nearly finished. She has a daisy in her hair. "It's a complicated situation; there's truth to what both of you are saying. We should all just want to live in peace, no?"

"Mars, I love you, but this is not the time for your liberal Zionism. If we want justice, if we want a just solution, which you do, right, Marula, then the only answer is dismantling the Zionist state, making Palestine a place for all its inhabitants, Jews, Palestinians, and everybody."

Fischer's face is as red as the nipples on his toilet. He flutters his fingers through his hair, fixing and adjusting the gelled spikes. "You've gone fucking insane, Ruby. That land is ours, it belongs to us! It was given to us by God in the Bible! The Palestinians had chance after chance to come to a peaceful agreement, yet all they could think was Jew-hatred and strapping bombs to themselves. Don't you see, their whole society is diseased, rotten. The only 'solution,' as you so ignorantly put it, is to keep the Palestinians under lock and key. Or to remove them from our land entirely." The Grizzly song had peaked, is now in a slow, atmospheric space jam, lasers and whooshes of digital sound.

Ruby laughs. "Why do you love Israel so much? What did that country, all the way over there, ever do for you, except turn you into an unapologetic racist and advocate for ethnic cleansing? I really don't get it. Tell me, please. Why do you care?"

"*I* care because the one thing I want this summer is to bang a hot Israeli soldier!" Ari Dressler blurts out, eliciting laughter, ending the discussion. Fischer keeps his head down as he finishes shading his toilet. Ruby, breathing hard, grabs Danielle's hand under the table. Later, standing at the toaster oven, watching her Shrinky Dink buckle and bend as it shrinks down into its tough final form, Ruby couldn't help but laugh: the funny thing was that even Ruby, radical anti-Zionist that she was, meaning every word she had said to Fischer, had started entertaining the idea of there being a soldier for her. Since she and Phil had broken up, she was ready for some fun—why not hate-fuck an Israeli cousin or two? It wouldn't mean anything.

Once everybody's Shrinkies are done, it's well past midnight. Leaving A&C, Ruby makes sure to turn off the lights and lock the door, pocketing the key she has to return to Andrea at breakfast. Standing on the A&C porch, Ari and Marula sharing a cigarette, a cold rain sweeps across the camp; everybody scatters. Ruby and Danielle run screaming for their cabin.

That night, strange dreams, brought in on the rain, infiltrate the camp. Tom dreams that he's at the centre of the Earth; the solid iron core hums with knowledge of the cosmos: Tom shuts his eyes to absorb as much as is humanly possible. Debs first dreams she's floating in a sensory deprivation tank, everything calm, at peace, smooth; then she's getting an ultrasound, a steady, small heartbeat on the monitor. Brett dreams he's the Green Bay Packers' QB, throws the winning touchdown at the Super Bowl, Ruby watching from the stands. Stolow dreams of falling through endless trees without a harness, guitar in hand. Ruby dreams that Phil is in the IDF. He comes back to Thornhill for weekend leave, his uniform ill-fitting, his usually shaggy hair cropped, his hands covered in gun grease, his eyes dead, flashing like mortar rounds. They fuck on the scratchy carpet of Ruby's parents' bedroom closet, go out into the broiling backyard heat to eat heaping ice cream sundaes with small wooden spoons. "How many people did you kill this time?" Ruby asks casually, licking her dream spoon. Phil doesn't answer, keeps eating his sundae. "How many people did you kill? How many?" Ruby's yelling now, is boiling with anger and hatred. "How many people did you fucking kill, Phil? How many?!" She wakes up horny, nauseous, slick with rage.

— DAY —

Strange vibrations in the camp—the first collective sour mood of the summer. Is it because of last night's dreams? The general ebb and flow of human emotions? The phase of the moon, carefully charted on a white-board inside the S'Nature hut? Or is it because, with the Israelis' arrival tomorrow, today is the last day of the old Camp Burntshore? Whatever the reason, it's a cool, dewy day, campers and staff alike sluggish. Still, there are pockets of excitement. Any camper or staff member that has an IDF T-shirt, sweatshirt, or toque, or anything with Hebrew writing really, are wearing them; the boys talk about guns, kill counts, uniformed breasts; the girls, about bravery, tanned arms, the careless hotness of a soldier in his loose-fitting olive green pants and shirt. Everybody is asking the same questions: What will they look like? What will they talk like? What will they be like?

What will happen to camp once they arrive?

Ruby is in a piss-poor mood, has a splitting headache even though all she did last night was smoke a couple of joints, take a few bong hits and some pipe hoots with Danielle in the thick green dark behind the cabin before they went to bed. She had decided to fuck worrying about getting caught—she was smart, she knew how to behave—and had fallen back into smoking with a vengeance. But here she was, confronted with the downside to living sky-large: she's super brittle, anything will set her off.

This camp she loved more than anything else, about to change irrevocably. These people and their pretensions, their performances, their props. Casey and his Oakleys. Dawn and her constant need to sleep. Debs and her clipboard, her mountain of orange hair, her fucking swear jar. Marula and her new-age hippieness, her centrist politics, her new daily routine of staring at the sun in the early morning and late evening in order to decalcify her pineal gland. And what about you, Ruby? What do you hold onto to feel real, alive, like a person who matters?

Fuck off, Ruby says to herself.

— NIGHT —

Raskin leaves for Toronto. Geoff shows up at the ski docks for the first time that summer. He doesn't join in the jam, just watches, listens. Casey convinces Stolow to let a bunch of them run high ropes in the dark. Ruby, after a ninety-minute nap, feels rejuvenated, her old self. She puts on a sweater and leaves her cabin to find somewhere to hang out. Fischer, standing on top of the high diving tower, his spiked hair catching what little light there is, his friends drunkenly cheering him on from the beach, pisses a high, clean arc of piss into the dark frothing lake.

— DAY —

The sun rises behind a grey sky, but by 10 a.m. it's all burnt off; the crappy weather has moved on to lower the temperature and screw with the brain chemistry of another lake. Today's the day: the Israelis are arriving. Raskin is supposed to pick them up at the Toronto airport around noon; without any major delays, they'll be at camp by three o' clock.

Ruby's at main gate when they arrive. The newcomers jump out of Raskin's van, a few of them still wearing their army fatigues, others shorts and tank tops, green army duffel bags over their shoulders. Their soldier shoulders, Ruby thinks, leaning against an oak. The anger she felt towards dream-Phil translates easily enough. They certainly look glamorous, Ruby admits—tall, confident, competent, hale. Not out of place at all. One of the girls is very tan, very gorgeous, with lush black hair and a mouth of straight white teeth that light up everything around her when she smiles; the boys will not be leaving *her* alone. Some of the guys are pretty okay too; one of them, tall with broad shoulders and a buzz cut, is holding a hardshell guitar case. Should she yell out "colonizers!"? (Should she ask them how many they've killed?) Might as well wait to get to know them better first.

A crowd quickly gathers. Boys and girls reach out, grab the fatigues, ask questions. One of the boys mimicks firing a machine gun. The Israelis, bombarded, under siege, look collectively unsure, off-balance, lost. Chaos. Debs is running around, trying to keep everything organized. A pen flies off her clipboard. Finally, Tom and Jenna show up, start ushering the new staff members towards the office. Debs has a Debs-level scowl on her face.

Well, here we go, thinks Ruby.

— NIGHT —

The low-yet-forceful wind folds the yellow yolk of the sunset into the blue batter of the lake. Once the wind settles, the lake's crust hardens into a verdant cerulean, soon to be glazed with sugary moonlight. All of the staff who aren't on cabin or night duty are in the dining hall with the Israelis, who prepared a little skit to introduce themselves, which they perform standing on one of the long tables. Four of them sit on the table and one—the tall, vigorous young man Ruby noticed earlier, with long solid limbs and a buzz cut—is lecturing them, mimicking the cadences of an Israeli general. "Now, troops, here comes your most important mission yet: watching over young Canadian Jewish yeladim in a faraway land."

The seated Israelis gasp in exaggerated, surprised shock. "Ken, there will be some cultural differences. Ken, they will not know what hot shalosh is. Ken, oh, ken, they will cry if you yell at them, so, please, try to yell only ten, fifteen times a day. Ken, it'll be cold there, so remember to wear your army-issue parkas." The staff laugh. All five of the Israelis mime putting on heavy winter coats, boots, hats, gloves, but it's not enough: they still shiver violently. When the skit is done, they jump up one at a time and introduce themselves: Dov, Orit, Michal, Etai, and Yehouda. Michal is the gorgeous one Ruby noticed at main gate, Dov the tall one with excellent posture who led the skit. Tom gives a short speech of his own before leaving, about welcoming the newcomers, taking some time to get to know each other. "We will all be learning lots over the coming days." Once Tom's gone, Raskin casually delivers a wine box filled with forties of vodka, gin, and tequila. "Yehouda was asking if we knew how to drink here at Burntshore," Raskin says, arranging the bottles on the table. "Well, let's find out!"

The contents of Raskin's wine box gets spread around; the drinking begins. Ruby is sitting with Marula, Stolow, and Tova. Talia is at her most flirtatious. At first the Israelis are clumped together, but as the night progresses the two groups start to intermingle. Brett, Casey, and Fischer are laughing and talking with Dov and Orit. Ruby is surprised to see Fallon there; she usually keeps either to herself or with other head staff at night. Tyler starts speaking to Michal in what sounds to Ruby like perfect Hebrew.

"Wow, I didn't know you went to Hebrew day school, Tyler!" she says.

Tyler laughs, combs back his hair with his fingers. "I didn't, my Filipina nanny taught me."

Outside the dining hall windows, whole genera of bugs flitter and flap.

By midnight they're at the paddle docks, sitting around a blazing fire. Most of the younger staff had wandered off, the guitar players are at the ski docks; it's just the older counselors, the Israelis.

"Your commander-sergeant, Tom, is a very interesting man," Dov says. Dov has the heaviest Israeli accent of all of them, pronounces Tom to rhyme with "roam."

"He told us all about the geological history of this part of Ontario while we were in his office," Orit, who went to high school in Ann Arbor, Michigan, and speaks perfect English, says with a mix of incredulity and sarcasm.

"I'm surprised Tom managed to leave out the rocks and the ice from his little speech just now," Ruby says.

"'I will never be flippant towards rocks again,'" a number of them say in unison.

They pause to drink, smoke, watch the fire. Ruby notices Dov looking at his surroundings, taking it in, surveying.

"What are those?" Dov asks, motioning with his head towards the lights on the west side of the bay, twinkling across the water. Somehow, Ruby knows Dov doesn't mean the cottage lights or the lights of Spitsville.

Apparently, so does Talia. "It's the First Nations reserve," she answers, practically sitting on Yehouda's lap, the two of them having quickly progressed from flirting to pawing. "Geoff, and most of the other kitchen staff, live there, and Cindy, the head chef, is from there too. Have you met her? She's fantastic, but don't double-cross her!"

"It's why the food is so good! You should consider yourself lucky you weren't here before Cindy arrived."

"Reserve? What is this?"

Ruby explains: the arrival of Europeans, the broken treaties, the wars, the forcing Indigenous people into small parcels of land, the residential schools. She doesn't know the history well, but she knows enough to be repulsed. The history she doesn't tell Dov: Holleander Spitz buying all the land around the lake, except for the reserve—which is probably why he treated the inhabitants viciously the rest of his vindictive life. Spitz giving most of the land to the government upon his death; his sons selling the rest to cottagers, and, eventually, to Tom's father, Dan, who built the camp.

Dov looks interested. "You have this here? Ra'atem ?" he asks, turning to his fellow Israelis. "Yesh lahem raion nahon."

"What's he saying?" Ruby asks.

"He's saying we should try that in our country," Michal answers, slightly disgusted.

"Are you fucking serious?" Ruby's heart is pounding in her throat. Here we go.

Dov looks at Ruby, the firelight flicking off his face as he studies her before responding. "No, no, of course not. Of course not!" Dov raises his hands in exaggerated innocence.

Talia and Yehouda, who were making out with increasing intensity, tip off their log and fall onto the ground, dangerously close to the flames. Yehouda jumps up and pulls Talia away from the fire. Talia, laughing, smudges some of the ash that had gotten onto her top across her face, runs into the woods, giggling. Yehouda looks back, shrugs, and jogs after her.

The excitement shoves the fire past the tense moment. Tova rearranges the burning logs. Multiple conversations branch off. Ruby stays by herself for the moment, packs and lights a bowl, exhales out the side of her mouth. Did Tova, talking with Casey and some of the Israelis, just wink at her?

Later, the Israeli named Etai sits down next to Ruby.

"Don't mind him, eh?" he says. "Dov is, how do you say, a fucking asshole?"

Ruby smiles in a way she knows is bitchy, but she doesn't care. "So what, you don't agree with him then?"

"Who, me? Oh no no no. I am not like my fellow Israelis. Can I tell you a secret?"

Ruby raises an eyebrow.

Etai's face drops into intense seriousness. "I'm not supposed to be here," he says.

Ruby stares at him. His black hair sits in wide curls on his forehead. His face is big and open, his brown eyes full of emotion. He's like a teddy bear. Ruby's hands rest on the log she and Etai are sitting on; she can feel the hard, grooved texture of the wood. "What do you mean?"

"When I refused to serve in the Occupied Territories, the army threw me in jail. I've been in jail three times so far for this refusing."

"Why'd you refuse to serve in the Occupied Territories?"

"Lama at choshevet? Why do you think? I saw the way you looked at Dovi. Trust me, I hate the occupation as much as you. Maybe more. I hate all of it. The whole shebang. That's why I refuse." He pronounces *shebang* like it was two words, subject and verb.

Ruby bites her lip. "When you're not in jail, what are you doing, though? Are you in the army?"

Etai shrugs. "Sort of yes, sort of no? It's hard to explain. I'm not serving, exactly, basically waiting to be given orders again, which I refuse, and then back to my cell, which is very nice, I must tell you. Very cozy."

Ruby laughs, half in disbelief, half in delight. "I find it hard to believe the Israeli government would send a soldier who doesn't follow orders to represent Israel at a Canadian Jewish summer camp."

"Did I not say that I'm not supposed to be here?" Etai smiles, his eyes catching the starlight.

Ruby is beginning to enjoy the rhythm of this conversation.

"Well, then, Etai, why *are* you here?"

Etai leans in close. Ruby can smell his body wash, the vodka on his breath. Etai's seriousness has descended into a new register, well below ground-level. "I will tell you why. It was . . . a clerical error."

"A clerical error?"

Etai nods gravely. "Yes. Is that not how you say? An error of a clerical nature? Can you believe? Is it not too perfect?"

Ruby laughs, shakes her head. Of all the soldiers to send to her camp. "Where'd Tom place you?" she asks.

"On Ski." Ski. It was a good fit. The kids would love him, would feel comfortable with him behind the wheel of the boat, would try their best to impress him, to get up on the skis, to cut through the wake.

"Maybe I'll come visit you tomorrow."

"I'd like that."

A pair of loons call in the distance. Everybody turns to the lake. Ruby wonders for how many of the Israelis it's their first time hearing the unique sound. A cackling, haunting, melodic laughter, impossible to describe. It wouldn't be long before the sky to the right of them, the exact direction of the loons' metaphysical lament, will show the first signs of morning.

— **DAY** —

There's a lineup at the infirmary. There's a lineup at the tuck counter. There's a lineup at the showers. Geoff stands at his workstation, cutting onions and carrots, playing through last night's jam at the ski docks, imagining where he could enter, what he would play. Stolow writes Vlada a song he will never perform for her. Casey Mustard's kids, with Yonatan's help, are filling in the potholes on all the camp roads, loudly singing The White Stripes. Dawn comes into the cabin, says how exhausted she is, collapses onto her bed. A pre-CIT boy, his chest tight with desire, watches Yehouda, one of the new Israeli staff members, a big, smiley lunk, eager to please, perform a crisp, perfect dive off the high jump tower. Yehouda knifes into the water, barely disturbing its calm surface, his plump toes visible for a perfect instant before being sucked under.

— **NIGHT** —

Tuesday night, Debs decides a cookout would be a good idea to help welcome the new staff. Counselors man the long tables set up in centre field, doling out hot dogs, burgers, veggie burgers, buns, fries, and salad. At either end of the tables are the condiments: ketchup, mustard, relish, pickles, Tabasco. The plates are paper, the cups of bug juice, plastic. After dinner Tom leads the entire camp in a garbage pick-up (Ruby can still remember when the weekly cleanup was called a "buffalo hunt," before Cindy came on and had Tom change it). Every camper has to find at least six pieces. All five of the Israelis collect massive amounts of garbage, exude friendly competitiveness, egging the campers on, holding up their garbage bags in triumph. Ruby notices Fallon talking with Etai, laughing, touching his arm. Is she wearing makeup? Ruby blinks, looks away. Debs sits on a picnic bench near the flagpole, watching the cleanup, senses attuned for any and all atmospheric changes.

The lake is a cake with knife-carved icing. Clouds pile up on the horizon like dollops of whipped cream.

It's going to be a fantastic sunset.

Later. The staff lounge. Another night of drinking and smoking with the Israelis. Ruby, a little too high, her fingertips tingling, her stomach crampy, sits in an easy chair, watches Etai and Fallon at the computers, the only place in all of camp with internet access. Fallon's showing Etai pictures on Facebook of a trip she took to Israel. They're leaned in close, whispering, laughing, their bodies bright. Ruby has never seen Fallon without her glasses before; she must be wearing contacts for the first time in her entire Burntshore career. Ruby knows she's acting irrationally—why else had she worn her tightest, scoopiest black T-shirt, combed her hair?—but can't help it. What does he see in Fallon, anyways? Ruby has to admit that Fallon is okay-looking, in a tall, flat-chested, horsey sort of way. But she has the personality of a tree. She's so . . . mainstream. Not that Ruby knows what part of the stream Etai swims in, but their conversation last night had apparently left its mark. His face when he told her about the clerical error. But still, he's a soldier, an oppressor, if not directly, then still part of the machine.

Marula crashes down on top of Ruby. "What's up, bitch?" Marula's wearing her yellow sundress, blue eyeshadow, smells like sweat and patchouli. "What d'you think of our new colleagues?"

Ruby laughs, bites her lip. "The jury's still out I'm afraid."

Marula giggles, squeezes Ruby's cheeks. "I think it's great! Jews from very different places, different cultures, bonding over our shared peoplehood. Such good energy!"

Ruby has stopped listening. Fallon is telling Etai a story of some kind, her face more animated than Ruby has ever seen it. Ruby pats Marula, wiggles out of the chair, makes her uneasy way to the couch, sits next to Casey, who is drinking a beer, fiddling with his Oakleys. So beautiful. So stupid.

"Hey, Casey," Ruby says. When Casey turns, she puts her hand on his bicep and starts to make out with him. For a long, swirling minute they're really going at it. Everybody in the lounge cheers. When Ruby pulls away, Casey looks stunned, dopey, pleased. Ruby's disgusted—Casey tasted like beer and beef jerky, his tongue a steel probe—but hides it, shrugs playfully.

Her eyes catch Etai's. He's smirking, staring at her over Fallon's shoulder, who's still talking, oblivious.

Only a handful of hours until sunrise.

CHAPTER 7

DEBS HAS A SLEEPLESS NIGHT; THE FLAG AND THE KNAPSACK; RUBY AND ETAI IN THE SKI BOAT

Debs couldn't sleep. Her suite in the staffies was too hot; she opened a window. Then it was too cold; she shut the window, leaving the tiniest crack. Despite the uncomfortable temperature, Debs knew the real reason she wasn't able to sleep: Burntshore was going through the most momentous change since Tom took over from Dan, his father. She couldn't help feeling that Brett had thrown a wrench into the summer's gears, and she was doing everything she could to keep the machine running at whatever efficiency she could manage. Sooner than she would have liked, the windows of her cabin started to glow. Stolow would be lacing up for his morning run about now. Most mornings Debs would be on the staffies' second-floor porch having her first cup of tea by the time Stolow jogged past, but not today. She closed her eyes, went through her mental clipboard of the new staff, placing imaginary checkmarks, making notes.

Overall, the Israelis themselves were friendly, gung-ho, industrious. They had no trouble adjusting to the particular communal rhythms of Burntshore. All this was good. Yehouda was a sweetheart. Strong as anything, a team player with infectious energy; the campers loved him. He was placed with the CITs, though he would have done well anywhere. Not the most seaworthy canoe in the fleet. Etai, at twenty-one, was the second oldest of the Israelis, and he seemed it: the most mature, the most patient, the most even-keeled. Ski was a good fit for him; he would ramp up the pros, make the beginners and the fearful feel at ease. Dov, not only the oldest but the only new staff member not in the army—he had finished two years ago, backpacked through South America, was getting ready to start university—Dov was going to be trouble. Debs had known staff like Dov her entire camp career, arrogant, intelligent, knows the one right way to do things, a natural leader (and always, *always*, male); mix in Dov's Israeli bluntness, his knee-weakening attractiveness, and his foreign allure, and it was a recipe for disaster, or at least some broken hearts. And too many broken hearts do not an amazing summer at camp make. She'd have to keep an eye on Dov, not least of which because Brett had seemed to take a particular liking to him; she had seen the two of them coming back from the Crown land, crossing the river, arms around each other, laughing (the question of what they were doing out there in the woods flitted through Debs's head, but it didn't seem worth catching, holding, worrying). Placing Dov on Ropes made sense. During the day he was removed from the regular goings-on of the camp, and Stolow could handle his brash forwardness. And, hey, might as well put his strength and charisma to work.

The two new female staff were similar to the guys in terms of competence and outgoingness. Michal was easy to talk to, upbeat and fun, her campers seemed to have taken to her. If she didn't have a boyfriend back home, she would soon have any number of suitors here (even if she did have a boyfriend back home). Orit was a little harder to read, quiet even in her team-playerness, eyes that took everything in but didn't reveal much—maybe because she spent her teenage years in America and was therefore neither all Israeli nor all American? Debs would seek her out this afternoon at the swim docks.

In any case, it wasn't the Israelis as individuals that were the issue, it was what their arrival precipitated in the camp. In a way—though would a stranger walking through centre field notice anything different?—Camp

Burntshore had transformed overnight. The IDF shirts and sweatshirts were still out in force; Debs had no idea so many campers and staff had them. For the most part, the staff had kept their collective cool, unlike the vast majority of the campers (a few, though, like Ari Dressler and Fischer, had gone overboard in their adoration). It wasn't just *one* thing, it was a series of little things. The Israelis had been invited to do morning song two days ago, and they chose "Anachnu v'Hem," a popular Israeli pop song, hip-hop lyrics over techno beats and Mizrahi melodies. Yesterday morning, a girls' cabin in unit 1 picked the same song, a rarity in the history of morning songs. Well, maybe Debs was overreacting. And besides, if it doesn't hurt the camp, what's the harm?

Debs rolled over, pushed Raskin. "Rask, time to get up." Raskin moaned, turned to Debs, put an arm over her, his face in her hair.

Later, as Debs emerged from the bathroom, Raskin was standing in the middle of the cabin, in the process of putting on a T-shirt, one thick arm held straight above him, nearly touching the exposed ceiling. The small, old, barely waterproof staffies room was just big enough for the two of them. "What do you have going on today?" Debs asked, flicking on the kettle, pulling a long orange hair off of Raskin's face.

"Running into town to pick up some extra clay for pottery, taking the bus and canoe hitch up to Algonquin after lunch to pick up Tova and the unit threes."

"Ah, yes. How'd the weather seem during their trip?" Raskin made a habit of closely following the weather of all camp trips.

"Not too bad, maybe some rain on the second day. I'm sure Tova gave them the time of their lives."

"No doubt about that," Debs said, pouring the boiling water into her blue Camp Burntshore travel mug. Debs often thought that Tova was among the best staff ever to pass through Burntshore. Tom luring her away from Outward Bound had been a terrific boon for the camp. Slathering sunscreen on her face and arms, Debs was excited to hear her thoughts on the Israelis; Tova's opinion she could trust.

"See you later." She pecked Raskin on the cheek, grabbed her walkie, her clipboard, her fanny pack, her mug, and headed out the door.

Debs had a whirlwind of a morning. Her walkie squawked: a camper twisted her ankle, was crying that she wanted to go home; Debs went to the infirmary to make sure everything was copacetic. Her walkie squawked: Yonatan needed her at the maintenance shed to discuss plans to fix the toilets in cabin 15. Her walkie squawked: a whole box of chocolate bars was missing from the tuck shop, could she come right away?

She didn't get to speak to Orit until after Rest Hour. She found her at the swim docks, watching campers practise front crawl in second area. Orit had on a black one-piece swimsuit, had her orange whistle on a *Burntshore Staff* lanyard, her hair in a tight bun, an orange swim board snug under her left arm.

"How are you finding things so far?"

"Oh, things are good. Very comfortable. The camp is very beautiful. On my first day off Yehouda and I are going to explore the lake in a canoe." As she spoke, Orit's eyes followed the pre-CIT boys as they swam their laps. "Elbows in!" she called. Not for the first time, Debs thought about how similar Orit and Fallon were: both serious, responsible young women who chose their words carefully and didn't readily show emotion. Orit could easily be running swim.

"That sounds great! You can camp on Big Rock Island if you want, just check with Tova that none of the unit ones are there for a cookout. The black sand is also worth the paddle."

"We will definitely keep that in mind." Orit turned to Debs, switched her board to her right arm. A volcano of joyful shrieking erupted from the little kids playing in first area. "Deb, can I ask you something?"

Debs blinked. "Yes, of course, that's what I'm here for."

"Well, some of us shlichim are still a little unclear on what is expected of us here. Are we to be simple staff members, or should we be bringing more of Israel into what we do? We've been trained to be representatives of our country, but we feel that's not really what's expected of us. I know Tom covered this topic on our day one, but we are still unsure. Are we here simply as hired hands?"

Debs nodded along. These were the exact things that kept her up at night. The docks rocked with the waves created by the ski boat zipping past. Etai, topless, waved from the wheel. "Yes, well, as far as I'm concerned, you are here as staff, with the same responsibilities as any of the other staff. Feel free to be yourselves, of course."

Orit glanced at the swim lanes. "Two more laps! Hey, I saw that! Thanks, Debs, I understand. At the camp I went to in America, we were told for the first few weeks to leave our Israeli flags in our knapsacks. When the campers are more comfortable, when we all have become friends, only then do we take out our flags."

"Metaphorically speaking." Debs meant it as a question, but it came out more as a statement.

"Metaphorically speaking."

"Could you give me an example of what you mean by Israeli flags?"

Orit stared at Debs before responding. "Oh, like Hebrew word of the day, little history lessons, things like that."

"These are good questions, Orit. I'll have to confer with Tom. This is all new to us as well."

"Thank you, Debs. Like I say, some of us are more . . . passionate about bringing Zionism to the diaspora children. Things are very different here in Canada than in the camps we went to in America."

Debs wasn't sure if the difference was really between countries, or just between other Jewish camps and Burntshore.

Yonatan's voice crackled over Debs's walkie. "Raskin's pulling into the gate."

Debs always tried to be there when a trip returned. "Okay, Orit, it's been great talking. Feel free to come to me or Tom whenever something is on your mind."

Orit was already turning away. She blew her whistle. "That's enough. Everybody out of the water! Good job. Tov meod!"

Debs left the docks, which were shuddering with twenty teenagers pulling themselves out of the bucking lake.

By the time Debs got to main gate, Raskin was unstrapping the canoes from the hitch. Tova and her tripping staff were throwing packsacks out of the back of the bus. The kids were all standing around, looking dazed.

"Okay, okay, everybody to the showers!" Debs called out.

"Debs, is it true the new staff are here?"

"Yes, it is. Don't bother them too much, though, they're a part of Burntshore now just like all of us."

"What are they like? Did they bring their guns?"

"No, of course not. They're not soldiers here, they're just staff. They're our friends."

They're our friends.

After dinner, Debs managed to sneak away to her room. She had to close her eyes for at least a minute; her sleepless night was making itself felt. It was a camp-wide EP tonight, and she was needed. For the first time this summer, she turned her walkie off.

~~~

While cabin 9 was at Swim, Ruby picked her way along the shore to Ski. It had been a few days since the fire at the paddle docks. After making out with Casey, Ruby had decided to not visit Etai at all, but that morning she woke up knowing she was going to; there was something compelling about him that she needed to investigate, pull close to, scratch til it bled. If it made Fallon—who Ruby had spotted with Etai in the dining hall, at the office, walking cabin line—angry, even better.
~~~

A cabin of unit 2 boys were at Ski, the campers waiting on the wooden seats along both sides of the dock for their turn; some of them wore unzipped life jackets, others held theirs in their hands. Ruby's brother was there; they said hello before he quickly looked away. A Justin Timberlake song was coming out of an old battery-powered boom box set to The Otter 95.9, "Muskoka's Most Trusted Summer Rock Station" (no relation to her brother's nickname, "Otter"; at least, Ruby didn't think there was).

When Ruby heard the motor of a returning boat she looked out over the lake. There was Etai. He was topless, wearing black sunglasses, his curly hair wild in the wind. His arms were muscled, his stomach flat and rippled. He pulled up cleanly to the dock, slowing down so the skier he was towing could gently sink into the water. He drove the boat well.

When Etai saw her, he grinned, beaming in the beating sunlight.

"Come aboard!" he said. "Yalla!" Ruby grabbed a yellow life jacket from the rack and stepped into the boat, smiling at the first-year Ski staff stationed in the back as a spotter.

Ruby's brother's turn was next; when he was set up, Etai drove the boat away from the dock. Otter's real name was Jordan, though everybody at camp, Ruby included, called him Otter. He was one of the rare younger kids that everybody at camp knew: loud, hilarious, athletic, with unkempt sandy-blonde hair, willing to talk back to anyone, climb anything, be stupid and smart-alecky and embarrassing. He was advanced enough to do a dock-launch and was soon up on the skis. Etai revved the engine, and they were barrelling towards Big Rock Island, the boat leaning into its speed, the wake's spray, the green trees, the hot sun in the blue sky.

"Where'd you learn to drive a ski boat?" Ruby asked, yelling over the engine. Etai pulled a graceful curve around Big Rock Island, Otter riding the wake, white spray exploding like icy fireworks all around him.

"My cousins used to have a cottage in Vermont. I spent my summers there."

Ruby's hair was whipping her in the face, not unpleasantly. She felt on her wrist for a hair tie but didn't find one. She should have shaved her hair off before camp started instead of just cutting it to her chin. She bit her lip. Etai's English had improved vastly since his first night here, had regained its apparent past fluency. Its Vermont fluency.

"So, tell me more about your adventures as a deserter," Ruby said.

Etai laughed. "Not quite a deserter. Though I probably should have been."

"What do you mean?"

"I still enlisted, I just refused to serve. I should have refused to enlist. Selective conscientious objecting, where I should have gone full conscientious. Sarvanim, it's called in Hebrew."

"What would have happened if you did that?"

Etai turned to her, lifted his sunglasses off his eyes. "Execution, most likely."

Ruby laughed. Just like at the docks, the conversation thrilled her.

"Haha. No, seriously. More jail time, more court dates, more social ostracization. Do you have any idea what it's like there? If you don't join the army, people will treat you like you've got the plague. The only thing worse would be to be an actual Palestinian."

"What do your parents think?"

"My dad's a dove. He's actually really proud of me. My mom is more hawkish, so she wasn't too happy with me for a while, but she seems to have gotten over it. Not worth being estranged from your only son, I guess."

Ruby nodded. The boat was bouncing along. Ruby stepped closer to Etai.

"Well," she said, pulling her hair out of her mouth, "if you refused to enlist, if you went full CO, you wouldn't have been able to come here, right?"

They were passing the reserve now. Ruby could make out the rental cottages along the shore, the band office farther back. Cottagers splashed in the roped-off swim area, canoes and kayaks scattered along the shore.

"There would have been no chance for a clerical error, that's right."

"Do you think whoever made that clerical error got in trouble?"

Etai shrugged his shoulders. “I doubt it. The only reason it happened at all was because of how short notice the call-up was. The agency can’t admit a mistake now, it would make them look bad. Outreach to the diaspora is of utmost importance, you know.”

“The never-ending PR battle.”

“Now you tell me something about yourself,” Etai said, slowing down the boat to make a wide, arcing turn. “What makes you, Ruby Shacter, tick-tock?”

They were passing the other Burntshore ski boat. Etai and Ruby waved at David Stein, who was driving one-handed, the other hand down his swim trunks. Stein pulled his hand out of his swimsuit to lift his sunglasses off his head, surprised to see Ruby on the boat. He waved with his whole free arm. Otter whooped from the water.

Ruby bit her lip. “Well, let’s see. Nothing as exciting as serving jail time, I’m afraid. I love camp, have been coming here since I was a little girl.”

“Uh-huh.”

“I’m studying poli-sci with a minor in English.”

“Ken.”

“I’m treasurer of York University’s chapter of Students Against Israeli War Crimes, and undergrad member-at-large for the part-time faculty union.”

“B’emet?”

“Oh, and that’s my brother, Jordan, sorry, Otter, back there.” She motioned behind her, Etai’s eyes going wide with surprise.

“B’emet . . . ” Etai raised his eyebrows, drew out the Hebrew word. “Fallon tells me you are also recently broken up from a serious relationship.”

Ruby guffawed. Fallon. That bitch.

“It’s true. B’emet. At the start of the summer I had a boyfriend. Phil. But I don’t any longer. He’s not even here anymore—in fact, you are here to replace him. Did Fallon tell you that?”

Etai laughed. “Not exactly.”

"What's the deal with you two anyways? I doubt she is as excited about your jailtime as I am. Fallon's a, how shall we say. A stickler for the rules."

"Tell me about it. Every time we talk she tells me about Israel. What Israel means to her, what it means to Canadian Jews. It's exhausting. Can you imagine, explaining Israel and its central role in the life of the Jews to me, an Israeli? She doesn't have a clue. She wants to work for the UJA, has mentioned many times the excellent reference letter Tom will write for her."

Etai maneuvered expertly around a difficult, shallow area of the lake, Otter cutting and slicing at the end of the ski rope. He learns quickly, Ruby thought, trying to suppress a smile.

"Tom is famous for his reference letters, it's true."

Etai looked at Ruby. "You are nothing like Fallon. Nor are you anything like the run-of-the-mill JAP I had you pegged for. No. You are something else entirely."

Ruby couldn't tell if he was joking or not, but he was smiling.

"Jewish *Canadian* Princess," she corrected.

The spotter waved at Otter that they were returning to the dock. Otter gave a thumbs-up, let go of the ski rope, slowly sank into the water, a satiated grin on his small, mischievous face.

"One other thing you should know about me," Ruby said, her head turned to watch her brother, her mouth nearly touching Etai's ear. "I despise soldiers. Especially Israeli ones."

Etai cut the engine, pulled parallel to the dock in one smooth turn.

"That, I can tell," he said.

That night, after lights out, Ruby and Etai paddled a canoe over to Big Rock Island, Ruby in the stern. Compared to their earlier journey in the motorboat, their passage across the lake barely disturbed the gently lapping water.

EVERYBODY DOES IT

Once their counselors are gone for the night—except for Dawn, snoring from the staff alcove—cabin 9 has a shaving party: a bucket of hot soapy water on the floor in the middle of the cabin, disposable razors that June brought and distributed to the girls with ritualistic solemnity. Those who have no hair have to decide: do I shave and fit in, or do I not and risk ridicule?

The boys in cabin 8 show each other their penises, talk about the first time they jacked off. "Has anyone ever had a wet dream?" one boy, quiet, prepubescent, asks.

Fischer masturbates thinking of Jenna, his face in her chest as he cries; he had had an affair with a friend's mom in high school, ruining him for anybody but older women. Stolow masturbates thinking of a threesome with Vlada and Tyler. Talia masturbates while fantasizing being in a threesome with Dov and Brett; when that isn't working she subs out Brett for Eddie Vedder. Much better. Many boys and a surprising number of girls masturbate thinking of Michal. Brett, as usual, masturbates thinking of Ruby, though Michal is there too, until she isn't.

Tyler sees Danielle leaving the shower in nothing but a faded yellow towel and three-inch pink plastic pumps, her toiletries basket swinging water droplets on the ground, fights an overwhelming need to lie down. Dov tries not to jack off fantasizing about Marula—he is constantly testing himself like this—but on the third night he gives up. Marula, lying by the river on Rest Hour, the sun hot, the ash and birch rustling above her, the river tumbling beside her, her hand up her sundress.

Hand stuff. Mouth stuff. Under the shirt stuff. Over the shirt stuff. Underwear stuff. Tongue stuff. Ear stuff. Butt stuff. All-the-way stuff. Are-you-sure-you-want-to stuff. Slower stuff. Faster stuff. Just-right stuff. Ruby-and-Etai-in-Marula's-room-in-the-head-staff-lodge-across-the-road-for-the-second-night-in-a-row-lying-together-entangled-they-had-already-fucked-four-times-in-the-last-two-hours-Etai-hard-against-Ruby-again-Should-I-put-a-condom-on-Etai-asks-by-which-he-means-should-we-fuck-again-No-cum-in-me-Ruby-says-misunderstanding-besides-she's-on-the-pill-so-Etai-doesn't-put-a-condom-on-that-time-or-any-time-after-that-holy-shit-holy-shit-holy-shit-holy-fucking-shit stuff.

A twelve-year-old boy, his first summer at camp, so overcome with horniness that he can't think straight, walks back to his cabin after lunch in a disgusting daze, his erection real and embarrassing in the jeans that his mom carefully ironed a nametag into. The thoughts he is having! He's a sick person. He's revolting. What can he do to bring some relief? Where can he go? Everywhere there are people. There is no such thing as alone. What can he do? What is he supposed to do?

Feel bad for him, sure. But he'll figure it out eventually—one way or another, relief will find him.

CHAPTER 8

WHAT EXACTLY DOES IT TAKE TO RUN A SUMMER CAMP?; THE TWO JAREDS; WHO IS OMER STRINGER?; GETTING TO KNOW EACH OTHER; RAIN DAY!; THE FIRST SOCIAL

The end of the second week, and, even with the recent upheavals, if an outsider were to leave the Big Wide, cross main gate into the world of Burntshore, walk the oak-tree-lined road past the tennis and basketball courts, through centre field, and then up any of the three paths of cabin line, there would be no doubt that camp was a single unified community. The pattern of the daily routine had become rote. Those new to camp, six-year-olds and staff members alike, had begun to understand the geography of the camp in all its tightly packed mystery: the trail behind cabin line 1 that led to the White Pine River; the shortcut from the top of the cabin lines to the basketball courts; the roof of the dining hall, the best vantage from which to see Big Rock Island and the black sand beaches beyond. The small, cascading falls beside the river's pink rock, one of camp's few forbidden spots. The cabins had solidified—hard not to after spending nearly fourteen nights together, showering together, swimming together, swinging on ropes through the sky together, paddling together, eating together, listening to each other use the bathroom together, gossiping and laughing and sharing inside jokes together. The camp had become a collective. To an outsider, what would be hard to believe is that the community of Camp Burntshore had only existed in its current form for fourteen days, not fourteen years, fourteen lifetimes, and that it would dissolve in forty-one more.

Tom loved this particular juncture of the summer, when all the disparate rocks and pebbles combine to produce the conglomerate—the tripartite pressures of proximity, heat, and time. Sitting on his office's small porch, on the wooden rocking chair his father had made over half a century ago, Tom could easily hear the hidden machinery of the camp. He closed his eyes, saw it all, the complex Earth systems that kept the camp whirring along. Cabins' laundry was picked up once a week, trucked to the laundromat, laundered in big loads, returned folded and smelling of lavender. Everybody drank from the same water, swam in the same lake, flushed the same toilets (the plumbing under everyone's feet its own networked world). Food was delivered, prepared, stored, doled out. The same trails were walked, canoes paddled, plates eaten off of. Friday night was always roast chicken, Saturday lunch always deli meat, Sunday always salad bar. It was the same sometimes choppy, sometimes calm, always majestic lake that held them in its drainage basin. The choral rhythms of 418 humans living communally in twenty-six cabins on the edge of a freshwater lake.

And all of it had a cost. The laundry service. The water filtration system. The septic system. Maintenance on the docks, cabins, buildings. The weekly food deliveries. The staff salaries. The bus. The boats. The golf carts. The gas for the bus and the boats and the golf carts. Permits for canoe trips. Materials for arts and crafts (tempera, watercolour, construction paper, clay, glaze, newsprint, pencils, pens, pencil crayons, Shrinky Dink, string, fishing wire, boondoggle, beads, beads, beads, wooden spoons, felt, pompoms, brushes, googly eyes, tie-dye). Basketballs, footballs, tennis balls, baseballs, gaga balls. Tennis racquets. Repaving the basketball courts. Repaving the tennis courts. The various insurances. Property taxes. Hydro. Camp association fees. Internet, printer paper, phone service, propane, plates, cups, cutlery, tuck, food barrels, paddles, paint, chlorine, swabs, bandages, thermometers, wax paper, pots, pans, glass jars, lightbulbs. On and on.

In many ways, Tom's job as owner of Camp Burntshore was to make sure there were enough funds to allocate to all of the above. To take money in, spread it around, put it back out. And he loved every minute of it. Some summers he and Jenna cleared a profit; others they did not. What was important was the balance sheet: just enough in to put just enough out. To run this camp, where kids had fun, bettered themselves, made friends and memories, learned how to play guitar or hold a tennis racquet, became confident, unlocked their inner selves. Tom, as he often was during the few quiet moments that puncture the camp owner's day, was full of mission, of purpose.

He stood up.

Time to get back to work.

At Friday night dinner, Ruby and Etai were sitting across from two fifteen-year-olds. Pre-CITs. Skinny boys, their hair gelled, smelling like cologne, wearing collared shirts. The one with short curly hair in tight black whorls had a small Star of David on a silver chain; the one with brown hair combed forward and flipped in front had a hemp necklace with an acorn-sized wooden bead, already faded from the sun. They both had braces. They were known as the two Jareds (Finkelstein and Silver). They were obsessed with Etai, were peppering him with questions. "Have you killed anybody?" "Have you seen any action?" "What's it like being in the army?" "Have you ever met a Palestinian?" "Do you speak Arabic?" "What do you think of Canada?" Etai, who was holding Ruby's hand under the table as he ate a drumstick with the other, answered candidly. As always, the way he handled himself in front of what Ruby saw as the obsequiousness of both camper and staff impressed her, thrilled her, worried her. If only she could bring Etai's calm, rational forcefulness to her own political struggles. On top of that, she hoped Etai wasn't taking their . . . encounter too seriously; as she said to Danielle that afternoon, it was purely physical. Purely, throttlingly, blissfully physical. Though that wasn't entirely true either: they talked *a lot*, about their lives, their families, what they read. When she found out Etai had never heard of Ursula K. Le Guin, her favourite author, Ruby immediately ran to her cabin to lend him *Always Coming Home*. Etai hadn't brought any books with him, but he printed out some stories by Etgar Keret for her. Still, that was all part of the attraction, right? It's not like they were going to declare their love for each other, go steady. She squeezed his hand.

"Can I ask *you* a question now?" Etai said after the boys' interrogation petered out, brandishing the half-eaten drumstick at the two teenagers, who raised their eyes in amazement.

"Sure!" Jared Silver exclaimed, his voice cracking mightily.

"Who is this Omer Stringer person? He is on so many of your shirts and sweatshirts. Sounds like an Israeli name."

The name *did* sound familiar, but it took Ruby a moment before she could place it: Omer Stringer, the name on the Roots shirts and sweatshirts. She could see the logo now: *Beaver Canoe, built by Omer Stringer*. To her, those words were always just what a Roots sweatshirt looked like, nothing to think about or even notice. At Burntshore, they were ubiquitous, more so than Phish or Grizzly shirts, even IDF shirts. She herself probably had three or four pieces of clothing back in her cabin that had the name on it; she looked down at what she was wearing, half expecting to see the logo.

"We have no idea!" the fifteen-year-olds said in unison. Ruby chewed a mouthful of potatoes; she was slightly embarrassed that she didn't have any idea either. She looked away. At the other end of the horseshoe she noticed Yehouda standing behind the CIT Ayelet Cho, giving her a backrub. Where was Martin, her boyfriend? She scanned Ayelet's vicinity, didn't see him.

Uh-oh. She sensed drama there.

That night, after FEP, the Israelis ran a "Let's Get to Know Each Other" staff EP. Dov had roved all over camp that afternoon, getting counselors to write down any "burning questions" they had for the new Israelis. Now, with the five Israelis up on the rec hall stage, and five staff volunteers up there as well—Marula, David Stein, Stolow, Casey Mustard, and Talia—the ten of them forming a rough semicircle, Dov pulled slips of paper at random out of a baseball helmet. Ruby was sitting with Danielle and Dawn along the wall near the piano. Seeing Etai up there with his fellow Israelis made Ruby uneasy. She couldn't stop thinking about Seema and what she would say when Ruby told her she was sleeping with a soldier, even one who had refused to serve in the West Bank (she could barely believe it herself, felt like she was falling down a hill and was powerless against gravity's gargantuan grip). She decided, watching him up there, that she would stop putting it off, would write to Seema that very night.

Dov trilled a piercing whistle with his two fingers. Usually, it took minutes to get everyone quiet enough to start a staff EP, but Dov's one whistle had them all at attention.

"B'seder. Welcome, everybody. We thought it would be good to play a little icebreaker game. Lama lo? Why not! Okay. Let's begin. Yalla. The first question is from me, and it's to both groups. We'll start with the Canadim. The question: 'What do you hate the most about Israelis?'"

Everybody laughed. Getting right into it, Ruby thought.

"Their arrogance!" David Stein exclaimed, his hands down his green Roots sweatpants.

"How they think they are true Jews, and we are not," Marula said, looking thoughtful.

"Their dark sense of humour."

"How hot and sexy they are!" Talia.

Dov raised his hand to stop the yelling and catcalling. "Tov. Here is the second part of the question, to us shlichim. 'What do you hate the most about Canadian Jews?'"

"When they criticize what we do to survive from their place of complete safety," Orit said matter-of-factly.

"Their materialism," Michal said.

"Boo!" Fischer called from the audience.

"Their diasporic weakness," Etai said, winking at Ruby.

So went the night, Dov working through the questions, the representatives answering seriously, funnily, bitingly.

"What is your favourite physical part of camp?"

"Where to start," Marula said. She closed her eyes. It looked like she was meditating. "Every path, trail, and beach. The different sounds of the different dirts and gravels of the different paths. The red pea gravel in front of the infirmary. The wood chips outside of the trip shed. The packed dirt trail on the way to CIT Town. The river stones in front of the Monolith. The field behind the head staff building. And then there's the trees. The red oak beside—"

"Tov, tov, thank you, Marula, toda," Dov said, cutting her off.

"What are your favourite sexual positions?" This was to the Israelis.

"Whatever hers is," Yehouda said.

"The one where you ride him, how do you call this?" Michal asked. Staff in the audience called out suggestions. "Ah, yes. The 'cowgirl.'"

"A more serious one now. For the Canadians. What do you think of Zionism and its place in the contemporary Jewish world?"

A chill spread through the rec hall. Ruby knew what a fair number of staff were thinking: it was good she wasn't up there.

Marula went first. "Well, I obviously don't support the occupation, but I do believe that Jews need a strong, defensive state of their own so their enemies can't kill them. We were defenseless for too long, and because of that we were almost eradicated. We just want to live in peace."

"I don't know about Zionism," Stolow said, "what Zionism means now, what it meant in forty-eight, so forth and so on. But Israel exists, and I support it."

It was Casey's turn. He moved his Oakleys from his hat to his eyes. "Don't listen to these spoon-fed liberals. We love Zionism, and we love Israel. Why else would we invite you here?" Whooping and hollering from the audience. Fischer stood up and repeatedly punched the air.

Ruby was so full of disgust she could spit. The taste of beer and beef jerky washed through her.

David Stein pulled a hand out of his sweats and grabbed the microphone from Casey. "What if we turned the question around. What do *you* upstanding Israeli citizens think of the occupation?"

Etai motioned for the microphone, leaned forward. "Against it," he said. Had Ruby imagined it, or did Dov just grimace?

Etai passed the mic to Orit. "Listen, as some of the Canadians said, it's not as simple as for or against. It's a working solution to a complex situation."

"Bull*shit*," Ruby said, not loudly, but with enough volume for the people in her immediate vicinity to hear. Her armpits were sweating. Her mouth was thick with saliva. Talking about the dispossession and occupation of millions of people as if they didn't exist. A "complex situation." Holy fucking moly. She was paralyzed between wanting to shout and not wanting to get involved. Danielle put a hand on Ruby's thigh, squeezed.

Dov took the mic. His demeanour had shifted from affable host to stoic message-bearer. He looked very determined, very serious, very potent, up there pacing the stage. He rubbed his shaved head with his calloused hand. "The truth is," he said, "none of you know what it is really like there. Our country started with five Arab states declaring war on us. We lost many men and women to make a safe haven for Jews, only to have to live with the fear of bombings, to know people who lost parents on blown-up buses. It's *them* who are killing *us*. From the beginning we offered peace, but the Arabs didn't want peace. The Palestinians don't want peace. If they did, things would be quite different. They only wanted us gone. But where were we supposed to go? What are we supposed to do but protect ourselves?"

Ruby leaned into Danielle's ear. Her mouth touched the soft, warm concavity, Danielle's hair in her face. Dov's false pragmatism, the outright lies, the historical untruths, the twisting and hypocrisy, the dehumanization, the knowledge that most everybody else was imbibing it as unimpeachable truth; it was too much for her.

"Bullshit, bullshit, bullshit," she sang.

Afterwards, some of the staff ended up at A&C, making Mr. Noodles and Kraft Dinner with the white electric kettle that had A&C head Andrea's name painted on it in multicoloured letters. They waited for the water to boil at one of the long wooden benches, covered in paint, Fimo, campers' names, Rorschach blotches of dye. Around them were shelves and shelves of materials, paints, paper. In the adjacent room was the kiln, the fired pottery waiting to be glazed. There was a misshapen slab of discard clay on the table, left over from the day's pottery period; Casey ripped it into chunks and passed it around. Ruby held her chunk in her hand, weighing it, while with her other hand she slurped her burning hot noodles. She decided to make a pipe. Would Andrea fire it for her in the kiln, or would that be too bait? Andrea was hard to pin down when she wasn't in the A&C building—she moved around camp like a spectre, was only fully formed in this very building—but Ruby would try to find her tomorrow.

Someone put *Tel Aviv!* on the speakers—it seemed to be the only CD Andrea had—and everybody bent down to work on their clay, eat their food. The whole time Ruby was shaping her pipe, digging out the trigger with a toothpick, Dov, sitting across from her, meticulously turned his lump of clay into little round balls. He had quite a pile of them. Dov noticed Ruby watching him, caught her eye.

"You see, Ruby? This is what it's like in Israel." He placed roughly half the balls in a big pile. "We are all together as a collective, a society. The needs of Israel outweigh the needs of the individual." He then separated the rest of the balls, setting them inches apart from each other. "And here, here are you Americans—sorry, *Canadians*—all alone in your materialism and manifest destiny."

Ruby put her pipe down, swallowed a mouthful of spicy, salty broth. She wished Etai or Danielle were here, but Etai had gone with the other Ski staff for a nightcap at the head staff lodge, and Danielle had gone to bed. "You misunderstand me. Fuck American individualism. And fuck your chaverim Zionist bullshit. If every one of those balls has to be Jewish, then it's not a revolutionary collective at all. It's an ethnostate."

Dov smiled affably. "You wouldn't say that if you came over and lived a day in our boots."

Ruby looked around her. Everybody was working on their clay, pretending not to be listening. It was the song from *Tel Aviv!* where the characters sing about the wonders of the Jewish New Society in Palestine, which Herzl had imagined from Austria in the early 1900s. Ruby thought about the basketball game called American: everybody for themselves. One on one on one on one on one on one. Total chaos.

"I would rather die than put on your murderous boots," Ruby said, trying to channel Etai's calm, straightforward demeanour. She worried she had gone too far, but Dov just laughed.

"Typical diaspora leftist," Dov said quietly, stacking all his clay balls up again, smooshing them down with the flat, wide palm of his right hand. "You wouldn't survive a day in a place where you had to fight just to live. The kibbutz I grew up on would spit you out alive."

The song reached its climax and some of the girls started to sing along. Ruby gave a quick smile. The conversation was over. The fact that she couldn't get Dov riled, while inside Ruby was all squirming agitation, left her even further frustrated.

On the way to her cabin—after Casey, swinging his Oakleys around his fingers, asked if she wanted to make out again and she told him that that, my friend, was a one-time thing—Ruby breathed the cool wet air.

Either the whole camp smelled like clay, or the scent was stuck in her nostrils. She felt better for saying something to Dov. At least now he knew where she stood. Ruby breathed in deeply again. It was a gorgeous night, loamy, rich, fecund.

The next morning the rain was falling so hard that alarms rung out unheard, unheeded. When staff belatedly started to rouse their campers, it was a lugubrious affair for all. Even with the overhead lights on, it was heavy and dark in the cabins; even as the storm raged outside, it smouldered inside. The wet, cedary must of a cabin in the rain. Hair in buns, rain jackets broken out, rain boots looked for, the mad dash through sunken, sodden trail and field, the rain cold and sharp. It was dark enough in the dining hall that the lights had to be turned on. Rain jackets—yellow, blue, orange, grey, red—hung from every available surface: the rows of hooks near the front doors, benches, chairs, corners of tables, weighted down with napkin dispensers, dripping along with the sounds of forks, knives, spoons. The smells of mud, grass, lake, fog, fused with the smells of coffee, hot chocolate, syrup, body wash, sweat, cleaning solution, morning farts. Campers and staff sipping hot chocolate, tea, coffee, a forest of steam and burnt tongues. After the meal and the subdued camp announcements, Debs went to the microphone and made it official: the first rain day of the summer. Open activities: A&C, gaga in the rec hall, board games in the dining hall. There would be movies playing in the CIT rec hall. Don't go anywhere without your counselor's permission or supervision.

The rain jackets begrudgingly went back on; more than a few are soaked through, while others are left behind to begin the slow, sometimes summer-long journey to the lost and found. Outside, the camp was a swamp. The rain had yet to let up. Mist boiled up from the cauldron of the lake. Centre field was a shallow sea straight out of the Cambrian. The storm and its hands of rain engineered streams, rivulets, fast-running tendrils, all reaching, reaching, reaching towards the lake. The terraforming downpour, adding its mark. Most campers stayed in their cabins that morning, wrote notes to each other which their staff ran back and forth between cabins.

There was a knock on cabin 9's door. "Everybody decent?"

"Come in!" Ruby called out. It was Etai. He was dripping wet, wearing a big yellow rainslicker, black gumboots with green heels. He stepped into the cabin, flung his hood off. His curly hair was sparkling with droplets, his forehead damp. The rain seemed to have energized Etai; he burned with intensity.

"I just learned this expression. Everybody decent? Everybody decent? I love it. Eh, what are you ladies up to?"

Ruby, Danielle, and Dawn were sitting on the floor with their campers surrounding them, most of them wrapped in their blankets, the Hip's *Day for Night* on the stereo.

"We're playing five," Ruby answered. "Everybody has to say the five types of profession they'd want to have with them in a post-apocalyptic survival scenario. It's Arielle's turn. Let's see. So far you have cook, farmer, and waitress. What're your last two?"

"Umm . . . saucier, and pastry chef."

"Arielle!"

"My turn! My turn!" This was June.

"Okay, this is easy." June closed her eyes, pretended to think really hard. Etai leaned against the wall, watched with a bemused expression, nodding curtly after each item in her list. "Okay. One. Fireman. Two. Soft porn actor. Three. Helicopter pilot. Four. Bodybuilder. And, last, but definitely not least . . . water ski instructor!" June opened her eyes in triumph, her face bright, her mouth open in a big, goofy smile. The whole cabin screamed and cackled. Etai shook his head, laughing, water flinging from his hair.

"Let's take a break," Ruby yelled over the laughter, "I have to pee."

"I might go lie down real quick," Dawn announced. Everybody scattered. June scampered onto her bed. Arielle went to get her insulin kit to prick her finger. Danielle looked out the window longingly; she was supposed to play tennis with Raskin at Rest Hour but it didn't look likely to happen.

While Ruby was in the first stall, Etai read aloud the sign on the open door of the second stall. It was written on pink Bristol board with black Sharpie, in carefully formed block letters, hung at the perfect height to read while sitting on the toilet. "'Have I ever told you the story of the ghost shit?'" Etai read. "'There are three kinds of ghost shit. 1. The Happy Ghost Shit: a normal shit, but surprise! No need to wipe. Cause: Lots of fibre. Enjoy it while it lasts! 2. The Frustrated Ghost Shit: there's no shit, but LOTS to wipe. Cause: improper diet. Stay calm, take a breath. Fix yo'self! 3. The So-So Ghost Shit: you shit, but it disappeared down the bowl before you could see it. Medium amount of wiping. Cause: the whim of the great shit goddess. Nothing to do but pray for better luck next time.'"

Etai laughed. "Who wrote this?"

Ruby flushed the toilet, exited her stall.

"June," she said, standing next to Etai, admiring the Bristol board.

"She's hilarious."

Ruby stepped closer to Etai. From where they were standing, they were out of view of the girls, blocked by the sink and the wall of mirrors above. "You can take off your jacket, you know," she said, her face an inch from his. She stuck her hand down his pants.

"I looked up Omer Stringer," Etai said.

"That's funny, so did I."

"He was born in Algonquin Park, revolutionized canoe paddling."

"Led trips in the backcountry his entire life." Ruby was really working her hand.

"Helped start Camp Tamakwa."

"Invented a non-electric dentist drill."

"A white man living on Indigenous land, claiming an Indigenous tradition as his own, helping both become an integral part of Canada. Would you not call Omer Stringer a settler?"

"I guess so." Ruby pulled her hand out of Etai's pants just as Danielle came into view. Danielle opened the front door, to see if the weather had changed, but was greeted by Fallon, who was walking up the porch steps in a knee-length blue raincoat with big wooden buttons, letters from the boys' cabin in her hand. The rain had yet to let up.

As Fallon handed out the letters, the girls swamped Etai, bombarding him with questions, statements, observations.

"Hello! I'm June. Aquarius, Ravenclaw, Carrie-Samantha, top bunk, ugh, obviously. What about you?"

Ruby went to the sink to wash her hands, fighting back a smile.

After lunch, Dov, Orit, Michal, and Brett went up and down cabin line to arrange a coed mud football game, the three Israelis wearing thin plastic ponchos with enormous hoods, black zinc angled under their eyes. At the new field soccer pitch, they quickly divided the thirty or so campers into two teams. The rain, somehow, was coming down harder than in the morning; it was difficult to see through the deluge. Dov ran backwards with the football, the grass squelching under his bare feet, yelling a mixture of Hebrew and nonsense words, and the game started. It was loose, fast, wet, and loud. It wasn't so much a game as it was bodies running and jumping and screaming and catching and throwing and rolling in the mud. Lots of adrenaline and touching and wrestling and sopping grass-stained clothes clinging to skin. Rain and trees and wind and grey and burning chests. Bodies at play. At the arbitrary end of the game, the score abandoned twenty minutes in, both teams ran screaming and hollering down to the lake, following Brett and the three Israelis. They happened to meet up with Yehouda, who was leading most of the CITs running over from CIT Town in their underwear. Both groups converged on the shoreline, screaming and laughing. They thundered down the dock and, without pausing to even take off their shoes, jumped in in their clothes, heads surfacing into the cold shower of the rain.

A roiling sea full of panting Jews, a platoon exercising in the worst the hostile world could throw at them.

By dinner, the rain had stopped, but the sky was still a sopping bandage. There was a line at all the showers, campers shivering in their towels and bathrobes, waiting for what they knew would most likely be ice cold showers, but, hey, gotta be clean for the social. The Israelis held a Havdalah ceremony before the social, Burntshore's first in over twenty years. The entire camp stood in a large circle in the giant septicy puddle of centre field, many still in their rainboots, dresses and black jeans and fancy shirts hidden under raincoats. Dov strummed his classical guitar, singing the wordless melody, as Michal and Orit walked around the circle, putting the box of spices under everybody's nose, the Havdalah candle. Ruby, secular to the extreme, found herself enjoying this communal farewell to the Sabbath, swaying with the whole camp in the wet grass, the lake a black swirling galaxy. Every seven days, a little taste of the divine. She felt the ritual awakening Burntshore deep in her gut. She couldn't stop thinking of Etai, no matter how she tried to mentally shrug him off.

After Havdalah, the camp burst into the rec hall, which was already stuffy and humid. The perfect conditions for adolescent love. Tyler deejayed, standing behind a folding table with his gear, headphones over one ear, still in his Cowichan sweater, hair constantly falling into his eyes. Everybody ran onto the dancefloor and scream-sung along to "Call Me Maybe." June breakdanced to "Gangnam Style." Ruby and Etai slow danced to "Kiss from a Rose," their bodies doing inappropriate things. Otter flung himself around like a trapped sparrow to "Party Rock Anthem." As the night wore on, Tyler sneaked in a few Grizzly and Phish tunes. Michal, Marula, and Danielle led the girls in the "Cha Cha Slide." After multiple requests, Tyler acquiesced and put on "Anachnu v'Hem," to which the kids went nuts, performed a choreographed dance they somehow all knew. The staff who had migrated outside, including Ruby and Etai, ran back in for "Blurred Lines." Ruby and Etai swung each other around, laughing, tingling.

In the wake of the storm, the next two days will be pleasant, cool, a light breeze blowing off the placid lake. Kids will complain about swim, the rain having churned up the cold water, the nights will be jacket-worthy, wet clothes will get funky in corners of cabins as they wait for laundry day. The younger campers—and some older campers—will not be able to sit still for visitors day excitement. But for now, the camp danced.

A LETTER FROM SEEMA

July 7, 2013

Dear Ruby:

Thank you for the flag keychain! I absolutely love it! I've given it the place of honour on my knapsack, hanging off a zipper right above the No Bombs No Wars patch.

Well, I asked for the juicy gossip, and I got it! Is what you're telling me true? Oh, habibti! If I know you, Ruby, you won't give those Israeli soldiers a moment of peace—they don't know what they signed up for. If I didn't understand Jewish sleepover camp and your love of it before, I am definitely confused now. What will they be doing there, setting up checkpoints and searching cars? (I know, I know, they'll be taking kids water-skiing and telling them about Tel Aviv's amazing, tolerant nightlife.) I can just picture you telling those soldiers off, never leaving them alone, ruining their summers. It brings a smile to my face. It'll be just like Central Hall when we table there and get into fights with the hasbarists—nobody can make them cry like you, Ruby. Imagine, the soldiers who are now swimming and farting at your camp could literally have been working at the checkpoint my cousins have to wait hours to get through every day. I know you'll be doing everything in your power to make sure they won't be coming back next year. Remind them for me that while the two state solution is nice—two Palestinian states side by side!—one would be just fine. Haha.

Anyways, back here in Toronto it's Jamil's trial all day long. Trial trial trial. He and some of the other defendants have been doing research on the senate members at York. They're multi-millionaires, CEOs of mining companies and multinationals, capitalists all. They donate millions of dollars to the university, get buildings named after them. One of them was arrested for insider trading, but he made a major investment at York and—surprise!—the charges were dropped. They are quite literally using the university to launder their money and reputations. So much for the university being a place to challenge power, eh? Amazing that on the same campus we can sit in Zipperstein's classroom and discuss the brutal violence of enforced hierarchy, these bigwigs sit around smoking cigars while discussing their latest investment in a strip mine in Central America.

Some amazing weed has been going around the city lately. It's called Rocket Fuel. Should I mail you some? Haha, joking. Unless . . . ? Oh, Guess What?! We're going to Jordan for my cousin's wedding after all, so I won't be able to come up for the second visitors day like we had planned. Oh well! I'm excited for the trip. It'll be nice to visit family, be so close to home. I think Jamil was worried that I was going to ask him to come, but I spared him.

Yours in Keychains and Solidarity,
Seema

CHAPTER 9

THREE FIRES

Last night at the ski docks Vlada had suggested they jam by a firepit, for a little "scene of changery" as she put it, so tonight Stolow grabbed his guitar and walked over to the pit behind the dining hall. Vlada was already there. She was alone, sitting in the middle of one of the five logs that made a pentagon around the firepit, head down, playing a rocking groove, a small fire burning in the pit. Stolow sat down on the log to her left, not wanting to disturb her. He watched her play, the flicking tongues of the fire caught in the sheen of her guitar, the skin of her forehead. She was playing in B minor pentatonic, a raucous mixture of chording and lead lines. Her fingers, flashing up and down the fretboard, were magnetic, mesmerizing, magic. Still playing, Vlada looked up, saw Stolow, smiled, nodded in invitation. Stolow rubbed his pick between thumb and pointer, poised on the strings, waited for Vlada's loose progression to start over, and then, when it did, leapt headfirst into the jam. They trucked along for ten minutes, bouncing rhythm and run off each other, moving this way and that, deking and charging forward, the music coming to a tremendous crashing peak of stiff-wristed strumming and twanging high-neck bends before abruptly ending.

Silence.

Vlada smiled. She rested her guitar against her log, squatted down, added sticks to the fire. "Some nights I feel like there's all this music coiled up inside me, and if I don't let it out, I'll be all blocked up." She didn't look up as she said this. Stolow watched the top of her head. A few flakes of dandruff rode the river of her part. "At other times, the music is gone, like it was never there, and I'm bereft." Here she did look up, locking eyes with him.

"I know what you mean," he said, keeping her gaze, but with difficulty.

He could hear Tyler and the others approaching from the other side of the dining hall before he could see them.

"Michal and I can't get over how popular the Herzl play is," Orit said. They were sitting around a roaring fire at the paddle docks: Orit, Michal, Dov, Brett, Ruby, Etai, Marula, Polina, Tripper Steve, Barry Blum, taking up the first row of the theatre-style benches that could fit 150 campers. Tova dropped a pile of logs and went back to the maintenance shed to get another load.

"It's true," Michal said, nodding. "In Israel, we do not understand the obsession with this play. Why make up a different version of Israel? Why not a play about the real Israel? Isn't it dramatic enough? You are so strange, you diaspora Jews."

"First of all, the music is amazing," Marula said. A crown of daisies was in her hair, her cheeks flushed from the fire, her body hidden under layers of Mexican blankets. "Second, it makes Jewish people proud. It shows them what Israel could be, how given the right circumstances we can solve any problem."

Michal looked at Marula like she didn't understand.

"But Israel *is*," she said. "It *is* what it *is*. Why imagine it different than it is?"

Marula shrugged. "By bringing to life a world that could've been, the play shows what's at stake in our own world."

"Marula's right," Dov blurted out. "The play celebrates the Jewish, eh, how do you say, *compulsion* to constantly better our surroundings. Look at what they have that Zionist leader, David, build in twenty years. Herzl understood what it meant to make something fast and strong and lasting."

Michal looked from Marula to Dov, raised her eyebrows at him.

"Look at all that government land over there," Dov continued, nodding towards the Crown land across the river, "nothing but trees and rock and beaver pond. If we had *half* of that land back in Eretz Yisrael, imagine what we could do with it."

"I wrote a paper on the play for a class," Ruby announced, desperate to change the subject, not engage. "I compared it to Herzl's original novel."

"So did I!" said Polina, her shorn blonde-dyed hair and square freckled face making her look a bit owlish. Polina had taken three summers off before coming back as CIT staff; Ruby didn't know her too well, but she seemed like somebody she could be friends with. "Not comparing it to the novel, though, but looking at how its music and choreography mirrored its subject matter."

"What did your paper say?" Brett asked. He was drinking a beer, sitting between Dov and Michal. Ruby had noticed Brett and Dov were spending a lot of time together; it didn't surprise her that Brett would be drawn to somebody like Dov, he was the masculine ideal Brett would forever feel short of.

His question startled Ruby. "Well, uh, basically, I argued that where the novel, written in 1902, imagines a Jewish society in Palestine that was not based on violence and military dominance, the play, written in 2009, simply uses Herzl to whitewash what is actually going on in Israel-slash-Palestine, the actual violence, military dominance, and ethnic nationalism. In the gap between reality and the play, the Nakba disappears, the eight hundred thousand displaced Palestinians, the destroyed villages. In other words, it's liberal Zionist propaganda."

Michal was staring at Ruby. There was definitely a hot intelligence between those sultry eyes. Maybe Ruby had misjudged her.

"Feh. This still does not explain why the play is so popular," Michal said.

Polina nodded aggressively. "She's not wrong. I think it's even more popular than *Rent*. Every single CIT girl is obsessed, and a good part of the boys, I'd wager."

"Sure, the music is fantastic," Brett said, watching Ruby for her reaction, "but nothing really happens."

Polina and Marula both scoffed. "Plenty happens! Friedrich and Miriam fall in love. Kingscourt learns to love humanity again. There's the election between David and Rabbi Dr. Geyer. We learn about the utopic Jewish New Society, where everybody gets along and everything is flowers and sunshine."

"Yeah, but the flowers and sunshine are all a fantastical lie," Tova said. She was standing behind the group, holding a load of logs. "What's next, *Hebron! The Musical?*" Everybody laughed, even Dov.

"Has anybody else besides Ruby and I read the novel?" Polina asked, taking a ChapStick out of her vintage MEC fanny pack, uncapping it, applying it to her lips. "It's bananas. Pages upon pages describing the perfect newspaper syndicate."

"Hard to believe they turned those pages upon pages into a song millions of thirteen-year-old girls sing to themselves in the shower," Etai said. Etai was sitting across from Ruby; she didn't look at him as he spoke.

"That's what I mean! What is it about this play that's so struck a collective nerve?"

"Sometimes the right thing just comes along at the right time."

"It's cause it tells a story we all desperately want to believe."

"And what is that story?"

"That we're innocent."

There was a quiet moment of contemplation. Tova added some birch logs to the fire, the white bark on the logs flaring up.

Brett broke the silence. "And what's with the scene with what's that guy's name? The false messiah from the eighteenth century that we watch a fake opera of? Shibboleth Susie?"

"Sabbatai Zevi?"

"Yeah! Sabbatai Zevi. Seems random."

"I think it's meant to show that Zionism is the new messianism. I found an article on the real Sevi and his inclusion in both Herzl's novel and the musical. It's really far-out stuff! Bananas, as Polina would say. Nearly the entire Jewish world believed he was the Messiah. Jews in Amsterdam were selling all their worldly belongings to begin the trip to Palestine for the coming messianic age."

"Mashi'ach achshav!" Dov yelled out, laughing.

A shooting star curved across the laden sky.

Ruby was watching Etai add wood to the fire. They had paddled over to Big Rock Island with a knapsack of beer and pot, a pack of hot dogs Ruby got from Cindy. Etai fiddled with the fire, moving the sticks around too much, not giving it enough time to take. Ruby didn't say anything, though, just watched. Seema's last letter had startled Ruby out of what had been an idyllic few weeks. Seema was exactly right—how had Ruby let this happen without even putting up a fight? Dov, Orit, Yehouda, and their brand of fun, harmless Zionism had infected the entire camp. They were singing Hebrew pop songs at morning song now, had started doing a "Hebrew Word of the Day" during lunchtime announcements. Not that there was anything wrong with learning Hebrew in the abstract, but this wasn't in the abstract: this was Hebrew in the specific, Hebrew in the ideological, and she had barely noticed. Ruby was not the Ruby she normally was, the Ruby that Seema loved (and that Ruby was proud of being). Ruby desperately didn't want to disappoint Seema. She had never had a best friend like her before. But then, there was Etai, standing up from the fire, sitting down beside Ruby, the smell of smoke in his hair, his arm against hers, making her incredibly horny.

After cooking and eating the hot dogs and smoking a joint Ruby turned Etai's wrist so she could see the time. "That's not right," she said.

It had taken her a minute to realize the time was seven hours off; at first, she thought she was looking at the watch wrong.

Etai looked down. "Oh. It's still set to Israeli time."

Ruby bit her bottom lip. Israeli time. Of course. His family, his friends, his life, his struggle, is still out there, over there. Unlike Ruby, who had nearly forgotten her life in the Big Wide (like she did every summer) Etai was living in two time zones. A sinking sensation flushed downwards through her body. "I gotta pee," she announced. Using the flashlight on her phone, she went to the other side of the island, pulled her sweatpants down, squatted next to a tree. From this vantage, she could see a big bonfire at the paddle docks.

For the first time since she and Etai hooked up, Ruby wondered what the rest of the camp was up to.

Stolow could hear Tyler and the others approaching from the other side of the dining hall before he could see them. Vlada had seriously built up the fire; by the time everybody was situated and had their guitars in their laps, it was raging. Stolow was thrilled to see that Geoff had joined the jam, had brought his fellow kitchen-worker Jojo along.

They played through the usual Dead, Phish, and Grizzly jams. By the time they took their first break, they had accrued a substantial audience, way more than the usual one or two onlookers (most often whomever Tyler was sleeping with at the moment plus one of her friends she dragged along). Someone asked if anybody played any *Tel Aviv!* songs. "I could figure something out," Tyler said, his fingers already ghosting along the fretboard. Everyone watched as he seamlessly found the melody line of "Misanthrope Anthem II," the chords swiftly following. The other guitar players joined in, and everybody sang along with Kingscourt as he explained to young Friedrich his hatred for all humanity and his plan to retire to a private island to live out the rest of his days. After the singing, they moved into a jam section, which Tyler made up from the main chords of the song's chorus: C, Em, Asus2, Em. Stolow was enjoying himself until he broke his G string, which snapped after a massive bend, catapulting him out of the river of the jam. He sat back, took in the music. A bong with a fresh bowl ended up in his lap, and he gladly smoked it down.

Stolow hadn't just watched a jam for a while. As usual when observing others play, whether his friends, a concert, a guy at a park, or a video on the internet, his thoughts turned to the wonder of music: the making of it, the listening to it, the contemplating of it. He could never get over the fact that this was something he, himself, could do: his limbs holding the guitar, music coming out. The flatness of the fretboard, the curvature of the back of the neck, the higher reaches of an electric guitar. How lucky was he that he could pick up this piece of perfection and, with nothing but his hands, create meaning? (Not that it came easily, without hard work, without the ten thousand required hours, the early years of non-stop practice—oh, the practice.) What else was guitar playing but celebrating what it is to have hands, fingers, arms, a mouth, a heart, a circulatory system? To exist in a world that is made of pattern, rhythm, melody, shape, and time? To know something so well that you detach from the process of doing it and become pure conduit?

All around him, the music chugged along.

The shooting star curved across the star-laden sky.

"So, what, the idea is that once the Messiah comes, Earth will become a paradise?"

"'I will bring forth fruit, I will bring forth honey, la lai lala lala lai lai,'" Polina said, quoting from the Sabbatai song.

Barry Blum used his Maglite to spotlight his wide face, spoke in his deepest stentorian voice. "The twelve tribes will return from their wandering, their leader will speak every language known to man. The temple will be rebuilt. The righteous will be sanctified. The temporal world will melt away."

Laughter.

"Yeah, basically, Earth *will* become a paradise," Marula said. "We have been waiting ever since biblical times and will probably continue waiting for quite a while. That's the whole idea: to live as if the Messiah will come tomorrow, but also as if she will never come."

"Fuck that!" Ruby said. "If we want a different world, a better world, we have to build it ourselves."

"And how will we do that?" Orit asked. She seemed genuinely curious.

"Join communes, fight for justice, redistribute wealth. Change the way we live, change the stories we tell about ourselves."

"My father always said the best way to tell if somebody is your friend is if you'd want them on a commune with you."

"*My* father always said Communists are godless fools."

"This we already have at the kibbutz," Dov said, running his hand along the top of his head. "As far as I'm concerned, it is the only way forward. Small, intimate communities, living off the land, no one better or more powerful than anybody else, a place where you can see and know everybody, not polluted with screens and billboards."

Ruby swallowed. She had to respond. "But didn't the kibbutz movement fail?"

Dov nodded his head woefully. "Yes, b'emet. It is very sad. Some kibbutzim, maybe most now, have been tricked by the Moloch of capitalism. My kibbutz, I'm proud to say, has yet to fall. We've reached a compromise between pure socialism and pure market competition, between raising kids as a group and stifling them in the nuclear family. It is much like the new society of your musical *Tel Aviv!* How do they say, 'the best of both worlds'?"

"Egalitarian socialism for Jews only is not egalitarian socialism," Ruby said, her eyes on the fire.

Dov shrugged, as if he were finished with the conversation. "It is either that, or death."

A quiet moment watching the flames.

“I don’t know.” This was Tripper Steve. Ruby sat back. Her battle of words with Dov had once again reached a stalemate. Tripper Steve continued: “Would you really give up all the trappings of the modern world, as fucked up as it is, and just start over?”

“In a second.”

“Haha, yeah fucking right.”

Brett added three big logs to the fire.

“I don’t know,” Barry Blum said, “I really feel that nobody can be truly free until everybody is free. We can’t just bounce out of civilization and start our own thing. We’re responsible for our fellow brothers and sisters.”

“I agree.” This was Etai. Ruby felt her heartrate rise. “It’s exactly why I stay in Israel. To fight against the occupation, to fight against apartheid. I could easily leave, but how would that be fair or right? We have to try to fix what is broken, not just look out for ourselves.” Did he look right at her when he said apartheid?

“Okay, that’s all well and good,” Tova said. “But where do you draw the line? Let’s say, for example, that through a powerful telescope we could see and hear a planet, somewhere out there, where a whole race of people are treated brutally. Absolute brutality. Millions of them under the whip. What could we do about it? Are we not free until they are free?”

“Build a fucking spaceship and go get them!” Etai said.

Dov was shaking his head. “Eh, why should I care about the millions of humans, or other lifeforms, who have given up? I need a community of people I can see, touch, talk to, gossip about. If thirty, a hundred, three hundred of us can live how do you say, ethically, isn’t that the best we can hope for?”

Brett’s logs had smothered the fire, killing the flames. Ruby was following this exchange attentively. She wanted to agree with Etai, but felt herself also seeing Dov’s point of view, which left her mostly confused.

“It’s too late for either one of those options,” Barry Blum said. “Capitalism is terminal. And we are all along for the ride, whether we like it or not. Now that people can lead seemingly innocent lives while in actuality being a part of horrific, unending global crimes, how could there be any possibility but total civilizational and planetary collapse? This thing is going to play itself out, and it's not going to be pretty."

The fire sputtered, smoked, called out for help. Everybody sat with Barry's words. Ruby and her hope for a better world felt small and childish in the shadow of Barry's booming pronouncement, of Dov's solipsistic certitude, of Etai's need for justice.

Tova got to work fixing the fire.

For the first time since she and Etai hooked up, Ruby wondered what the rest of the camp was up to. She stood, pulled up her pants. Being alone in the woods on a small island, the weed, the cooling breeze, the encircling lake: it all hit her at once. She felt better. She felt silly. She felt sparklingly, blisteringly alive.

"Do you know how to play horse?" she asked, bounding out of the woods and plopping down beside Etai, who reacted with nearly imperceptible surprise, a jerk in the shoulders that would have been invisible to everyone but keyed-in Ruby.

"No. What is this?" Etai asked, laughing. He had stoked the fire into a roaring blaze. They were alone in its warmness, everything beyond its glow black lake, indistinct, unimportant.

"You have to copy what I do. If you don't do it right or if you fuck it up you get a letter. We keep going until one of us spells out *horse*."

"And they win?"

Ruby smiled. "They lose."

Ruby went to the opposite side of the fire, sat on the seat stump. She grabbed her left breast. Etai stood, leaned over the fire, put his hand on Ruby's other breast.

"No! H! You have to do it to yourself. You get an H! And be careful!" Ruby yelled, pushing Etai back away from the flames. Etai put his hand on his own chest. Ruby put her finger in her mouth. Etai did likewise. Ruby put her hand down her sweats. Etai followed suit. She started rubbing. Etai followed suit.

Followed suit.

Followed suit.

Followed suit.

The music was still chugging along. Casey Mustard had left the jam, had returned with some bigger logs, added them carefully to the fire. The guitar players were all locked in, the audience rapt. The fire was sucking the music out of them; Stolow, still not playing, rode the updrafts and surfed the downdrafts. Tyler had taken his ponytail out, his hair was all over his face and arms. Vlada was curved over her guitar, her sparkly purple fingernails dazzling on the frets. Geoff was soloing, playing short phrasal runs in the higher registers of the neck. Stolow wished he could take the jam apart, place the solos front to back in time, untangle them, sequentialize the multiple stacked tracks of the music. Lay them out. Understand them.

The bong came back around. The bowl was black, nearly cashed, but Stolow put his lighter to it nonetheless and patiently sucked out what smoke remained locked in the nearly combusted combustible plant matter. He exhaled, his throat pulsing with heat. Ah, the glories and horrors of the material we live in, live through, live among. How amazing, how unearthly: as molecules, those tiny fragments of matter spinning around each other, affect us, so do the geographies of where we live—the buildings, the paths, the waters, the commons. How we organize ourselves, what we surround ourselves with, what we tell ourselves matters, becomes us. And, Stolow saw with cannabinoid clarity, so it was with the jamming: the music creates a space we can live in, breathe in, communicate, see each other. We're nothing but creatures moving around in a world we create, that creates us.

Stolow put his guitar back in his lap, found his place in the jam, started in again. In a world of material laws, five strings are still better than none.

Tova was at work fixing the fire. Everybody watched: she tilted the big logs to the side, pushed the embers into a tight pile in the centre, and rearranged the bigger sticks and logs on top of the new heat source.

"Talk about the need for some structural change," Barry Blum said.

"Redistribute that wealth!" Ruby called out.

Tova grabbed a Frisbee and used it as a fan, aiming the air through the big logs and into the embers inside. The embers glowed redder and redder, the sound was louder and louder, the flames reached higher and higher, Tova kept fanning and fanning, until she finally stopped and the fire continued roaring.

"Now that's a blaze!"

"Look at that motherfucker burn!"

Tova sat back down. "Sometimes, nothing will do but a total reset."

They segued into a quiet part of the night. Ruby watched the fire, the endlessly proliferating facades—so much better than television. Once the logs had burned down considerably, Tova added another layer, creating a new shape, instigating a new pattern, the heat pulled up from the furnace deep inside to create new hot space, the air sizzling, the flames licking madly.

They had finished following suit. Etai was using two long sticks, one in each hand, to move around the logs and embers in the fire. "This is how we do it in the desert," he said. Etai started to tell Ruby about growing up in Tel Aviv: the beach, the shouk, the used bookstores, the restaurants, the hot food market in the basement of the Dizengoff Center.

"Would you ever think of leaving Israel?" she asked.

Etai stopped. "And go where?" he asked.

"I don't know. Toronto, let's say? Thornhill?" What was Ruby doing? Inviting Etai to move in with her? Ruby bit her lip, hard enough to draw blood.

Etai stood up. God, he was tall. "I'm needed there."

"Why did you come here, really?" Ruby asked suddenly, feeling deflated, clear-eyed, practical. "Why come to this summer camp halfway around the world for no money?"

"Beat sitting in a jail cell," Etai said. He sat down, stared at the fire. "No. That's not it. I don't know. I was ready for a change, I guess." He continued staring at the fire. Ruby watched him. What was he seeing in the yellow-and-orange TV screen of the flames?

Etai blinked, looked at Ruby. "You know, this camp is more like the army than you'd think."

"What do you mean?"

"The bunks, mealtime, the intensity, being outside all the time, the sense of Jewish purpose."

"Yeah, except the IDF's Jewish purpose is war and dispossession. Camp's Jewish purpose is to swim and make friends and French kiss."

Etai poked the fire with his sticks. "B'emet," he said.

"I think we should go back," Ruby decided aloud, her desire to leave the island suddenly all-consuming. She wasn't sure exactly why, but this conversation was making her upset. Etai looked disappointed, but he went with the old island bucket to get water to douse the fire while Ruby pushed the canoe into the lake, gathered their garbage and knapsack and paddles. They didn't speak on the way back to camp. About halfway across the glassy lake they could hear loud guitar music, but Ruby couldn't see anybody from the ski docks. What a cacophony of noise.

"We should end this," Ruby said. Etai didn't respond, but she knew he had heard. "We barely know each other. I just got out of a serious relationship. It was fun for a few days, but I think that's all it was."

Etai paddled for a few strokes. "Yes, of course. Consider it ended. Fallon's already called dibs, anyways. That's how you say it, right? *Dibs*?"

Ruby laughed. "Fallon will be good to you. And we can still be friends, right?"

"Ken, of course. Friends. Chaverim. Nachon."

They pulled up to the paddle dock beach. A bunch of staff were sitting around the firepit. Everybody was excited to see them. "Come, sit, sit!"

Ruby found herself next to Barry Blum. Etai had gone over to Brett, Dov, and Michal; Ruby could hear them speaking Hebrew.

"You and Etai out for a little paddle?" Barry asked. He was obviously drunk.

"Just plotting the overthrow of the camp." Ruby herself was a little drunk, a little high, a little confused, a little determined to have a good time.

Barry laughed. "Tell me, Rubele, what are you going to do with your one precious life? Where are you going to put all that revolutionary energy? What, will you teach at a university? Write a mind-blowing book a few hundred will read, while across the quad they'll be making weapons of mass destruction?"

"You're in a saucy mood, Barry," Ruby said, laughing.

"Don't mind me, the fire has a tendency to burn off all pretense and bullshit."

"Must be nice."

There was a moment of relative quiet. The sound of a half dozen guitars playing "Misanthrope Anthem II" drifted over on the breeze.

"Michal and I can't get over how popular the Herzl play is," Orit said.

CHAPTER 10

**VISITORS DAY; THE FUTURES MARKET;
DR. STRANGE; DOV AND BRETT IN THE CROWN LAND;
CINDY IN THE KITCHEN; SUGAR HIGH**

The sun rose on Camp Burntshore. Tuesday, July 16, 2013. Visitors day. Debs had beat the sun by a few hours, had stood in the dark of her room eating a bowl of instant oatmeal, was currently at new field with Yonatan and Raskin, discussing the coming chaos.

"Say goodbye to this pristine grass," Yonatan said, cigarette in hand, kicking the field with his work boot. Yonatan and Raskin were both wearing fluorescent vests, had pyloned out parking rows for the mini-vans, SUVs, and sports cars that were right now, from motels and hotels and cottages and even from as far as the city, closing in. In past summers Yonatan had asked to have the parents meet at some other locale and for Raskin to bring them in the bus, but not only would that be a logistical nightmare, the parents would never agree to it. Debs was happy that Yonatan had dropped it, but still, he had a point: every summer, the field barely recovered from being turned into a parking lot.

"Remind me why we have to do this twice a season?" Raskin asked.

Debs knew his question was rhetorical but answered her husband anyways. "To keep the parents happy. To keep the campers happy. So

Tom can show the camp off. To keep the numbers up for next summer. At least it hasn't rained in a few days." A wave of static issued from Debs's walkie. She looked at her watch. "Shit, it's almost breakfast. Let me know if there's any problems here," she said, already walking away. There's one for the jar.

"Yes, boss," Yonatan and Raskin said at the same time.

The camp didn't technically open for visitors until 9:00 a.m., after breakfast. The cars started arriving at eight. Eight-thirty found a small crowd of the most eager parents, usually of the youngest children, already gathered at the main gate; by quarter to nine, a hundred or so adults were impatiently waiting.

Debs was on the inside of the gate with her clipboard, a fluorescent vest over her black *Program Director* long-sleeve, her orange hair, recently shampooed, bouncy and glossy. Well, here they were: the parents. The eponymous visitors. The fathers holding Thermoses of coffee, the mothers looking feral with need to see their children. Lots of coolers, lots of plastic and reusable shopping bags, lots of two-fours of bottled water. These were the people who, for whatever reason—they themselves went, their kids begged to go, they saw a Facebook ad, the grandparents offered to pay, so they could have some peace and quiet at the cottage, for some light Jewish community out in the rugged Ontario wilderness—paid the quite hefty fees to send their children to Camp Burntshore. A cross-sampling of upper-middle-class Jews of Toronto, Montreal, Ottawa, New York. As usual, a surprising number of fathers were wearing ill-fitting baseball hats with logos for obscure tech companies, tourist attractions, banks they have never and will never have an account at. Where do these hats even come from, Debs often wondered. Are there bank open houses that fathers go to for the free merch? Is there a mail-order subscription service for terrible hats? At what point do these men start wearing these hats? As soon as they had children, would Raskin show up with a puke yellow *Visit the Erie Canal Museum* cap? The women were a more varied demographic. There were mothers in top-of-the-line exercise clothes, mothers in summer dresses, mothers in shorts and T-shirts, mothers dripping with makeup and jewellery, mothers who looked like they just got back from a hiking trip (usually these mothers came with a father who looked likewise, except wearing a dumpy baseball cap that said *Linda's Windshield Repair* on it).

Well, here they were—and they were getting restless. "This is ridiculous, can't they let us in?" Shouts and nods of agreement. "We pay your salary! We want to see our kids!" A baby was crying. At ten to nine Casey Mustard showed up, crunching an apple, the dogs in tow, Oakleys on, his staff shirt a size too small, showcasing his bulging biceps, his chest muscles as defined as two salad plates, the ring in his left nipple clearly visible.

Just before nine Debs heard breakfast let out, could picture the hundreds of children streaming out of the dining hall, about a kilometre from where she stood at the gates, and heading her way fast. A few minutes later she saw them. The parents were about to explode; Debs wouldn't be surprised if they started rattling the bars of the gate. Casey wasn't helping, was in fact egging it on, the dogs barking encouragement, bowing at the fence, black tails wagging furiously. An instant before the rush of kids crested the top of the hill, Debs opened the gate, Casey yelled "go go go!" and it was a double-ended stampede of parents, campers, siblings, staff in their staff shirts and name tags.

Hugging, crying, screaming, shouting.

Debs let it engulf her.

Visitors day had begun.

Weather-wise, it was the perfect morning. The cooler temps, the preceding storm, had left everything replenished, had tamped down the dust and dirt, had cleaned the air, greened the trees, plants, and grass. All signs pointed to a pleasantly warm, lightly clouded day. For the next seven hours, the camp would exist in a strange interstitial, the two worlds of Burntshore and the Big Wide colliding, combining, sharing fluids before being ripped asunder again. The youngest campers excitedly showed their parents their cabins, their beds, introduced them to their counselors, their friends, their favourite parts of camp, crooned with story and anecdote. The older kids played it a little more chill but still listened to the family gossip, stood by as girlfriends and boyfriends and parents met, shook hands, made terrible, terrible jokes.

For those who wanted to do more than see the cabins, eat a meal, take in the trees and the lake, all of the activities were open. Ski, Paddle, Ropes, Sail, Tennis, S'Nature. You could bead a bracelet with your too-young-for-camp-maybe-next-year sister at A&C, show off the bowls you made and glazed in pottery. Prove to your dad how you can drop a ski now. Some of the more adventurous parents go for a swim. Tova was answering questions about trips past and future, had set up a little portage obstacle course for the parents to run. From eleven-thirty til one there was a buffet lunch in the dining hall, Cindy standing big and beaming in the kitchen doorway. A good number of parents brought food from the city. Deli, bagels, takeout. The Chos always brought Indian food, ate it on the pink rock by the waterfall.

Some of the parents were as fawning over the Israelis as their children were. Brett had convinced most of them to wear their uniforms. Etai was the only one who didn't comply, wore his usual outfit of hemp pants, his staff shirt, his *Shalom Achshav* button pinned to his chest. As Ruby was walking to lunch, she saw a group of fathers standing around Dov and Michal like they were rock stars. Did one of them actually mime firing a machine gun?!

Ruby was in the staff lounge. It was after lunch, and she was taking shelter from all of the parents, the general visitors day intensity. A few other staff were there, at the four humming computers, checking their email.

Talia was scrolling Facebook. Ruby had had a busy morning of meeting people, saying hello to parents she knew but hadn't seen in a year, fielding questions, showing off shelves and beds, introducing them to Fallon. She forgot how quiet June's dad was; her mother, on the other hand, was an adult clone, loud and quick and funny and observant. Arielle's parents were downright aggressive in their questions to Ruby, to Danielle, to Fallon, which made sense but was still a lot to deal with. Arielle's dad looked like Wallace Shawn, and her mom looked, well, also like Wallace Shawn. Arielle was set on going on the upcoming camping trip, but her parents didn't want her to. Ruby and Fallon, working in tandem, seemed to have convinced them of its safety and necessity; it was the most time they had spent together since Ruby started sleeping with Etai. She briefly saw her parents in Otter's cabin. As usual, the Shacters and Margolises—who were there to visit Marula's younger sister, Jaida—ate lunch together. Ruby half expected David to show, but as Marula informed her, he had decided to sit this one out, unsure of the amount of bad blood between him and Tom. The two sets of parents always brought deli; it's the only non-vegetarian meal Marula will eat all year, a tradition she's kept since she was twelve.

Whatever else it was, visitors day was always a good reminder of what actually allowed camp to exist: money. Direct lines could be drawn from the renovated cabins, the food delivered by truck twice weekly, the canoes, the campfires, the salaries of the staff, to the banking accounts of the campers' parents, to words like GIC, high-interest savings accounts, tax deductibles, dividends, annuities, bonuses, the futures market. Ruby, on the couch in the staff lounge, in that sweet spot right before sleep where the mind has near-hallucinatory free rein, found herself standing smack in the middle of this river of Jewish wealth: the money of grandparents filtered down to parents, who are now teachers, bankers, doctors, lawyers, business partners, allowing these temporary societies to exist, these respites from the city, this communal communing with nature. Ruby's own recent ancestry fit this description to a tee: all four of her grandparents came over from Europe with nothing, sacrificed plenty, and all so Ruby could grow up in a big house in the suburbs never wanting for anything. At least Ruby knew it was wrong, this blatant concentration of wealth while others starve. It was a bitter pill, but there it was: it required vast ranges of exploited labour and ravished landscapes laundered hundreds and hundreds of times for a place like Burntshore to function, to exist.

Etai and Stolow came in, giggling.

"What's so funny?" Ruby asked, sitting up, blinking sleep from her eyes. They plopped down on the lumpy blue couch on either side of Ruby. The dream, the vision, whatever it was, was nearly gone.

"Nathan Goldberg's grandfather was regaling Etai with stories of Tom from his wilder days," Stolow said, still laughing.

Etai calmed down enough to take a breath. "We were at the ski docks, I was helping Stein organize the kids to go out on the boat, and Mr. Goldberg starts telling me all about Tom. Back when Dan was alive and still ran the camp, and Tom was in his twenties, still a pharmacist, he would apparently show up every summer with all sorts of pills, LSD he made himself. They called him Dr. Strange. Apparently, he gave it out like candy, his dad none the wiser."

Ruby knew who Mr. Goldberg was. A bigshot Montreal lawyer, he and Tom were the same age, were cabinmates when they were campers. Goldberg came up to visit camp once or twice a summer, would stay at Tom's cabin, sit at the head staff table, wander around chatting with staff and campers during the day.

"He must have been trying to impress you," Ruby said. She and Etai had not fooled around since the fire at Big Rock Island. Ruby had almost written Phil an email the night before but talked herself out of it at the last minute. Why confuse things even further?

"I can't imagine Tom as a pill-popping pharmacist," Etai said. "What made him decide to go into geology?"

"'I will never be flippant towards rocks again.'" Ruby and Stolow, who both knew Tom's first-day speech nearly by rote, burst out laughing.

"Basically, he had a vision of a rock speaking to him," Ruby added for clarification. "Dr. Strange, indeed."

"Also, according to Mr. Goldberg, Tom is quite the baker."

"I heard he makes a killer mandelbrot."

"What?! How come he's never made it for staff snack?"

"Probably doesn't want to step on Cindy's toes."

Stolow sat back, his hands behind his head. "Camp must have been a crazy place in the seventies," he said wistfully.

Talia swivelled away from the computer to face them. "You have no idea. Even besides the drugs. My dad always talks about how each summer their mothers would send them with a full salami, and the boys would hang their salamis from the rafters of their cabin and eat them all summer. He doesn't shut up about it."

They were laughing so hard Ruby was crying. "Oh my god. My god. The smell."

Stolow slapped his knee, wheezing. "I think some of the cabins on line two never lost it. That meaty smell, it's soaked right into the wood."

There was a relaxed day off kind of vibe brewing, the exuberance of released pressure. The staff lounge was more or less the only place in all of camp where there wasn't a fear of running into parents. Talia and Ruby locked eyes through the laughing. They hadn't spoken since Ruby walked in on her and Phil in the girls' washroom at Muskoka Grill during pre-camp, only three weeks ago but might as well have been three years, three planetary epochs. They kept laughing. Ruby's stomach was starting to hurt. Etai was hiccupping. Ruby felt like she was high, whether from the lack of oxygen making it to her brain, the laughter releasing globs of serotonin, or something else, she couldn't tell.

"What time is Tom's big welcome-slash-goodbye speech?" Ruby asked when the laughter had died down.

"Three-thirty."

"Should we see what Cindy's up to? See if she has any treats for us?"

"Let's go."

Ruby was mildly surprised, but not necessarily annoyed, when Talia got up to join them as they left the staff lounge. The screen door squealed on its rusty hinges and banged shut behind them.

They entered the kitchen through the back door, found Cindy working on order forms at her small desk in the back of the kitchen, wearing a pair of reading glasses, receipts and invoices tacked up on the walls. Geoff was the only other person there.

"Hi, Cind."

"Well, hello, hello. Aren't you supposed to be out there manning your stations?" Cindy laughed.

"Dov and my CIT are on Ropes. It's only the climbing wall that's open right now," Stolow explained.

"I'm on break," Etai said.

"I was hiding out in the staff lounge from being ogled by all the fathers," Talia said.

"We're hungry, Cind, anything for us to eat?"

"Let's see what we can find for you." Cindy got up, tapped her pencil against her mouth. "Ah! I know. Plenty of left over muffins from this afternoon." Cindy went to one of the racks and pulled out a tray. Everybody gathered around and grabbed a muffin. "You can thank Geoff for these."

"Thanks Geoff!"

Geoff, who was cutting vegetables, bobbing his head, his headphones on, didn't hear.

"How long do you think the CITs will last at the waterpark tomorrow?" Cindy asked.

Ruby laughed. "I don't know, what was it last year, they made it just until lunch?"

"Something like that. I don't know about this year's group though. They might survive through the whole visit."

"That would be a Burntshore first," Talia said.

Etai, Stolow, and Talia went over to talk to Geoff, who took his headphones off and smiled at the visitors. Cindy leaned in towards Ruby, who was still peeling the frilled paper cup off her muffin. "Hey, do you have any idea what's going on with Brett and Dov?" she asked.

"No, what do you mean?"

"They've been spending a lot of time together. I didn't think much of it til I saw them in the woods across the river with a man I didn't recognize a couple hours ago."

"Interesting." Ruby took a bite of muffin.

"I'd mention it to Tom, but he has beans in his ears when it comes to Brett."

"I'll ask around, Cind."

Lots of noise from outside. "Tom's speech!" They left the kitchen through the dining hall and out onto the balcony.

Cindy watched them go. One of her favourite parts of being head chef at Burntshore—besides the pay, which had kept Cindy there a few years longer than she had planned on staying, delaying her plans of opening an Anishinaabe catering business in Toronto—was watching the kids grow up, turn into young adults (it was an utterly different experience than at the Spruce, where the children were a part of her community, were her children, in a way the Burntshore kids were not). Ruby, in particular, had always been one of Cindy's favourites. She reminded her of Cindy's youngest son, Giiwedin, who had from a very young age been inquisitive, quick-witted, preternaturally attuned to issues of fairness and justice. *Un*fairness and *in*justice, more like it. Ha! Ruby was just the same. There was a fire in her. When Cindy had seen Dov and Brett come back across the river, with that man that had "government" written all over him, she had a bad feeling in her gut and had decided almost immediately to tell Ruby. Cindy had watched the Israeli soldiers come and be welcomed into camp with open arms, which left her with mixed feelings to put it mildly (for a few days it was all anybody talked about at the reserve; one of Cindy's aunts was a hardcore Christian Zionist, believed that not until all the Jews were in Palestine would the rapture come). And though Cindy considered herself an important part of Burntshore, she often stayed out of the camp's problems. There were enough issues in the Spruce that required her attention. Though, if her intuition was correct—and seriously, she was old enough to know that it rarely was wrong—whatever was going on across the river, in that land the Canadian government considered theirs but that had been part of the Black Spruce traditional territory since time immemorial, was going to spill into the confines of Camp Burntshore.

Cindy got up and opened the back door. She could see across the river and into the trees. She thought of her son Giiwedin. When he was young, Giiwedin just could not stomach the stories told to him of what happened to his people, to Cindy's sisters and parents and aunties, to the Black Spruce. One of the many reasons he left the reserve (Giiweden still didn't approve of Cindy working at the camp, brought it up every time they spoke). He was now a lawyer in Syracuse, visited the least of her three children, even though Freddie lived much farther away, in Vancouver. Maybe when the summer's over she'll plan a trip down into Haudenosaunee territory to visit Giiwedin, cook his old favourites. Speaking of food, dinner wasn't going to prepare itself.

"Geoff," Cindy called out, startling her young worker. "Can you go get the lettuce from the fridge? Miigwetch."

Meanwhile, outside, Tom and Debs were standing near the beach on a little stage made out of scaffolding, with the parents and kids spread out on the hill and up centre field. Raskin was fiddling with a microphone. Behind Tom, the lake was a slab of liquid marble. Ruby hung her arms over the balcony railing, searched the large crowd for Brett. Sure enough, there he was, standing at the top of the hill, Dov beside him, both of them talking with a short man with a comb-over and shoes that were much too fancy for a summer camp.

What were they up to?

As Tom's speech was ending, Debs was heading towards new field. For some of the younger kids especially, saying goodbye to their parents could be rough.

Debs looked at her clipboard and its record of the day's events. Out of the three kids—two unit 1s and a unit 2—who said they were going to go home with their parents, only one—a sweet nine-year-old who was there for his first summer, had fun during the days and made friends but was terribly, existentially homesick at night—actually left. Debs herself helped him pack. One camper: might be a record, she'd have to check.

By a quarter after five, the last car had left new field. Debs looked it over. Hmm. Not so bad. Yonatan will be relieved.

She breathed in the lingering smell of trodden grass, mud, exhaust, and temporary goodbyes.

The parents gone, the camp begins to return to itself, to disentangle from the intrusion of the Big Wide. Dinner is salad bar, usually reserved for Sunday lunch. Kids and staff alike take a small plate, barely eat. The Evening Program, as always, is a bunk night, to allow campers to reform into cabins, share bounties, gorge on candy, gossip about what was learned about city friends, reassuringly work through the summer's catalogue of inside jokes, make new ones, ride the sugar as high as it allows, the cool summer night air comimg in through open windows, until exhaustion takes you and tosses you into a slightly sad, slightly relieved, sleep.

From above, the camp and the lake look calm, still, at rest. The pine and oak trees, the buildings and tetherball poles are sure of their place in the world. There's enough of the summer left that you still can't hold it all, it spills out of your outstretched arms, recedes into the ever-expanding future.

CHAPTER 11

HEATWAVE; SKINNY DIPPING; THE THEME OF COLOUR WAR IS ANNOUNCED

Lake Burntshore was in the throes of a heatwave. The thick, wet heat rolled into camp overnight, gummy, cloying, quickly everywhere. Cabin 9 woke up, staff and campers alike, with their blankets thrown off, sleepwear stuck to skin, mouths dry, hands clammy. As Ruby, Danielle, Dawn and their girls blurrily performed their morning ablutions, gargled away sticky throats, splashed cold water on their sweaty faces, looked for shorts in their shelves, slipped into sandals and flip-flops, and escaped the stuffy cabin for the cottony air of outside, the cool early mornings that had been a constant so far this summer already seemed like a season long distant. How could there be anything else except this dreadful heat? The walk to morning song was a chorus of groans amid the whir of handheld fans, pink, blue, black. For Hebrew word of the day, Dov and Orit did *heat*. Ruby didn't think a single person was paying attention; a passing pleasure. The windows in the dining hall were all open, the ceiling fans wobbling at full RPM, but there was no cooler air for the fans to circulate: everything was still, suspended, hot. When Tom got up after the morning announcements and said, "Don't forget to drink lots of sunscreen," the entire camp mumbled back, "and wear lots of water, it's going to be a hot one!"

The day's rhythm modulated to the furry tempo of the heat. Everything slowed. Cindy was stationed at the dining hall stairs, handing out giant freezies from a blue-and-white cooler. There was a lineup at the infirmary of campers with heat-induced headaches, nausea, dehydration. There was lots of low moaning, lots of sweat, lots of batteries bought from tuck for fans, lots of spray bottles of water, lots of freezie-stained tongues. Piper and Daisy were splayed out under the dining hall porch, the heat and sun too much for their black fur. It wasn't quite hot enough to call a lake day—that would require thirty-eight degrees on the thermometer on the office door—but Debs did announce at lunch that Swim, Paddle, and Ski would be open at Rest Hour for swimming. After lunch most of the camp slugged their way to their cabins for swimwear, towels, books, water, sunscreen, before tromping back to the lakefront to claim a spot.

Ruby was sitting with Marula, Stolow, and Yehouda on the picnic bench next to the volleyball court; they were currently in the shade of a burly maple tree but would not be for much longer.

"So, what happened with the CIT trip to the waterpark yesterday?" Stolow asked, wearing a sky-blue tank top, his skinny ropey arms resting on the table. "I haven't heard anything yet."

Yehouda shrugged his bear-like shoulders. "Oh, we had a great time! Yofi tofi. Weather was metsuyan, I learned all about poutine, ate two bowls of butternut squash ice cream."

The Canadians laughed. Yehouda made a quizzical face.

"I think you mean butterscotch, honey," Marula said.

Yehouda smiled, his affability a cool balm on burning skin. "Ah? Butter*scotch*? Nachon. I like this flavour very much."

"I heard the CITs lasted until late afternoon?" Campers were walking by from the tuck shop with sweating cans of soda; Ruby spotted Otter with a can of Nestea held to his forehead.

"Yes, they clogged the slide. What fun!"

Ruby remembered her CIT waterpark trip well. It was a scorching hot day; not humid like today, but dry and fiery. She and Phil gave each other hand jobs in the change room before sharing a large poutine. By two o'clock they had clogged the super soaker slide with all forty-two CITs; when they finally all tumbled out of the slide yelling and shaking their arms, the management had asked them to leave. Two kids, stinking of whiskey, were booted before they had even boarded the bus.

"Seems like a rather tame bunch," Ruby said.

"You say that every year!" Marula said, hitting Ruby's arm.

"Well, it is! Our year, kids were getting kicked out every week for drugs or alcohol or fucking a staff member."

Marula shrugged. She had had a steamy affair with a first-year staff—a one year difference!—but, unlike some of their other fellow CITs, did not get caught. Camper-staff relationships were as verboten as open drug use.

"They are a good group of kids," Yehouda said, sounding the most serious Ruby had ever heard him. "Inspired, team-oriented, respectful. We could use teenagers like that ba'aretz."

"When we were CITs and were out of camp, we'd steal anything that wasn't bolted down," Stolow said wistfully.

"Fuck, this fucking heat."

Etai was jogging past, from the direction of his cabin. When he saw Ruby, he stopped, looking bashful. He was wearing flip-flops, a red bathing suit, a white tank top, and had an orange whistle hanging off his neck. His tanned shoulders were starting to freckle.

Ruby was undeniably happy to see him.

"Hey."

"Hey."

He continued jogging. Everybody at the bench laughed at the imagined hookup. Only Marula knew the truth: that Ruby had ended it.

"Did any of your campers get anything good from their parents?" asked Stolow.

"One of my girl's moms brought like a trunk of Montreal bagels," Marula said.

"What?!" Ruby exclaimed, tuning back into the conversation. "How did I not know that?"

"Well, they're all gone now."

"Besides, don't you only like Toronto bagels?"

"No! Who says that?"

They were all laughing. Ruby was in the sun now. She was sweating.

A chorus of shrill whistles rose from the lakefront like a flock of birds taking off. Rest Hour was over.

Ruby's thighs stuck to the bench as she stood up.

That night, the heat had not budged. Campers were melting in their beds, tossing and turning, adjusting fans, getting up for the blissfully cold water running from the sink taps. Staff were in the dining hall for staff snack: Cindy's famous three sisters soup. Yehouda was shovelling it into his mouth. "Mmm-mmm. What is this? Ze tamid. Ze metsuyan. This is large soup."

"Large soup is right!" Casey Mustard exclaimed. The heat had made everybody a bit stir-crazy.

"Let's go for a swim!"

It was unclear who removed the first piece of clothing—there was very little clothing in the first place—but as two dozen staff ran down the hill towards the swim docks, they left behind a trail of tank tops, basketball shorts, T-shirts, bras, boxers, panties, and a wide assortment of ball caps, sunglasses, and sandals, leather, pleather, and plastic. Forty-eight bare feet thundered down the wobbling docks, screams and shrieks as bodies pushed off, jumped, and dived into third area. The dark shock of plunging out of the hot night air into the cold, bracing water.

After a few minutes of chaos, splashing around, calling for each other, they formed a rough circle, everybody treading water. Barry Blum's large body, his scruffy hair. Stolow, stuck between trying not to look at Vlada and trying not to look at Marula's breasts floating on the water. Ruby and Etai ended up treading next to each other. The docks and ropes of third section created a home, a room, a safety from the wider lake.

"Ah, that's better," Blum sighed.

They floated in the cool water, the stars above, the sharp crowns of the trees, the heat sticking to their faces. Danielle started a game where you have to yell out your "large soup" and your "small soup," sort of a modified roses and thorns. Danielle went first: "My large soup—tennis. My small soup—this fucking heat!" "Large soup—that soup we just ate. Small soup—that we're not right now eating this soup!" When it was Ruby's turn, she couldn't think of anything, so she just went for it. "Small soup—uhh, late capitalism. Large soup—Etai's large . . . face!" She put on a shocked expression, plugged her nose, and submerged to get away from the cheering, whatever Etai's face was doing. Barry Blum passed his flask around. Talia straddled Yehouda, who sank under the water before popping back up. Stolow clambered onto the dock, ran to the high diving tower, climbed up without using the ladder. He released a whooping yell and jackknifed into the water, bulls-eyeing in the middle of the circle, everybody shouting and hollering. The moon rose. So this is what it means to belong somewhere: to be consensually naked with a group of people you've known for a lifetime, to feel utterly safe, for harm to be a foreign word. "Ani ohevet et kulchem!" Michal announced. Ruby stuck out her leg, tentatively brushed Etai's thigh with her foot. Without turning his head, Etai reciprocated. Their feet tongued each other beneath the lake's surface.

Afterwards, everybody back on the shore, the spell broken, hands covering private parts, the search for clothing began. Ruby caught sight of Michal's body: it was stunning, deep brown, her ass and back, her thick black hair catching silver. She was easily the hottest girl at camp, maybe tied with Talia. Dov scooped up Marula in his long arms and, both of them laughing, ran full throttle—and fully naked—back towards the deep end, the dock juddering with his massive strides, launching himself and Marula into the lake, making a tremendous crashing splash into the water. Ruby watched them swim out to one of the two floating rafts that marked the outer corners of section three, their strokes messy and urgent. When did *that* happen? They climbed out of the water and onto the raft, and Ruby wrenched her eyes away.

Where her eyes landed were on Brett, who was standing by the swim shed, buck naked, his jean shorts balled up in his hand, his penis—the only untanned part of him—flaccid under a flagrant black bush of pubic hair. He was staring at her, his eyes bright. When he realized Ruby was looking back at him, he turned away, called for Casey, who was tripping and swearing into his own shorts a little farther down the beach, his nipple ring catching moonlight, his Oakleys perched atop his head.

Etai was walking towards her, proffering a white towel. Though it wasn't strictly necessary, Ruby already nearly bone dry, Ruby took it and wrapped it around herself. She grabbed Etai's hand. "Let's go find something to eat," she said.

Etai smiled. "I have some Mr. Noodles in my cabin, we can make them in the staff lounge."

"Perfect. I'm sure Cindy won't mind if we borrow some eggs from the kitchen."

"Ramen time!"

Yehouda and Talia ran by, disappeared into the swim shed.

The group dispersed. The experience was over. The sand was in a new, novel shape. A pair of sandals was left under a picnic table. Except for the rhythmic displacement from the floating raft Dov and Marula were on, as far as the lake was concerned it was as if nothing had just happened.

The heat lasted through Friday, making a sludgy Friday night dinner. When, instead of the usual announcements, the lights in the dining hall were turned off, the communal energy shifted, ramped up. It could only mean one thing: colour war! Ruby perked up; how had she missed that colour war was going to be tomorrow? A soundtrack of explosions and harried yelling started piping through the speakers, and in through the main doors burst Dov, Michal, Casey, Fischer, and Orit, dressed in army uniforms, holding intricately detailed cardboard machine guns. Dov was leading them, crouching low, directing with hand signals. The track changed, and they mimed being in fighter planes, swerving and firing. They strapped themselves into parachutes, and jumped out of the plane, floated throughout the dining hall. Finally, they put on sailor hats and were on a submarine, moving as one. The break was very well rehearsed; the campers cheered in each iteration. More staff ran in, holding up a big banner that read *IDF DIVISIONS*. There was whooping and catcalling, table banging and whistling.

Ruby was flabbergasted. IDF divisions? What the fuck?! Usually, the themes for colour wars were things like superheroes, cereal mascots. This is worse than she could have possibly imagined. She caught sight of Tom—did he look surprised as well? Ruby had been too distracted with Etai, with worrying about what Seema would think of their on-again, off-again relationship. She didn't even know Dov was on the colour war organizing team.

The camp rose as one in a surge of excitement, crowded around the lists taped to the front table to see what team they were on, grab the booklet that detailed the events, the complicated points system, the timetable that, down to the minute, would organize their day tomorrow. Red was air force; blue was navy; purple was army; white was paratroopers. Ruby had been put on air force. She didn't think so! She found Marula. "Did you know about this?"

"Yeah, didn't you?"

"No!"

Marula shrugged. "It's different. Should be fun."

"Ugh, Mar."

"Do you want to come with me tonight to charge my crystals? It's a full moon."

"I don't know. Maybe."

She went to look for Etai, found him surrounded by his campers. She pulled him aside.

"Did you know about this?!"

"Yeah, Dov really pushed for it apparently."

"Why didn't you tell me?"

"I didn't want to upset you." Etai looked sheepish. Last night after the skinny dipping and Mr. Noodles, they had had explosive sex in Marula's room in the staff lodge; afterwards, lying with their faces close Ruby had said, "I feel like I've known you my entire life. It's so stupid," to which Etai responded, "gam ani." And now Ruby was suddenly questioning if she knew him at all, if last night had been a mistake.

"Fuck! I could have tried to stop it."

Ruby was walking away.

"Ruby! I'm sorry!" Etai called after her.

All through FEP, bedtime, roses and thorns, Ruby thought about how this was all her fault. She had let her guard down, had let Dov and Orit hijack the camp. They were going to *celebrate* the Israeli army now?! An army that, when it was born, ethnically cleansed 800,000 people, destroyed four hundred villages, and currently kept millions of people locked in the open-air prison of Gaza?! It was like a terrible, terrible dream. The girls, of course, had the usual colour war excitement, were asking Ruby to help her pick which clothes to wear for tomorrow; Arielle, in particular, was highly enthused. Danielle, knowing Ruby was upset, took over. After lights out, Ruby went to the staff lounge.

It was time to write Seema an email.

CHAPTER 12

COLOUR WAR

Ruby woke up from a toss-and-turn night feeling much calmer. She was back to her usual resilient self, someone who is not surprised by the bullshit and hypocrisy of others. Venting to Seema had helped; it was the longest email she had ever written her. (She also told her about Etai, "this Israeli refusenik boy" who she was "sort of seeing" and who "wasn't like the others." Just writing it out had lifted an enormous weight.) After sending the email she had grabbed her toiletries from the cabin and took a late night shower. She hadn't showered this late all summer: not only was she the only one there, but, miracle of miracles, there was actual hot water. She had slipped her one-hitter into her toiletries bucket, and, baitness be damned, took a few luxurious shower tokes, exhaling into the streaming water. Lathering her hair, singing the Hip as loud as she could, her skin burning pleasantly. A little buzzed, she decided the best way to deal with tomorrow's colour war would be to just check out for the day. This particular battle for the soul of Burntshore was already lost. For now, Ruby would hang back, regroup, gather resources. She left the showers into the humid night, the crickets and bullfrogs singing their night songs as if they had just learned the rest of the tour was cancelled and this would be their final concert of the summer.

That morning Ruby's girls were up early, chattering and excitedly putting on their team colours; for the rest of the day, their allegiance wouldn't be to the cabin, but to their team. Their colour. Their division. Practically the only day all summer they didn't need cajoling to be at morning song on time—which was "Hatikvah," fittingly, awfully. The heat hadn't broken, but there was a cool breeze blowing hard off the lake. At breakfast everybody sat according to their team colours; Ruby sat with Tova at the white table. If, to the kids, camp was a twenty-four-hour barrage of activity and game and friendship and inescapable sociality, colour war was camp's camp: Ruby doubted the radicals she met at protests or in class believed in their cause as much as these kids believed in their one-day team and wanted them to win. Was it just the human condition, Ruby wondered, that when you're partitioned into groups you start to see the world through the prism of us and them?

Even though Ruby was technically assigned to air force, sticking to last night's decision, she was just going to float around, wearing her green Camp Burntshore staff shirt from three years ago. And after breakfast, she did just that, wandered the camp, trying not to get involved or be too conspicuous. Everywhere she went there was an activity, a race, a contest, a song-writing team, kids cheering and clapping. What seemed like typical harmless colour war fun soon got darker. Kids playing capture the flag, firing fake Uzis and throwing fake grenades. Kids pretending to jump out of planes deep into enemy territory. She passed Fischer, in his IDF shirt, his spiked hair looking extra sharp, and a bunch of young boys in blue, pretending to interrogate Barry Blum, who was tied to a chair. Ruby was walking through a nightmare; she had to get inside. She darted into A&C. There was Marula, working on team plaques with Andrea, the CIT Ayelet, and representatives from each team. It was a factory of paint, glitter, and plywood. Andrea's naturally pale skin—which barely saw the sunlight all summer—looked even whiter compared to Marula's tanned face and arms. The Otter played quietly from the stereo. At least kids weren't fake torturing somebody.

"How are things with you and Dov?" Ruby asked, a little spitefully perhaps, but in her desperate need to talk about anything but colour war, of the camp being taught to see everybody who wasn't Jewish as an enemy, to think about something other than her growing feelings for Etai, it was what came out. Of course, Dov *was* colour war this year.

Marula made a face. "I don't think I'll be doing that again. Though every time I think that, he comes to find me, and we do it again. He says he wants to bring me back to his kibbutz, that I'd love it there."

"And what do you think?"

"That he's probably right, but, ugh," Marula said, making a face you'd make biting into a rotten pear.

Ruby laughed. At least Marula wasn't as enamoured with Dov as the rest of the camp was.

"It's fucking dark out there," Ruby said, unable to keep it in.

Marula raised her eyebrows. "What, the colour war? It's not so bad, is it? I mean, armies are not automatically bad, right?"

Ruby blinked. Dov was rubbing off on her more than she had realized. "Uh, yes, Mar, armies are always bad. And this army in particular is bad."

Something flashed across Marula's eyes, but in a second it was gone. "Whatever you say, bitch," she said jokingly.

Ruby escaped A&C and wended her way to the kitchen, where she would definitely find some respite from the war games. Cindy wasn't there, but Geoff was, prepping chicken fingers for the deep fryer. As they chatted, Ruby made herself a tea.

"Hey, I finally burned that CD for you," Geoff said, dumping another huge bag of frozen chicken fingers into a stainless-steel bowl. "Twenty-three songs that have the name 'Ruby' in the title!"

Ruby took the CD, smiled her thanks.

"Can you believe this?" she asked.

"Believe what?" Geoff asked, grinning.

Ruby wasn't exactly sure how to put it. "What's happening to this camp."

Geoff looked around the kitchen, as if the changes Ruby was referring to would be in abundant evidence.

Ruby hit him on the arm. "The soldiers, well, mostly Dov and Orit, trying to turn Burntshore into an IDF base! Do you see what's going on out there today?!"

Geoff smiled. "You have no idea."

Ruby's stomach tightened. "What?"

"Dov asked me and Jojo to dress up as Palestinians, with keffiyehs he had and everything, for an event today he called 'meet your enemy,' where the campers would yell and tell us off."

Ruby was going to vomit. "What did you say?"

"What do you think I said? I said no thank you. Apparently Yehouda and Orit did it instead."

This was worse than her worst fears. She pictured Geoff and Jojo up there, hate raining down on them from the camp. She pictured Etai up there. She pictured herself. She pictured Seema. Oh god. What had she let happen to Burntshore?

Geoff shrugged. "To be honest, until Dov spoke to me yesterday, I didn't really notice any difference."

Ruby was thrust back into the kitchen, into the conversation. Of course Geoff hadn't noticed—why should he have? Ruby had barely seen what was going on until it was pushed into her face through a camp-wide program. A bubble of doubt rose to the surface of Ruby's consciousness: was she overreacting? No, there was no way. Right?

"What I did notice is that you and Etai are spending a lot of time together," Geoff said. "What, no more time for your old Geoff and our freewheeling dorm room conversations that leave us energized and exhausted?"

Ruby laughed, happy for anything else to talk about. "Yeah, Etai and I are *this* close to solving the growing Israel-diaspora divide. But that's not the point, Geoff! Don't you care that the camp is turning into a settler-colonial outpost?!"

Geoff put his hand on Ruby's arm. Jojo pushed open the kitchen door, walking backwards, mopping as he went, his headphones on, his hair down to his ass.

"Honey," Geoff said, "not only is that entirely your problem, but, from my vantage point, I don't see all that much of a difference. Besides the Israelis being a bit more in-your-face about it, it's the same attitude to this land, this place, that the camp has always had."

"Which is what?"

Geoff raised an eyebrow. "That it's yours."

Ruby bit her lip. This was turning into quite the day.

Debs loved mealtime during colour war. And perhaps lunch most of all. Camp spirit, camaraderie, friendly competition, the decibel level, none of it was ever higher. The teams screaming their team cheers, a mixture of old reliables and newly minted. The colour-coded tables. The good-natured insults. The timbre of the eating itself seemed different somehow, elevated, purposeful, insatiable, *louder*. When the meal was finished, each team started their cheer, competing with the others, faster and louder, slamming the tables, Cindy, Tanya, and Jojo at the kitchen door watching. "Up there, in the sky, all other teams better look out, you're going to die!" "Parachutes! Parachutes! Parachutes! Yeah!" "Give me an S! Give me a U! Give me a B! We're coming for you under the sea!" "Left one two three, right one two three, we're the army, and you're the enemy!"

After lunch, Debs visited the different stations. The heat was still thick; the morning breeze had abated. Dov and Orit had put together an excellent day of activities and had chosen the team captains well. The Israelis had seemed to adjust to the Burntshore culture without much of a hitch. They were undoubtedly a part of the camp fabric now. They had been here, what, two weeks, and were already running a successful colour war? They were performing well above her expectations. Not for the first time, Debs was amazed at camp's ability to absorb whatever was thrown at it. Not that she was particularly enthused about this year's theme—she had thought it would be something like kinds of bagels, what with all the bagel discourse this summer—but she had to admit that Dov was doing a decent job of keeping any politics or propaganda out of it, at least as far as she could tell (she had heard about an event this morning that involved staff pretending to be Palestinian, but she hadn't been there and hadn't heard how it had gone yet). It reminded Debs of Israel Week at Brandeis.

There was Stolow and a few kids on the roof of the showers with their guitars, working on their team song. She'd go say hi.

The relay race was the crown jewel of colour war. Like at most other camps, the race used to be called the Apache, but in her first summer as head chef Cindy had Tom change the name. Since then, it had simply been called the relay race, but Ruby was not surprised when she saw that it was now being called the Maccabiah. Ruby used to love this part of the day. Now she couldn't wait for the entire spectacle to be over, to find out tomorrow how much damage a day celebrating war and the mechanisms of war had wrought on the camp.

The race started—and would end—at the lake. Brett blew the starting whistle, and each team's competitor dove off the dock and swam to Birchhead Island and back. Clambering onto the dock, they tagged in the next camper, who had to run out to new field. After new field was completing the high ropes course, running to the paddle docks, kayaking to the sail docks, shaving whipped cream off a balloon without popping it, the greased watermelon race, and the three-legged race. There was one new addition to the relay race this year: the David Margolis Memorial Vacuum Challenge, organized and overseen by Yonatan. A representative from each team, Shop-Vac in hand, had to suck up a ten-metre-long jagged line of soil. The participants seemed to love it.

As with every year, the relay culminated in an egg race back to the swim beach for the egg boil—the grand finale of the relay race, the climax of colour war and possibly of first session in general. At the beach, the assigned eight campers waited impatiently to be tagged in. Each two-person team had to start a fire, boil water, and hard-boil an egg with nothing but a single match. Otter and June were two of the combatants; they had their twigs and bigger sticks and birch laid out in neat piles, waiting for the eggs to arrive. Once they did, the whole camp screamed themselves hoarse as bundles were arranged, matches struck, heads bent over blowing, sticks added, smoke rising. Dov stood on the beach in his army fatigues, his arms crossed on his chest, looking supremely proud of himself, shouting encouragement in Hebrew. All four fires were going now, though one was having trouble staying lit. Pots of water were placed on the fires, which were being carefully, lovingly tended. Lids were lifted to inspect for telltale bubbles. Everything was extremely serious.

Ruby saw that most of the kids doing the egg boil, including her brother, were wearing a strip of cloth over their watches; she had noticed Dov doing this earlier in the summer and had asked Etai about it. "It's so our watches don't flash any light when we're out in the field. It's more just force of habit now."

Ruby felt the anger rising from her gut, everything she had kept at bay all day storming the siege walls, just as the whole camp rose in cheers: Otter had got his egg to cook before two of the other teams had even gotten their water to boil. Brett took the egg, held it aloft like a grenade, peeled it, and ripped it in half, telltale crumbly yellow yolk falling to the ground. Otter had won! His team surrounded him, Dov swooped him up, threw him onto his shoulders, paraded him around.

Ruby's brother, victorious.

Before the closing ceremonies, the word spread: a CIT had been kicked out. Scharfy, the lovable dreadlocked skateboarding hippie who had already broken his arm a week ago; this was *not* his summer. The reasons varied: smoking pot, taking mushrooms with a camper, being drunk. Staff discussed it in hushed circles. Yet another casualty.

The rec hall during closing ceremonies was stifling. Ruby wasn't going to go, but Danielle had grabbed her arm and forced her along. After the four teams presented their songs, Dov took the mic and gave a short speech about the importance of the IDF in maintaining Israel's security, how he hoped it was now apparent to the campers what it meant for the Jewish world that Israel was as strong and secure as possible. Dov took a breath, palmed his head.

"And now, the moment we've been waiting for: the winner."

Everybody cheered.

"It was a tough battle, but the undisputed champion of the day is . . . the air force!"

Eruptive cheering from a quarter of the audience.

Debs watched everybody file out of the rec hall. Now the work of transitioning from colour war teams back to cabin, to unit, to best friend would begin. One of the many transitions that make up a summer at camp. Debs supposed she should go hang around CIT Town, see if any trouble was brewing now that Scharfy had been sent home. Debs herself had ordered the spot check; some of the CIT boys were getting rather cavalier with their pot smoking. If Tom had been the one who had noticed, it would have been much more severe. Hopefully now they'll take better care to not stink like weed in the camp's common areas.

Tomorrow morning, the heat will break.

CHAPTER 13

THE RIVER; RUBY LEAVES ON TRIP; STOLOW AND VLADA FIND RELEASE

The White Pine River runs for over a hundred kilometres before it passes the eastern border of the camp and empties into the lake. One of its tributaries, a narrow stream that as far as anyone at camp was concerned was unnamed—but that has had an Anishinaabemowin name since long before the first Jewish immigrants arrived on the continent—flows for a tenth that distance, mostly through the Crown land that makes up thousands of acres east of the lake. Sunday morning, early enough that the day's dimmer switch is still pulled all the way down, a black bear and her three cubs visit this stream. The cubs' three butts align perfectly along the rocky shore as they bend down to drink. The mother bear, who is also drinking, has her senses tuned to the varying frequencies of the entire forest; the boundaries between camp, reserve, private property, and Crown land as meaningless to her as the airplane drawing a white river in the sky above her. She hears deer, the water of the lake lapping against Big Rock Island, mice scurrying; the wolf pack is far enough away that she can just barely make them out. They are many kilometres from the camp, but the mother bear clearly hears when the backdoor of the kitchen is propped open—probably by Geoff, who will shortly go out onto the porch to watch the sunrise. In the winter, hunters from the Spruce will set traplines, there will be snowmobiles, there will be snow and ice and January quiet, the mother bear can smell all of it, its seasonal residue still apparent, never totally banished, but for now, it is the height of summer, green and brown and alive. The bears continue to drink. The stream will take the bears' comingled saliva down into the White Pine, where it will flow past the camp and into Burntshore, dispersing itself into the body of water, adding its infinitesimal texture to the near-infinite brew of the never-finished lake. A little farther upstream, there's something new to this part of the forest: a surveyor's marker, a squared stake of wood, three feet tall, painted grey with a red tip, has been hammered into the ground—the first of many. The mother bear knows it's there but ignores it. Just another foreign oddity of the forest, meaningless unless assigned meaning from the outside. The bears leave the stream, the sun comes up over the lake, bright fresh light hits the red face of the marker.

Ruby and Danielle were getting their girls ready for their canoe trip. A three-night loop in Algonquin Park. Ruby used to hate canoe trips when she was a camper, but now, as staff, she loves them. When the campers do most of the work, what was to hate? "Okay girls, you know the drill. You have to fit everything into one dry bag. No sneaking of extra shirts or socks."

"Ruby, do we have to go?"

"Ruby, what's the weather going to be like?"

"Ruby, which trippers are coming?"

"Why doesn't Danielle have to go if I do?"

Ruby watched June help Arielle close her dry bag, which she had to borrow from an older cousin in unit 3. It was obvious to Ruby that Arielle was hyper with excitement, but she was doing a good job of hiding it from everyone else. After dinner, Ruby had a phone call scheduled with Arielle's parents to go over the logistics of the trip and to assure them once again that she and Tova had all the necessary medicine safe in a special waterproof container and knew how to dispense it, and, yes, of course, we'll make sure the sat phone is charged up before we go.

When all the dry bags were packed, they threw them thudding out the cabin door before dragging them over to the trip shed.

That night, Ruby was smoking a joint with Marula at the lake. They had climbed up the high diving tower with Marula's portable speaker, were listening to a Grizzly show. Marula had some of her crystals arranged in a crescent between them. Ruby was trying to focus on her girls, on tomorrow's trip. On her job.

Marula ashed the joint off the diving tower. "When you get back, I was thinking we could go to my cottage for a day off?"

"Sounds great!" Days off at Marula's cottage were always wanted.

"Did you hear that Fallon's been trying to sleep with Dov?"

"What? No!"

"She can have him, for all I care."

They laughed through the smoke.

Afterwards, Ruby went to find Etai, but he wasn't in the dining hall, the ski docks, or the trip shed. They didn't have a plan to get together—they were just friends, after all—but Ruby really wanted to see him before she left camp for four days. The desire was almost painful, shocking in its persistence. Friends shouldn't want friends this badly, right? At midnight she gave up the search and, with a serious case of what Casey Mustard would have probably called "lady blue balls," went to her cabin to try to get some sleep.

Early the next morning, Raskin was waiting by the bus. The canoes were already strapped down, the food barrels and stuff sacks loaded on the floor of the canoe hitch and in the back of the bus with the paddles, life jackets, water jugs, tarps, and maps. It was a cool, misty morning; if it wasn't quite raining, it could be at any moment. Spirits were low. Ruby's girls stood beside the bus, quiet, sleepy, hair in braids, their breath coming out of their mouths as gentle fog. Even Arielle seemed cowed by the early hour, the unpromising weather. Tova had run back to the trip shed, and when she returned, her black cherry paddle in hand, Ruby sensed some of the girls' moods lift.

"Okay, who's ready for a little adventure?" Tova called out, hoisting herself onto the canoe hitch, smacking one of the boats with her hand. At the last minute, Etai appeared through the worsening fog, wearing his yellow rainslicker and black gum boots. Ruby thrilled silently at the sight of him. He gave Ruby a big hug, handed her a letter. He must have run out of his cabin before brushing his teeth; she could smell his morning fug. "Where were you last night?" Ruby asked. "Looking for you," Etai said.

"Will you write me while I'm gone?"

"Every day."

"Aw, he's not coming?!" June said, as they watched Etai walk away. Ruby put her arm around her young camper. They boarded the bus.

Stolow returned from his run just as the bus and the canoe hitch were pulling onto the road. He watched them move away from him, the hitch kicking up dust as it trundled along. He looked at his watch. He was soaked through with sweat and dew; he had just enough time to grab a shower and make it for breakfast. He jogged towards his cabin to grab his shower kit.

By the time the camp was flowing out of the dining hall after breakfast, the mist and clouds had burned off. Stolow took a deep breath on the dining hall porch, looked out over the blue lake. It was going to be a beautiful day at Ropes. Later, while a cabin of unit 1s ran the low course, supervised by Dov and their CIT, Stolow's thoughts, as they did constantly the past couple of weeks, turned to Vlada. They had yet to hook up, but Stolow couldn't get her—nor her captivating, flawless music—out of his head.

He couldn't tell if she was into him or not, or if she just enjoyed jamming with him. She *definitely* enjoyed jamming with him. (Right?) Stolow hadn't had a crush like this on a girl for years; his last string of sexual encounters had all been with men. He felt a bit uneasy about the age difference—six years—but they were more than equals musically, and they were both staff, so it wasn't, strictly speaking, verboten (if she were still a camper, or even a CIT, that would be a different story). Yeah, she was seventeen and he was twenty-three, which seemed unsurmountable; but when he turned forty-eight, she'd be forty-two, which was basically the same age. Right? Or was that a bullshit way to justify something that was on its face wrong? For these reasons and more, Stolow reasoned, he didn't feel any compulsion to do anything, to act, to reach out. Not yet, at least.

That night, at the ski docks, Geoff showed up to the jam, which he had been doing more lately, his Martin acoustic in hand. They worked through the usual assortment of Phish, Dead, and Grizzly jams, other classic rock staples. Stolow and Vlada traded fours. Brett, Dov, Yehouda, Talia, and Fallon appeared, reeking of tequila and pot, laughing and chumming around. They were deep into a "Layla" jam when Stolow felt the rhythm begin to change, new chords edging in, new tonal possibilities opening up on the fretboard. Stolow closed his eyes to concentrate. It took him a minute to realize what song they were collectively moving into, like inexorable hands on an aural Ouija board. It was the jam from Phish's "Stash": D minor 7, B flat 7, E diminished, A7. A fast, jazzy tempo. It was not an easy song to jam to, the chording and scales were advanced, and most of the players slowly stopped playing, except for Vlada, Stolow, Tyler, and Geoff. For the first few runs of the progression, they each took turns soloing in the D melodic minor scale, which fit the chords well with its overall minor sound and surprising major seventh, each player bringing it to a short fast peak before dropping back into the chords and letting somebody else go. Eventually, Tyler and Geoff started sitting on the E diminished chord, vamping on it in different voicings and rhythms, leaving Vlada and Stolow to slip into the corresponding diminished scale. Since the scale doesn't land back on the D, the home key of the progression, it doesn't allow the melody to resolve, and Stolow and Vlada were bent over, digging into their guitars, ratcheting the tension up higher and higher, getting further from resolving the more impossible it became to not resolve. Tyler and Geoff slammed diminished chords all over the neck, Tyler switched in and out of bass lines, Stolow and Vlada ratcheted and ratcheted and ratcheted. Tauter and tauter and tauter. Stolow fell into a wacky four-note riff, which he repeated louder and louder, the D just out of reach, yet unattainable, Vlada's fingers wide on her fretboard as she ran the diminished scale up and down. The peak must be close now, all four players were locked in, bent over, wrists swinging, the tension was unbearable, near breaking, it had to break soon, it had to, what would happen if it didn't break, the music got faster as the tension got slower, pulled tighter, the break was never going to come, they were trapped in this gyre of swirling tension and pressure and tautness forever, this was the world now—and then, break it did, Tyler and Geoff landing exquisitely on the D minor chord exactly as Vlada and Stolow relieved the jam into the D, slid home, hit the tonic, made landfall, broke the atom of the jam, torrents of released energy geysering over everything. Riding the high, the four of them played through the progression in perfect sync once, twice, three times, stopped.

The jam over, everybody clapped.

"That was cool, what song was that?" Geoff asked. His brown forehead was beaded with sweat.

"'Stash.' You just figured that out by ear?!" Stolow asked, impressed.

Geoff looked at his guitar neck, shrugged. "Yeah, I guess so."

"You guys are freaking incredible," Brett said. "Holy fuck." Though it was a general statement, Stolow knew he was talking about him and Vlada. The two lead guitarists' eyes locked, and they smiled shyly at each other. Tearing his eyes away, Stolow busied himself by flipping over his guitar and rolling a spliff on the smooth back of the momentarily-at-rest instrument.

"We need a palette cleanser after that," Fallon, exuding surprising playful energy, said. "Play us something, Tyler!"

"Yeah, play us something!"

"Play us something!"

Tyler obliged, jumping into one of his earliest songs, now a camp classic: "Intergenerational Wealth."

Stolow watched Vlada, puffed on the joint. He couldn't figure her out. Was he supposed to make a move, say something? Usually, whether boy or girl, Stolow was clear when there was a green light.

For now, he would let the tension brew. See how taut it could get. Why not? There was oodles of summer left.

He handed the spliff to Yehouda, tossed his attention back to Tyler, started singing along with the chorus. Everybody—including Dov, including Brett, who sang loudly, wildly, a bright gleam in his eyes—joined in. Vlada was beaming.

> Why not be born wealthy?
> Why not be given everything?
> Isn't that the goal, isn't that the dream? Have you tried it?
> Drowning in green.

CHAPTER 14

ETAI AND RUBY WRITE EACH OTHER LETTERS ACROSS A VAST EXPANSE OF TIME AND SPACE

ear Ruby:

Some of the boys in my cabin were talking about bus letters, so I thought, lama lo, I'll try my hand at one. I'm sorry we didn't see each other last night. I looked everywhere for you before giving up, ended up playing Asshole with Barry Blum and some others in the head staff lodge. (As it turns out, I am often the Asshole. Tonight, maybe I will try for President, but I will settle for Vice Asshole.) I am looking forward to having some low-key nights, maybe catch up on my sleep, write my parents an email (which, negligently, I have yet to do since arriving . . .). I hope you have fun with your girls and with Tova. Will you think of me, your good friend Etai, while you are exploring the wide forests of the Canadian wilderness?

Etai

Dear Etai:

Thank you for your bus letter! I read it with keen interest. The keenest of interests, you might say. Our first day of the trip is done, and boy was it a long one. For most of the drive to the park, it was pouring. The girls were freaked about the rain, as was I. But before we turned off the 11 and onto the 60 the rain had stopped, and by the time we got to Canoe Lake the sun was out. While Tova was in the park office, I helped Raskin take the canoes down. Canoe Lake was bustling with people getting ready for trips, returning boats, eating chicken fingers on wet picnic benches. We sorted the packs, organized the boats, and we were off! The landing at Canoe Lake is a long beach, and we paddled our little hearts out. I'm in a canoe with June, Clara, and Dalia. The first portage is barely a portage: a short, wide path around a dam to Joe Lake. Back into the canoes. Up the Teepee River, into Tom Thompson Lake, where we stopped for lunch. The girls were already tired. Tova told me that a big first day would mean we leave most of the crowds behind. From Tom Thompson we did a huge portage. I doubled a canoe with Arielle. At the end of the portage there's a wooden staircase! It leads down into this small pond called Ink Lake, and then there's a windy river, and, finally, we arrived at McIntosh Lake. Tova knew the perfect campsite for us, a short paddle from the river, with a huge rocky outcrop. After we set up, and the girls started collecting wood for the fire, I sat down by the lake to write you this letter. (Being staff on trip is sooo much easier than being a camper: you don't have to collect wood, you can look at the map and know what time it is, you don't have to do the dishes.) Here is a drawing of our canoes paddling up Canoe Lake, and another one of the staircase that leads down into Ink Lake.

While we were having lunch Tova told me that just a few hundred metres from most of the lakes we paddle, the loggers are at work. Even a place like Algonquin can't escape the teeth of industry. What a world.

We're having pasta for dinner. I'm happy to be away from all the current camp bullshit for a few days, but I didn't think I would miss you as much as I do. You jerk. I can't wait to hold your big face in my small hands. (As friends, of course . . .) Whatever the cards say, you're my President.

Ruby

Ruby:

Hello! Are you decent?! Camp is not the same without you. Breakfast was egg log, lunch was mac and cheese, dinner was chicken chow mein. It was an uneventful day in the ski boat. Get this—some of the CITs actually went on strike today because of Scharfy getting kicked out. I think it lasted until just before third period! What else. Oh! Casey Mustard ran a half-day program for his unit. I saw some of it from the docks: it looked fun. The program was to design, build, and advertise a car. The unit was divided into three teams, each one their own car company. One of the teams asked me to be in their commercial! For EP tonight the unit met in the rec hall to screen the commercials, unveil the cars, and declare a winner. The commercials were very funny. I'll describe them to you now. Commercial 1. A person in full winter gear, ski jacket, hat, goggles, gloves, at first you can only see the sky so it looks like it could actually be winter, and he's moving along and the camera pans down and you see it is actually summer and the person snowshoes right into the lake until he disappears. A cue card comes up: Burntshore Auto, *Built for All Seasons. Commercial 2. The first part of this commercial is stop-motion animation. It's a big truck with huge tires, rolling all over A&C. A voiceover says, "This car is the ultimate survival vehicle. On road, off road, in road, road road. And, in dire situations, the tires are a hundred percent edible." The commercial then cuts to somebody in full army attire, their face painted camo, sitting in the forest shovelling bits of tire into their mouth. (That's me! I'm the guy eating tire!)* Big Buck All Terrain Survival Vehicles: We've Been Munching Tire Since 1989, Baby! *Commercial 3. The final commercial shows a hand loading smart phones into a wood-burning stove and setting them on fire.* Get Away from the Modern World for a While. Take a Trip in a Mustard Gas RV. *The commercials are great, eh? So creative. Anyways, Casey decided to not declare a winner, to let the game continue. A strange choice, but, hey, Casey is a great counselor. I'm learning a lot from him.*

Tell me everything! Did it rain during your first day? Who did you end up in a canoe with? Did you go swimming? Did Tova build a raging fire? How is Arielle managing? What's the food like? Did you see any shooting stars? Did you make a wish? If so, what was the wish?

I eagerly await your "reply."

באהבה
Etai

Etai:

Today was a good day. Tova is the best. The weather was great. No injuries or complaints. We are on a peninsula site on

Big Trout Lake. It is really beautiful here. The farthest into the park we will go. When we got to the site and set up, we all took a nap. I played cards with the girls—who are being extra hilarious (you're right, June is a little comedienne, and she and Arielle are becoming inseparable)—and helped Tova organize the food barrels. Tonight for dinner is TVP chilli. The paddling was really special today. I wish you were here with me. Between White Trout and Big Trout there's a narrow channel—Tova says it is technically part of the Petawawa River—and we waited there for the slower canoes to catch up. I can't really explain it right now, but it was a very meaningful place, just floating there between two massive bodies of water. Tova is in her tent writing "sex letters," as she called them, to her girlfriend in the city. Tripper Steve is telling stories of being a tree planter in BC, June is asking him a thousand questions. (I think she has a little crush. Looks like you have some competition . . .)

UPDATE: Etai it is 1:30 in the morning now Tova and I were sitting at the fire I was pretty blitzed and she was telling me about how the Indigenous people were forcefully removed from the area when it was turned into a park when Clara came out of the tent and said she had to go to the bathroom she was scared though and wanted me to go with her so I put my headlamp on and we walked to the kybo she did her business as I waited a few feet away standing in the woods in the dark I just got so full of life and what it means to be here on this planet even with all the fucking bullshit I must not have realized quite how high I was anyways I'm back in the tent now writing this to you in my sleeping bag I wanted to get it down to capture this moment I couldn't wait to tell you I can't wait to be with you I didn't think I'd miss you like this I don't know what I'm saying maybe we are *more than friends would you want that*

I don't know I think I want that okay the bugs are attacking my face I miss you so much

With loon,
Ruby

Ruby:

So much for my plan to take it easy while you were in the bush. I've been partying pretty hard. David Stein brought back some hash from his day off in Toronto, and let's just say that the past few nights have been seen through a hashy haze. Last night I ended up at the ski docks with all the guitar players. I know you don't like it, but the music they make is really something else. Afterwards, Stolow took some of us to the ropes course, and we climbed up to high ropes and smoked bowl after bowl of hash. Stolow put me in the harness and I ran the tire swing in the dark! It was like basic training all over again. JK, JK.

I don't know exactly how, but being here this summer has changed me. Or maybe it was meeting you. In any case, I feel myself expanding, sinking into the ground, wanting more from life. I can't quite explain.

I'll see you tomorrow.

Etai

Etai:

Well, the trip is done. I am sitting on the bus, beside Tova. We spent last night on Burnt Island Lake (a cousin of our own Burntshore, I guess, eh?!). We got to the lake early in the evening, the sky was insane with cloud and colour and sunlight, and we were paddling like a real unit. The lake is long with many twists and turns. We'd paddle a short section, follow the turn of the lake, and at the end of the new section there would always be a small island that we would head towards. We'd get there, paddle past the island, swing around again to another vista, another island. The world shifting and throbbing as we paddled our canoes through it. We ate pea butter sandwiches for lunch, a massive snapping turtle sunning itself on a rock right beside where we stopped. I think Clara got a picture of it on her disposable.

We haven't gotten back to the 11 yet. Still a few hours away from seeing you. I miss you like crazy. I can't stop thinking of you sitting in that Israeli jail cell, all alone, doing what you feel is right. What is *right. What have I ever done that can compare? I've basically let the camp get turned inside out by Dov and his comrades. What should I do? I should fight for the camp, I know that, but I don't even know how, or what the point would be (and, trust me, I'm usually not a defeatist). Shit, I really didn't think I would miss you like this. (I had a strong desire to cross that line out, disappear it with a block of ink, but have decided to leave it.)*

All of which is to say, we're all going to Marula's cottage for a day off later today, and I hope, I pray to the camp gods, that you will do me the privilege of coming with us. Imagine it? We could, for the first time since we met, be alone *alone.*

Until then,
Rubes

CHAPTER 15

**MARULA'S COTTAGE; SEX AND A FIGHT;
STOLOW DECLARES HIS FEELINGS; PHIL RUNS INTO THE WOODS**

Raskin levered open the bus's front door, and out erupted forty bus-crazed eleven-year-olds, Piper and Daisy eagerly giving wet hellos to each child. Tova and Tripper Steve threw open the back doors and started to toss out the gear. Ruby was the last to exit. She stood on the bus's grooved bottom step, her hand on her forehead to block the sun's glare, and took in the camp. It was a sunny, hot summer's day. The trees rustled gently in the breeze. She was home. She jumped onto the dirt ground, her mud-caked hiking boots, which she was wearing without socks, sending up little explosions of dust. She was sore and dirty, exhausted and muddled, emotional and contemplative, full of competing wants and needs. She badly needed a shower. At the end of the afternoon, like a sparkling, expansive lake on the other side of a hot, buggy portage, waited Marula's cottage. Ruby went wobbly with desire just thinking about the coming delights. But first, she had to take care of her girls.

"Okay, my stinky little camperettes," she yelled, "don't say hi to your boyfriends or girlfriends, don't say hi to anybody, find your dry bag, dump it at the cabin, and get right into the shower! You know the drill!"

The last hour of the bus ride had been a little nutty, lots of filthy songs and screaming and laughing, and that depraved energy persisted as they moved as one through the camp and to their cabin line.

Before Ruby herself showered, she went to find Marula, who was at S'Nature, making pinecone peanut butter bird feeders with unit 1s. Ruby gave Marula a questioning thumbs-up, and Marula responded with her own. The cottage was on! Ruby asked if it was okay if Etai came, and Marula said she had invited him while Ruby was gone. Ruby called Marula a bitch, the unit 1s gasped, Ruby apologized to the kids, her heart fluttering, told Marula she would see her later. Ruby had to shower and pack. The urge to go to the ski docks and see Etai was elemental in its force—she was the kind of horny where she had to shit and fuck and pee and cum and run and eat and swim and scream and sleep in a pile of violently thrashing bodies—but Ruby wanted to draw out her desire for as long as possible.

She walked back up to her cabin.

Two hours later, everybody met at the staff lot, a patch of hardened dirt next to the tennis courts, the lake just visible through thirty feet of white pine and birch. Dropping her knapsack and small duffel bag next to Marula's car, Ruby saw Marula and Dov having words by the main gate rock. Dov was much taller than Marula, was gesticulating with his hands, was the image of masculine virility and strength, but it was obvious even from that distance that Marula, standing straight, a detached, bemused smile on her face, was the one controlling the conversation. Ruby bit her lower lip as she watched them. Dov finally threw his hands in the air and marched off, smacking an oak tree with his open palm as he passed the lot. "What was that about?" Ruby asked as Marula walked into earshot.

Marula shrugged. "Oh, I wouldn't let him come to the cottage. Get this, he says he's in love with me. He wrote me a song about it and everything."

Ruby guffawed. "What did you say to that?"

"I told him to calm down." Ruby stared in the direction Dov had skulked off; he could probably have almost any girl at the camp, and he had fallen in love with Marula. Unbelievable.

When Etai showed up, Ruby ran to him and jumped into his arms. They hugged long and hard. The air hummed with bugs, sunlight, loose electrons.

They packed the cars. Marula, Ruby, Etai, and Stolow were riding in Marula's car; Orit, Tova, and Tripper Steve were in Tova's. As they were getting organized, a bunch of first years were impatiently waiting for Raskin to drive them into town for their own day off. Marula went up and started speaking with Vlada, who was part of the group. They had a quick conversation, Vlada nodded her head enthusiastically, and Marula skipped back to Ruby and the others.

"Vlada's coming with us!"

Stolow, bent over Marula's trunk, arranging the knapsacks, mesh bags of laundry, and loose shoes, froze. Did Marula invite Vlada for *his* benefit? No, it couldn't be. The familiar desire to climb something, to pull himself off the ground, handhold by straining handhold, swelled through him. He continued packing.

Finally, they were off. It was about a seventy-five-minute drive to the marina, where they would transfer to Marula's family's boat and motor to the island cottage. Ruby and Etai were in the back, holding hands. Ruby was sitting in the middle seat, laundry and its sour funk piled high beside her. "Ani retuva," she whispered into Etai's ear. "Where did you learn that?" Etai asked, laughing. "I asked Tyler." At some point during the canoe trip, Ruby had decided to stop fighting against what her body, her mind, her being, were telling her about Etai, to give in to the sweet rush of it. Without having to verbalize it, Etai seemed to be right on board. While the others were in the grocery store in Huntsville, Ruby and Etai elected to stay in the car, let the others decide what food to buy. As soon as they were alone, they threw themselves at each other, making out, pushing and grabbing, hands down pants, a frenzied reintroduction. Tova's loud laugh as they came back with their grocery carts forced them to unclamp. "How are we going to fit all this food?" Ruby was painfully aware of Etai's erection, her own swollen areas.

"Oh! I almost forgot. Your letters." Ruby handed Etai her three letters, each in their own envelope, decorated with little sketches and stickers. The letters Etai had written were in brown ink—where did Etai even find a brown pen!—were folded into thirds, were sans envelopes. They devoured their respective missives, still holding hands, the frenzy momentarily abated, the cars continuing on their tandem journey.

They pulled into the marina; Ruby hadn't even noticed when they had left the highway. Marula headed to prep the boat as everybody else emptied the two cars. She came back too soon, shrugging in her white peasant dress; her boat wasn't in its slip. "That's weird. I'll go call my folks." Marula went off to the pay phone outside the marina office's front door.

"What's her place like?" Etai asked. He and Ruby were sitting on the dock, throwing pebbles into the lake. "I've never been to a cottage on an island."

"Marula's cottage is . . . its whole own world," Ruby responded. "I've been going there since I was nine."

Marula came over, sat down. "Guess what? My brother's up. He's going to come collect us in the pontoon." Hearing that Margolis was there deposited a shovelful of moist soil into Ruby's gut. Oh, fuck. "I wish he had told me," Marula said, perhaps thinking the same thing as Ruby.

Ruby grabbed Etai's hand. They waited on the docks for Margolis, Ruby and Etai sitting close (Ruby trying to stay calm, not freak out, Etai still trying to hide his erection), Stolow, Tova, and Tripper Steve tossing a Frisbee, their feet crunching on the gravel as they jumped and swivelled, Vlada lying on the roof of Tova's car, her headphones on, Marula picking wildflowers in the field behind the marina: Queen Anne's lace, bellflower, buttercup, chickweed. The business of the marina frothed all around them: boats coming and going, tanks being filled, cars loading and unloading, cottagers laughing and calling out, motors sputtering, gas attendants gossiping with the regulars. The sweetly rotten smell of the lake, diesel, cut grass, cheese sandwiches. They waited, the summer afternoon moving to its own internal count. Eventually, Marula, who had joined Etai and Ruby and was trimming her bouquet with a pair of scissors she got from her glove compartment, stood up and pointed out onto the lake. Ruby followed her finger: there was the pontoon, Margolis standing topless at the wheel, a cigarette behind his ear, approaching quickly. Margolis cut the engine and steered the large unwieldy boat on its two steel pontoon tubes parallel to the dock. He tossed the rope to Marula, who tied it off, and crisply jumped onto the dock.

"Sis! Rubes! Welcome!" He gathered them into a three-way hug, slapped high-fives with Tova, Steve, and Vlada, and brought Stolow, Frisbee in hand, brown arms and face glistening with sweat, into a bear hug. "I fucking missed you guys!"

"And who are you?" Margolis said to Etai after releasing Stolow.

"Oh, that's Etai. He's one of the Israelis," Marula said. Margolis stuck out his hand and Etai shook it. "Ah, so you're one of my replacements," he said, glancing meaningfully at Ruby, waggling his eyebrows. Ruby turned away, her bottom lip tight between her teeth.

They tossed their bags, the laundry, and the food into the boat, jumped in. Ruby knew the boat ride well, but it still seemed to take forever. They bounced along the water. Nobody spoke. Islands passed, peninsulas, cottages large and small, other pontoon boats, ski boats, a few canoers and kayakers. Seagulls wailed.

Finally, there it was: Margolis Island, unmistakable with its long flat rock on the island's backside. Margolis took the boat the long way around. Ruby stood up, peering through the trees for the first sighting of the cottage. Sure enough, once they pulled around the island and the dock came into view, there he was. Phil, reeling in a fishing rod, wearing his favourite neon green tank top, a bathing suit Ruby had never seen before. She laughed to herself. Fuck me.

They docked the boat, unloaded, said their hellos. Phil practically ignored Etai, nodding stiffly in his direction. Ruby watched Etai carefully. She had mentioned Phil to him, but had he put together that that was who this rude person was, wielding his fishing rod like a weapon?

They all walked up to the cottage, talking and filling Phil and Margolis in about what they'd missed at Burntshore. Apparently, the two ex-Burntshore staff had quickly found landscaping jobs in the city, had been working outside every day. "It shows," Vlada said, "you're both übertanned." Ruby felt nothing except embarrassment towards Phil, who was acting crazy, making awful jokes and attempting to do physical comedy, which, Ruby saw now, was never his forte; though she had to admit, Vlada was right—he was super tan, his arms defined, both he and stocky Margolis radiating masculine health. Maybe she did miss him, a little bit. Ruby could feel Phil's disdain towards Etai reverberating off him like heat off a recently parked car. Did anybody else notice? Marula put the flowers she had picked at the marina into a glass vase, Orit unpacked the food, there was a mad rush for the old laundry machine. There had been no room in the cars for guitars, but there was an old classical at the cottage, and Stolow picked it up, attempted to tune it the best he could. It only had four strings, the A and the three highest strings. He tuned the A by ear, moved on to the G string.

After the food was in the refrigerator and the laundry was rumbling away (Orit having organized the order for the in-demand machine), it was time to determine rooms. The cottage was a series of low buildings in a loose semicircle, huddled around the dock. The main cottage was a sprawling bungalow with three bedrooms, two bathrooms, a large common area with a stone fireplace, big windows that looked out onto the lake, a screened-in porch. There were also two bunkies, one with a bathroom, one without, and the boathouse had a loft space which was mostly taken up with a double bed. Besides those buildings, the island was forest: oak, birch, hemlock, cedar, white pine, and spruce. "Well, Phil and I are already in Ma's and my room," Margolis said. "Shotgun red bunkie!" Ruby called out. Marula listed off the remaining beds on her fingers. "Okay, so me, Orit, and Vlada will take the last room in the cottage, a.k.a. my room. Tova, you can sleep in the boathouse. And Stolow and Steve can take the blue bunkie."

"Sounds good to me, okay, I absolutely *have* to take a nap! See you sweethearts later!" Ruby grabbed Etai and left the cottage for the bunkie, Etai weighed down with their bags. Ruby ran up the three wooden steps and opened the door for him. Once inside, she shut the door, lowered the blinds, and undressed Etai. They were both standing, he was completely naked, she was completely clothed. She jumped on him and they made out in the middle of the small room, eventually toppling onto the springy bed. They fucked three times. She wiggled and bucked; he came on her tits. Fifteen minutes later they were screwing again. Having given in totally to her desire for him, the sex was more open and full and physical than anything she had experienced before. They pushed and pulled until they were satiated and then they pushed and pulled some more. They crashed into a deep, fathomless sleep, both waking up exactly twenty minutes later, parched, disoriented, groggy. It was stuffy and hot in the un-aired bunkie; the light had softened, late afternoon shadows creeping into the room.

Ruby opened the blinds and, with grunting effort, cracked the window. She got back into bed. They could now see the shoreline, the water.

"Fallon says hi," Etai said.

"Fuck off!" Ruby said, slapping Etai's chest. "Seriously, though, you guys didn't do anything, right?"

"Ani? Of course not! I don't know if you've noticed or not, but I've developed pretty strong feelings for you."

Ruby hit him again, snuggled closer.

"This is just like camp, but without the campers," Etai said into her side after a few minutes of comfy silence. Though he was talking about camp, his thoughts were zeroed in on all the food in the cottage. The cornucopia of food. He would literally kill for a burger.

Ruby adjusted. "Yeah, I guess so."

"It's like a kibbutz without the, you know, work."

"Or the imperialism," Ruby said, almost unintentionally.

Etai shifted, turned onto his back, looked at the cobwebbed ceiling. "Hey, yes, the country is beyond fucked up. Ethnonationalism is evil. What the government and army do to Palestinians is reprehensible. But there was still something special about the kibbutzes, the early kibbutzes. They really tried to live differently, for each other, with each other."

Ruby stiffened. It was like she was in bed with Dov. Anger gushed into her as forcefully as the earlier orgasms. "Socialism for Jews only, no matter how revolutionary or successful, is not socialism. And besides, you know as well as I do—you do know this, right?—that the kibbutzes were used as the original facts-on-the-ground, pushing the Jewish settlement farther and deeper into Palestine, acting as armoured outposts on the colonial frontier." Etai was standing now, naked and sticky, his hands in his hair. He was thirsty and hungry and seeing red. Ruby was struggling to think of something, anything, from the books she'd read, from the history she knew so well, from Seema or Prof. Zipperstein or anybody, but, of course, could come up with nothing. Maybe Etai wasn't as much on the same page with Ruby as she thought he was. "I thought we agreed about this stuff. I guess I was wrong," she said.

Etai was pacing. "I don't know about that, Ruby, I really don't. All I'm saying is that it wasn't all bad, it wasn't all a hundred percent genocide and ethnic cleansing and dehumanization. How could it have been? These were people too, Ruby, radicals and socialists and starry-eyed romantics and refugees. The country did not have to be this way. That's all I'm saying. Besides, how different is camp than a kibbutz really? You said yourself the land used to belong to the Indigenous. Is what you call the imperialism of the kibbutz so different from the imperialism of Burntshore?"

Ruby was sitting now, the sheet pulled tight across her chest. She was seething. She flung off the sheet, stood up.

"I knew you were a soldier. Are a soldier. I knew it. I shouldn't have been convinced by your feelings towards the occupation, confused by our obvious attraction. Seema's right—you're no better than Dov!"

Etai stopped pacing, turned to the bed. "Who's Seema?"

Ruby was gobsmacked; she had not told Etai about Seema, her best friend? Could that be possible?

"This whole thing was a mistake!" she said, her voice raised.

Etai waved his hand in a shooing-off motion. "At chaia b'seret."

"What does that mean?!"

"You're living in a movie!"

They were really screaming now. Ruby was out of bed, unpacking her knapsack, throwing her book and clothes and toiletries everywhere. She found her bathing suit, put it on.

"I know you want me to hate Israel," Etai said, putting on his boxer shorts with one hand, the other emphasizing his words, "but I don't, not all of it. I was born there! My family and friends are there! Yes, I hate the army. Yes, I hate the government. Yes, I hate what the country has become, but I'm a realist, Ruby. The reality: the occupation can be ended. Beyond that, I don't know." He had wrapped himself in a blue sarong.

"Fuck! Whatever! Why do you have to go back there? Why can't you stay here with me?!" For what felt like the millionth time that afternoon, the room shifted.

Etai stared at Ruby, his hands collapsed at his side, his usually flouncy hair flattened from the bed. Ruby made a noise and stomped out of the bunkie, coming back in to grab a towel before stomping out again, slamming the door extra hard.

Etai, wrapped in his blue sarong, went back to the cottage, fiddled with the barbecue, and made himself three hotdogs, which he ate right off the grill, burning his fingers. Inside the cottage, he bent into the fridge to find more to eat. The fridge was decades old and had a bad, wheezing cough. Etai could still taste Ruby on his lips. He grabbed a peach, took half of it into his mouth as he went out to the porch. The air was scented with pine, the smell of far-off bonfires. He was calmer now. He hoped he hadn't fucked things up too badly. Did she actually want him to stay in Canada? To stay with her? Or was it just something she said in the heat of the moment? They weren't even really together, until this afternoon. If they *were* still together. The peach finished, he popped the pit into his mouth to suck out the juice, poison be damned.

Ruby found everybody else at the docks, swimming, playing in the water, sunning on beach towels. As she approached the group, she distinctly heard Marula say "they're still in the talking and fucking phase." Ruby pretended she hadn't heard, slumped down into an available beach chair. She couldn't believe she had said that to Etai—stay in Canada? Where had that come from? Not that the thought of it wasn't pleasing.

It was early evening now, hot and sultry. Ruby picked up the bong she found next to the wooden bench built into the dock—it was Phil's from home, transparent glass with purple speckles, she knew it well—packed a bowl, and took it all in in one gargantuan hit. She sat back in the lounge chair and closed her eyes. She was high enough that, laying there in the chair with the sudden breeze stroking her exposed skin and the sun beating down, it felt like she was floating. She opened her eyes. A water skier knifed past them, the ensuing waves bobbing Orit and Tripper Steve, who were *actually* floating on the lake. The fight with Etai seemed ridiculous now. Orit had rolled off her float and was splashing around with Phil near the shore. Her brown hair was down and she was wearing a cute black high-cut one-piece; Ruby had never noticed how pretty Orit was, she always seemed so severe. Phil had not said a single word to Ruby since their arrival. Well, fuck him. And fuck Etai too. Fuck them all. She would stay on this island all alone for the rest of her life, grow peas and potatoes, forgo the ways of men. She closed her eyes again. Floated off.

For dinner they barbecued steaks, hot dogs, burgers, veggie dogs, onions, peppers, corn. Etai cooked a massive pot of mashed potatoes loaded with garlic and sour cream. Marula made a big salad with some foraged greens. For dessert, Orit—now wearing a white blouse and jean shorts, her hair in a loose bun—made two chocolate cream pies, a "family speciality."

They ate outside, swatting mosquitoes, drinking beer, hitting joints, and packing bong bowls. Etai and Ruby were sitting beside each other, though they weren't speaking; Etai was still wearing nothing but his sarong. Phil and Orit were loudly flirting, Phil going on about the landscaping industry—repeating the word *industry* over and over again—as if it were his life's work and not an emergency summer job; Ruby was sure Phil was just trying to piss her off. Well, congrats to you. The others were deeply engaged in a conversation of their own, discussing this summer's CITs: who was hot (Tori, Ayelet, Becca, booted Scharfy), who had potential as staff (Martin, Becca, Ayelet), the rumours that at camp bred and bloomed and died like ragweed ("I heard Yonatan had a threesome with Ayelet and Tori." "What? No!" "Poor Martin—he's so good with those little kids"). Marula told Vlada all about the pineal gland, its connection to the third eye, how modern society had gunked it up, disconnecting us from the natural world. At one point Ruby overheard Tova telling a story from their trip. Hard to believe that she had woken up in a tent in Algonquin Park that very morning. Hard to believe she woke up consumed with longing for Etai. Ruby took a long drink from her beer, asked Phil to pass her the bong.

The washing machine beeped from inside the cottage, and Orit and Phil ran inside, yelling and pretend fighting about whose turn it was to go next.

Stolow and Vlada were finishing the dishes when Stolow suggested they go down to the dock to watch the sunset. It was just the two of them, standing beside the large oak tree rooted next to the dock. The lake lapped against the rocky island. The sunset was fantastic, like it was being drawn with pastels in real time just for them. They could see the cottages on the mainland, the lights turning on in the big windows of the A-frame directly across the water. A cooler breeze cut through the warm evening air. The smell of pine, campfire, sun, night, lake, barbecue. The bugs were getting worse.

"It's a real E major kind of night," Vlada said wistfully. A big open chord of desire reverberated within Stolow.

Now or never.

"Vlada, I'm really into you."

Vlada smiled, laughed, looked away. Looked back.

"Stolow, I'm into girls," she said. "At least, I think I'm into girls. No, I'm definitely into girls."

Stolow laughed. Well, at least the tension had been broken.

"Too bad you didn't know I existed until this summer," Vlada continued, laughing also. "When I was younger, I was *obsessed* with you. Like obsessed obsessed. You're one of the main reasons I even picked up the guitar."

"Before this summer would have been a forbidden CSR. You know what's the funniest part about this? You're the first girl I've liked for a long while."

Vlada rested her head against Stolow's shoulder. They watched the latest of the sunset's pinks and lavenders seep into the trees. "But we can still jam together, right?" she asked.

"Yes! Of course!"

The cottage door opened, feet on the stairs.

"Vlada, Vlada, want to go kayaking with me?" Marula called out from the top of the hill. "We can check out the beaver lodge one bay over, see if anybody's home. It's the perfect time of night!"

Vlada looked at Stolow, who nodded. "Yeah! Sure!" she called back up to Marula. She ran off.

Alone now, Stolow clapped his hands, swung both his arms behind him, and jumped, grabbing onto the lowest branch of the oak tree. He swung himself up, and, hugging the trunk now, shimmied himself more than halfway up the old tree, scrambling into a split between two thick branches. The sky was deep purple, black, blue. Stars were starting to appear. The lake was burbling its nonsense words. He could hear laughter, music from the cottage.

He was going to stay up there for a while.

Soon after Vlada and Marula returned from their paddle, the drinking started in earnest. Tova made a bonfire. Tripper Steve rolled an absolute beast of a joint. The four-stringed guitar got passed around. Margolis came out of the cottage with a bottle of whiskey. Vlada pulled gorgeous improvised music from the handicapped guitar, reams of silk from a busted spinning wheel, playing a bass line on the A string, chords and melody on the G, B, and high E strings, all the more expansive since it was from a shrunken palette—and all of it in E major, Stolow half-noticed. More beer. They were screaming camp songs at the top of their lungs, climaxing in a feverish rendition of Tyler's "Intergenerational Wealth." The moon, nearly full, rose above the trees.

Ruby was very high and quite drunk. I am very high and quite drunk. The nearly unbearable sexual tension of earlier in the day, the glorious, hours-long breaking of it, the explosive fight, all of it were objects of the deep past, valleyed out by the orogeny of Ruby's inebriation. As Ruby looked around the fire, at her friends, the trees, the water, the phrase *cottage industry* began repeating in her head, the words turgid with meaning, fecund. Cottage industry, cottage industry, cottage industry. Ruby looked at Etai and smiled. Etai returned the smile.

Phil sat down next to Ruby. After the singing, the group had split up: some had gone down to the water, others into the cottage. Ruby, who had been staring into the depths of the fire—cottage industry, cottage industry, cottage industry—was surprised to find herself and Phil the only ones still there. When had Tova left?

"I said I'd wait for you," Phil said with disdain, disbelief, a dash of hurt. An afterthought of hurt.

Ruby took a breath. Her head was spinning. There was no point beating around the bush. "Yeah. So? There was nothing to wait for. We were broken up. We *are* broken up."

Phil scoffed. "I loved you, Ruby. I *love* you. I've thought of nothing else all summer. I've been waiting. And trust me, I had *plenty* of opportunities to, uh, not wait. But that's not the point. That's not the point. I love you. I'm sorry. I fucked up. You know that. What happened with Talia at pre-camp, was . . . was—"

"Listen, Phil. First of all, it's only been, like, three weeks—do you want a medal or something? Second, I don't care about Talia anymore. We're over. We're through. Get on with it. Go get those 'opportunities.'"

Phil's long face, illuminated in the firelight, turned sour, turned knowing.

"Oh, is that what this is about?" he sneered. "Your Israeli fuckboy? When Margolis told me about him, I couldn't believe it! You, of all people, rebounding with a soldier of the Jewish state, oh my god. So much for the moral high ground! Does dicking an active member of the IDF not violate BDS? Did you tell Seema yet?"

Ruby wanted to smack him. Instead, she turned away. "Fuck off," she said, adding, a beat later: "he's a conscientious objector."

Phil snorted, liquid and nasal. "I thought you believed *so* strongly in your politics, in your belief in the power of non-oppressive diaspora, and I'm gone for, what, three days, and you turn into a freaking Zionist, of all things?"

A small part of Ruby's brain was touched that Phil had, in fact, actually been listening to her all those years. The rest of her brain was plotting murder. "It's nothing, Phil," she said, pretty much yelling. "It's nothing. Ya know what, you're right, it *is* just a little rebound fling. We're not even really together. Are you happy now?!"

Phil guffawed, triumphant. Ruby looked up. Etai was standing on the other side of the fire, his face fallen.

"Do you copy that, soldier?" Phil said. He grabbed his bong and stomped off towards the woods.

When Ruby turned back from watching him go, Etai had also vanished.

"Phil! Etai!"

Ruby heard the bunkie door swing shut.

Ruby couldn't find Phil anywhere. She went into the cottage, where everybody was slung in various states of repose. Janis Joplin was singing about hope and heartbreak from the speakers. "Phil's gone, he's run off into the woods." Tova grabbed some flashlights, and they went looking for him. They called his name, split up in the trees, the beams of their flashlights lopping through the forest. A few times Ruby thought she smelled the sour odour of spilled bong water, but Phil did not materialize. The moonlight grew brighter, everything backlit with a blue glow.

"Hey guys, he's over here!" Margolis finally called. Phil was passed out against the massive root wad of a collapsed oak tree, the exposed roots and dirt and pebbles cradling him, the bong tipped over on his lap, making an uncanny tableau. The moon shone bright enough now that the flashlights were no longer needed. "Either he's pissed himself, or that's bong water all over his pants."

"Narsty," Tripper Steve said. They helped Phil up and carried him back to the cottage. He was muttering inaudibly. They threw him onto his bed, left him there, still in his clothes. Tova offered to make everybody grilled cheeses; the Joplin was turned up; the washing machine and drier rumbled on. Ruby pretended not to notice when Orit slipped into Phil's room.

Ruby returned to the bunkie just after 4:00 a.m. Etai was asleep, lying on his front on top of the sheets, still in his sarong, his arms and hairy legs splayed. His watch, however, was on the night table, ticking loudly. Ruby picked it up. It was still set to Israeli time: over there, it was eleven in the morning, the new day well underway. Ruby pulled out the dial and set it to the right time, to Canadian time. To Burntshore time. To their time. She replaced the watch, stood watching Etai for a minute, his tanned taut back, his smooth shoulder blades—soldier shoulders, she thought bitterly—before she took her sandals off and got in beside him. "Promise me you won't go back," she whispered into his arm. "Promise me."

They woke around ten, went for a swim, had a late breakfast before Margolis boated them back to the marina; he and Phil were planning to stay through the weekend. At breakfast, nobody mentioned what had happened the night before. Marula and Vlada came out of Marula's bedroom together. "I had *too* much to dream last night," Marula said. Ruby glanced at Marula's open door, saw the bedsheets on the floor, bras and underwear, the dresser littered with crystals and pinecones and rocks and feathers and pieces of wood. Margolis, messy-haired and looking groggy, poured a cup of coffee, cut a slice of Orit's leftover chocolate cream pie, dumped the whole thing into his coffee, stirred it with a fork. Phil didn't make an appearance; Margolis said he was still sleeping it off. Orit looked circumspect. They all stood in the common room folding their newly laundered clothes. When they got back to the marina, Ruby called shotgun, and Stolow rode in back with Etai. Ruby had a splitting headache. "Let's stop for ice cream sundaes," she said. Heads nodded in assent. Ice cream sundaes it was. "Butternut squash ice cream sundaes," Etai said.

They arrived back at camp with an hour to go before Friday night dinner. Ruby hurried to her cabin, to catch as much sleep as she could before dinner. She was more tired than when she got back from the canoe trip, which, oh my god, was only yesterday.

She couldn't wait to tell Danielle everything.

CHAPTER 16

THE LAST WEEKEND OF FIRST SESSION; ABSOLUTION; THE SOCIAL

Ah, the last weekend of first session. A strange, bittersweet time, the knowledge of forthcoming change thick in the air. Though the impending changeover was a more significant event for the younger kids—more of whom stayed only one session—it was felt by the older kids and the staff as well. The halfway point of the summer brought out all the feelings.

At Rest Hour, Ruby had filled Danielle in on the goings-on at Marula's cottage. "I asked Etai to not go back to Israel." "Why, are you worried about him getting hurt?" "What! No. I don't want him to be the oppressor anymore. To *do* the hurting." What she didn't say was that Etai's comment about camp and imperialism had thrown Ruby for a major loop. Sure, she knew Canada was a settler-colonial nation-state, but she had never let that knowledge seep into her understanding, her love, of camp. She still wasn't sure what to do with this new knowledge. For now, she simply put it aside.

During Friday cleanup, Ruby went to the office to call Arielle's parents. After the canoe trip, Arielle had decided that she wanted to stay second session. Arielle and Danielle had already spoken to Arielle's folks while Ruby was on her day off, and they had said no. Arielle was beside herself, and in an H2H with Ruby—heart-to-heart—asked for her help, so here Ruby was, listening to the phone ring. Arielle's mom picked up.

"Trust me, it's not the money. I don't want you thinking it's the money. We're just so worried about Arielle all the time. It was hard enough for us to say goodbye to her for four weeks, but another four? I don't think I can bear it. She needs her mother!"

"I hear you," Ruby said. "But Arielle's a really strong girl, really strong and independent. You should have seen her on the canoe trip, portaging a canoe like a warrior. I think her staying could be really good for her."

"Well, even if we said yes, she wouldn't have enough medication. She needs more insulin. We'd have to drive some up."

"I'm sure that could be arranged with Tom or Debs."

Arielle's dad took the phone. "What about this June character? I feel she could be a bad influence on Ari." Bad influence? They were eleven-year-old girls!

"June's terrific. They've really become good friends."

Fifteen minutes later, Ruby came up to Arielle, who was making her bottom bunk bed. She looked at Ruby with expectant eyes. "Guess who's going to be a full summer camper?" Arielle squealed with delight, squeezed Ruby. "Oh my god, thank you so much, Ruby! June, did you hear that?"

For Friday night EP, the campers put on the play they'd been working on for the past two weeks. *Fiddler on the Roof*. Now this was a play Ruby could appreciate: each of the sisters' personal rebellions against Tevye, the father, the patriarch, resonated with Ruby (especially Hodel's relationship with Perchik, the Communist). It mourned something lost, however romanticized, unlike *Tel Aviv!*, which celebrated something that never existed. And the music was funny, catchy, emotional, diasporic to the extreme. During the curtain call Ruby wholeheartedly joined in with the rest of the camp in applauding the campers.

Saturday: the last full day for those who only stayed first session. There was packing, there were serious discussions, there was the exchange of phone numbers, emails, addresses. There were tears. Ruby, on her way to the staff lounge to check her email—something she had been compulsively doing since returning from Marula's cottage, waiting for a response from Seema—was surprised to see so many kids wearing buttons from one of the three car companies from Casey's half-day program. *Burntshore Auto*, *Big Buck All Terrain Survival*, *Mustard Gas RVs*. Ruby had heard rumours that more and more kids were joining the companies, there was some sort of tuck buy-in; Ruby wasn't exactly clear what the payoff was. Just a fun camp activity that had stuck. The staff lounge was empty. Ruby logged in, opened Hotmail. There it was. A message from Seema. Ruby was irrationally nervous. She opened the email. It was short.

> *Hi Ruby, I don't have long to respond; I'm at an internet café in Amman. I have to say, I was a bit taken aback by the tone of your email. It was almost like you were expecting absolution from me. I'm surprised I have to remind you of this, Ruby, but not only am I not going to absolve you, absolution from me is not something you need or deserve. Am I surprised, a little hurt, that you are fucking a soldier of the army that oppresses my family? Yes. Of course. Why shouldn't I be? Do I hate you now? No, of course not. Why should I? What do I know? Maybe this Etai is one of the good ones. That's up to you to decide, Ruby. As we talk about constantly, we are only as good as our actions. Jordan's a trip, can't wait to tell you about it. Seema.*

Ruby was surprisingly calm. Seema was right: what *was* she expecting? And to top it all off, Ruby and Etai weren't even speaking to each other! All at once, she felt a powerful urge to be with her girls—four of whom were leaving—to laugh and be silly with her cabin. Heading to cabin line she saw the DJ's van, pulled up to the rec hall doors to unload gear for tonight's big end-of-first-session social. Tyler was talking gear with the DJ as he hacked a butt beside his van with Yonatan.

Ruby spent the rest of the day with her girls, with Danielle and Dawn, helping the four who were leaving pack up, telling stories, helping everybody get dressed for the social. Etai, Seema, and Dov were as far out of her mind as possible.

It was a beautiful, warm night. Everybody was dressed in their camp finery, cameras in hand. Lots of teary eyes during Havdalah, a new camp tradition. In the rec hall, the DJ spun all the bat mitzvah classics, the kids sweated and danced under the light show. Couples hugged and swayed, nervous boys asked nervous girls to dance. Ruby watched as some first-sessioners gave their Israeli sleep-ins big tearful hugs. The Israelis had really become a part of the camp, Ruby had to admit. I guess there's nothing wrong with that, in practice. It's the militarism, the Zionism, the ethnic superiority that could easily come along with it that Ruby would have to watch for, fight against. (Like she'd fought against their indoctrination of the camp? Jesus, Ruby, way to fail the one thing you truly loved!) Ruby happened to be watching the DJ spin his turntables when Martin, the CIT—wasn't he one of the ones she had seen late the first night of camp?—approached the DJ's female assistant, said something that made her laugh. Were he and Ayelet still together?

Ah, young love.

Ayelet ran to the river, sat down on the big pink stone, caught her breath. The river was running fast and loud, rushing over the small falls. She could still hear Beyoncé's "All the Single Ladies" pounding in the rec hall. She watched the river. She sighed.

What a summer it's already been.

CHAPTER 17

THIS CURVED AND CURVING WORLD;
OR, BEING SIXTEEN AT THE END OF THE ANTHROPOCENE

The night before Ayelet Cho left for camp, she got high with her best friend Tara Goldfarb. They had both only been smoking since winter break, but it had quickly become their most cherished pastime. They walked the quiet late-night streets of Thornhill, keeping the skinny joint discreetly by their side when not taking quick tokes, Ayelet wearing old sweats, a ripped camp sweatshirt she had decided, after much hemming and hawing, not to bring this summer. Tara still had another few days in the city before she left for her own camp, Bilium, in the mountains north of Montreal. Ayelet had spent the day organizing her toolbox, going through her toiletries one more time. After dinner, her dad had taken her and her sister Rebecca to Shoppers Drug Mart for some last minute items. The Shoppers was bustling with girls and their fathers; Ayelet said hello, goodbye, and "have a great summer!" to four different girls from her high school, all setting off for different camps. Ayelet's boyfriend, Martin, had arrived from Montreal two days ago, was staying at his best friend Simon's house in Forest Hill. They were supposed to get together yesterday afternoon, but Simon's ride up to Thornhill had fallen through.

"Still not planning on smoking weed at camp?" Tara asked, as they walked down Centre Street towards Bathurst. They were nearly at the massive intersection; Ayelet could see the skyline of traffic lights. To their left was some of the last undeveloped land in Thornhill: forest and scrub. To their right, the Promenade Village Shoppes. The big green glass temples where, among restaurants and video game stores and chiropractors, Ayelet's orthodontist was. Ayelet took a last hit on the roach, coughed heartily.

"Don't think so. Not worth the risk, ya know? I'll miss this though." When Ayelet was high, especially when she was high with Tara, she felt smart, funny, tremendously alive.

"What about Martin?" Tara asked, tossing the roach onto the street.

"Oh, I'm sure he will. He's *obsessed*. And Scharfy's a bad influence."

"Imagine Martin got kicked out!"

"I'd die! And then I'd kill him!"

This, apparently, was a stupendously funny thing to say. Waiting for the lights to change at Bathurst, which from where they stood shot south straight through the entirety of Toronto until hitting Lake Ontario, standing on the engorged suburban median as cars sped past them, they nearly toppled over laughing.

"You think you're going to go all the way at Billy?" Bilium was a notorious sex camp—a hundred-plus barely supervised sixteen-year-olds in glorified tents, each year supplying salacious stories, rumours, and STI scares to the Jewish teenagers of Canada. Tara had been dying with excitement since last August.

Tara looked over her shoulder coyly, flipped her hair. "Depends on what the boys are like, I guess. What about you? Are you and Martin finally going to do the deed? You visited him enough times in Montreal this year."

Ayelet batted her lashes. "Well, unlike you, we'll actually have *responsibilities* this summer. We'll be CITs, we won't just be lounging around in our tents all day, making out."

"That's not all we do!"

"Oh, yeah?"

"We also have programming, and activities, and themed days, and fawning over the Israelis, and . . . other stuff."

This led to another fit of giggling. They were nearly back on their street. They stopped at Tara's house, a block and a half from Ayelet's. They hugged long and hard on Tara's driveway, their faces buried in each other's sweatshirts, breathing each other in, saying "I love you" in rhythmic succession.

"Write me, like, all the time!"

"I will, and you do the same. I'll see you in August!"

"And, Ayelet . . . if you do do it, let me know right away!"

"I swear!"

Ayelet walked home from Tara's through the suburbs she knew so well, felt a familiar love for her neighbourhood, where people of all races and religions lived and worked. Her love also enveloped Tara, her best friend; they had both been worried when after grade eight Tara had gone on to Westmount but Ayelet had transferred to CHAR, the private Jewish high school, but the daytime separation, if anything, had made their bond stronger, as did their summers apart. She smiled thinking of the coming camp season. For the six years she had been a camper at Burntshore there was always a nervous excitement the night before camp, but tonight was different: she was no longer just a camper but a CIT. A counselor in training. The responsibility left her giddy, nerves and expectation in alternating bursts of weighty feeling. What did the summer have in store? She stopped on her porch, looked out over her street, smelled her hands. Did she smell like pot? Was she still baked?

She opened the front door. Her parents were watching TV in the family room in the back of the house; it was usually around the time they'd switch to Omni for the Mandarin-language news, her dad explaining things her mom missed (Ayelet hadn't watched the news with her parents since she was a little girl; the political had not yet come for her). Sure enough, slipping off her running shoes, she heard the familiar voice of the Chinese announcer, as much a part of the house as Alex Trebek's. She padded up the carpeted stairs. In her room was a mess she was not ready to deal with. She'd wash her hands and face and go annoy her sister, who was undergoing her own pre-camp rituals.

Tomorrow morning had never been closer.

Twenty-four hours later, and from the profane, empty time of the city, the suburbs, of parents and school and paved streets and homework and television and being alone—from all that nothing, the sacred time of camp had come. For the CITs, the first three days of the summer, before they were assigned their placements, were theirs; a strange, borderless limbo—not quite campers, not quite staff, they waited, got used to finally being CITs, to living in CIT Town with its own geography, buildings, and shoreline, to not having staff sleeping in their cabins, to, in a strange, still-paying-to-be-there way, *being* staff. Barry Blum, CIT head, was one of the most beloved personalities at camp, funny, kind, brilliant, his girth enormous, his coolness infinite, enlarging everything it touched, and besides speeches from both Tom and Debs and mandatory workshops on what it means to be a Burntshore counselor, Barry made sure the sixteen-year-olds had plenty to do if they wanted but also let them chill, relax, hang, sleep. And chill, relax, hang, and sleep they did.

That first night, to celebrate their new roles as CITs, Martin Gold and his boys stood on one of the dirt roads outside of camp, which they had struggled through thick forest to get to. It was just after midnight. They had already polished off the rum Josh had finagled into a pack of juice boxes—"the secret is to open from the bottom, fill it up, and then close it back up with a glue gun." Josh had rolled a massive joint standing in the moonless Muskoka dark, the only light emanating from Martin and Scharfy's plastic lighters. They were too afraid to turn on their flashlights.

The five of them—Martin, Scharfy, Josh, Simon, quiet Babka—huddled close. Scharfy offered his still-flaming lighter and held it under the joint as Josh puffed it into alightedness. The cherry was quarter-sized, burning orange-red as it went around the circle. Lighters away, the red cherry of the spliff was the only light, a bobbing fiery tear in the black velvet night. Scharfy had snuck in a half ounce of weed in the tongue pocket of his size-thirteen Chad Muska skateboarding shoes. Josh was supposed to bring a half ounce of his own, but his mom found his stash while labelling his clothes, and, after getting thoroughly reamed out, had been lucky to sneak his juice boxes past her, let alone be allowed to board the bus that morning. Martin was also supposed to, but his "dealer bailed" on him (in truth, he had been too afraid to risk getting busted).

"Scharfy, you champ, you saved our summer!" Josh said, his pimply, rebellious face lost in smoke.

Scharfy cough-laughed. Tall, athletic, with a new set of amazing dreadlocks, the Muskas were not just for the zippered tongue pocket: everything about Scharfy, from his low jeans and large shirts, to his ironic detachment, was modulated to fit the label *skateboarder.* Martin had been jealous of Scharfy and the ease with which he existed in the world since puberty. "When Glazer found the weed during the search this morning, I thought I was going to die! He only pulled out the bag of pre-rolls, though, didn't realize there was a bag of fresh nugs snug at the bottom." He tapped his left foot on the road.

"Fuck! At least he didn't rat you out."

"Yeah, 'cause then the rest of us would've been stone cold sober all summer."

"He's probably smoking them right now, the prick."

The joint went around, an EKG of the night's steady beat, its rises and drops getting steeper as the spliff got smaller and they became higher. Though they had spent the last three nights together partying in Toronto, walking the sidewalkless, mansioned streets of Forest Hill, debating whether or not Scharfy should bring his skateboard for the summer, tonight was the first night of camp, and the sense of reunion, of being together again at long last, was potent, was deeply intoxicating. Five best friends, back at Burntshore.

"Ayelet's looking mighty hot," Josh said, his cheeks collapsing as he sucked in smoke. "You finally going to put it in her, Martin?"

"Fuck off!" How could he tell them that the last time Ayelet came to Montreal she was more than ready but Martin had chickened out and they just did their usual stuff? He'd never hear the end of it.

The joint was nearly done. The cherry was no longer the blazing noon sun, but minutes away from dropping below the horizon, blinking out of existence. It was suddenly cold in the near-absolute dark.

"I'm high as low-hanging balls," Scharfy said.

"What should we do now?"

"Let's order a pizza!"

"Are you sure? What if we get busted?"

"Don't be a pussy! We're CITs now, as good as staff!"

So, order a pizza they did. To get back into camp they walked along the road to main gate, no longer worried about getting caught. Standing behind Tom's office, Martin ran to the pay phone and placed the order. "Too bad we don't have our cellies." "There's no reception up here anyways, dumbass." Martin's heart was jackhammering in his chest as he messily explained the directions, hung up, ran back to the others, lit with accomplishment. They waited at the gates til the lights of the delivery car appeared in the distance, and they flagged it down, waving their arms above their heads. They ate the pizza—extra large, pepperoni, sausage, hot peppers, and garlic—standing near the gate, multiple slices in each boy's hands. They were not as drunk as they were when they fought and scratched themselves through the trees to get to the road, were slightly less high, were satiated on the greasy food and the cool cottage-country night.

"Oh, fuck, do you see how late it is?"

On the way back to CIT Town, near A&C, they ran into Ruby. Martin's heart cracked his ribcage. Josh had always had a huge crush on Ruby—fuck, she was so hot—and, drunk, stoned, and petrified, was utterly tongue-tied, as were Simon and Babka. Scharfy, as usual, handled it. Ruby must have known they were fucked up but let them go anyways.

Ruby was the exact kind of counselor Martin wanted to be, that he was going to be this year during his placement.

They were back at CIT Town. A peninsula at the far end of camp that dipped into the lake, CIT Town was made up of the CIT cabins, the CIT staff cabin (Barry Blum had his own cabin across the road beside the head staff lodge), a small rec hall, the CIT Pit, the Sitting Tree, three tetherball courts, benches, two bathrooms (the TITs and the showers), and a rocky shoreline full of cedars and white pines. To a sixteen-year-old normally bounded by the walls of his parents' house, it was the clearest form of freedom they had ever known; it had the potential, especially late at night, full of intoxicants and pizza, to make one feel boundless, unappeasable, huge.

"I'm going to go to the girls' cabin," Martin announced. "Anybody care to join me?"

Scharfy let out a whoop.

"Have fun, you fantastic fuck," Josh said, slapping Martin's hand.

Martin tiptoed up the steps of the cabin. Trying to open the door as silently as possible, he realized how blasted he was. Once he was in the cabin, he was at an utter loss. Ayelet had told him at dinner where her bunk was, but he had never been inside the cabin and couldn't get his bearings (and barely remembered what Ayelet had told him—back left? behind the sinks?). He stood for a moment in the cabin of sleeping girls, most of whom he had known since his days as a shy, prepubescent boy. The first night and this was already clearly a place where teenaged girls lived. It thrummed with female energy. He would have liked to have just stood there forever.

He couldn't just stand there forever.

"Ayelet? Ayelet?"

"She's over there, in the corner," somebody angrily whispered.

He looked in the corner, caught sight of Ayelet's red knapsack hanging off a hook.

He climbed the ladder, his face now inches from Ayelet's beautiful sleeping face.

"Psst . . . Ayelet!"

Ayelet opened her eyes. Her face brightened.

"Martin! Come up. Be quiet!"

Martin got into the bed with Ayelet. They were holding each other tightly.

"I missed you so fucking much."

"I missed *you* so fucking much."

Ayelet took Martin's hand and put it on her crotch. They commenced giving each other quiet, unreal hand jobs before falling asleep in each other's arms in the skinny twin bed, Martin still in his clothes, his shoes.

The night before they were given their placements, the CITs gathered in the CIT rec hall to watch a movie. Barry Blum stood in front of the television with a DVD in each hand. "Alright, gang, what should it be? *Night of the Living Dead* or *Titanic*?" He held up one DVD, then the other. The response to *Titanic*—carried by the girls—was the clear and obvious winner.

Barry popped the DVD in and pressed play, went to sit in the back with the other two CIT staff. The CITs, on their pillows and blankets, in their sweatshirts and sweatpants, sitting or lying on their stomachs with their heads in their hands, heads in laps, girls braiding hair or knotting string bracelets, eating candy from home and chocolate bars from the tuck shop, settled into the luscious, exposed-cedar smell of the building for the three-hour movie. "Show us your tits!" Scharfy yelled at the old Rose in the opening segment. "Shut up!" "You're disgusting!" The girls swooned—half ironically, half earnestly—when Leonardo DiCaprio first appeared on screen. For the first ninety minutes, while Jack and Rose fell in love, while Billy Zane scowled, while the lower-class berths and the upper-class splendour were crudely juxtaposed, the boys—mostly Scharfy and Josh—booed and threw candy at the television, only momentarily switching registers to catcalls and hooting when Kate Winslet's breasts appeared, when Rose and Jack fucked in the sweaty carriage. "Shut the fuck up, you pervs!" Becca yelled. And then, on a cold, breath-fogged night, the ship slammed into the iconic iceberg, and the movie turned inside out. Now the boys roared and cheered as carnage visited the boat, as the ship cracked in half, as extras died their gruesome deaths. By the end, Rose and Jack floating on that once-stately door, there was very little noise at all from the audience, except for some quiet sobbing.

The movie was over. The sleepy CITs rose, gathered their blankets and pillows, filed out of the rec hall into the treed, solid world of CIT Town. Ayelet and Martin were holding hands, Martin's sleeping bag draped over his shoulders. She pulled him behind the building, kissed him. Her face was wet with tears.

"Draw me like one of your Jewish girls, Martin." Ayelet was pushing herself against him. He could feel himself getting hard.

"Come by my cabin tonight," he whispered in her ear.

"I'll try. Maybe Becca will come with me."

"Hey, lovebirds!" They pulled apart. It was Jeremy Kraftchuk, their counselor, walking past. Ayelet blushed. "You're one to talk!" Martin shot back. Jeremy was from the famed 2005 CIT year—hot, cool guys and gorgeous, cool girls. Martin and Ayelet were eight years old in 2005, but still, they knew the stories, the myths, filled with wonder when they saw Kraftchuk's name scrawled on a cabin wall. It was unreal that he was now both of their counselors, this larger-than-life figure from Burntshore's deep history.

"I'll see you later," Ayelet said, pecking Martin on the cheek and running to catch up to her girls. Martin watched her small butt in her plaid pyjamas, her pillow tucked under an arm.

Back at the cabin, the guys were sitting in their folding chairs, talking once again about how Glazer had gotten kicked out.

"Dude, do you think it was *your* spliffs he got caught with?" Josh asked.

"Who the fuck knows, man," Scharfy said, shrugging, taking a chug from his can of iced tea. "Serves him fucking right for taking my shit." He crushed the can and threw it on the floor.

"We've gotta be careful. Don't want to become the next Glazer." Since they got the news that Glazer had been booted, Martin was terrified of getting caught with pot or leaving camp.

There was a knock on the door, and Ayelet, Becca and some other girls came in. Their energy spilled into the boys' cabin like bubble bath into warm water. Becca jumped onto her boyfriend Simon's lap, tugged on his neat, manicured dreadlocks.

Martin sat there, taking it all in.

The night glimmered with possibility.

The next morning, huddled around the CIT Pit, they were given their placements. Before reading them out, Barry gave a little pep talk. "Camp is going to be a little different from now on. Welcome to the other side of the divide. Don't forget, if you ever need help with anything, if you're unsure of your role, if your staff is being unkind to you—anything at all—please come talk to me, Jeremy, or Polina. That's what we are here for this summer. Okay. You folks ready for this? Let's do it." Ayelet got A&C—her first choice! Martin, who didn't really care what he got as long as it was staff, was placed in a unit 1 cabin. After breakfast the next day, they would start. That night, Ayelet, Becca, and Natalie snuck to the rocks on the far side of the peninsula, stripped out of their clothes, and dove into the water, naked, unsupervised. It was just after a fish spawn, and the lake was riddled with fish eggs; it was like swimming in bubble tea.

"I hope we don't get pregnant!" Becca said, tittering, which was extra funny because she was the only one of them that was sexually active.

The next morning, they heard, first as rumours, then as confirmed fact (from Barry's mouth, no less) the terrible news: Jeremy Kraftchuk was no longer employed at Camp Burntshore. He, along with three others, had gotten fired. Kraftchuk, gone? More than a few girls openly wept at the news, some guys got teary and tried to hide it. The CIT boys who had smuggled in weed were petrified, stopped smoking for a whole night. They had a hushed discussion about it in the showers.

"If Kraftchuk can be booted, any of us can."

"We've got to hide this shit better."

"Fucking Tom, he's such a fucking Nazi. Didn't he used to be a pill pusher himself?"

"Let's start hiding it in the woods. We shouldn't have any of it on us or in the cabin at any time."

Martin now spent his days keeping ten-year-olds in order, wrestling with them, answering an unending barrage of questions, playing sports and cards, making up elaborate jokes and insane stories, which they ate up like candy. Ayelet was in A&C, learning the ins and outs with Andrea, who, though off-putting in her quiet, tall, wispy way, was an excellent teacher who knew a hundred creative uses for every spool and safety pin; they made bracelets and Shrinky Dinks and glazed pottery, either singing along to *Tel Aviv!* or listening to The Otter.

One evening, Josh and Martin, wandering around the camp dump—on the other side of the road, adjacent to the head staff lodge and cabins, a whole world of discarded bunk beds, mattresses, propane tanks, punky wood, old furniture—found an old poker table and carried it carefully back to their cabin. They now spent their evenings—when not at their "spot" in the woods getting high—playing Texas Hold'em, five card draw, seven card stud.

Ayelet was loving being on A&C; she felt she had made the right choice. The endless possibilities! Not to mention that she had had no idea that A&C was such a hot spot for camp gossip: with all the cabins coming through, Ayelet learned more about camp hookups, politics, betrayals, and secrets than she thought could possibly exist. She was the first CIT to hear about Tom's hiring of the Israelis, information she dutifully brought back with her to CIT Town, basking in the easy glow of having shocking news. Saturday night, sitting on the rocks with Becca, watching the lake, Ayelet realized a whole week had passed already. She and Martin had yet to go beyond what happened that first night; since then, it had only been kissing, some light clothes-on grinding. Was she supposed to make the first move? Hadn't she given him all the signals? Martin seemed to like fooling around with her, though he was mostly focused on getting high and playing cards with his boys. She wondered what Tara would think. With a sinking feeling, she remembered she hadn't yet written Tara a letter. She had been waiting for the big news to share, but who knew when—or even *if*—that would happen? First thing tomorrow morning, she'd write. She suddenly knew what she would tell Tara. About how amazing camp was, how terrific her summer had been so far, how she couldn't believe that next summer she would get *paid* to do this. How at camp time is both slow and fast. How even boredom, when it visited the girls' cabin, was suffused with contentment. How she was sixteen and today, this very moment, right here, on the rocky shoreline of Lake Burntshore, *this* was the universe. How it was almost too much, this curved lake all golden and shimmering on this curved and curving planet.

When the Israelis arrived, the CITs were spread out across camp at their placements so some met them before others. Word spread swiftly, though, and by dinner first impressions had been solidified: the hottest girl was Michal, black-maned and sun-kissed, the hottest guy, Dov, tall and muscled. However, the moment Ayelet laid eyes on Yehouda—who was replacing Kraftchuk as CIT staff—she disagreed with the consensus; she had never seen anybody like him, dark skinned and hunky, happy and confident. Unlike some of the other girls in her cabin, Ayelet hadn't been particularly enthused about the incoming Israeli staff. Not like Becca and Tori, who had become obsessed, had talked about nothing else in the days leading up to their arrival. Not only were there plenty of opportunities to meet Israelis, young and old, soldier and civilian, at CHAR, not only had she heard countless stories from Tara about Israeli counselors, but she had a boyfriend (which, come to think of it, so did Becca, but that hadn't stopped her). Yet when Ayelet first saw Yehouda, a glacier that she didn't know was in her chest receded, leaving a deep, sparkling lake. Ayelet, gifted at languages as she was, spoke a more-than-passable Hebrew, could easily eavesdrop on whatever Yehouda was saying when he was talking to the other Israelis, but for days she was too shy to say anything to him. But she watched him, drank him in.

Yehouda's second night there he gave a welcome talk to all the CITs. "Who has grandparents who were in the Holocaust?" he asked, standing in front of the thirty-six sixteen-year-olds in the CIT rec hall. Barry Blum, who was leaning against the wall near the door, looked a bit taken aback. About half of the CITs raised their hand. Yehouda nodded, like this was the answer he was expecting. "And I'm sure none of us wants anything like that to happen again. That's why we need the state of Israel. You Jews in the diaspora do not understand what it is like. When I first get here, I say to Dov, 'Where are all the checkpoints? The security?' I was happy there was a gate, but all you need to do is walk around it. Not even the medical personnel carry weapons. It is very strange. Then I realized: you are entirely safe here. This, this safety, is new to me. I realized: this safety is because of Israel, because of the sacrifices we make for you. I have two older brothers. One of them lost a leg in the Second Lebanon War. The other took part in the evacuation of the Jewish towns in Gaza. What a horrendous thing to do, eh? For Jewish soldiers to kick other Jews out of their homes. Imagine if Canadian soldiers came down and closed this camp, pulled you away screaming and crying. That is why we must stand together, as Jews, against all our enemies."

When Yehouda finished, everybody was quiet. They filed out of the CIT rec hall into a warm, skunky night. Ayelet had heard plenty of speeches about Israel, but she had never listened as she'd just listened to Yehouda; she had *heard* him. Ayelet had rarely felt so awake, her aperture cranked world-wide. Here they were, in a forest of hemlock trees, their cabins' roofs dusted with their needles. Bats were swooping. Soon owls would start to call. She could see stars out over the lake. How lucky we are to be outside *all* the time. Yehouda was right: she did feel safe here. More than safe. She belonged in this terrestrial night world. Was it really because of a country halfway around the world? Maybe it was.

Later, she sat with Becca, Simon, and Martin on the steps of the TITs. The two interracial couples of the summer. "Well, that was heavy," Simon said.

"I heard Barry giving Yehouda shit afterwards," Martin said. "I was walking by, and Yehouda said something like, 'What, I thought that was why we were here?' Barry told him to tone it the fuck down, that's not what he meant when he asked Yehouda to introduce himself."

"He just doesn't understand how much Yehouda cares about us," Ayelet found herself saying.

Ayelet lay in her top bunk, her headphones on, thinking of Yehouda, her new nightly ritual. Yehouda was big, eager, a caring, gentle giant. Where Martin's skin was pale and burned easily, Yehouda's was rugged, deeply tanned. Where Martin was saying he wasn't going to go to CEGEP but move to Toronto and get a job at Simon's dad's company, Yehouda had plans to become an officer in the army. Where Martin suddenly seemed to Ayelet to be a boy, naive and unaware of the ways of the world, Yehouda, only three years his senior, was a man, with all that entailed. Yehouda had lived life; he had lost friends and family in battle. What did Martin know except the suburbs of Montreal? What hardship had Martin endured besides running out of weed during a dry spell, flunking a French test? Yehouda seemed to be good at everything, game for anything, strong and loyal and willing. Ayelet shuffled through her growing collection of images of him. Here was Yehouda helping Yonatan fix a broken lawnmower. Here was Yehouda doing push-ups under the Sitting Tree. Here was Yehouda telling a story about losing his best friend in Lebanon, everybody crying. Here was Yehouda volunteering to take Scharfy to the hospital in town when he broke his arm at the ropes course. Here was Yehouda sitting by the fire, the sleeves of his various layers: blue long-sleeve shirt, green sweatshirt, grey jacket.

Ayelet was obsessed. She knew she was obsessed, but knowing she was obsessed made her even more obsessed. Does he even notice you're alive? Why would he, you never talk to him, you don't stand out compared to Becca and Tori, you're just a child!

Meanwhile, Yehouda had started to make nightly visits to both the girls' and guys' cabins. He'd sit down, surrounded by the girls, and tell stories, answer questions. "You are all such fresh bread, eh?" he said once, laughing. Ayelet squirmed with delight along with everybody else, sure he didn't mean her, because why would he? (It wasn't for many years until she realized how inappropriate saying something like that was.)

During the rain day on the second Saturday—the rain coming down stunningly hard, a bottomless lake fed through the great shredder in the sky, CIT Town a swamp—the CIT girls played MASH. Ayelet swooned when she ended up with Yehouda in a shack. What did it matter where they lived, Yehouda would fix the roof, put in a fireplace, dig out a garden for Ayelet to grow the vegetables they would eat all year round. Ayelet folded up the MASH paper and put it in the bottom of her toolbox.

It was shortly after the Israelis arrived that Martin and the boys planned a raid on the tuck shop. Well, Josh planned it, and the rest went along for the ride. On the predetermined night, they got high at the spot, played poker with the cabin, pretended to go to sleep. At two-thirty they woke up, silently put on black sweatshirts, scrunched their hoods over their faces, covered their watches with arm bands, and left the cabin on bare feet, their shoes in hand. They snuck along the waterfront, cut across centre field, jimmied the door, and were inside the tuck shop. They stuffed their knapsacks with chocolate bars, chips, batteries (which Josh claimed he was going to sell to other CITs). Martin grabbed a half dozen Oh Henry! bars, which were Ayelet's favourite. They ran back to CIT Town, didn't stop until they were in the TITs, laughed and ate chocolate in the heady afterburn of the heist. The bright glare of the bathroom lights, the smell of piss and disinfectant, the tiled floor, nighttime air blowing in through the screen windows, bugs buzzing, the toilets with their black clawed seats up.

The girls listened to *Tel Aviv!* in their cabin, sang into their hairbrushes, gossiped about the boys, made each other friendship bracelets, sunned themselves near the Sitting Tree, snuck out to watch the stars. Andrea taught Ayelet how to fire the kiln. Ayelet watched Yehouda, building up the nerve to talk to him. She and Becca had a heart-to-heart by the water. Ayelet said she still loves Martin but has an insane crush on Yehouda, and, besides, Martin is so busy with his boys. Becca said Ayelet should totally go for it. Ayelet laughed. On visitors day, Ayelet's parents came up to visit her and Rebecca. Ayelet took her parents up to Yehouda, standing in CIT Town, introduced them. It was the first direct thing she'd said to him. "Ayelet is one of our best CITs," Yehouda said, "conscientious, attentive, showing real leadership qualities." He smiled at Ayelet, and the lake in her chest glittered in the sunlight.

For the CITs, the day after visitors day meant one thing: the waterpark. Every camper under the age of sixteen waited for their turn at the mythical park, which had opened in the mid-1970s, ten years after Camp Burntshore's inaugural season, and was where the CITs had been spending the day after the first visitors day ever since, except in '85, when the waterpark was closed for the entire season due to flooding. It was amazing the waterpark still allowed them to come: it was a rite of passage for the CITs to get kicked out every year, at any and all costs.

Martin was psyched. He was sitting at the back of the bus beside Scharfy, who had his Muskas on, the right tongue fat. Barry led them in camp cheers, Yehouda clapping and yelling out even though he barely knew the words. Martin didn't make as big a deal of the Israelis' arrival as his boys did; he had Israeli first cousins, spent every second winter break in a suburb of Tel Aviv. Yeah, Michal was freaking hot, but so what, Ayelet was freaking hot!

The bus pulled into the parking lot. Barry motioned for them to stay seated. "It's going to be a hot one. Lots of water, lots of sunscreen, etcetera. Now, I know we're all here to have a good time, and, trust me, we will. But try to keep the monkey business to a minimum! Don't forget, we're here as representatives of Camp Burntshore. In other words, don't be total fucking jackasses." They piled out of the bus and were let loose inside. They threw off their clothes. They waited in short morning lines for hot dogs and poutine. They stood in the wave pool. They baked in the sun. They rode the slides. They played mini-putt. They lounged and they sunned. They drank water and slathered themselves in sunscreen and gorged on ice cream. Everything was bright, pastel, hot. Barry lay on a lounge chair, a tanning mirror unfolded across his chest.

By lunch time the sun was broiling. Every surface was burning hot to the touch—plastic chairs, cement floors, skin, hair, tabletops, the railings as you stood on the stairs waiting for your turn to go down one of the six slides ranging from one to fifteen stories, picnic benches, the mini-golf clubs, the lockers, the silver Zippo Scharfy used to light the spliff the boys smoked in the sweltering parking lot, their senses on high alert for a counselor or waterpark staff.

Ayelet was standing near the edge of the wave pool, letting the waves wash over her, trying to be inconspicuous, half wondering where Martin was (though she had a pretty good idea). It took her a second to realize that Yehouda was calling her. "Hey! Ayelet, right? Bo-ee, bo-ee! Yalla!" He beckoned her towards him, his whole arm sweeping. Ayelet pushed herself off the edge and walked over, painfully aware of her bathing suit, her legs and arms and face, half of her body submerged in chloriney water, the other in the smouldering air. Once she was close enough, Yehouda picked her up and swooped her onto his shoulders. Ayelet couldn't believe it—she was giggling, her thighs were on Yehouda's hot and meaty shoulders, his hair was in her hands, Yehouda took big, exaggerated steps towards Becca, who was on Simon's muscular shoulders, the girls pushed each other, laughing, their hair in their faces. Ayelet could feel Yehouda's head and neck against her crotch. The sun slamming down all around them. The waves stopped, and Yehouda moved in such a way that Ayelet knew they were about to flip into the pool. Ayelet pre-empted him by tipping herself backwards into the water, plugging her nose, her eyes closed tight, the waves in her heart's wave pool cranked all the way up.

After the wave pool, Ayelet was sitting with Yehouda on hard plastic stools as he ate two poutines, one with smoked meat, the other with extra curds. Yehouda was shovelling the food into his mouth in big gooey forkfuls. Ayelet couldn't look away; she had never before enjoyed watching somebody eat, but here she was, transfixed. She heard laughing: most of the boys, Martin included, were standing around Tori and Natalie near the bathrooms. Tori was wearing a tight yellow bikini, her boobs enormous.

Yehouda finally took enough of a break to speak. "I've never had food like this before. What is it called again?"

"Poutine. It's from Quebec. The owners of the park are Quebecois. This was the first real poutine in Central Ontario." Yehouda nodded vigorously, resumed stuffing his face. Ayelet was proud to be so knowledgeable, even though she had taken this information right from the billboard next to the menu.

"Mmm . . . mmm . . ." Yehouda said, swallowing, "so, are you related to the head Ropes staff? Stee-low?"

Ayelet swallowed. Even though they had just come out of the wave pool, her skin was dry and hot. Until this moment, Ayelet had been feeling happy in her pink bikini. "What? No, ha ha. Not at all. Besides, Stolow's mom is Korean, and my dad is Chinese."

"Enh, so you are only half Jewish?" Ayelet was used to questions like this from kids at CHAR, from synagogue, from everywhere, really, but still, it was disappointing. Weren't they used to Jews of all kinds in Israel?

"What? No! I'm fully a hundred percent Jewish! I'm Jewish *and* Chinese." The disappointment from Yehouda's stupid question had morphed into the thrill of talking forcefully this way. He won't forget her so quickly now.

Yehouda stared at her, wiped his mouth with a napkin, nodded.

"Ah, yes. I understand now. My grandparents were Jews from Iraq. So were Michal's. And Etai's great-grandfather came from Turkey."

"Oh wow! So do you speak Arabic?" Ayelet couldn't believe it—she was having a real, meaningful conversation with Yehouda!

Yehouda fake-spat on the ground. "No, no. Arabic is the language of the enemy."

"Oh," Ayelet said.

Yehouda laughed. "Anyways, I am a proud Israeli. Are you a proud Canadian?"

"I guess so. I never really thought about it."

Yehouda nodded knowingly. Ayelet felt she was losing the thread of this conversation. Were they talking about something besides what they were actually talking about?

"Is it true Etai and Ruby are hooking up?" Ayelet asked, in perfect Hebrew, trying to steer the conversation into less subtexty-terrain, trying to impress him.

Yehouda smiled; if he was surprised, he didn't show it. "Ah, Ruby and Etai," he said, answering in English, nodding with his entire head. "Ruby and Etai. Ruby v'Etai. Yes. They make a cute couple, do they not?"

Heat rushed to Ayelet's face.

Fifteen feet away, Martin was standing with the guys around Tori, everybody trying to make her laugh, looking at her breasts. Martin was a little too fucked up; his heart was racing. He should get a drink, go for a swim. Yet he just continued standing there. He noticed Ayelet sitting with Yehouda, laughing. Before he had time to register what he was looking at, there was a big commotion from the slides.

"Scharfy's clogged the mega whirler!" Simon called out, running towards the tall trunk of central slides. "Let's go! Let's go!" The CITs ran for the slides from all over the park, whistles shrilling. Ayelet looked apologetically at Yehouda, jumped up, and ran with the others. Yehouda drank his soft drink, watched them go. Next up: ice cream.

By the time Ayelet had gotten to the top of the slide platform, pushed past the harried attendant, and jumped into the mega whirler, it was clogged nearly all the way to the top. Thirty CITs were in the enclosed slide, stacked up close. Body heat, sticky chloriney skin, mouths red and blue from cotton candy, the light waving on the plastic tube they were stuck in like underwater shadows.

They started singing the CIT song, belting it out, the words echoing and warbling in the curved space of the tube. When they got to the verse that was just a list of the camp's bathroom huts—"There's Rigor Tortoise, there's the Monolith, but nothing beats the TITs! No, nothing beats the TITs!"—they repeated it four times, screaming at the top of their collective lungs.

By the time Scharfy let go of the plug and they all slid out into the pool one after the other, the waterpark owners were standing there waiting for them, their arms crossed. Barry was there too, trying to keep back laughter, a smudge of sunburn on his face where he had failed to adequately apply sunscreen.

On the bus home, Ayelet sat next to Becca, Becca's sweatshirt spread over both of them like a blanket, an earbud in each of their ears playing *Tel Aviv!* Ayelet could barely keep her eyes open, kept fluttering into and out of sleep, the music soaking into her unconscious. She had always considered herself a Miriam and saw Martin as a Friedrich—young, innocent to the ways of the world, newly in love—but now she wanted to be a Sarah to Yehouda's David: builders of nations, parents of new worlds, steadfast life partners with more than their fair share of suffering but also of pride in what they had accomplished together. Martin passed out almost immediately, his head lolling on Josh's. Tori was sitting with Scharfy, laughing at the smallest thing he said, touching his shoulder.

Barry and Yehouda played spit, the sounds of them slapping the bus seat puncturing the otherwise quiet journey.

Friday night dinner, and Becca was telling Ayelet and Natalie about the sex she had had with Simon the night before. She was talking loudly; the younger boys sitting across from them were quite obviously listening, their mouths agape.

"And then we did it from behind. It was so hot and sweaty, liquid was like literally dripping off us! Simon put the condom in one of Babka's shoes when we were done! And the rest of the cabin slept through the whole thing. I couldn't believe it."

Ayelet wanted that for herself: to do something illicit, something hot and forbidden. She finally spotted Yehouda, sitting at the other end of the dining hall with Dov and Michal. Why would he ever want to sleep with somebody with no experience? She needed to be more like Becca. She needed to be fearless, to reach across the CIT-staff divide and take what she wanted. She was terrified the first time she smoked pot, but, guess what, she ended up loving it! It was fun and giggly. All she had needed was to smoke the first joint, cough her lungs out, to get past the fear.

She scanned the dining hall until she found Martin. He was with his boys, talking to some pre-CIT girls sitting across from them, the girls flirting and smiling, their mouths full of braces. Ayelet felt two big hands on her shoulders. "Shalom, Ayelet." It was Yehouda. Ayelet's whole body went stiff.

She hoped Martin was watching.

After the second time Martin and the boys raided the tuck shop, they got bored of it. They already had more candy than they could eat, and it was so *easy*, there was no sense of danger anymore. So, after Josh made a joke about stealing a pair of basketball shoes they saw unattended at the ski docks, they started stealing people's clothes. Shower sandals at first, then sweatpants, sweaters, anything that would not be immediately noticed missing. Simon was the only one who vocalized any dissent, but after a few days he went along with the group.

They had never been closer. During the day at their placements, learning, as Barry put it, "how to run the camp, how to be counselors, how to be adults." Martin loved his kids, felt that he was a great counselor. He loved tying his kids' shoelaces, telling them stories, playing basketball with them. During the unit 1's army night—where the staff woke the kids up in the middle of the night, made them run some obstacle courses, and in the morning pretended nothing had happened—Martin gave it his all, covering his face in paint, barging into the cabin, shouting, "They're coming, they're coming!" "Who?" asked a bleary-eyed camper. "The enemy! Quick, grab your stuff, we've got to move!" And after the days were the nights: they would go to their spot in the woods and get high, go back to the cabin, play poker, listen to music. Laugh and laugh and laugh.

Since the early days when all those staff got booted, they had remained super careful: all the weed, papers, pipes, everything, hidden in the woods. The spot they found had a big fallen tree they could sit on. They took off their shirts and sweatshirts, hung them from branches, Purelled their hands, Visined their eyes before heading back to camp. Becca had come a few times, and Martin had tried to get Ayelet to come, but she refused. He knew they weren't spending too much time together, but he was so busy with his kids and his boys—and she was busy with A&C and her girls—that Martin didn't give it a second thought.

"How come a dime in Montreal is a full gram, but in Toronto it's point-seven?" Martin asked one evening, everybody pitching on a joint.

"Capitalism at work, baby!" Simon said, licking the paper of the spliff before rolling it into a massive canon.

"How are your plants doing, Simon?" Martin asked. Simon supposedly had six weed plants growing somewhere in the woods. Simon took a hit from the joint.

"They're coming along nicely. And don't ask again, I'm not telling you where they are."

"Dude man, Scharfy, Tori is so fucking into you. Why aren't you doing anything about it?"

Scharfy shrugged, his dreads shrugging along. "I don't know, I don't know what you guys see in her, to be honest."

"She's fucking hot, that's what!"

Scharfy shrugged again, took a massive hit off the joint.

"Get this," Simon said. "Yehouda asked me if I was related to Barnie Ratner."

"What, doesn't he know any Black people in Israel?"

"Guess not."

"Funny thing is, if he had asked Mira Ratner if she was related to Barnie, the answer would have been yes."

"Why's that funny?"

"'Cause they *are* related."

"You're a fucking idiot, Josh."

That night, Ayelet, Tori, and Becca visited the boys' cabin. Ayelet sat down on Martin's bed. He became painfully conscious of the state of their cabin: clothes everywhere, sweat and boy and wood and dirt, the faintest underwhiff of dried cum. The poster board hanging in the bathroom keeping track of how many shits each boy had taken so far that summer (should Martin be embarrassed that he was well in the lead?). The poker table covered in chips and crushed soft drink cans.

"Hey, let's take our sleeping bags down to the rocks, check out the stars," Becca suggested. The three girls, Simon, Scharfy, and Martin headed down to the rocks.

Dear Tara:

Well, we did it. We did the deed. Martin and I. It was during colour war, yesterday. During the relay race I grabbed him by the hand and marched him to his cabin, and there was nobody there. An empty cabin! What could be sexier? It was short and sweet. But I really feel like my life is starting now.

Remember that Israeli counselor I told you about in my last letter, Yehouda? Anyways, we had a girls only EP with the staff. All about being strong, well-rounded young women. Yehouda says that to be Jewish means to always be on the lookout, to be vigilant. I've never looked at the world this way before. He really knows what's important. He's lived through sooo much.

*OMG! I almost forget to tell you: Scharfy got kicked out! They caught him with a dime bag of pot in his wallet. A random spot check supposedly. It was d*r*a*m*a*t*i*c. First he breaks his arm, and now he's gone. Tori is mucho upsetto. Some of the boys say they want to do something to show to the staff how unhappy they are.*

Sorry I haven't written as much as I promised. It's been a crazy summer. What's going on at Billy? Who's hooking up? Has anybody gotten kicked out? Dish, girl!

Xoxoxoxo

Ayelet

Ayelet had just finished writing the letter when Yehouda, Polina, and Barry walked in. "Hey guys, we're here to talk about Scharfy." Tori was still quietly crying.

"It doesn't seem fair. Pot's barely illegal anymore," Becca said.

Polina nodded, taking a tissue out of her fanny pack and handing it to Tori. "We have rules here, you know that."

"You act as if Scharfy has died," Yehouda said finally. Everybody in the cabin held their breath. Here was Yehouda, who had *actually* lost friends, lost them to *death*! "You will see him in a few weeks."

Tori raised her head, spoke through tears. "You don't get it. Camp is not just the normal world. You don't get it."

After the talk, the staff were milling around. Yehouda came up to Ayelet's bed. "Hakol b'seder?"

Ayelet smiled. "I'm good. I'm fine. I'll miss Scharfy, but I totally agree with you that it's not such a big deal. Not compared to what . . . what you've been through."

Yehouda put his hand on Ayelet's shoulder. "I do it for all of us," he said in Hebrew. Ayelet nearly fainted.

"Okay, girls, lights out! Tomorrow's another day!" Ayelet fell back onto her bed, kicked her legs in private joy.

Martin and the boys were slumped in their chairs around the poker table.

"I can't believe Scharfy. Why did he have to go grab a piece of stupid fucking weed and put it in his wallet?" Simon wondered for the hundredth time.

"And why did they have to spot check him that same afternoon?" Martin asked. Since Scharfy had left, they'd been smoking with abandon, and not just at night: before breakfast, at Rest Hour. They knew they were pushing their luck, but it just made them push it harder.

"He was bummed about hooking up with Tori," Josh said, disbelief in his voice. "He said it was like fooling around with his grandmother."

"What the fuck does that mean?"

"What a strange guy."

"Scharfy's grandmother must be fucking stacked."

"I'll miss him."

"Maybe I should try to comfort Tori."

"Too soon, Babka. Too soon."

Later that evening, the cabin was deep into a game of Texas Hold'em when Yehouda came in.

"How are my chaverim doing?" Yehouda said, sitting on Scharfy's old bed, the mattress bare, already collecting dirty clothes and garbage.

"Martin and Ayelet finally boned!" Josh announced.

"Josh!" Martin yelled, tossing his water bottle at him.

Yehouda jumped up, smacked Martin on the back, hard. "Martin, kol hakavod!" Martin nodded through the pain, his lips tight.

In bed that night, he thought about Ayelet. They'd had sex a few times, and it was fucking fantastic. Short, but fantastic; he was getting better at getting the condom on. He couldn't wait to have more alone time with her. Since Scharfy got kicked out he had started to realize how important this time at camp was. It could be taken from him at any moment. For second session, he was going to spend more time with Ayelet. Less weed, more Ayelet.

Less weed, more Ayelet.

He fell asleep happy.

Ayelet had done it. She had gotten herself alone with Yehouda. During the Friday night bonfire she had asked him if she could talk to him in private. He said sure, and she took his hand and walked him into the CIT rec hall. Nobody saw them. "So, ma koreh?" Yehouda asked. Ayelet jumped on him and they fell over. They tousled and rolled on the floor before coming to a stop against the cedar-planked wall. They didn't kiss, but just held each other tight. Ayelet was wearing her coziest sweatshirt, her sexiest underwear under her jeans. Yehouda was hard against her. Ayelet bucked her hips. His body was big and powerful.

"We should wait til after camp," Yehouda said. "I'll be in Toronto for a week."

In response, she nuzzled into him. Put her hand into his sweatpants. Yehouda didn't say anything for an agonizing minute.

"Okay, if you are sure."

"I am sure," she said.

Later, Ayelet was sitting with Becca on their cabin's porch.

"Ooh, that chocolate cake is not sitting well," Becca said, her hands on her stomach.

"Maybe it's because you ate four and a half pieces," Ayelet said, laughing.

"Ugh, having an upset stomach makes me so horny."

"What? Becca!" Ayelet laughed. Becca vogued.

"So? How was it?" Becca asked, whispering, everything suddenly very serious.

"It was . . . so different than with Martin. It lasted so much longer. Maybe too much longer. Though I had, like, three orgasms. Oh, Becca, I think I'm in love with him. I think he is too."

"Oh my god!" Becca said, twittering with excitement. "What are you going to say to Martin?"

"I don't know yet. I don't know."

"Blow him off, who needs him!"

Ayelet thought of Martin, his sweet, adorable face. Ayelet's stomach felt queasy, and she didn't think it was from the chocolate cake.

Ayelet and Martin were slow dancing at the social when Martin mentioned Babka saw her and Yehouda running into the rec hall during the Friday night fire. Ayelet knew she had to tell Martin eventually, but she was still caught totally off guard.

"You're in love with him, aren't you?" Martin said, reading it on her face.

"No! Maybe. So what if I am?" They had stopped dancing, had let go of each other.

"So what if you are?! We're together, Ayelet. Aren't we? We had sex for the first time last week!" Martin was crying. "How could I have been so stupid!"

"Ugh, Martin! I don't know! I need to be alone!" Ayelet ran out of the rec hall, almost colliding with Yehouda, who was sitting with some other staff and Israelis, talking and laughing. He was wearing a black silk button-down shirt, his hairy chest peeking out through the open top.

"Yehouda, can I, can I talk to you a second?" she asked, sniffing back snot.

Yehouda jumped up, a worried look on his face, the other staff making fun.

They went behind the rec hall, sat down on the big rock.

Before Ayelet had the chance to say anything, Yehouda, rubbing Ayelet's back, started talking. "There, there. You know there can be nothing between us, right? Don't misunderstand, Ayelet. Last night was lots of fun. Lots of fun. But, you know, in Israel, we often don't start relationships until after the army, until after we travel and university. You know this. There, there. You understand? At mahveena?"

Ayelet had her head between her knees, but she nodded meekly. His tone—half comforting, half lecturing—was confusing her.

"Good. Tov. Tov tov tov. I'll see you tomorrow, okay? Laila tov." He patted her head.

Ayelet sat there for a while, in the dark, the trees rustling behind and over her, the music from the social reaching her as muffled sound. Eventually she went to the river. Sat down, let the rushing water flow over her hands, wet the bottom of her skirt as she thought through the last four weeks. What had she done? Had she blown it with Martin? What had she been thinking? The cold water on her hands, the sound of the river, the cool night, it was like waking from a dream. Martin, her sweet, funny boyfriend. What had she done?

She had to find him.

CHAPTER 18

RUBY CONFRONTS BRETT; DUDDY KRAVITZ; MORE DREAMS

The social ended at eleven. The lasers were turned off. The lights came up. The DJs unplugged and packed up their gear. The kids and staff left the hall, talking and laughing, headed towards cabin line.

Ruby was sitting on the stairs with two of her campers, one of whom was leaving at changeover the next day, when the CIT Ayelet Cho ran by them and into the rec hall.

"Nobody's in there!" Ruby called after her, but she was already inside.

Ruby stood up, clapped her hands.

"Okay, gang, back to the cabin."

Putting the girls to bed on the last night of first session was an emotional experience, but Ruby, Danielle, and Dawn got through it without crying too much. They stayed in the cabin til everybody was asleep. Danielle and Dawn went to bed, and Ruby went to the kitchen to try to find something to eat. Cindy was there, doing paperwork. She offered Ruby some leftover mac and cheese from lunch.

"So did you ever find out what's going on with Brett and those land surveyors?" Cindy asked, looking at Ruby as she signed her name with a practised flourish.

Ruby had a forkful of the cold pasta in her mouth. She swallowed loudly. "Uh, no. Land surveyor? What do you mean?"

"Brett has something cooking with the Crown land," Cindy said, motioning with her head out the kitchen door and towards the river. "He and one of the Israelis—Dov, I'm sure—were at the band office a few days ago, looking at old maps."

Brett. Old maps. What the fuck?

"You might want to ask him what's going on. And then let me know. Hah."

"Thanks, Cindy!"

"Anytime, Ruby."

Ruby left the kitchen to go find Brett. She was crossing the road to the head staff cabins when she ran into Etai. By the way he had called her name and jogged over to her she knew he had been looking for her. They hadn't spoken much since Marula's cottage.

"Hey, Ruby. Listen. You're not mad at me, right?"

"What? No."

"Good, because, because . . . I think I'm in love with you, and I didn't want to ruin it just because of one stupid fight."

Ruby stopped walking. Etai was in love with her?

Etai took Ruby's silence as an answer. "I'll stay. I'll stay here with you. I won't go back!"

Ruby laughed. "Nothing was ruined. You're just an asshole!" She kissed him on the cheek and ran across the road, calling out, "Can't talk! On important camp business!"

Etai watched her go. After a minute of standing there, fireflies blinking in the bushes, he started for his cabin.

Sure enough, the lights were on in Brett's cabin. Ruby knocked once on the door before pushing it open.

Brett was there with Dov, Talia, Michal, Casey Mustard, Yehouda. There were beer bottles and ashtrays all over the place. Jimi Hendrix's "Izabella" was pounding from Brett's surround sound speakers. They all looked at Ruby, standing in the doorway.

"What's this I hear about you mucking about in the Crown land, at the band office?"

Brett stared at her, a sickening smile on his face.

"You haven't heard?" Dov asked, yelling over the music, whether totally oblivious, totally arrogant, or totally smashed, Ruby couldn't tell. "Brett is buying up all that empty land across the river. Imagine all those resources just sitting there that will now be Burntshore's. The things this man does for this camp! To Brett! L'chaim!" Dov held his beer up in a cheers that everybody took part in. Ruby glared at Brett and left the cabin to calm down on the porch. Once again, Ruby felt her ignorance about what had been going on this summer.

The cabin door swung open and slammed shut. Brett was standing beside her. He lit up a spliff, got it going, passed it to her.

"Don't be so dramatic. What's wrong with wanting to enlarge the camp, bring in some extra money through some, uh, light resource extraction? Think about it, all that land, just sitting there."

"How are you even buying the Crown land? Isn't it, like, protected?"

"Dov has a second cousin who works in the Ministry of Natural Resources. MNR Micky! He came up on visitors day. Great guy. His parents were Holocaust survivors. Anyways, it's all sorted. A long, complicated process, but Micky knows what he's doing. Don't look at me like that! Do you think if the Jewish people in Poland, in Spain, in Palestine, in fucking *England* had access to so much land we would have been persecuted, evicted, fucking genocided like we have been for the past two thousand years? I'm doing this for you, for us, for all of us."

"This is some real Duddy Kravitz–level shit, Brett. I knew you were an asshole, but I had no idea you were so fucking greedy! And don't give me that Jewish survival bullshit, I've heard it before." Ruby knew anger was the right response to this news but also could see that she was overreacting, maybe because it was Brett. All the anger she'd suppressed over the past four weeks had found an outlet.

Brett smoked the joint pensively, exhaling a long thin line of smoke. He turned to her. She had never seen his face so bare of pretense, so nakedly mean.

"That night, when I saw you leave the swim shed and told Pa that Phil and those idiots were getting high in there, I thought I would finally have a chance with you. But I guess with your misguided politics and all, that was wishful thinking."

Ruby blinked. She couldn't believe what she was hearing. Brett ratted out Phil and Margolis and Kraftchuk and Aimee? So he could *get* with her?

She took a sharp breath.

"What. The fuck. Is wrong. With you?"

Brett smiled. Shrugged his shoulders. Laughter and Hebrew erupted from the cabin. Something momentously funny was going on in there. The disbelief and anger washed out of Ruby, leaving only tiredness.

"You know," Brett said, "maybe I *will* clear-cut all ten thousand acres, make a killing."

Ruby laughed derisively. "Have fun with your fucking land," she said. She jumped off the porch and headed towards the road. She had to find Etai. Brett watched her for a moment, a smirk on his face, before going back inside to join his new friends.

Hours later, and most everybody is asleep. Soon, there will be teary goodbyes, there will be disbelieving hugs. Buses will depart. But for now, the camp dreams. A ten-year-old boy, who's leaving tomorrow after his first summer at camp, dreams he's in the IDF. He is arguing with his commanding officer, walking through green canvas tents during wartime, a machine gun strapped to his chest. He keeps taking off his glasses, but they keep multiplying in his hands. Ruby dreams that she's floating in a canoe in the narrows between two lakes, the sun at a slant, the shoreline rising into treed mountains. The other boats are on their way, she knows this, though she can't see or hear them. They have to be on their way. They have to. Then she's running through an endless hallway, salami hanging ominously from the ceilings. She is looking for a door, but there is no door. She is afraid. Debs dreams she's in a university lecture hall. It's Brandeis, but it's not Brandeis. The professor, who looks exactly like Einstein, writes *Kill the Lake, Kill the Dream* on the blackboard in big swooping script. Brett dreams of Ruby. Not the usual sex dream, just the two of them sitting on a log in the forest drinking cold tea. All around them, giant yellow machines dig up the trees, the rocks. They're looking for gold. Yehouda dreams he is being tortured. He will not cave. He will not cave. He will not cave. Stolow dreams he's a luthier, he's making a guitar as a wedding present for Vlada and Marula. Ayelet dreams she and Martin are on a roller coaster, humpback whales swimming through the starry sky. A unit 1 camper has a nightmare that camp is invaded—it's like army night but real—and they have to evacuate, quick! Now he's walking on the road in a thronging mass of people, they have become refugees, bombs explode over the camp, it's chaos and confusion. He realizes he forgot to grab the unopened letter from his mother, and now he'll never know what was in it. He gasps awake, terrified.

June dreams that at the end of every summer, faceless loggers show up, cut and hack and saw down every building, tree, utility pole, bathroom. They clear-cut the entire camp, load it all up onto trucks, leave nothing standing. But soon after, the planters arrive, replant everything—a seed for the tennis courts, a seed for the rec hall, for the dining hall, for every water fountain and tetherball pole and light post and cabin and rock and tree. Everything grows anew, ready just in time for the first day of camp. The whole thing repeated the next summer. And the next. And the next.

It's a good dream.

PART 2

CHAPTER 19

CHANGEOVER; SUMMER LAKES AND ICY DAWNS; ODE TO THE KITCHEN

Tom sat on his porch in the early morning, drinking his second cup of coffee, an indulgence allowed on only the most important days of the summer. He could hear the White Pine behind his cabin, moving sediments, feeding the lake, rushing its unique chemical and mineral brew from here to there, continuing its ceaseless work of thousands of years. The gurgle of continual, unending change; it comforted him, this sound he had known since a young child. Unending change, indeed: it was only ten thousand years ago, a cough's cough of geological time, that the ice retreated, leaving behind a climate steady and fecund, as well as the ice's orphaned offspring, the lakes, that for four months a year refreeze in memory of their distant progenitor. Do summer lakes dream of icy dawns from long ago? Above Tom the blown-out crowns of the white pines swayed in the still air. After breakfast, the buses would take away just over a hundred kids, whose summer at Burntshore was at an end; sometime after lunch, the same buses would bring in forty-five kids, whose time at camp was just beginning. The ice comes in, the ice goes out. Changeover was a pivot in the middle of summer, a cleave, a boundary, a rive. As always, second session would be smaller. Smaller, looser, faster. Cabins would re-form, staff would move around, friendships would realign, new loves would erupt through the planet's crust. The sudden changes that hold up a geography as unavoidable in a timespan of millions of years as it is in eight weeks, fifty-six days, 1,344 hours.

Tom sipped his coffee. A loon sang from the lake. As usual these last few mornings, his thoughts turned to Brett and Brett's plan to buy the Crown land. Ten thousand acres, at a cost per acre that was laughably low. Tom had colleagues who occasionally did governmental or industry consulting work (work Tom had always himself avoided), so he had an idea of how land transfers like this worked, yet he was still surprised by how quickly Brett had put all this together. Surprised, and a little impressed. To turn Crown land into private property should have been a long, drawn-out process, but MNR Micky sorted it all out in a matter of weeks; since the camp was already incorporated, all he had to do was pull the appropriate strings to move the land onto the market.

The moment Tom shook his hand on visitors day after Brett brought him by the office, Tom knew he wouldn't want to be across the table from MNR Micky; he had known people like that, ruthless, well-connected, brilliant-in-very-specific-but-useful-ways, back in his pharmacist days. The type of man who made things happen, whether those things were supposed to be able to happen or not. Canada had been built by such men (perhaps all countries were). And now Brett had mixed himself—and therefore the camp—up with this man. Tom himself had made some major changes when he took over the camp from his father, toning down the religious aspects to the point of non-existence, expanding the tripping program, building the new rec hall, putting in the ski docks; Brett was just doing the same. Was he not? Tom trusted his son. Most of the time. At least, he *wanted* to trust his son. Tom having to fire Brett for getting the entire swim staff inebriated had been the hardest moment in his life as a camp owner, as a father, as an adult (except for his own father's death). But that was years ago. Brett was no longer a misguided youth but a young man trying, in his way, to make Burntshore better. Brett was his son. Tom should not only support him in this endeavour but be with him a hundred percent. The more land, the better.

Having made his decision, Tom felt relieved, resolved. Restored.

Daisy and Piper ran out of the woods, collapsed on the porch in curved black puddles. An alarm went off in a distant cabin, buzzing faintly. A great blue heron flew low across the lake, majestic, Mesozoic. Tom finished his coffee, savouring the last still-warm sips. The camp was stirring from uneasy dreams.

Breakfast. Geoff was on dish duty. Transferring the stacks of dirty plates and plastic bins of cups and cutlery from the dining hall window to the dish station, loading up the dishwasher, unloading, loading again, stacking, shelving, classic rock blaring from The Otter 95.9. Cleaning the big pots in the industrial sink, bent over with the sponge and hose to get the gunk at the bottom, saying "behind" as he maneuvered to reshelve them, scrubbing the stainless-steel worktables at the end of the meal, joking with everybody, peppering his speech with Anishinaabemowin—aanii, miigwech, piizhan oma (this had recently intensified, since it was the first summer there wasn't a single white person in the kitchen).

Geoff loved the rhythm of the camp kitchen, the comradery, the infinitely repeatable daily pattern. Food gets prepped; food gets cooked, boiled, baked, fried; food gets served; food gets eaten; dishes go out clean, come in dirty; waste is disposed of; surfaces and utensils and cookware get grimy, gunky, grubby; surfaces and utensils and cookware get clean; the dishwasher beeps, belching hot steam. The dumpsters are emptied once a week, the truck carefully picking its way down a road that a nine-year-old kid could suddenly jump into at any second; fresh food is delivered, whoever's on duty kibitzing with the deliveryman as he has a smoke before heading off to the next camp kitchen to deliver lettuce, tomatoes, chicken, beef, onions, garlic, flour, eggs, milk, cheese, bread, rice, pasta, breadcrumbs, coffee, tea, juice crystals, radishes, potatoes.

When handled properly, Geoff often thought, the industrial kitchen is the ultimate renewable resource. He felt similarly about the land: the trees, the grasses, the flowers, the bushes, the rocks, the soil, the bugs, and the animals, all constantly change, die, grow, but the land is always still the land, even with, no, *because* of the constant change. (In Geoff's Intro to Greek Philosophy course, the professor—an energetic white man always in leather pants—had introduced them to the Ship of Theseus problem: if you take a particular ship and replace every component in it, one after the other, is it still the same ship? Most of the class thought it was not the same ship. "Ugh, that's cause you're all materialists," the prof had said. Geoff disagreed with the majority of the class. That's how it was with the land. Lifeforms come and go, but the land is the land.) Maybe Geoff should try to write a Tyler-style song about it. Call it "Ode to the Kitchen" or something like that. Bouncy verses of clever wordplay and a chorus of big chords and pithy one-liners. He'd see what came of it tonight when he was home, in the small room at the back of his mother's house. Lately he'd been spending two, three hours a night playing, the painting put on hold. He had been entertaining the idea of getting a degree in music when he finished his BA. He knew he had the chops; all he had to do was work on his reading comprehension. With his aptitude for languages, it shouldn't be too hard.

After he finished wiping down the last prep table, Geoff was going to put his headphones on, start Jefferson Starship's *Blows Against the Empire*, and go to the porch to watch changeover. Geoff often took an anthropological interest in the goings-on of camp (his observations often shared over a joint with Ruby, who would agree, disagree, or explain). His biggest takeaway: the inhabitants of Camp Burntshore took camp *very* seriously. On the last day of camp last summer, Geoff had watched teenagers bawl like they were at a funeral. Not that he blamed them. From the perspective of the kitchen—not to mention his friendships with the staff—camp did seem to be a special place, a place worth bawling over. It was amazing what the Jewish community did for their kids. Two months of friendships, activities, self-betterment, and experience. And to think, to compare to what the country and the country's religious institutions did to his people's kids, to his own grandparents—disgusting! Ruby would get a kick out of this line of thinking; he should bring it up the next time they hung out.

Walking through the now-empty dining hall, Geoff's sister Tanya and Jojo flipping the benches onto tables to sweep and mop, pushing open the screen door onto the porch, Geoff imagined the conversation with Ruby, comparing Indigenous and Jewish experiences of Canada. The Ruby in Geoff's head was getting angry, yelling in her direct, passionate way about the violent hypocrisies of this so-called free country.

Geoff laughed. He hadn't written a short story in a while; was his unconscious trying to tell him something? Whenever his head was swarming with characters running their mouths, he knew there was a story brewing. Stories, music, painting, languages, cooking (his first, earliest love, the reason Cindy asked him to join the kitchen staff four years ago)—sometimes Geoff felt like he had to pick one passion and stick with it, other times that it was perfectly acceptable to carry them all, take one out when the mood struck him, shelve it when he felt the tug elsewhere. The Jefferson Starship song was peaking. The campers who were leaving were saying goodbye. He watched two girls hug for an easy ten minutes. Just visible on the other side of the river was the Crown land, which he had been brought up knowing was his ancestral land, regardless of how it was labelled in some file folder in Ottawa (the land the camp stood on, the town, the cottages, the black sand, were also part of the Spruce's traditional territory, but as Geoff would joke with Tanya or Cindy, he was plenty willing to share). Maybe he'd draft out a story the inverse of Burntshore: the Jewish people have been confined to reserves, their languages and traditions stolen and suppressed, and the Native kids—untraumatized, unburdened, able to ignore or immerse themselves in their nation's rich cultural, linguistic, spiritual, and legal world as they saw fit—are at summer camp. Too on the nose? In any case, Geoff was flush with the thrill of creative potential.

The song was on its way down, towards its inevitable conclusion. A counselor was prying the hugging girls apart. Time to get on the bus.

And time for Geoff to get back to work.

CHAPTER 20

INFIRMARY VISIT; ALL HAIL THE QUEEN OF BURNTSHORE

Ruby was waiting in line at the infirmary with her camper Dalia. They had walked over together from the dining hall after breakfast; it was a warm, pleasant morning. Dalia had a cut on her ankle that Ruby was worried might be infected. Since Danielle took Arielle for her meds most mornings, Ruby hadn't been to the infirmary much at all this summer, unlike last year when she had been numerous times a week—besides the flu that had swept through the entire camp, a rash of impetigo burned through her cabin, and Ruby herself got pink eye the last week of the summer. The infirmary was a long bungalow on the far side of the tennis courts, with blue clapboard siding and flowerpots of red cone flowers under the windows. The second floor of the infirmary, accessed from its own wooden staircase on the side of the building, was the staffies, where Debs, Brett (who was technically assistant program director), and Cindy (though most nights she slept at her place on the reserve) had their rooms. Most of the campers in line in front of them were waiting for their daily meds: Ritalin, antidepressants, vitamins, penicillin. Ruby saw Danielle and Arielle leave the infirmary, chatting and laughing. Arielle and Dalia waved.

They were next in line. A small wood-framed chalkboard hanging beside the front door said in well-formed pink-and-blue bubble letters, *The Doctor Is In*. Underneath this, in a barely legible cursive, it read *Dr. Farberman* in white chalk. Along with the two permanent nurses, four different doctors spent two weeks each at the camp, working in the infirmary during the day and staying at the doctor's cabin next to the office at night; Dr. Farberman's placement had just started. As far as Ruby knew, the doctors were always men, always related to the camp in some way. One of Tom's oldest friends, Dr. Farberman had been a camp doctor at least since Ruby was in unit 1. His own young children from his second marriage, the twins, had started coming to camp last summer; they had a reputation for being whiny, difficult boys.

Ruby chatted with the nurse, and she and Dalia were led into the examining room. Shortly after, Dr. Farberman entered, stooping to get through the doorway without hitting his head. He was a tall, vigorous man with thinning silver hair and intense, intelligent eyes. Dr. Farberman, much more so than the other doctors, considered himself an important part of Camp Burntshore. He participated in EPs, attended Friday night campfires, water-skied and swam laps and played tennis. Every summer, he undertook a different initiative to improve either the infirmary or what he called the "general health of the camp": buying all new diagnostic tools, starting a food drive for the food bank in Barrie, donating his old telescope to S'Nature, paying to replace all the toilets in the Monolith. His most important contribution, though, as far as he was concerned, was the small library of books he kept in the infirmary's reception room.

"Alright, Dalia, let's take a look-see."

He investigated the wound, Dalia sitting on the examining table, one leg of her sweatpants rolled up, Dr. Farberman sitting in an office chair, bent over, Ruby standing in the corner.

"I heard you've developed a 'special' relationship with one of the Israelis," Dr. Farberman said in his pleasant doctor voice, shining a light at Dalia's ankle, not looking up.

Ruby bit her lip. He had only been here one night—news did spread fast. "I guess you could say that."

"That's great, Ruby. That's absolutely terrific! I think having these Israeli ambassadors here is a great leap forward for the Burntshore community. I've always told Tom that he should be doing all he can to deepen our campers' connection to their Jewish identity, and especially to the Jewish state. So many of the other camps do, it was a real shortcoming of Burntshore. I haven't had a chance to meet any of the new recruits—heh heh—yet, but I am planning on making it a top priority. Now, Miss Dalia, this is quite the humdinger you've given yourself. Are you sure you don't know how you got it? Okay, then. Well, it's not infected, but make sure to keep it clean and put some Polysporin on it. I'll have Nurse Bridgett give you some Tylenol and a bandage. And as for you, Rubele, please do make sure to take proper precautions with your new Hebrew friend. Things are different in the Holy Land—as they should be, of course. The only thing looser than their women is their men. *Trust* me, I know. Is it any wonder, with what they have to put up with out there?"

Dr. Farberman said all this in the same agreeable, easygoing tone, talking the entire time he examined Dalia, patted Dalia's knee, watched while Nurse Bridgett put on the bandage, walked with them both to the reception, put Dalia's folder on the reception desk, and brought them to the front door. The part about condoms sent both Ruby and Dalia avoiding eye contact.

"Do you need anything to read, Ruby? Feel free to take something from our little library. I brought up some new texts. Every year I tell Tom to make sure the library is set up at the start of camp, but, as these things tend to do, it always falls to me."

Ruby glanced at the bookshelf. The books all had some kind of Jewish content: novels by Mordecai Richler, Chaim Potok, Isaac Bashevis Singer, Cynthia Ozick; collections of Yiddish jokes; memoirs by Israeli statesmen; coffee-table books celebrating Israel's tenth anniversary, twentieth anniversary, thirtieth anniversary; the required Holocaust histories and testimonials; numerous biographies of Herzl; a half a shelf of books by Leon Uris, including three battered copies of *Exodus*. Ruby noticed a fancy hardcover book about the making of *Tel Aviv!*, which must have been one of the new additions. Ruby remembered hearing somewhere that Dr. Farberman had the largest collection of Herzl memorabilia in the world, that there had even been an article in the Jewish newspaper about it once. In fact, Ruby noticed now, on top of the bookshelf next to a JNF donation box, was a Herzl bobblehead figurine, as well as one of Max Nordau and David Ben-Gurion.

"No thanks, Doctor," she said instead. "I brought plenty to read from home."

Ruby and Dalia left the infirmary, holding hands, their mouths closed tight over their laughter until it burst out of them halfway across the hockey rink, and they started running back to their cabin. They passed Yonatan watering the flower beds beside the tennis courts from a long green hose, Casey Mustard and his campers running Ultimate Frisbee plays on centre field, older campers walking out of now empty unit 1 cabins with extra mattresses on their backs.

A little later, Ruby sat on her bed. It was nearly time for first period. Ruby's cabin had said goodbye to four girls yesterday and welcomed two new ones. They were still unpacking, organizing their shelves and bunks. June was telling some story from first session, but through the girls' laughter, Ruby couldn't quite make it out.

Ruby looked down at her hands. She hadn't yet told anybody about what happened with Brett two nights prior, his plan to buy the Crown land. To *annex* the Crown land. Ruby hadn't seen Marula or Etai except for quick hellos during meals, she hadn't wanted to burden Danielle, who was busy putting together a coed tennis ladder, and changeover had eaten up all her attention (by the time she had gotten to the dining hall after her confrontation with Brett, the desire to talk to Etai, to anybody, had faded; she stayed for a few minutes and then went back to her cabin). What could she do anyways? It *was* Brett's camp, or, if not quite yet, it soon would be. At the very least, she should tell Cindy what she had learned. She'd go visit her during Rest Hour.

Brett's revelation that he had ratted out Phil was another thing entirely. To purposefully get four counselors booted, most of whom would probably never return—it was unconscionable. A vivid image came to her of Brett on the second night of pre-camp, lighting a blunt he had rolled, taking a massive puff and blowing smoke rings. Ruby never much liked Brett, but she had no idea he was so willing to hurt others to get what he wanted. What a fucking asshole. Should she tell Phil? Did Brett really think getting Phil fired was going to give him a shot with her? The more she thought about it, the more obvious it was that Brett had always been into her. She pictured him during the heat wave, his penis looking unused, inanimate, guileless.

Ruby, not for the first time since their last encounter, let herself daydream what it would be like to be with Brett: a disgusting prospect in reality, but something still worth playing around with in fantasy. To date camp royalty, literally. All she'd have to do was put up with his arrogance, stupidity, greed, ugliness, and terrible politics, and she could spend the rest of her summers at Burntshore, grow old here, come up for winter visits, snowshoe on the lake. The camp, in a very real way, could be hers, and her children's, and their children's—not that she believed in the handing down of wealth and property, but hey, that was the world we lived in. She could write herself even more fully into the history of the camp, this place she'd loved since she was a girl, this home away from home, this yearly two-month taste of communal living—imagine all the good she could do as wife of the owner! As *partner* of the owner. As *business* partner of the owner. Stranger things have happened: she also never thought she would develop feelings for an Israeli soldier, and yet here she was, in stupid, gross love with one (admitting it, even to herself, felt delicious, felt freeing, felt terrifying). Imagine: she could be queen to Brett's (hopefully) absentee king. Her eyes fell on her Le Guin sitting on her shelf—so far she had done very little reading this summer, the short Etgar Keret stories the only thing she could get through besides her Paley, though she and Etai had had many conversations about *Always Coming Home*, both as he was reading it and when he finished, thrilling at the Kesh and their non-hierarchical, village-based society—and she laughed. Was that kind of power really what she wanted? Maybe it was.

Danielle came into the staff area, her face flush, tennis racquet in hand. "Do you think I have time for a quick shower before first period?"

Ruby glanced at the clock.

"If you run." Danielle kicked off her tennis shoes, slid into her shower heels, grabbed her towel, her shower bucket.

"Hey, guess what I found out?" Ruby blurted. Danielle stopped at the edge of the staff area, a study in pent-up motion. "It was Brett that ratted out Phil and them all to Tom, and he's going to buy all the Crown land and turn it into a mine or something!"

Danielle shook her head. "What a slimy bastard! Oh, Ruby, are you okay?"

Ruby nodded, though she felt tears stinging the back of her eyes. "Go, go shower before it's too late." Danielle looked at Ruby for a long second, nodded, and ran out of the cabin. Why hadn't she wanted to tell her? Danielle was a good friend, and the best co-counselor. The absolute best. When Fallon had given Ruby her mid-summer evals yesterday, she had even mentioned that she and Danielle were a good team, especially with bringing Arielle out of her shell, and that Fallon never had to worry about cabin 9. (Fallon had gone on to say that Ruby was perhaps spending too much time with Etai and not enough with her girls: a little bit of residual jealousy cracking through Fallon's otherwise imperturbable facade?)

Ruby stood. She had to change out of her sweats. It was going to be another hot day.

CHAPTER 21

COFFEE HOUSE; ATIVAN DUST;
"INTERGENERATIONAL WEALTH" IN ANISHINAABEMOWIN;
RIVER TALK

The staff EP that night was coffee house. The tables in the dining hall had been pushed to the sides, a stage of skids had been set up, the dining hall benches radiating out in a semicircle. Barry Blum and Tova hosted. Tova opened the night with a few minutes of stand-up.

"Hello, y'all. I'm not at camp as often as I'd like to be, in fact I'm leaving on trip tomorrow." "We'll miss you, Tova!" "Don't go, Tova!" "Sing us a song, Tova!" "Oh, I'll miss you too. As I was saying, I'm not here that often, which means I never got a chance to formally welcome the Israeli staff. Where are you guys? Well, welcome to Burntshore! Baruch haba'im! Boozhoo! And don't worry about feeling out of place, foreign. We'll do our best to make you feel at home. Trust me, I know what it's like. Some of my best friends back in the city, after all, are war criminals."

Ruby knew Tova could give it hard, but that punchline took even her by surprise. The Israelis loved it; Dov howled with laughter, called out, "I bet they are!"

Tova bowed and left the stage. Barry, very fat, very confident, very cool, wearing a black T-shirt and basketball shorts, took the mic off the stand and paced the stage as the laughter continued. "Okay, guys, we have a great night ahead. First up, our favourite resident war criminal, Dov!"

Dov jumped up, grabbed his classical guitar from the line of acoustic guitars that were leaning against the wall. He dwarfed the wooden chair that was placed on the skid stage for him. Barry helped him adjust the mic. Dov looked nervous up there, out of place, alone and with a guitar. The guitar exposed him. He lowered his mouth to the bulb of the microphone.

"Uh, thanks for having me." He palmed his head. "Toda raba. This is a song I wrote with my band back home, Judecca. I hope you enjoy."

Danielle leaned into Ruby: "Do you know what that means?"

Ruby, having just taken a world lit class, did in fact know. "It's the bottom of Dante's hell. Good name for a band." Ruby hated that Dov apparently had a sense of humour, at least where band names and being called a war criminal were concerned. Was there nothing that would rile him? Ruby already knew she was in a pissy mood, but her reaction to Dov up on the stage confirmed it. She should have smoked a bowl; she was being unkind to herself when she had decided not to, though she did have the foresight to bring along her one-hitter, freshly packed, in her hoodie pocket. She put the hood of the hoodie up, yanked on the flat white drawstrings, cinching it tight. It was her favourite hoodie, blue, soft, still fresh from the laundry at Marula's cottage, and the cozy hood made her feel slightly better.

Dov wasn't a fantastic guitarist, but the song he played, consisting of three or four power chords, wasn't half bad. It was mostly in Hebrew, though the chorus had some English lines in it; after the first chorus, his voice got more confident, and he started to really get into it. When he finished, everybody clapped, and Dov stood, smiling and waving, already back to his usual self. Ruby could practically see the arrogance return to him, a viscous golden liquid.

Next up were Stolow and Vlada. Their guitars and bodies angled towards each other, they launched into an instrumental piece they had been working on the past couple of days, with some short, complex composed parts, followed by improvisation. Ruby could acknowledge that the music was perhaps "good," but still, its repetitive dissonance did nothing for her. By the time they finished there were more than a few bored faces in the audience. Tyler sang "Ativan Dust," a song he wrote at Burntshore his first year as staff, using his whole body, striking the strings, lifting his knee, his mouth open, hair swinging, slapping the body of the guitar for its percussive response, the music easily getting under the skin, everybody, Ruby included, singing along. Andrea, Fallon, Barnie Ratner, and Ari Dressler did a puppet show with spoonie peeps, making fun of other head staff. Polina, Orit, and Michal got up to sing a medley from *Tel Aviv!* accompanied by Tyler. They started with "Welcome to the New Society," with its refrain of "How changed it all is! There's been a miracle here!" By the time they segued into "The Hydraulic Engineers," Ruby had had enough, was disgusted with the whole spectacle.

She snuck out of the dining hall, went over to the Rigor Tortoise to take a piss. She didn't bother to turn the light on, sat on the toilet in the dark. That fucking play. Fucking Dov, laughing at being a dickhole. Her bad mood was getting worse; she could feel it like a physical presence, bad mood pheromones buzzing all around her (BMP, she thought—I should tell the girls that one). Still sitting on the toilet, she took her one-hitter out of her hoodie pocket and took a long, patient hit, the small pipe growing hot in her hand. Fuck them if they catch her. She exhaled straight up, the smoke escaping the bathroom hut out the open top of the walls. She flushed, washed her hands in the dark, groped her way to the door. Outside, the night was heavy and fragrant. Might as well go back. She started humming "Ativan Dust." *Cut me a line, smoke me a bowl, powder me up in your Ativan dust, your Ativan dust, your Ativan dust.* She returned to her seat just as the applause for the *Tel Aviv!* medley was starting. Danielle glanced at her. "Maybe we should do that for the staff play?" somebody said over the clapping. Jesus god no, Ruby thought, could this summer get any worse?

Barry ambled back up to the mic. "Well, folks, we have a late final addition. Everybody's favourite chef . . . well, *non-head* chef at least, haha, our very own member of the kitchen staff, Geoff Anderson!"

Geoff got up onto the skids.

"So, I uh, I translated a song into my language, into Anishinaabemowin. You may know it. It's called 'Intergenerational Wealth.'" The audience went nuts. "You know what, Stolow and Tyler, come up here!" They both grabbed their guitars and sat down. Geoff played, singing in a low, slow register. Even though everybody knew the words, in English at least, it was silence as they took it in. Stolow took a raging solo.

Ruby had no idea Geoff had such a beautiful voice. When he finished, the applause was loud and hearty.

"Geoff, that was fucking terrific!" Ruby said, the staff EP over, everybody milling around.

"Thanks Rube, it was fun putting it together."

"Want to go hit a bowl, catch up?"

"Naturally."

"We'll go to the river."

"Right. I have to grab my stuff."

Ruby followed Geoff into the kitchen. The sight of Cindy's desk, her reading glasses sitting atop a stack of order forms, triggered a pang of guilt.

Behind the dining hall, the light over the kitchen deliveries door flickered. The ground was packed hard and smooth from countless truck tires, feet, paws. They walked into the trees. Above them, the sky was thousands of white and blue seed beads spilled across an expanse of black Bristol board. They sat on the pink rock, the river tumbling pleasantly beside them. Ruby took her one-hitter out of her kangaroo pocket, cashed the ashed bowl onto the rock, packed it with fresh weed.

"So," Ruby said, coughing from the first hit, "how has your summer in the kitchen been? I feel like we've barely hung out."

Geoff took the pipe and took a hoot. "Oh, you know. Cooking your daily slop has its ups and downs."

"Oh, eff off." Ruby took a deep breath. The river smelled like laundry detergent wants to smell, fresh and cold and alive.

"I've been playing guitar with the jam kids," Geoff said. "It's been super fun."

"Stolow told me you've become quite the impresario."

"I wouldn't say that."

They passed the pipe back and forth. After a particularly large hit, Ruby spat thick saliva in the river. Geoff followed suit, spitting into the bottom of the small waterfall. There was a sound in the forest, a rustling, a scrambling. The river was silver and white, a natural noise machine lulling Ruby into calm introspection.

"Hey. How would you feel if all that land over there were to, say, become part of camp?"

Geoff cashed the pipe, threw a stone into the river. "Cindy told me something was up. How would I feel? Not good. But how is that different than anything that's happened here? You do know that according to the treaty we signed, we were supposed to share the land. As far as we are concerned, the Crown land over there was never given up, never ceded. So, if it were to become part of the camp, to turn into private property, I don't expect that would go over so well."

Ruby nodded. She couldn't think of anything to say. "True. Jesus." This was all so complicated. But what was she supposed to do?

Geoff looked at Ruby. He could see the convo was upsetting her. Not that he wasn't upset himself, but the river was flowing, the air was warm, the trees were standing tall, the herb was hitting. It was a beautiful night. He decided to tell Ruby about his daydream, about his vision of Indigenous camp and Jewish reservations.

"Imagine!" Ruby said, laughing. "But does it really have to be either or? *That's* what should happen with the land over there. Burntshore should create a sister camp for Anishinaabe kids, hire Elders to teach the language, the culture. Isn't it the least we can do?"

"You know, my people have been meeting at this river mouth, holding ceremony on the black beaches, literally forever. Land that is considered desirable for Canadians to camp, live on, visit, was just as desirable a thousand years ago. Ten thousand years ago. That's why we had to be pushed out of the way."

"Jesus, Geoff. I'm so sorry."

"But enough of that serious business that doesn't concern us, two lowly employees of a faceless camping corporation," he said. "Tell me about Etai."

Ruby laughed. Just hearing his name warmed her belly. At Rest Hour that afternoon they had borrowed Marula's cabin once again. For foreplay they both apologized profusely, ripping their clothes off, declaring their love for each other, their hatred of everybody else.

"Etai, Etai, Etai. Where to begin," she said now, to Geoff. "Where to begin."

CHAPTER 22

COOKOUT; TELLING PEOPLE; GHOST STORIES

Ruby was outside the dining hall with Etai and Marula. They had signed up to work the grills for the Thursday night cookout and were busy at work with three of the CITs. Two of them, Ayelet and Martin, were laughing, fooling around; to Ruby, they looked very much together. Whatever had happened at the end of first session must have blown over. Ruby had heard that the third CIT, Tori, had been dating Scharfy before he got kicked out, which would explain Tori's black outfit, dark mascara: she was still in mourning for a lost summer. Nobody else was around yet; it was just the six of them. The counselors were starting the grills, the CITs still bringing out the bins of paper plates, cutlery, and cups, when Ruby finally told Etai and Marula about Brett's plan to purchase the Crown land. Even though it had only been five days, the secret knowledge had begun to fester, and she needed to disinfect with some old-fashioned sunlight.

After Ruby finished her story, embellishing Dov's smugness and Brett's cruel laughter, Marula looked sheepish. She was organizing the raw veggie burgers and veggie dogs into disposable aluminum trays.

"What?" Ruby asked, scraping the grills with a brush that was so old the bristles were mostly melted away.

"I already knew."

Ruby stopped scraping.

"What?"

Marula shrugged, a pack of veggie dogs in her hand. "Dov told me, back when we were . . . friends."

"Mar!" Ruby shoved her.

"I sort of forgot about it. What's the big deal?" Marula was prepping the veggie dogs again, slicing the pack open with a knife and squeezing the slimy dogs into the tray. A cloud passed under the sun, momentarily dimming the bright afternoon.

"It *is* a big deal! I can't believe I have to explain it. Camp is a good size, why should we keep eating up all the land? It's thousands and thousands of acres we're talking about here! It's greed, pure and simple. Jews have survived and thrived on way less for way longer than Brett. Besides, that land doesn't rightfully belong to us *or* to the government. How do you think Cindy and everybody at the reserve will feel about this?" Ruby felt like she was doing a poor job getting her points across.

Marula shrugged. "I don't know. Should we go ask them?"

"Maybe when Cindy gets back from her day off. They all went up to Nipissing for the pow-wow."

"This is how it always starts," Etai said as he tied a white apron around his waist. Campers and counselors were trickling into centre field.

"What do you mean?"

"It's just like what happened in Palestine: a little bit of land here, a little bit of land there. A loophole here, a we-know-what-the-settlers-are-doing-is-illegal-but-we're-going-to-let-them-do-it-anyways-and-later-when-everybody's-forgotten-we'll-enforce-their-right-to-the-land there."

Ruby blinked, bit her lip.

"Well, what should we do about it?"

"I don't know. Maybe talk to Debs."

Ruby took a drink from her water. She hadn't mentioned the other things Brett had confessed to her.

Lines for food were forming. Centre field was bustling with children. The smells of barbecue wafted over the frothy lake.

"Hey, Cind." The next night, during staff snack, Ruby went into the kitchen to speak with Cindy. Tonight's snack was bannock, one of Cindy's specialities. Ruby had been avoiding the necessary conversation; she was nervous about what Cindy's reaction to Brett's plans was going to be, felt like she was personally responsible.

Cindy was at the stovetop, frying the bannock. Geoff was beside her, kneading dough. Jojo was running the hot food out to the dining hall; he had gotten a new tattoo on his day off, and it took Ruby a second before she realized it was an outline of Lake Burntshore.

"Ruby, what can I do you for? They're through all that bannock already?"

"No, no, it's still going strong. Listen. I found out what Brett's up to."

Cindy stopped dropping dough into the frying pan and wiped her forehead with her forearm. She raised an eyebrow at Ruby. Continue.

Ruby swallowed. Nothing for it but to get it all out. "He's planning on buying the Crown land across the river. All of it. He says he's going to expand the camp and also grant mining rights. He's going to buy it, Cindy. He has a contact in the government."

Cindy chuckled, shook her head, flipped the bannock bubbling in the pan with the slightest flick of her wrist. "As if the land were something you could buy, as if it were theirs to sell. In any case, I figured as much. You know as well as I do, Ruby: That is not good. This is not good. We have a good situation, a good relationship, with the camp right now. When Tom's father bought this land from those Spitz pricks and founded the camp, he decided to be on good terms with us Black Spruce—that's what it was, a decision—we still talk about it, you know, he and his wife showing up with all that deli and matzo ball soup! Tom has continued those good relations, even strengthened them, given our youngsters good, well-paying jobs.

Perhaps the Spruce and camp don't see each other exactly as equals, but it's pretty close. But even so, it is a situation that could quickly change if Brett buys that land. Things aren't like they were fifty years ago. Hey, things aren't like they were one year ago!" Cindy belly laughed. "We've been okay with the situation, with not making waves, for a few generations now, but that can't last forever. Things are calm, Ruby, but if the land goes to Brett, to the camp, it could start something that won't just end at the river."

Geoff, who had been watching Ruby and Cindy, cleared his throat. "Guess it only took three generations of Balters before relations soured. The settlers—no offense, Ruby—always think they have time on their side, but what they don't realize is that we have the land on ours, and the land ticks to a different clock."

"Well, relations aren't sour yet!" Ruby said. Being called a settler, and by Geoff, stung, but she pushed past it. "I am not happy about this either, Cindy. I'm going to think of something I can do."

Cindy pushed the bannock with her spatula to gauge its bounce-back. "There's only one thing we can do, hon. Stop him."

Ruby nodded. She felt overwhelmed. How could they possibly stop him? How could she? Ruby had basically decided to let the camp be taken over by Dov, and now this. She was just lowly cabin staff. She felt alone, powerless, vastly outnumbered. She needed a drink. She needed a spliff. She needed a nap. She needed Etai.

Cindy lifted the bannock out of the pan and slid it onto the melamine serving platter. It was still sizzling, golden and oily, delectably browned at the edges. She handed the platter to Ruby, studied her face.

"Brett has always been a loose cannon. If this thing is already underway, it is going to be near impossible to stop it."

"Cindy, I'll think of something!"

She brought the bannock out to the waiting staff.

Later, a dozen of them, full of bannock and beer, not ready to call it a night, canoed over to Big Rock Island for a fire. Instead of the big firepit at the cookout site, they used the secondary pit at the flat top of the eponymous big rock, which from where they stood slanted at a decent angle for a hundred metres, straight into the lake. Ruby stood at the top of the rock as if transfixed. How many times had she ran screaming down this very rock as a young girl, splashing into the cold water in her frilly white bathing suit, surrounded by her friends, untouched by sex and politics and pot and climate change and oppression and genocide and Zionism and ethnic cleansing and justice, justice you shall pursue, the only thing on her mind scampering out of the lake, running up the hot smooth slate and barrelling down into the lake again? Hell, Ruby, you're in a contemplative mood tonight.

Geoff had been leaving the kitchen, about to get on his bike, as they were heading towards the canoe docks, knapsacks of beer and hot dogs and marshmallows swung over shoulders, Yehouda holding a bow saw, Barry Blum with a stereo in one hand, a mesh orange bag of firewood in the other. So, after telling his sister Tanya to leave her bike at the dining hall and get a lift home with Jojo on his ATV—to which Tanya made a sour, jealous face—Geoff had paddled out with them. The dogs had stowed away in Barry's canoe, so now Daisy and Piper were having a free-for-all on the island, chasing and digging and rolling.

With thirteen of them to collect sticks and branches, the two bags of wood they had brought, and the long, curled strip of birch bark Marula pulled out of her cleavage, within twenty minutes they had a raging blaze going. Beers were drained. Joints were burned. Orit sharpened sticks with her Swiss Army knife to spear and cook the hot dogs.

"Look up, bitches," Marula said. Conversations stopped, heads were raised. There were millions of stars smeared across the sky, trillions, a panoply of brightness. Clearly wending its way directly above them was a thicker river of stars, cloudy with gas and mystery, a split in the otherwise uniformly layered night sky.

"I wonder who named it the Milky Way."

"It was most definitely a guy, whoever it was."

"Someone should tell a ghost story," Michal said after the laughter had died down and attention had returned to the fire.

Orit volunteered to go first. "We tell this story on army basic training. It takes place on a kibbutz in 1948. This was during the war, most of the men off fighting in the south. The kibbutz was closed up tight as they waited for their soldiers to come home, for the fighting to be over. A young woman was stationed at the kibbutz's watch tower during the night shift. It was mostly waiting, mostly boredom. But one night, out of the blackness, a figure appeared. The woman was terrified. There were rumours of gangs of marauding Arabs in the valley. She held her rifle close, stood up tall. The stranger was an old woman. She was bone thin. Scraggly hair. Dressed in rags. The woman assumed she was an Arab. 'Please, let me in,' the old crone said, raising her arms in pleading. There was something strange about the words, but the woman understood them well enough. The old hag's lips were thin and crusted, her mouth groaty, the teeth gone. 'Go away!' the young kibbutznik said. 'Don't you know there's a war going on? Don't make me shoot you!' So the old woman left. The next morning, the men who were still at the kibbutz—the old, the young, the infirm—told her at breakfast that she must have been hallucinating. There was no movement last night. Maybe she should trade her night shift and get some sleep; she looked exhausted. The woman said no, she was up to fulfilling her duty. Her duty was all she had. She *believed* in her duty, in doing her part for the kibbutz, for the newly declared state. The next night, sure enough, the old hag was back, pleading, hands up in supposition. Again, she was told to go away. The third night, there she was once again. 'Please, let me in.' The old hag raised her arm, and the woman, for the first time, saw the number tattooed on her forearm. She knew what that tattoo meant (god, did she know). It wasn't until right then that she realized what was so strange about the old hag's voice: she was speaking Yiddish, a language the woman hadn't heard since she left her parents in Latvia and moved to Palestine. The woman was flooded with nostalgia, with love, with anger, with terror. But, mostly, with guilt. She opened the gate and let the old woman in. She brought her to the empty dining hall, fed her broth and tea and bread, let her sleep in her own room, in her own bed (the idealistic kibbutznik slept on the floor). When the woman woke up from the deepest sleep she had had since the British abandoned them to their fate, the kibbutz was eerily quiet. It had been ransacked, destroyed. The hidden weapons stolen. Three people, one of them a young boy—the first child born on the kibbutz—were dead. Apparently, in the middle of the night, the old hag had opened the gates, letting in a group of avenging spirits, whether Arab or Jewish or otherwise nobody knew (though most assumed). The young woman, feeling that she had failed in her duty to the young Jewish state, to the kibbutz, to her own dream of Jewish community, wandered off then and there into the swampy valley surrounding the kibbutz. She was never seen again. Though on hot summer nights, throughout the north of the country, even today, you can still hear her lament."

"That's fucking dark, Orit."

"Trust an Israeli to have the most moralistic ghost story possible."

"What's the moral, Mr. Smarty Pants?"

"Uh, to kill all the old women, duh!"

Next up was Marula. "This is a story about masturbation."

"Hell yeah, it is!"

Marula switched her headlamp to its red light setting, held it under her face. "Does anybody know where the prohibition against masturbation comes from? Well, surprise, surprise, it comes from the Torah. Here's the story. Judah had three sons. He procured a wife for the eldest son, Er. Her name was Tamar. However, Er did something to piss God off—what Er did is unimportant, God was often pissed off in those days—and so, naturally, God struck Er dead. As was the custom, Judah's second son, Onan, was now supposed to impregnate Tamar, his sister-in-law, to continue Er's line. However, that meant that Tamar's child would be considered his dead brother Er's official offspring, meaning Onan would lose out on some of his inheritance. Everybody with me? Complicated biblical math, but that's how it was. So, what did Onan do? He had sex with Tamar, alright, but, at the last possible moment, he pulled out and ejaculated on the ground."

"The first pull and pray!"

Marula flashed her light at the interrupting voice.

"Because of this," she continued, "God smote Onan. So, while it's most likely God was angry at Onan not for spilling seed, per se, but for not impregnating Tamar as was his duty, the sin of masturbation was established."

"Sounds like Onan was a fucking boss."

"The Hebrew word for masturbation is onanut," Michal said, intrigued.

"Anyways, from there it was established that demons, called mazzikim, were the after-product of wasted seed. In fact, it is believed that mazzikim, monsters of squandered cum, ruled the world until Solomon built the first Temple. Even now, here at Burntshore, demons and monsters from our wasted seed roam the lake. Don't worry, they mostly are just nuisances: stealing clothes, draining the hot water from the showers, guiding the mosquitoes and horseflies to our skin. But every now and again they get really angry, decide to eat a camper or two, a counselor who has been particularly wasteful with their precious life fluid. So next time you sneak out to the Monolith to rub one out, be wary!"

"Well, I'm good and terrified."

"Jesus, Marula."

"I'm never going to yerk it again."

"'Squandered Cum' would be a great name for a band."

"Joking, I'm going to yerk it any minute now."

"Yes! Spawn those demons!"

The two dogs exploded out of the forest, giving everybody a good scare.

"What about you, Geoff, you must have some killer ghost stories?" Barry asked, the stereo, which had yet to be turned on, cradled in his lap.

Geoff looked up from the fire, where he had been lost in thought, listening to the stories but also elsewhere.

"Who, me? No, not really. I know lots of stories, but nothing appropriate for the telling. Or the audience."

"C'mon, man, don't hold back!"

A chorus of "c'mon, Geoff" and "tell us, tell us!"

"Tell us a windigo story!"

"Yeah! A windigo story!"

Geoff smiled. Ruby could tell that he was in no mood to placate anybody (not that he ever was). "What do you want to know?" he asked. "That windigo's hunger is bottomless? That windigo won't stop until he has consumed everything between his dripping white lips? That windigo never forgets? That even now, windigo is out there, plotting, gathering dark forces, waiting for its moment to strike?"

Everybody laughed, and the conversation moved on. Still, most would be up late that night, every little sound ballooned to terrifying proportions.

Ruby left the fire and carefully picked her way down to where the rock lipped into the water. From here, you couldn't see the lights of the camp, reserve, or town. Only a few cottage lights dimly in the distance. If you listened closely enough, you could hear the White Pine River as it crashed into the lake. The forest on the opposite shore was dark-dark against the slate blue sky. Ruby could just make out the black sand beaches, an even darker band against the dark horizon. From the rock, looking across the lake, immersed in this living world, it couldn't be more obvious that it was impossible to own this land, this land that supposedly belonged to the government and would soon belong to Brett (supposedly). It was far too alive to be owned. The only thing you could do was live with the land, in the land, as part of the land. You could run down the rock and jump into the lake, swim back, climb out, make landfall; anything else was just hubris.

Anything else was against the land.

CHAPTER 23

THE FREE MARKET; THE HISTORY OF CANADIAN ZIONISM; MORNING JOG; GETTING ROASTED THREE TIMES

The car companies had begun to expand into oil production. It was pretty simple: to complement the three car companies, there were now three competing oil companies: Muskoka Oil, East Toronto Oil, and Petroleum Oil and Oil. To buy stock in one of the companies, you traded a piece of tuck for a stock card. The more stock an oil company had, the more oil it could provide to the car companies, the more cars the company could produce, the more stock cards the members of the car companies received, which could be traded for tuck or oil card stock (and vice versa). And Casey Mustard—chairman of the Muskoka Summer Camp Stock Market (the MSCSM), head of the Stock Regulation Authority (the SRA), founder and acting manager of the Burntshore Energy Board (the BEB), not to mention lead lobbyist for the Free Market League (the FML)—Casey Mustard, as arbiter of all things stock, naturally got a taste of it all; he was swimming in chocolate bars, chips, soft drinks, toothpaste, batteries, all of which his cabin organized into shoeboxes and carefully labelled.

Debs had known about the car game business since the half-day program that spawned it but had just figured it was a little harmless, role-playing fun. Now that campers were willingly giving up their tuck for shares in make-believe oil companies, now that they were apparently participating in a game called Playing the Market that consisted of rolling twelve-sided die and could potentially lose a camper their entire summer's worth of tuck, she felt like she had to do something about it. So at Rest Hour she went over to Casey's cabin for a chat. She knocked before opening the door. The lights in the cabin were off, the windows blacked-out with garbage bags duct-taped to the wooden window frames. The campers were in shadows on their beds. Were they all lying on their backs, pencil-straight, their arms crossed on their chest? It was a mystery how Casey could get twenty twelve-year-olds to be so still. Debs could tell the cabin was immaculately clean, every bunk's blanket folded neatly at the foot of the bed, which did nothing to lessen the eerie, off-putting vibe. It felt like an army bunker. "Where's Casey?" she asked.

"In the back," one of the campers said. Nobody moved.

Debs went into the staff area. It was even darker in there. Casey was sitting on his bed, his headlamp on, staring at a fat yellow binder open on his lap. Taking up most of the floor space were stacks of shoe boxes. Fischer was playing solitaire on his bed by the light of his headlamp. The third bed was covered in junk food, pop cans, floss, and travel bottles of shampoo, waiting to be sorted and boxed.

Debs felt rather bewildered.

"What's going on here, Casey? You can't be taking kids' tuck from them, no matter if they think they're giving it to you willingly or not. You know this."

Casey looked up, smiled his normal, brilliant, affable, no-worries smile. It might have been the first time all summer Debs had seen him without his Oakleys. Though she doubted they were far. "Don't worry, Debs. This is all just part of the half-day program, which, I admit, has gone on a little longer than originally expected. At the end, we'll be redistributing all the tuck. Obviously! Trickle-down tuck-onomics, haha. The campers will end up with more than they gave. That's the beauty of the whole operation!"

"Besides," Fischer interjected, slamming down his cards, "it's a great learning experience." He had borrowed Dov's army uniform, was wearing it, boots and cap and all.

Debs truly didn't know what to make of this. She had never liked Fischer, who was always a foul-mouthed smartass (if he kept a swear jar, he'd be rolling in it). Casey, though, Casey was one of the best counselors Burntshore had: always engaged, always creative, always making memories for the campers; did any cabin in all of camp feel as safe and beloved as Casey's boys in any given summer? She and Tom had often talked about how Casey was going to make a great unit head. This behaviour was . . . new. Or maybe Debs was just reading the situation wrong, was on edge because of all the changes happening to the camp? She looked at Casey. He didn't *seem* to be acting any different.

"Well . . . okay, Casey. Just, don't take any more tuck from the kids. And return what you've already taken."

Casey nodded. "Sure thing, Debs."

Fischer shuffled the cards. On her way out of the cabin, the campers had not budged.

Escaping into the sunlight, Debs felt like she had made it through some kind of ordeal. She hadn't sworn, which was good, though she had come close. It wasn't until she exhaled that she realized she had been holding her breath.

Ruby had been spending most of her free time in the staff lounge, researching Crown land, the treaties, the sordid history of Ontario cottage country. After her conversation with Cindy, she had decided the first thing she needed to do was educate herself; it was astounding how little she knew about the part of the world she called home. Her knowledge of the US, of Israel, of Palestine, of Jewish Europe, was deep enough to compose multiple books from, unlike the napkin's worth of notes she possessed when it came to Southern Ontario. And she was having trouble finding sources on the internet. She had put some books on hold at the Huntsville Public Library, would pick them up on her next day off. The best books, however, had to be purchased, and so she ordered them, hoping they would get to camp before the summer was over, though she knew trusting the camp mail system was a rookie mistake.

One evening, as Ruby read and took notes at one of the computers, Marula came into the staff lounge and plopped down beside her. She was wearing a hemp necklace with one of the Fimo bagel beads Ayelet had been making in A&C, holding a big hardcover book to her chest.

"What's that?"

"I was in the infirmary, and Dr. Farberman downright *insisted* I take a book. The blue on the cover caught my eye. Anyways, I thought you would get a real kick out of it." Marula held it up so Ruby could read the cover: *Rekindling the Torch: The Story of Canadian Zionism*.

"Let me see," Ruby said, grabbing it from Marula. Ruby had noticed more than one camper and a few staff leaving the infirmary with a book from Farberman's library. Such archival one-sidedness did not sit well with her, to put it mildly. Even Arielle, her own camper, sweet, innocent Arielle, had been reading a YA novel from Farberman, set in Israel, about courageous teenaged soldiers sacrificing it all to protect the homeland. "Do you think this is what it's like for Etai and the others?" Arielle had asked Ruby. Ruby had evaded the question.

Just as Ruby opened the book, Etai and Tova came in.

"How'd the game go?" Marula asked. Etai and Tova were co-coaching an intramurals boys touch football team. The two of them had become fast friends.

"We won!" Etai announced, collapsing onto the couch, his hands behind his head. "Otter threw up after the game. Apparently, he ate thirty chicken wings at dinner."

"Yeah, I heard his cabin cheering him on at their table," Marula said. "Your brother's a maniac." Ruby had still not looked up from the book.

"What're you reading?" Etai asked.

"Apparently it was some wealthy Jewish Canadian that invented the modern Hebrew word for mall," Ruby said, "*after* he built the first mall in Israel, of course."

"Good for him," Tova said. "Malls and mines, our two greatest exports. Give me that." She reached over Ruby and yanked the book out of her hand, started flipping through it.

Ruby looked up, saw Etai. "Hey," she said.

"Hey," he responded. Though they hadn't been spending much time together during the days, the nights—the glorious nights—were theirs. They would barely sleep, Ruby explaining the Hip's discography to him, Etai showing her Arik Einstein and other Israeli folk artists, both of them taking turns reading Stone Telling's narrative from *Always Coming Home* aloud. They talked about the important years of their lives: 1992, 2008. 2011. 1948, 1967. 2013. Etai questioned Ruby about Burntshore's history and personalities, and Ruby answered at length. Ruby told him about Chrissy Sugarman, about her acronyms, about her relationship with Phil, about Seema. Etai asked where the lake got its name from, if all Canadians were as aware of Indigenous peoples as they were at camp. And this was just what they did when they were not in the throes of their mountainous fucking, a conversation that had developed its own charged vernacular. The one thing they never talked about, at least since changeover: what would happen when camp was over. It hovered over these nights like a raincloud.

"There's pages and pages in here about how Canadian Jews helped ship illegal arms to Israel in the leadup and during the 1948 war," Tova said, the book open on her lap. "Wow. Listen to this: 'One of the more colourful underground arms merchants was a Winnipegger, David Harris. Harris . . . used Ben's Delicatessen in Montreal as his "purchasing office." Bent over a table, Harris quietly negotiated deals with a variety of suppliers, working with a code based on the restaurant's menu.'"

"Of course a book like that would celebrate an arms dealer," Ruby said. "My god."

Tova continued flipping through the glossy pages. "If we were a saner people, the characters being celebrated in this book would be considered war criminals," she said.

"They *are* war criminals!"

"No, c'mon," Marula said, snatching the book from Tova. "They thought they were doing the right thing. Is it their fault the situation got so, so out of hand?"

"Yes, it is, and even if they thought they were doing the right thing, it doesn't change what they actually *were* doing," Etai said, looking over Marula's shoulders. Ruby loved it when Etai said the exact thing she was thinking.

Marula, sensing she was outnumbered, dropped it. "Look," she said, "here's a list of all the Canadians who fought for Israel in the War of Independence."

"A.k.a. the Canadians who participated in the Nakba."

"Over two hundred and fifty of them, not all of them even Jewish," Etai read.

"Wow. Imagine believing in something *so* much that you'd travel halfway around the world and kill people, and even die, for it!"

"And imagine if that thing was ethnic cleansing."

Marula looked over the list of names. "I wonder what their stories are."

"Well, give us a name," Tova said.

Marula scanned the columns. "Milton Schacter," she said, a smile on her face.

"Schacter! A relation of yours?" Etai teased.

"I don't think so, there are lots and lots of Schacters," Ruby said. The truth was, she didn't know; they honestly *could* have been related.

Tova was thinking hard, her eyes closed, her head nodding: "Milton Schacter. Milton Schacter. Schacter. Schacter. Ah!" Her eyes popped open. "Got it. Milton Schacter. Was born in a shtetl in Russia. His family took a boat to Canada in the 1910s, settled in Montreal. Schacter's father was a butcher, and Schacter planned on going into the family business; he already had a reputation as an all-star with the cleaver. But that was before he attended his first Habonim Dror meeting, before he fell in love not only with the idea of a socialist Jewish state but with Gertie Goldblum, the socialist treasurer of their socialist committee. In 1948, when the state was declared, he was on the first boat out of here. He died on the battlefield, an unopened letter from Gertie in his pants pocket, informing him that she was pregnant. With twins."

Ruby, Etai, and Marula laughed. Tova's biography of Milton, succinct, complete, had the uncanny aura of truth to it.

"Okay, okay, give me one," Ruby said, biting her lip, getting into the game.

"David Tarnofsky," Marula called out after scrolling with her finger down the column of names.

Ruby took a deep breath, collected her thoughts. She could feel Etai's eyes on her.

"David Tarnofsky was born in Winnipeg to a poor family of tailors. His mother died when he was eight years old. When he was eighteen, he made his way by train to Toronto, where he wanted to study to become a lawyer but started waiting tables at a dairy restaurant in Kensington Market. On a street downtown one day, a homeless Indigenous person yelled at him to go home. And so he did—or thought he did—setting sail for Palestine in 1935, having never made it to law school. He fought in the battle for Jerusalem, saw some ugly things, but hey, creating a state required some ugly things, no? Afterwards, he stayed in Israel, became a lawyer, a respected member of the first generation of the Israeli judiciary. After the 1967 War, he couldn't shake the feeling that the country was heading in the wrong direction. He could have become a judge, some thought he could have gone all the way to the Supreme Court of Israel, but he closed his practice in Jerusalem and moved to Ramallah, where he represented Palestinians stuck in Israel's brutal military court system. He never stepped foot in Canada again."

"Hey, that's not how the game works!" Tova admonished Ruby. "These are soldiers, remember, not peaceniks! Etai, you go!"

Etai looked nervous. Making up stories was not his forte. "B'seder, b'seder. Give me a name."

"Samuel Goldstein."

"Samuel Goldstein." Etai stretched his interlaced hands in front of him, cracked his knuckles. "Born in Toronto in 1920. His entire extended family was killed in the Holocaust, his parents were the only ones not still in Europe. From a young age he heard stories of his ghost relatives, of his cousins that would have been, of the humiliation of the ghetto, of the horror of the camps, of what was taken away from him and his family by the Nazi monsters. It filled him with hate—is it any wonder? Who did he hate? He hated the Nazi monsters, he hated the British and the Americans for not doing enough, he hated the Arabs for rioting and being selfish when all the Jews wanted was a safe haven. He hated Canada for not letting refugees in. In fact, he hated anybody who was not Jewish. In '46, he left for Palestine. He spoke English, Yiddish, French, Italian, and within a few months had picked up Hebrew and a spattering of Arabic. For two years he helped smuggle in arms for the Palmach and settle Jewish refugees. He, in fact, smuggled arms for our friend at the deli, what was his name? Harris, right. Harris would always send Goldstein a big fat smoked meat sandwich hidden among the machine guns. It would be rancid when it arrived, but still, Goldstein, who had by then changed his name to Shmuel Goren, appreciated the gesture. It was only when he was doing this work that he didn't feel consumed by hatred. Anyways, when the war started, Goldstein/Goren was a proud member of the Irgun. He planned bombings against the British, went on raids for weapons, dreamed of a Jewish state in Palestine for Jews and Jews only, evacuated a few Palestinian villages in order to achieve it. On one particularly ill-fated raid, he lost his left arm when a grenade with a stuck pin detonated accidentally. He stayed in Israel until 1957, when he returned to Toronto, where he used his international connections and one-armed war glory to become a prominent businessman and a major macher in the Canadian Jewish community. He sat on boards, knew the premier, had halls of synagogues and universities named after him. He gave fifteen percent of his earnings to Israel. Both of his sons served in the Israeli army. By the time he died at the age of ninety, he had become obsessed with what he called the 'traitors,' Jews who didn't support the Jewish state, and spent most of his lucid hours penning letters denouncing them to the Jewish papers."

"Wow, Etai, that was deep."

"I doubt this is what Farberman expected us to do with this book," Ruby said.

"Hey, he wants us to learn about Jewish history, well, here we are, learning."

"What time is it?"

"Nine o'clock."

"Shit, I got to go, I promised my girls I'd play five with them tonight."

"Don't forget to include an arms dealer in your five," Tova called after Ruby as she left.

Dr. Farberman had started joining Stolow, Yehouda, and Dov on their early-morning runs. The three counselors discovered him at main gate one foggy morning, wearing a white track suit with matching headband, stretching his long legs.

"Shalom, boys! Mind if I tag along?" he asked, pulling his knee into his chest.

"Eh, doctor, you made it!" Dov exclaimed, slapping the older man on the back.

They left the camp and were soon jogging on the gravel road that wrapped around the west side of the lake until intersecting in the centre of Spitsville with the paved numbered road that led to the highway. The fog soon burned off, and it became a cool, windless morning. The running was good, the variegated horsetail plentiful along the sides of the road. Stolow hadn't really noticed when Yehouda and Dov had begun accompanying him on his morning excursions, but what had always been a solitary start to his day had now become a group activity. It hadn't bothered him too much; Yehouda and Dov were quiet runners, chatting to themselves in Hebrew if at all. It was nice to have some company.

Dr. Farberman, on the other hand, was not a quiet runner.

"Have you boys checked out my little library yet? I've been curating it for almost five years now. I think it's coming along quite nicely. Let me know if you think there's anything I should add. Any Israeli novels that I might not know about? They'd have to be in translation, of course. You men are both readers, are you not? Good, good. From what I understand, the novel is still an important mode of cultural transmission in Israel, unlike here. Postmodernism and identity politics killed whatever readers we had left. I tried to take a literature course at the university a few years back but had to drop out. Such nonsense! Phh! And try being a proud Zionist on campus these days—those so called 'anti-Zionists' are depraved! Anti*semites* is more like it. Speaking of translation, I'm thinking of adding a whole series of Hebrew language textbooks to the library. I know it's a long shot, but hey, if any campers want to turn their summer into a little mini ulpan, shouldn't they be able to? I heard you tried instituting a Hebrew word of the day last session. It didn't take, eh? Too bad. My boys loved it. Twins, you know. Have either of you boys found yourself a Canadian girl yet? I know Etai has. Whatever does happen, don't let yourself get too used to our Canadian comforts. Our homeland still needs you!"

They had reached town, which was usually where they turned back. Dr. Farberman, however, was not ready to turn around. They paused at the town's small waterfront. There were wooden benches and a walking path along a short length of the lake, posters for motorboat tours to the black sand beaches, a plaque detailing the history of the town, the Spitz family and their exploits. The famous ice cream stand, which figured prominently in the younger campers' letters to their parents, was just out of view.

"C'mon, we've barely got our hearts spinning. Don't tell me you're tired already!" He smacked Yehouda on the back. While the two Israelis and Stolow were breathing hard, their faces sweaty, it looked like Dr.

Farberman had just risen from the couch. He pulled his leg into a stretch. His tracksuit rippled in the breeze; it probably cost more than the entirety of Stolow's camp wardrobe.

Yehouda and Dov looked at each other. Shrugged. "B'Seder, doctor, you're on."

"Yofi tofi!" Dr. Farberman said, bending at the hips and touching his toes.

"I'm going to head back," Stolow said. He was not unhappy to leave the unflappable doctor behind. He decided to cut through the reserve, take the ATV trail. He ran as fast and hard as he could back towards camp, alone except for the rustling trees.

Casey Mustard's half-day program had nearly the whole camp in its ever-expanding grip. Not only were the majority of campers and staff now involved in either a car company or an oil company, owning and trading stock, designing vehicles, playing the market, but nobody was eating their daily tuck anymore, they were all hoarding it for trades and the stock cards that had become laden with value. Campers were trading shoes, shirts, even CDs for those little slips of paper. And, through it all, the tuck siphoned straight to the top. Casey Mustard's cabin had become the most popular cabin in camp, boys and girls asking for favours, girls trading kisses for stock, boys forming alliances with those deemed closest to Casey, betraying them when something better came along. At lunch and dinner, the tables were abuzz with the latest stock news, the most promising oil patch discovery, the forecasted quarterly earnings of the car companies.

In Debs and Tom's daily meeting, he asked her about it. Debs told Tom that she wasn't too concerned, the camp was having fun, they seemed to be learning how businesses and the free market worked. "Casey keeps introducing newer and more complicated ways to play: shorting the stocks, betting on futures." She had decided to give Casey space, he did have the whole camp energized and excited.

"Just don't let it get out of hand," Tom said. "I remember twenty or so years ago when Pog trading took over the camp, and we had to have an intervention."

"I'll keep an eye on it," Debs said.

"Anything else going on?" Tom asked.

"Well, some campers apparently are complaining that their clothes are going missing from the laundry. Only boys, though, so far. David Berens is beside himself. His signed Kyle Lowry jersey is gone. He says his dad's going to sue the camp if it doesn't turn up."

Tom shook his head. "I've told parents time and time again not to send expensive or meaningful clothes with their kids to camp. And anyways, why would Berens put a signed jersey into the laundry?"

"My thoughts exactly."

Ruby and Etai were on their day off. First thing in the morning they borrowed Marula's car and drove into Huntsville. Ruby picked up her books from the library, they ate lunch at the diner, visited the bookstore—where Ruby bought Etai a copy of *The Dispossessed*; after devouring *Always Coming Home*, she had promised him more Le Guin, and the successful anarchist society on the moon of Anarres seemed like the natural next stop after his time spent among the Kesh—and then drove back. They paddled out to Big Rock Island with a tent borrowed from Tova, groceries, wood, sleeping bags. It was a hot summer day, the kind where you get roasted three times: first by the sun, then by the firepit, and throughout it all, by the copious amounts of cannabis you ingest.

"It's good to get away from the research, from the girls, for a hot minute," Ruby said, as they lay in the tent, their bodies warm and entangled, leaf-light playing on the taut nylon walls.

"I've barely seen you the past few days," Etai said, nuzzling into her.

"Well, I'm nearly done."

"I get the sense you'll never be done."

"You seem to have changed your mind about some things, too," Ruby said. She had been nervous to broach the subject of Etai's recent comments about Israel's early years, but lying in the tent, his face in her neck, it just slipped out. Etai adjusted, pushed himself closer.

"It's been an interesting summer, there's no doubt about that," he said.

"Remember the first time we were here together?"

Etai moved some hair off of Ruby's face.

"You mean when I clobbered you at horse?"

Ruby closed her eyes. She was happy, cozy, warm. For the first time in weeks, sleep was deep, refreshing, a carwash of cold, sudsy flaps and soft heated rollers.

Moshe Zimmerman. Snuck into Palestine through Turkey with five others. Were given guns and set loose. Became a real estate speculator, bought land in Canada and Israel. Was given the Governor General's Award for his contributions to Canadian civil society.

Asaf Zadowolsky. Went over with his big brother, who died. Zadowolsky became a world-renowned poet, contemporary of Irving Layton and A.M. Klein. He was an esteemed professor of literature at McGill for forty-five years. Wrote venomous op-eds in the Montreal Gazette *about the Arabs, Palestinians, Jews stabbing themselves in the back for giving up land.*

Leonard Brown. As soon as he stepped foot on the Haifa beach, he knew he was home. He fought relentlessly. He changed his name to Lior Ben-Hoom. A week after the 1967 War, he was in the Occupied Territories. This was the Jewish home. He was never going to leave. He was going to fight until all the land was theirs.

CHAPTER 24

BUTTER LAKE ALL THE WAY DOWN

Here is what Ruby learned about the treaties: the land of Lake Burntshore, of all of Ontario cottage country, exists under treaty. But for most of the peoples who lived on this land since time immemorial, the treaties themselves were already a last attempt to protect themselves and their lifeways from annihilation. Throughout the 1700s and 1800s, treaties between the Anishinaabe and the Crown—first the British Crown, then Upper and Lower Canada, finally just Canada—were signed, a few in good faith, though most not, and all misused by the state. The Anishinaabe did all they could to hold onto their hunting rights, their fishing rights. The fish then were plentiful; a single giant whitefish could have as much meat as several caribou. Slowly, not so slowly, with the attrition of generations, the white man moved into Indigenous space. Non-voluntary surrenders, land cessations, verbal promises not included in the written documents, lost treaties, not to mention the language games played by the state: what counted as "land" or "water," fishing or hunting rights. The Anishinaabe were moved and relocated into smaller and smaller areas with less and less game and fish. And on every side, the encroaching white man. All of cottage country a result of this ongoing three-hundred-year cluster bombing; Ruby was surprised how many lakes she recognized the names of reading the history. All of it, what the world was, what happened to it, what it could be, erased.

The Anishinaabe fought back, wrote petitions, used the already-damaging treaties as legal leverage, brought their cases to court. The government sidestepped, loopholed, played hockey with jurisdiction. Even when courts agreed with the First Nations, it did little to change the actual situation on the ground. The relentless, inexorable push into their hunting and fishing territories; the total lack of recourse. Rights slowly, steadily annulled. And this was before Canada even became Canada; the country was being prepared for, acre by acre, tree lot by tree lot, fishing ground by fishing ground. Ruby copied out in her notebook: *In the years leading up to Confederation, white settlement in unceded lands of Ontario had taken place at an unprecedented rate, and in complete disregard of Aboriginal titles and rights. In some instances, the government encouraged squatters to take over unsurrendered Indian lands.* Eventually, enough time having passed, the Crown would simply let the squatters buy the land.

Imagine being a Jewish settler in Toronto in the 1830s. You could stand at the end of town, your European past and the trip across the ocean receding behind you, and look out into the Jewish unknown: where did the Great Lakes end, what was the shoreline like, what amazing peoples and lives and poems and forests were out there? What other forms could we as humans take? Typical, that the only way Ruby could see herself in the past was through the Jewish continuum.

The government, of course, had other ideas. If you want a neat, clean narrative, here is one: Representatives from the white man come and ask to make a treaty. Treaties are something you are familiar with; you have a treaty of peace with the Five Nations. So you make a treaty. The terms of the treaty are not adhered to. You lose access to your hunting grounds. You make a new treaty, where you agree to resettle on an island where you maintain full fishing rights. On the land of the new treaty, the settlers fish you out. You petition for decades. You go to court. At first the court agrees with you. But then they decide it's impossible to keep the white Ontarians from stealing the land and the food, so why even try? A new decree is decreed: non-commercial (as in, non-white) fishing is for recreation only, not sustenance. A new method is devised: assimilation. A new mantra: "The only good Indian is an assimilated Indian." A new horror: residential schools. Now, we will not just steal the land, we will steal your culture, we will steal your language, we will steal your metaphysics, we will steal your children, we will steal everything we can steal, until the land is ours or you are white men, just like us.

Ruby wasn't exactly surprised; she knew the history in broad strokes. But delving into it, even as far as being a busy summer counselor would allow, shocked and enraged her. How direct the line that could be drawn from the white settlers of the 1800s to Phil's dad, an avid fisherman who went up to Simcoe nearly every weekend year-round. How direct the line to every fishing line, to Marula's island cottage paradise, to here, right here, where Ruby sat in a swivel chair in the glow of the computer, to Burntshore, to the river, to Brett. To Tom and his friends fishing out Butter Lake year after year. It was *all* Butter Lake. It was Butter Lake all the way down. Ruby had known, yet she had not known. The machinery of disenfranchisement and ethnic cleansing that began in the 1700s just churning right along. Ruby's stomach turning.

Here is what Ruby learned about Crown land: it's surprisingly hard to find any definitive definition of what Crown land is, where it came from, its history. She typed in *what is Crown land? How did the land become Crown?* She pieced it together from scraps, whispers. Basically, Crown land is land that is owned by the government, federal or provincial (technically, it is owned by the British monarchy, which . . . yikes), that Indigenous peoples were supposed to maintain hunting and fishing rights on, but that varied from locale to locale. Forty-one percent of land in Canada is federal Crown land, and forty percent is provincial Crown land. Provincial and National parks are Crown land. Even reserves are technically Crown land. You can camp on unorganized Crown land for twenty-nine days before having to move. You cannot build permanent structures on Crown land. (Finding herself on a message board discussing what you could get away with building on Crown land, she read the following "Cree saying": "When the last tree is cut down, the last fish eaten, and the last stream poisoned, you will realize that you cannot eat money." Digging further, she discovered that the saying wasn't really a saying after all, and it definitely wasn't Cree. Alanis Obomsawin, the Abenaki filmmaker, is credited with its first utterance.)

She copied into her notebook, *Surface and subsurface rights to the mineral, energy, forest and water resources may be leased to private enterprise—a very important source of government income in Canada*, underlined *rights* and wrote *says who?* She typed: *What is land? What is the Crown? What is owned?* These words, these phrases: *fee simple*, *999 year lease*, *freehold*, *mining rights*, *memorandums of understanding*, *free and informed consent*, *real estate*, *private property*, *easement*, *cessation of all rights*, *trespassing*, *forbidden*, *profit margin*. *For the good of the economy.*

The Crown land didn't really belong to the Crown in any real sense, yet they acted like it did. Crown land was supposedly held in trust for all Canadians, when in reality it generated vast wealth for corporations. The Crown means domination. The Crown means extractive industries. The Crown means genocide. Crown is just another word for hierarchy, for capitalism, for private property.

And now, armed with this information, now Ruby has to decide what to do with it.

CHAPTER 25

BAGELS REDUX; AN ARGUMENT

David Stein was putting on a special staff EP. The counselors trickled into the dining hall to find, laid out on one of the tables, three separate mountains of bagels. Handwritten signs in front of each platter announced the city the bagels originated from: *New York*, *Toronto*, *Montreal*. Ruby was pleasantly surprised by the fun idea for an EP, was unpleasantly surprised to find out most everybody else knew about the bagel tasting but her. Brett, Tom, even Dr. Farberman, were there. The CITs Ayelet and Becca were set up at their own table, helping staff make bagel Fimo beads.

Once Stein deemed enough staff had arrived, it was time for the main event. During the raucous blindfolded eating contest—guys versus girls—nearly everybody was able to differentiate the Montreal bagels, with a little bit of confusion between the Toronto and New York varieties. Afterwards, everybody milled around, ate bagels, drank tea and coffee. With all the schmoozing, kibitzing, sly glances, cups of coffee and juice, and, of course, the bagels, there was a definite post-Saturday service kiddush vibe in the air. Stolow was talking to Geoff and Jojo at the kitchen doors, Jojo—his long hair, usually in a hairnet, down, his tattooed arms exposed—touching Stolow's arm whenever he said anything. Ruby ended up sitting with Tova, Etai, Vlada, and Marula, a half of each kind of bagel on her plate, some cubes of orange cheddar, two slices of cucumber. Stolow said goodbye to Geoff and Jojo, grabbed an orange from the fruit bowl, and joined Ruby and the others.

"You guys know about the New York bagel union, right?" Tova was asking, chewing thoughtfully, a nub of Montreal bagel in her hand. "The Bagel Bakers Local Three-thirty-eight. In the 1950s, you couldn't buy a bagel in the greater New York area that wasn't made by union labour. The bakers worked hard, long hours but made good money doing it. They even went up against the Mafia and won."

"What happened to them?" Ruby asked. She had never heard of the union before, couldn't believe what Tova was saying. A strong union of bagel bakers? Seema was going to love this!

"What do you think? Automation. Once a machine was invented that could roll bagels, the bakers lost their stranglehold. Montreal bagels, of course, are still hand-rolled."

Dov swooped in, crashed onto the bench. He had recently shaved his head, it was down to the skin. He was staring at Ruby, alert, mischievous. "I don't understand the obsession here with this Ashkenazi old world food. Does it not reek of diaspora weakness? Where are the falafels, the hummus, the good strong Israeli food? Now *that's* the food of a proud people. While you lead your hollow little diaspora lives, we are in our homeland, eating like free Jews."

"Except for the fact that all that food you just mentioned is stolen," Ruby said. Energized after learning about the bagel union, fully aware that Dov had come over just to antagonize her, how could she help but give him what he wanted?

"Etai, are you really going to let Ruby speak that way about your country, our beloved homeland?" Dr. Farberman asked. He was standing behind them, one hand on Dov's shoulder, the other on Vlada's, who looked—to Ruby—rather uncomfortable. Where had Farberman materialized from?

"What do you mean, doctor?" Etai asked. "Ruby can speak whichever way she likes."

"Enh, do you not know, doctor? Ata lo yodaya? Our friend Etai here is a peacenik. As is Ruby, obviously. They'd both rather there was no Israeli army at all, that we were pushed right into the sea, while they're over here nibbling on their bagelim."

"Is that true, Rubele?" Dr. Farberman asked, as if believing something like that was so far out of the bounds of normal thought that it was quite impossible.

Ruby shifted. "Well, not exactly. I don't think *any* armies should exist. And in terms of Palestine, the Israeli army *is* the problem. The occupation of the land, the erasure of Palestinian presence and culture, the appropriation of their food, is the problem."

Farberman looked like somebody had smeared shit all over his beloved library. "I'm sorry," he said, the rage checked just behind the gruffness in his tone, "do you use a smart phone?"

"Yes," Ruby and Etai answered.

"Do you use the internet?"

"Yes."

"Of course."

"If you don't believe the state of Israel should exist, just throw all those things away."

"Ah yes," Tova spat, having held back long enough, "the airtight argument that good technology comes from Israel, therefore Israel can do no wrong."

Ruby, Etai, Dr. Farberman, Tova, and Dov all started talking at the same time.

There was a shrill whistle. Marula removed her fingers from her mouth. "Everybody, just relax. We're here to celebrate the bagel, not argue about the merits of smart phones."

"More like smart bombs," Ruby muttered, but the storm had passed. Everybody seemed agitated except Dr. Farberman, who was already once again cool as a cucumber. A cucumber in a white track suit.

"Anyways," Dr. Farberman said, as if continuing a benign conversation. "I've heard the terrific news. The staff are putting on *Tel Aviv!* for the end of summer play. That's excellent! Just excellent. You know, there's a long history of American plays directly supporting the Jewish state. In '46, in fact, a Broadway production starring Marlon Brando raised funds directly for the Yishuv war effort. *A Flag Is Born.* The play raised enough money to buy a ship to help smuggle Jewish refugees into Israel. You don't believe me, look it up! Some of you may know this, but I've been somewhat obsessed with Herzl for my whole adult life, way before all this recent attention."

"You know the best thing about Herzl?" Tova said. "He was such a workaholic he died at 45."

Dr. Farberman nodded, missing Tova's sarcasm, and continued droning on about his extensive Herzl memorabilia. Ruby, who had been staring at the ground, clenching and unclenching her hands, glanced up, saw Brett and Fallon sneaking into the kitchen, holding hands. As they melted through the swinging door, Fallon glanced back and Ruby turned her head. Fallon and Brett? Was that a new thing, or something else Ruby had missed this summer? It made a sort of perfect, infuriating sense. Fallon couldn't land an Israeli, so why not go for the next best thing, the heir to the camp? The shock of seeing them together was quickly morphing into sugary anger.

"In fact, I have a CD of the folk-rock opera version of the play, signed by the original cast members," Farberman was saying. Ruby heard the words from far away. "The play is the greatest artistic achievement of the new millennium. And it's not just me saying that. Did you happen to see the roundtable discussion on the play in last week's *Canadian Jewish News*?" Farberman declared he had decided to buy the camp costumes for the play; he had already told Tom, had promised him to secrecy, but, what the hell, he might as well let everybody know. Ruby took a deep breath. Her skin was tingling, her head reeling. She leaned into Etai, put her dry lips on his warm ear.

"Let's get fucked up tonight."

FUNDRAISING FOR THE JNF

"When I first arrive, I wasn't attracted to any of the boys."

"And now?"

"Now, I inexplicably—eh, that's how you say it, inexplicably?—find myself attracted to . . . some of them." Michal was with Marula and Ruby on the benches outside A&C. It was Rest Hour, a cool, sunny afternoon. Tripper Steve had just walked out of the showers in nothing but a skimpy blue towel, his toned body, covered in a rug of thick black hair, on full display, fresh and clean.

"Three-nine-two in action," Ruby said, laughing.

Michal scrunched her face. "What is this three-nine-two?"

"Well, when camp first starts, everybody is a three. A three out of ten. Like, ugh, what am I even *doing* here?! Everybody sucks! But after a few weeks, with all of us stuck together, all those threes somehow, magically, become nines. Attraction runs rampant! You can't decide who is hotter! And then, when camp is over and we're all back in the city, boys we thought were nines are now twos. They're even worse than before." Ruby shrugged. "It's basic science."

Michal was listening intently, nodding along with Ruby's description. "Ah yes. Shalosh-tesha-shtayim. This I understand."

Three-nine-two in action: Otter had had a few orgasms before, at home, either in the shower or asleep in his bed; then, a few days after changeover, some secret switch inside him was flipped, and he, for the first time, noticed all the female beauty around him. It was a deluge! The camp was teeming with mouths and breasts and legs and arms and tummies and butts and hair and faces. So many beautiful women, from the girls in his unit to the CITs to the staff, all the way to Jenna and her sweatered bosom. And since everybody loved Otter, all that flesh was within arm's reach. At the gladiators EP a few nights ago, he had wrestled with Michal in a pit of squishy mud, both of them in bathing suits. That night, lying in bed, full of sweet warmness, he had to admit it: he was in love with her.

For Brett, Fallon had always been a four, and was still more or less a four. When they fucked and he thought about Ruby—a.k.a. every time they fucked, Fallon thrashing and yelling and rolling her eyes back into her head beneath him—Ruby's infinite ten rubbed off on his new girlfriend, and he bucked to climax. Before this week, Fallon would never have thought to rate Brett: he was the camp owner's son, much older; he existed on another plane. Though of course she had fantasized about marrying him, having a camp wedding, staying at Burntshore forever—who hadn't? Now that they were together, Fallon couldn't believe that this was actually a possibility. It made the sex that much better—she was having sex *with* camp. And she was filled, she was satisfied, she was forever wanting more.

Michal could have any unattached boy at camp, and probably more than one of the attached, but besides Tripper Steve and that Indian boy in the kitchen, she didn't lust after anybody, was perfectly content to flirt and be admired. When Marula and Vlada were together—ah, the benefits of being head staff and having your own room at the staff lodge—when Vlada was going down on her, Marula left this temporal plane, was transported to the realm of undying trees, was undying herself, was pure eternal reaching and blossoming and sighing.

Tripper Steve hadn't masturbated since the fire at Big Rock Island. Was it because of Marula's story of Onan and the demons that are the after-product of jacking it? Not exactly. Not a hundred percent. Well, maybe a little. . . . In any case, after watching Otter and Michal mud wrestle at EP, spill his seed he indeed did (Michal in a bikini, covered in sloppy mud, would be the catalyst for an entire spilled sea of Onanian ghouls and monsters). When Tripper Steve came after such a long abstinence, it was as if the universe unplugged and replugged him, the cosmic ingredients of life once again surging through him. If that created demons in the world, it was worth it. Danielle masturbated fantasizing about Tom, an odd, satisfying first. Polina masturbated thinking about Talia. Talia masturbated thinking about the wild career success—CFO, cardiovascular surgeon, premier!—that awaited her in the future. Stolow masturbated to a threesome with Vlada and Jojo. Dov masturbated to Marula, to Michal, to Fallon, who he should have fucked when he had the chance. Fischer masturbated to the nightly withdrawals from his thriving, varied spank bank. Girls and boys all over camp put their hands down their pants for the first time, the second time, the 411th time. Three-nine-two may be a science, but the sexual heat that results from it is an art, a feeling, a proving. A beating, shuddering art. Brett, even with the nightly sex with Fallon, still jacked off every morning in the shower, fantasizing about Fallon's body with Ruby's face.

Cabin 17 Naired their vulvae. Cabin 13 talked about their latest exploits—"So, did you guys hook up?" "Oh, we munched tires, alright," "Ew, dude!" Couples made out on either side of the rock-climbing wall. Eternal love was declared. Summer flings were flung. The coupling of the camp couples continued apace. The more sex Etai and Ruby had, the more sex they wanted. Barging into Marula's room after midnight, asking her to vacate, pretty please, b'vakasha, Marula grumbling but grabbing a sweater and a blanket to go find Vlada, mountainous sex amidst Marula's rocks, gemstones, and candles. Ruby had never had sex like this before. The sex with Phil had been good, great, often explosive; but this was of a different magnitude entirely. It was like Ruby was looking into the miraculously lit windows of Etai's house from outside in the dark, unfettered cryptoscopophilia. Every hidden corner, the deepest basement beam and the highest attic strut, felt and acknowledged. She saw right into the guts of him, and he her. Such illicit, elemental knowing.

Saturday night, a rumour spread through the staff like tainted water in a well. Dr. Farberman had tried to get Yehouda and Talia to let him watch them have sex.

The rumour was talked about around fires, in the showers, in staff areas.

"That's disgusting. That fucking prick," Ruby said, smoking a joint with Marula.

"I think it's kind of sweet," Marula said. "Wouldn't you want to watch two young beautiful people making love?"

"No! And besides, he's an old man, a doctor!"

"Is it true, Talia?" Talia's sleep-in asked her in the staff lounge.

Talia shrugged. "It's not the first time," she said.

"Not the first time what?"

"That I've been asked that. That *he's* asked that. Yehouda was down, by the way. Farberman said he would donate five hundred dollars to the Jewish National Fund if we let him."

"Oh my god."

"You're fucking kidding me."

"Anyways, I'm used to that sort of attention."

"That doesn't make it okay," Ruby said.

"What," Dov said, "I thought all members of the diaspora like to watch?"

"The only kind of abuse that is permissible at this camp is substance abuse," Barry Blum said, doing a near-perfect impression of Tom.

Far off, loons, delirious with want.

CHAPTER 26

A MORNING LAKE IN LATE SUMMER

Camp goes on: Like the sun traversing the sky, like birthdays piling up, like time, there's no stopping it. Daytime and nighttime swing back and forth like a tennis ball in a summer-long rally. The dawns cool. The evenings soften, spread out like a spill on a table. Mornings become afternoons become nights become mornings. Summer is something you can carry around easily now, a hearty meal that left you full and ready for the evening. Laundry accumulates. The dining hall gets messed, gets cleaned. Garbage gets picked up. The lakeshore exerts its centrifugal force. Hair is longer, morning hair messier, night hair moussed, gelled, brushed, straightened. The sewage collects in the septic tanks underneath centre field. The river pulls in water like a long ropey magnet, flows into the lake, drains out. The borders of the camp are porous yet solid. Bodies move through the camp in endless configurations. Animals eat and drink and fuck and sleep and kill and sing and die. Trees grow, like fireworks set to the speed of glass.

The CIT trip was a day away. Tova and Tripper Steve were busy studying maps, planning meals, packing food barrels, restocking first aid kits, counting and recounting the toilet paper, rolling up tents and tarps, running canoes on the lake to test their seaworthiness. Tova had asked Yonatan to pick up some boat paint and sealant, had spent an evening in the maintenance shed with him painting a little flair onto the dozen yellow canoes that were coming on the trip. On the deck of the bow, they painted *YES!* in blue, and under it they painted an upside-down red *YES!* When sitting in the bow, paddling into a rough headwind say, the blue *YES!* would be there to encourage you; when portaging the canoe, flipped upside down on your shoulders, up a steep rocky hill on an overgrown path, there would be the red *YES!* to give you a little extra pep. When they were finished the work, they hacked butts together, the twelve canoes lined up outside the shed drying in the warm night air. "Jealous?" Tova said, a splotch of blue paint on her forehead. "I'm always jealous of you, Tova. In another life I would have been a tripper." "It's never too late, Yonatan." "No, I guess it never is."

The CITs themselves were finalizing dry bags, getting ready to say goodbye to camp for eight days. The girls sat on their cabin's porch putting their hair into tight braids. The guys sat on their porch, doing nothing, pretending not to be nervous. The whole of CIT Town hummed with anticipation, hemlock needles falling lazily through the honeyed air.

In the rec hall, the Drama staff were holding tryouts for the staff play. Dr. Farberman attended all the auditions, ready with a measuring tape to get the sizing for the costumes. His two weeks at Burntshore were almost up, and he wanted to make sure he had all the measurements before his tenure ended. It was a big play with lots of roles, and Dawn, Jenna (who always helped out with the staff play), and the other Drama staff basically had to give every staff member who wanted to participate a part, sometimes two; there just weren't enough bodies to turn anyone away. The leads went to the usual candidates: Tyler, David Stein, Polina. Vlada, who always had a role in the camper play, got one of the lead female roles. Brett was going to have a small speaking role. Etai, to Ruby's chagrin and teasing, volunteered for a part in the chorus.

When the CITs left on their trip, the whole camp went to main gate to see them off. They'd be gone for eight days.

Upon their return, the summer would be nearly over.

The night after the CITs left, the staff had a bonfire at the CIT Pit. David Stein and Casey Mustard built a roaring blaze, stacking a dozen hefty logs onto the inferno. Brett and Fallon came back from town with three two-fours of beer. Casey shared around a knapsack filled with chocolate bars and chips. The mood was loose, rowdy, sexual. Ruby and Etai left early, to take advantage of Barry Blum's empty cabin. Marula and Vlada ran away from the fire shortly after, holding hands; they were going to paddle across the lake to collect black sand for a sand jar activity at S'Nature. Fischer burst out of the CIT boys' cabin, holding a can of hairspray aloft. He commenced lighting a long stick from the bonfire and spraying the hairspray at it, creating a beautiful crackling whoosh of flame, moving his hands and acting as if he were firing a machine gun. Everybody cheered. *Encore, encore!*

Stolow had taken the night off from jamming and was there with Jojo. Stolow's summer at the ropes course was going well. There had been no accidents so far; he had some excellent climbers: Otter, in particular, was a natural. Stolow and Vlada had indeed remained friends, and jam partners. There was talk of starting a band back in Toronto. Mornings running on the road, green life thronging all around him. Days getting high and running the ropes course. Evenings at the ski docks making music. Nights with Jojo. And, best of all, the Grizzly concert, the jamband's first in Toronto, was just days away. "Wanna go for a ride?" Jojo asked. They got onto his ATV and revved off, Stolow's hands on Jojo's bony hips.

Brett had his arm around Fallon. They were both hammered, cackling at Fischer and his hairspray-flamethrower antics. "C'mon, let me show you our new land." Fallon looked at Brett with wet, drunken eyes. *Our land*. "Okay!" They stumbled away from the bonfire. As they traversed the entire camp, the moon a crushed tennis ball behind a net of gauzy clouds, Fallon talked non-stop about her dad, how she couldn't wait for Brett to meet him, he's the smartest person she knows, she thinks they'd really get along. Brett picked up his already fast pace. He hated when girls said their fathers were smart. At the river, a few metres upstream from the pink rock waterfall, Fallon took a wrong step and soaked her sandal and leg. Brett lifted her up and placed her on the opposite shore. On the Crown land. On Brett's land. *Our land*.

They walked through the trees, and Brett told Fallon all of his plans. "This is where the new staff lodge will be. We'll cut down all these trees, of course, sell them to the pulp mills. We'll probably lease some mining rights, naturally. MNR Micky says there's mica, gypsum, calcium carbonates, all kinds of good stuff. Fal, you should see this guy at work. Wheeling and dealing, calling in favours, making favours, playing people off each other. The man's a bureaucratic magician."

"Are you going to have Yonatan help you with the building? Doesn't he do construction in the winter?"

Brett laughed. "Yonatan? You mean my dad's little 'charity project'? A little secret, doll face, Yonatan's days at Burntshore are limited. Oh! And here Dov is going to help me put in some mountain bike trails." They were picking their way through heaps of exposed rock; Brett's headlamp made the mossy fur of the rocks glow green-blue. "Can you believe it was barely a month ago that Dov arrived and I told him I wanted to buy this land and he told me about his second cousin who works in the MNR? How was this not meant to be!" Ever since Brett had returned to Burntshore he had wanted two things (well, three, if you counted Ruby): to bring in Israelis as staff and to buy the Crown land surrounding the lake. He was already pleased enough to have achieved the former, but then he met Dov and the rest clicked into place. That first night they stayed up until sunset, talking on Brett's porch about their fast-developing plans: Israel has lots of history and no land, Canada has lots of land and no history, why shouldn't they take advantage? This is what he and Dov (and MNR Micky) were going to give Burntshore: Permanency, protection, at-homedness. A final refuge from the long nightmare that was Jewish history.

Fallon laughed. Brett was funny when he was being serious. Funny, and a little sexy. His black hair as cute and endearing as a newborn with a full head of shaggy locks. She lifted her dress, squatted down to take a piss.

Just being on his new land filled Brett with power, with purpose. He was engorged with it. He still thought he could convince Ruby—to love him, to love the new camp Brett was going to build. But in the end, what did it matter? The land was his. The camp was his.

Fallon squealed as Brett grabbed her, picked her up, spun her around, the world all giggles and warm skin. They fell onto the soft, mossy floor.

The next morning, Dr. Farberman was in a rage. Apparently, in the middle of the night somebody had broken into the infirmary and added some books to Dr. Farberman's library. *All That Remains: The Palestinian Villages Occupied and Destroyed by Israel in 1948. The Ethnic Cleansing of Palestine* by Ilan Pappé. *Footnotes in Gaza* by Joe Sacco. *Unsettling Canada* by Arthur Manuel and Ronald M. Derickson. The book that had Dr. Farberman completely apoplectic, however, was *Herzl's Dirty Little Secret: A Critique of* Tel Aviv!, *Its Reception, and the Misguided Veneration of the Early Zionists* by Jasbir Khalidi, Canadian-Palestinian scholar and activist.

"Listen to this!" Dr. Farberman said, pretty much yelling, at the head staff table during breakfast. He had brought *Herzl's Dirty Little Secret* with him, and he read from the first page, his voice dripping with scorn, bewilderment, disbelief, and hatred. It would have sounded no different if he had been reading about how Jews were made of cheese and came from the moon. "'Tel Aviv, the city named after Herzl's novel which has now given its name to the Broadway phenomenon, is touted as the first truly Jewish modern city, built out of the sand and waste of the desert. This, as so much of Israeli historiography, is simply not true. There were at least four Palestinian villages in what is now considered Tel Aviv, to say nothing of Jaffa and its depopulated neighbourhoods. The villages' tragic histories—the inhabitants removed, every trace erased, explained away, ignored—encapsulate the history of the Palestinians writ large. The remains of Summayl still stand in the heart of Tel Aviv. Over two thousand people lived in and around al-Shaykh Muwannis, land on which Tel Aviv University now sits. One beautiful building from the town, in fact, is now the university faculty club and restaurant. Just like the city hides its atrocities, so too does the play that bears its name obfuscate the ongoing horrors that are the bedrock of the Israeli state.'"

As he read, nobody at the table looked at him. Even Tom, one of Dr. Farberman's oldest friends, kept his eyes on his plate as he ate his eggs with extreme focus. Dr. Farberman barked in disgust as he finished reading, slammed the book shut.

"What are you going to do?" Debs asked, taken aback by this out-of-character outburst, a little intrigued. Dr. Farberman was red in the face, spittle on his mouth.

"I'd like to burn them, that's what I'd like to do! Four hundred destroyed villages! Who gives a fuck?! The Indian army just destroyed four hundred villages in the southern forests, I don't hear everybody going on and on about it!"

During breakfast announcements, after a small scuffle with Debs, Dr. Farberman was on the mic. Ruby had never seen him so angry before; his calm, confident, jokey veneer had been peeled away. He was screaming mad, entitled, affronted. "I know one of you thought this would be a hilarious prank. Well, I am here to tell you it has gone too far. This is beyond the pale." Tom was rising from his seat, but Jenna put her hand on his arm, pulled him down. She had never liked Farberman and was happy to see him self-implode in front of the entire camp. "If you are responsible for this flagrant disregard, this clearly antisemitic behaviour, this nonchalance about the survival of the Jewish people, shame on you. If you agree with this kind of behaviour, please, throw out your smart phones right now. Bye-bye. Just beyond the pale." Most of the camp didn't know what was going on, but the usually grandfatherly doctor was screaming into the mic, and that was enough to hold everybody's attention. "If you know who is responsible, I expect you to do the right thing and report them to Tom. Behaviour like this needs to be punished."

"Why, so you can sit in the corner and watch?" David Stein called out, to a few scattered guffaws. Dr. Farberman looked like he had been stabbed. He handed the microphone back to Debs and huffed out of the dining hall. Tomorrow, his time at Burntshore would be over.

Underneath the dining hall—which was experiencing a rare moment of stunned silence—there are folded layers of rock and soil, tree root and grub. Water. Underneath the soil and the rock is the crust, seventy kilometres thick, the plates grinding and bucking and shoving in a timeframe not of the human, ice on a frozen lake in March slowed down by a factor of a million. Beneath the crust is the mantle: two thousand kilometres of solid olivine-rich rock holding the world up, scored with vents, openings, release valves and sluice chambers, doors and hallways. And inside the mantle, secure like a nut in a basketball, the two storeys of the core. The liquid outer core, the ever-growing solid inner core, both made of the nickel and iron that sank to the centre shortly after the Earth's tumultuous birth, pulsating magnetic force, burnishing heat, slowly hardening, a chord of cosmic resonance set to infinite sustain, a single guitar-strum of the universe made manifest, vibrating out to every grass tip, every hawk wing, every pinecone pulling on its branch, every radio tower's sharp striving, every mind's secret thought, every mote of dust floating over a morning lake in late summer.

CHAPTER 27

CANVASSING

Ruby had been busy the past three days. When she wasn't with Danielle and their cabin—talking through Dalia's boy problems, visiting Arielle in the infirmary where she spent a night with a bad cold, suffering through June's transformation into a vegetarian ("Why aren't you a vegetarian, Ruby?" "Listen to what Marula told me about factory farms!" "I'm going to upchuck, Ruby, I just learned how veal is made!"), giving the cabin an early-to-bed for misbehaving on the ski docks, making games, participating in activities, leading by example—she was talking to the staff, getting opinions, seeing what kind of opposition she could muster against Brett. "If I get enough people on my side," she said to Etai, sitting with him at the ski docks, their feet in the water, "maybe I could get Tom to stop Brett from buying the land. It is still his camp, after all." Ruby could feel herself swinging towards the most radical extreme of her inner pendulum. She thrummed with possibility. She was thrilled, a little nervous, trilling with energy sexual and profound.

She was ready to canvass.

The first person she spoke to was Debs. Ruby caught up with her after breakfast, walking towards the main office, clipboard in hand, walkie on belt, orange curls loose and colossal. Ruby accompanied her to Debs's office, sat down on the one extra chair, explaining the situation the whole time. Ruby hadn't been in there all summer: Debs's diplomas were on the wall, a broken canoe paddle in the corner, her famous swear jar on a bookcase, half full. Debs seemed distracted. She kept looking at the door, as if she expected Brett himself to barge in at any moment. She wouldn't tell Ruby if she thought it was a good idea or not for Brett to buy the land, but she did say if Ruby got enough people against it, Ruby should definitely bring it to Tom.

Next was Barnie Ratner. Head of Sail, friends with everybody, Barnie was always a good barometer for how the staff in general felt. They were walking along cabin line 2 during the post-breakfast cleanup. It was a flip-flop and rubber boot kind of morning—sunny one minute, pouring the next, the dewy grass sparkling in the wet, bright light. "I don't know if you've heard or not, but Brett is trying to buy the Crown land across the river." "What? No shit!" Barnie hadn't put his contacts in yet; his glasses gave him a serious, thoughtful demeanour. "Anyways, some other staff and I are pretty upset about it. That land rightfully belongs to the Black Spruce. As much as land can *belong* to anybody. It's more about territory over private property. Anyways, I don't think we have any more right to it than the government does." Barnie scratched his two-day stubble. "Makes sense," he said eventually. "So, if I go to Tom to try to stop it, would you support me?" The cuffs of Ruby's sweatpants were wet enough that her ankles were cold. "Hell ya, Ruby! You're out there fighting the good fight. Be careful with Brett, though, he won't go down so easy." It had started raining. Ruby went up on tiptoes to kiss Barnie on his scratchy cheek before running towards her cabin.

First period her cabin had Landsports. As her girls crashed and clacked on the ball hockey rink, the sun now out, hot and thirsty, the edges of the rink momentarily still wet, she spoke to Ari Dressler. At A&C, making spoonie peeps—Ruby making one of Etai, brown yarn for his shaggy hair, blue felt for his sarong—she spoke to the A&C staff, except for Andrea, who was on her day off. At Rest Hour, she spoke to David Stein. She spoke to Marula, who took her across the road to pick spiked blazing stars growing in the meadow beside the dump in vibrant purple abundance. She spoke to Tyler. She spoke to Vlada. She spoke to the other counselors in her unit; she spoke to counselors in other units. She spoke to staff young and old, new and veteran, friend and foe. At free swim she was speaking to the head of Swim—who was saying if the land is on the market, it's on the market—when Orit, overhearing, came over, an orange float under her arm.

"If the people at the reserve want it so bad, why don't they just buy it?" Orit asked.

"It wasn't available for them to buy. Dov has a cousin or something who works in the government—they set it all up. Also, it's incredibly difficult for a First Nation to legally acquire land. Also, they don't have that kind of money. Also also, that is so not the point."

"Ah, yes, Dov told me this plan of his and Brett's they hatched when we arrived."

So that's when all this started: that night at the fire, the first time she spoke to Etai; was Brett even there? Nothing about Brett and this summer surprised her anymore. (Whether he was avoiding her or it was just the randomness of a camp day, Ruby hadn't seen Brett since she started talking to the staff, wasn't sure what she'd say when she inevitably did.)

In the quiet before dinner, she found Stolow sitting on his cabin's porch, restringing his guitar. The white paper envelopes of individual strings were fanned out on the porch, sprinkled with porch dust, and he was in the middle of unwinding the G string. It was the warm, scented beginning of a long August evening.

"How many times a summer do you do that?"

"Usually once, but I've been playing more than I ever have. It's Vlada and Geoff, they're running me ragged. I can't get enough."

"How's it going with Jojo?"

"We're having a good time. I heard you're going around asking everybody what they think about Brett and the Crown land." The G string free from its peg, Stolow popped the pin out of the bridge and pulled out the depleted string.

"That's right."

Stolow looked at Ruby. "I think I'm going to sit this one out, Rubes. The Israeli soldiers was one thing. That, I get. That would—that did, I'd say—change camp forever. But this, this just seems like how these things go. If the camp is doing well, why shouldn't it expand?"

Ruby nodded. "And there's nothing I can do to change your mind?"

Stolow had the new string in and was tightening the peg. "Sorry, Ruby. Good luck."

He hit the newly installed string with his pick. It rang out, sharp and golden.

Ruby spoke to a group of first years, smoking joints at the CIT Pit. She spoke to Dawn, busy at the rec hall blocking out scenes for the play. She and Etai spoke to Michal at the tennis courts as they watched Danielle obliterate Ari Dressler, who was swinging his racquet in frustration; Michal was furious at Dov for bringing his politics to camp and said she was on board to stop any purchase of land. Tova was on trip, but Ruby was sure she knew how she would feel. She spoke to Casey Mustard. She spoke to Fischer, which, even though a foregone conclusion, needed to be done. Fischer actually called Ruby an antisemite for trying to stop the camp's growth, said that Brett and Dov were the best thing to happen to Burntshore since grilled cheese. She spoke to Yonatan, who she found behind the maintenance shed, chopping wood. "You guys are having a lot of fires this year," Yonatan observed, not unaffably, setting the next log onto the chopping stump. Ruby told him about the situation, not sure how much he already knew. "I'm behind you a hundred percent, Ruby," Yonatan said. He raised the axe above his head, brought it swinging down onto the waiting log. There was a sharp crack, and the log was lying in two clean pieces on either side of the chopping stump. Just like that, what was once one was now irreversibly two.

Ruby had been keeping Cindy apprised of her progress. "Most of the older guys who are friends with Brett or Casey are sticking with Brett. Two of the Israelis are with me, three are with Brett. I think we've got enough to stop him, Cindy, or at least make a good show of it for Tom."

Cindy tasted the soup she was making. She had put an *Idle No More* poster up over her desk. It showed a fist holding a stylized eagle feather, all reds and blacks and off-whites. "That's fantastic, Ruby. Keep going. Have you been following the news, out there in what you call the Big Wide? Things are changing. Indian country is rising up. The Black Spruce never stopped fighting for our traditions and our way of life, though the fight has taken different forms over the years. But now we've had enough. Hell, we had enough three hundred years ago!"

Cindy laughed, plucked a clean spoon from the shelf, and offered Ruby a taste of the soup. Ruby took a spoonful into her mouth. As always, it was delicious.

"I spoke with Tom, you know," Cindy said. Ruby raised her eyebrows, spoon still in her mouth.

Cindy had gone over to Tom's cabin a few evenings ago. He offered her a beer, and they sat on his porch, listening to the crickets, bullfrogs, and mosquitoes, the camp slow and peaceful, the lakey air sweet and warm. Cindy had been getting more involved in band politics over the summer, and with what was going on across Canada—Theresa Spence's hunger strike at parliament, the hundreds of protests and rallies and blockades occurring across the country, the self-declared Summer of Sovereignty—she found herself compelled to speak with Tom.

"I don't know how aware you are of what's going on across the country right now," she'd begun.

"I read the papers, Cindy." Cindy had sensed Tom's usual friendliness had been curbed back; this response only confirmed it. No reason not to plow straight ahead. Cindy sighed.

"It's a bad time to do something like this, Tom."

Tom, holding his beer with his thumb and pointer, tipped it into his mouth. "I don't see what this has to do with Idle No More, which I am totally behind of course. This is between the camp and the federal government."

"You know as well as I do that that's bullshit. You know the history of this lake as well as anybody, Tom."

"Brett's a good kid, he has all of our best interests at heart."

Cindy sighed again, took a slug of her beer. There was a lull in the cricket drone, a brief set-break; the roar of the White Pine, flowing behind the cabin, filled the sonic space. The stories I could tell you about that river, Cindy thought. Best interests, my arse.

"Tom's beans in his ears when it comes to Brett have bloomed into full bean-trees," Cindy said now to Ruby, laughing.

Ruby licked the spoon, put it down. "So, what happens next?"

"Next, we make some noise."

At dinner on the third night of canvassing, Ruby went out onto the dining hall balcony to get some air. Fallon was standing at the railing, watching the lake. Ruby wasn't planning on talking to Fallon, obviously—her and Brett's relationship was now very much public knowledge—and she tried to sneak back into the dining hall.

Fallon, apparently, had been waiting for Ruby.

"I really don't see what business this is of yours," Fallon said, not looking at Ruby, who had stopped at the door. Ruby hesitated, then went back to the railing; Fallon was, after all, her boss. "You're a counselor, the lowest rung on the employee ladder. You should have come to me if you had any problems, not gone around spreading unrest amongst the entire camp."

Ruby couldn't believe this. She never liked when Fallon lorded her unit head role over her; Ruby could have been head staff if she wanted, she had *chosen* not to. Fuck this hierarchical bullshit.

"Whatever, Fallon. I'm just getting people's opinions before I talk to Tom about it."

Fallon turned to Ruby finally. Her brown eyes were brick walls, her blonde hair near teeth-white. Had she always been so tall? "Are you not listening to me, Ruby? I'm telling you *not* to talk to Tom about this. What the owners of the camp decide to do is their decision. If you go over my head on this, I'll make sure you don't get asked back next year."

Ruby blinked. Fallon, as the one who wrote Ruby's evals and participated in the hiring process, definitely had this power. At least she was being her usual forthright self with this ultimatum.

"Is this 'cause of what happened with Etai or because of what is happening with Brett?"

For an instant Ruby saw through the walls, saw surprise, saw hurt, but then the bricks mortared right back up.

"Don't be ridiculous, Ruby. This is your unit head telling you to not be a shit-disturber. Actions have consequences."

"Yeah, well, at least I didn't spend fifteen years at camp for nothing but a shitty reference letter I probably won't even need anymore," Ruby heard herself saying.

"Enjoy the view," Fallon said, ignoring her last comment, pulling her hair off her face, going back inside. The swinging door let out the usual dining hall cacophony.

Later, after lights out, Ruby rolled herself a joint and went up the high jump tower to smoke it. She was exhausted, her voice reedy, still shaken from her encounter with Fallon. Her fight against the Crown land suddenly had real weight.

Ruby reflected on what was happening, what she was doing. A self-canvass. Was she acting crazy? Was it totally normal for a camp to expand? Did the history of the land really matter? Was it worth severing her connection to Burntshore? She had been planning on coming back as staff at least until she finished her undergrad—would talking to Tom really be worth losing camp over? Was she thinking poorly because of Dov, seeing everything through the lens of Israel? Southern Ontario was not Palestine. On the other hand, Etai had given up a lot, risked a lot, for what he believed. What was Ruby risking—not going back to summer camp? Still, for the first time since this all started, Ruby wasn't sure what she was going to do.

There was a noise out on the lake, a fish, a turtle, maybe a beaver. Ruby took a big draw on the joint, ashed it off the tower. Was she acting totally unhinged?

Or, maybe, was she finally seeing things clearly?

Isn't every single lake a Sea of Galilee to somebody, every river a Jordan? Isn't that worth fighting for?

Well, Southern Ontario was not Palestine.

Was it?

CHAPTER 28

CONVERSATION AT THE FIREPIT

"What does being Jewish mean to you guys?"

"That's a stupid fucking question."

"It means adhering to a desert religion, so nothing much!"

"No, no. Jews are the persecuted of the human race. It means surviving."

"We were the others of Europe."

"It's about social justice."

"It's about believing in God and following his laws."

"It means we are special. It means we were chosen."

"Chosen by whom?"

"By Tom!"

"It means growing up in the suburbs and being rich."

"It means studying the thousands of years' worth of religious texts, arguing about them, critiquing them, making new ones."

"Jewishness is simply one particular way to commune with the divine, with the human, with the mystery of the universe."

"It means supporting Israel!"

"Oh, blow me! Being Jewish is about shared history, about kinship, about stomach problems. About living in diaspora. About being guests."

"What do you mean, 'being guests'?"

"We didn't have a home for so long that now we'll never have one. Isn't that great? Isn't that freeing?"

"We do have a home now. We have a state and an army and a language reborn. You and I could immigrate there tomorrow and be welcomed with open arms. You've been brainwashed by antisemites who don't want us to have a home so they can kill us easier."

"Open arms, as long as we're willing to stand on some Palestinian necks."

"You don't know what you're talking about."

"You're the one who has been brainwashed."

"What were we supposed to do? After the Holocaust, tell me, what were we supposed to do?! No other countries would let the Jews of Europe in! If Israel had existed, do you know how many could have been saved?"

"Yes, that's why instead of creating states at the expense of others, we need to change the existing countries from within. All borders need to come down! All armies need to be disbanded! All hierarchies abolished!"

"Without an army, Israel would be destroyed!"

"It's terribly sad, isn't it, that the one thing all Jews were made to believe in the past fifty years is such a terrible lie."

"Fuck that! If it wasn't for the Holocaust and Israel, Judaism wouldn't have come back as strong as it did."

"Instead of six million dead and Judaism revitalized, wouldn't you rather Judaism disappeared and six million lived?"

"Dude, that's fucking heavy. I'm too stoned for this shit."

"Maybe he's right. Maybe a complete genocide is better than a partial genocide. No one left with trauma, except for the perpetrators, and that's the least they deserve."

"That's not what I said."

"Jesus fucking Christ, dude, you're going to give me nightmares."

"Maybe if there were no Jews at all, humans would have a much better time getting along."

"If there weren't Jews, somebody would invent us. They'd have to."

"Maybe. Maybe not."

The fire picked up in the briefest of breezes, calmed down, crackled and spat.

CHAPTER 29

GRIZZLY CONCERT

Stolow, Tyler, Geoff, Vlada, Michal, and Dov were driving to Toronto for the most hotly anticipated—and hotly contested—day off of the summer. Grizzly was playing their first ever show in Toronto, and the Burntshorers had three hours to get to the amphitheatre at the bottom of the city. "This will be my first Grizzly," Dov said, his knees at his chest in the front seat, wearing a too-tight Grizzly shirt he had borrowed from Stolow. "They were going to play in Tel Aviv two summers ago, but the BDS social justice warriors forced them to cancel."

"It'll be my first show too," Geoff said, watching the pines one-two-three out the back passenger-side window, which he was smashed against. Geoff was looking forward to a night in Toronto; since starting school there last September, he had fallen in love with the city, with his neighbourhood of Parkdale, the bike ride to the university, sitting under a horse chestnut tree in Queen's Park working on a difficult book, looking up at the sky after every sentence. He had yet to go to a concert at the amphitheatre.

"Well, you're in for an experience," Tyler said, his hair in a loose bun, wearing his Cowichan sweater even though it was hot hot in the car. He was sitting on Vlada's lap in the back driver's side, with Michal in the middle seat pressed up against Geoff. The fourth guitar was across all three of their laps, the neck-end in Tyler's stomach, the body end on Geoff's legs—Geoff hadn't planned on bringing his guitar, but before they left Tyler and Vlada had convinced him and they stopped at the reserve on their way out for Geoff to grab it; they had to drive through the rally being held at the Spruce's entrance, twenty or thirty Indigenous protestors walking in a circle, drumming, holding signs. As they drove through, nobody spoke, though Geoff had the distinct impression they would've had more to say if he wasn't in the car. After all that, the guitar wouldn't even fit in the trunk, but Tyler still insisted it came. Tyler adjusted his weight, shifted the guitar. "There's nothing like live Grizzly. It puts our little ski dock jams to shame."

"Every jam has its place," Vlada said, giving Tyler a push.

"Fuck, are we going to make it on time?" As he drove, Stolow's eyes kept darting from the rear to side mirrors.

"We better. I've never missed an opening song."

"And he doesn't plan on starting!"

The city loomed. They had left camp later than they had wanted, and now they were in a race to get to the venue on time. They were in King City, a mostly rural area before the urban behemoth. The trees and rocks had long before become subdivisions become farmers fields become suburbs and suddenly, just like that, they were in the northern reaches of the city. As they passed Wonderland, Tyler took out the LSD, placing a hit on his tongue, Stolow's, Dov's—Tyler straining his hand across the entire length of the car—and Vlada's, before getting to Geoff, who shook his head no, and Michal, who also said no. Geoff watched a roller coaster train tip from the peak of its track and plunge car by car out of sight. They got on the 401, crawled across the city's midriff. There was another traffic snarl merging onto the DVP, though this one mercifully minor by comparison. They curved into the valley, were surrounded by hills of green trees, snatches of the low, slow river, curved into downtown, sped through the industrial area along the water, passed the SkyDome and CN

Tower and Air Canada Centre. And, finally, the exit for the amphitheatre. After an interminably slow red light, Stolow followed the traffic attendees with their fluorescent vests and waving batons and parked in a distant lot in a sea of cars. They piled out, got their backpacks and sweatshirts and tickets and drugs organized as quickly as possible, Tyler clapping impatient encouragement, and jogged to the bridge over the highway and into the funhouse of the amphitheatre.

On the cement steps outside the venue, Geoff and Michal bought a pot brownie from a shirtless dreadlocked hippie, his pants made from sewn-together green and brown patches, his Cheshire grin both contagious and off-putting. Geoff ripped the plastic-wrapped brownie in half, and they quickly scarfed it down before running to catch up with the others, already near the front of the ticket-taking line. They were searched, knapsacks opened on plastic tables next to grey bins of verboten water bottles. Their tickets were scanned. They were inside.

"Plenty of time to spare," Stolow said, finally taking a breath.

Geoff took in the scene. It was a wild place; it was a circus. They definitely weren't at Burntshore anymore, though, Geoff had to admit, there was something oddly similar about camp and the thousands of colourful (mostly white) people thronging all around him: something about feeling safe, feeling secure, being in an environment where you could act with such freedom, such abandon. Would Geoff ever experience such assuredness that the world was with you?

He and Michal ended up in line together at an ice cream truck. The others had vanished. They ordered two Oreo sundaes and ate them with long white plastic spoons while standing near a bridge over a manmade inlet of the lake, fans hurrying past in both directions.

"Do you listen to Grizzly a lot?" he asked her, trying to make conversation.

"Hmm? Ah, yes. I love Grizzly. In Israel, they are one of my favourite bands."

They ate their ice creams.

"How're you liking camp?"

Michal's eyes were sparkling. Her joy was infectious. "Camp? I love camp. And I love Canada! This is my first time in Toronto, and it also seems amazing. When my service is done, I think I will move here. Everything is so green, and you aren't surrounded by death and war and violence."

Geoff nodded. Should he say what he was thinking, that even in Canada—*especially* in Canada—you are surrounded by those things, it's just harder to notice, the remove is a little bit wider?

"I'm not feeling that brownie at all yet," he said instead.

Michal concentrated. "I think I am being to feel."

"I'm more buzzed from the ice cream than the pot. Hey, we better go find our seats."

They found the others near the back of the pavilion. Geoff and Michal sat down. Though Geoff knew how to play plenty of Grizzly songs, had heard the most famous jams, he was still not sure what to expect at a live show, still felt more than slightly out of place, a tourist, especially compared to fans like Stolow and Tyler who ceaselessly chased every recording the band made. Well. Time to see what all the fuss is about.

The house music stopped; the stage lights came on. The audience cheered. The band took the stage. Halfway through the first song, Geoff understood. The playing was fierce. And the risks they took as a band! Sometimes Geoff could sense where the jam was going, and when it went there it felt amazing; at other times, they went in an entirely surprising direction. Janice, the guitar player, was a wizard. His intuition, his chops, the vast array of styles and attacks at his disposal, raised the band into the stratosphere. Geoff drank it in, just one amoung thousands of Torontonians worshipping at the altar of amplified electric sound.

At set break, without the music to focus on, Geoff realized how high he was. The pot brownie had floored him. Was flooring him. He looked at Michal and smiled. She beamed back at him. He was high enough to feel the acid lapping at his feet. The bodies and fans and noise and laughter blurred and melted all around him. He couldn't follow the conversation—were they talking about Janice or Brett? Geoff felt himself getting higher and higher. The brownie was turning on him. He was becoming afraid. He grabbed Michal's hand. Was he going to hurl? Maybe he should hurl. The sky overhead was too many colours, was changing too fast. Tyler came back with water bottles and fries. Geoff wanted to hug him and his stupid sweater, but instead took a bottle and chugged, the water turning into sand in his mouth. "What do you think of the show?" Stolow asked, his voice coming from far away. Geoff smiled, nodded his head. When the sun had fully set and it became dark, Geoff irrationally wished for the lights to be flipped back on. He squeezed Michal's dry hand.

Finally, the stage lights went down. The thousands of humans surrounding Geoff rose as one. The second set had begun. Once Geoff was able to latch onto the music, his high and his mind stopped their vituperative bickering. And what music it was! Rolling, guitar-led peaks, deking and swerving, peaking again and again. Electric soundscapes unfolding against the cool night. And then, out of the aural fabric of a deep crunchy jam, out of nowhere—out of the mystery—a new motif, a new melody never played, the whole band jumping on to explore, to tease out, to connect to the rest of the show. Geoff could feel the energy transferring, the band pulling in the audience, the city, the huge mysterious lake, and weaving it into music. Geoff had become conduit. Geoff let go. Still holding Michal's hand, his eyes closed, he danced.

After the show, they took their time leaving the amphitheatre. Everywhere they looked it was a party. The slow walk out of the venue, over the bridge, into the parking lots, laughter and energy and subversive celebration. Back at the car, they pulled their guitars out of the trunk and walked to a grassy spot Tyler knew, on the lake, under galactically unfurled maple trees. They jammed, high off the show (and the drugs). The musical energy they had spent the last weeks riling up from Lake Burntshore was now being poured into Lake Ontario; Geoff could feel it moving through his body. Long-limbed hippies passed by, dancing to their music; for a while somebody with a djembe joined in. Dov was wild-eyed, his overgrown buzz cut askew, a beatific smile on his face; he hadn't said much since the show started, the LSD had rendered him mute, introspective. Tyler used his poster tube as a guitar slide. Vlada was plugged deep into the cosmic furnace. Geoff was intensely aware of Michal staring at him as he took a solo. The music coming out of his fingers, a revelation.

Eventually, the jamming petered out. They got up, walked through endless, empty parking lots until they found the car. They crammed in, Vlada sitting on Michal's lap, the fourth guitar once again on top of everybody. On the drive up to Tyler's parents, Geoff—high but not set-break high—was hyperaware of his surroundings, both the city outside the backseat window and Michal's body squashed up close to his. Tyler, who claimed to be the most clear-headed and was therefore driving, worked his way over to Bathurst and then started north. King, Queen, Dundas, this was part of the downtown core Geoff knew well; he'd often bike these streets after class. Tonight Toronto was a ghost town, eerily quiet, every intersection empty. At Bloor there were some cars, huddles of people, but once they passed Dupont the city was once again deserted. They were now at the limits of Geoff's knowledge of Toronto, a void on his mental map. Somewhere north of St. Clair they pulled off of Bathurst and were on wide, winding streets of mansions and huge manicured lawns, each with at least one tremendous oak or blue spruce. The houses! Geoff couldn't believe it. Unreal, how much wealth was concentrated in these streets. What could it be, a hundred billion dollars? A trillion? A hundred trillion? Where did it all come from? (He knew where it all came from.)

By the time they got to Tyler's parents' house it was four in the morning. The entrance to the circular driveway had a wrought iron gate, which slowly swung open for them. At the front door Tyler made an exaggerated *ssh*ing sound before turning his key in the lock and opening the large door. Once inside he tripped over a side table, crashing onto the floor. "That wasn't there before," he said, everybody laughing silently. Geoff had never been inside a house like Tyler's. It was massive, expansive, soaked in style and taste. It felt like he was inside a bottle of high-end Scotch. Drowning in green is right. Ho-ly. Tyler led everybody down to the basement. Geoff could hardly believe what he was seeing. It wasn't the flat screen television, the pool table, the couches and recliners, the high nap of the carpet; it was the guitars. The guitars! Hanging off two whole walls. Electric, acoustic, bass.

"Why did you make me bring a guitar when you have all of these?" he said.

Tyler laughed. "How else were we going to jam after the show? Grab whatever you want, man, my parents won't hear anything." They had a few jams, everybody trading guitars, trying out different amps, and then, sunlight coming through the windows, it was time for sleep. Tyler went upstairs to his bedroom, everybody else rolled out sleeping bags on the carpeted floor or couch. Geoff was already half asleep when Michal climbed into his sleeping bag. Her body was warm and very, very pleasant.

Three hours later, Geoff opened his eyes. The basement was flush with light from the large windows. Michal was sitting on the couch a few feet from Geoff, gently plucking one of Tyler's acoustic guitars, singing quietly in Hebrew. Nobody else was around. Geoff sat up on his elbows, watched Michal.

"Did you write that?" he asked when she was finished. Michal nodded shyly.

"Yes. It is a song about wanting all mankind to live in peace."

Geoff nodded.

"Maybe I could teach you the words and you could translate it into your language."

Geoff continued nodding. "Maybe," he said.

They went upstairs. Tyler, Stolow, Vlada, and Dov were in the kitchen, sitting around the white marble island. Tyler's mom, hair dyed platinum blonde, wearing a red and green apron, was in the midst of making pancakes, bacon, eggs. Geoff was groggy, disoriented. He sat down, poured himself a glass of water from the clear glass pitcher sitting on the counter.

The backyard out the big windows looked like a little piece of paradise, rolling downhill until a low fence demarcated where the property ended and the ravine began. Stolow obviously spent a lot of time here, was making himself right at home, taking orange juice out of the fridge, getting glasses from the cupboard, joking with Tyler's mom. Tyler's dad, who looked exactly like Tyler if you aged him thirty years, cut his hair, kept him in good shape, and gave him all manner of personal, financial, career, and social success, was listening to Dov—who was wearing the Grizzly shirt he had bought last night and which fit him much better than Stolow's—tell a story about his kibbutz and the microchip factory they were trying to start up.

"What did you say the name of your kibbutz was again?"

Dov told him.

Tyler's dad jotted it down on a notepad. "I'm going to have the firm invest some money. I watch the technology markets closely in Israel. This seems like a worthwhile project."

"Wow, sir. Toda. Toda, toda! If you ever come visit, we will treat you like a king."

The eggs were ready. Tyler doused his in Tabasco sauce. "Oh," he said, his mouth full of food, "this is Michal, and Geoff. Geoff is from the Black Spruce First Nation."

This piqued Tyler's dad's attention. "So, you're the Geoff that works in the kitchen, then?" he asked.

Geoff nodded, his mouth full of fluffy, delicious pancake.

"That's fantastic! I've met Cindy a couple of times. She's a terrific woman."

Later, after they had gathered their stuff and were about to depart, Tyler's dad called Geoff into his office. Like the rest of the main floor, it was dripping with taste and wealth. It was all wooden furniture, the wall covered in framed degrees and pictures of Tyler's dad shaking hands with men and women of all colours, in all matter of dress. An etched Coast Salish canoe paddle hung prominently behind the desk.

Tyler's dad put his hands behind his head, swivelled back and forth in his chair. He gestured for Geoff to take a seat.

Geoff sat. "The name's Adam. Ty was telling me that you're a bit of a musical prodigy."

"I guess." Geoff was uncharacteristically nervous. "That's quite the compliment if it came from Tyler," he added.

Adam smiled. "You're at U of T, is that right?"

Geoff nodded. A chequebook the size of a road atlas had materialized under Adam's hands; he was writing a cheque.

"I feel very strongly for the struggle you and your people have gone through. My firm, in fact, has done some pro bono work for some of the tribes out on the West Coast. I've actually been adopted by one of them, given a name and all. Purely symbolic, of course. What an exciting time to be Indigenous in this country." Tyler called for Geoff from the foyer as Adam signed the cheque with a flourish of his fountain pen. Geoff began to rise from his chair. "Sorry, I won't keep you much longer." Tyler's dad ripped the cheque out of the leatherbound chequebook and proffered it to Geoff. "I want you to take this money, to help with your studies."

"What? No, I don't think I can take that."

"I insist. Any friend of Tyler's is worth it."

"Dad, he doesn't care about your adventures in Kitimat! We gotta hit the road!"

Geoff stood. He took the money. Hell, why not?

They were barrelling out of the city. Once they left Toronto proper, Geoff watched the cities' and then towns' signed populations dwindle the farther north they got. Vaughan: 323, 281. Barrie:135, 711. Orillia: 30, 586. Gravenhurst: 11, 640. (Until, eventually, Spitsville: 596.) Welcome to the land of proliferating lakes and rivers, rocks and trees, what in Toronto they call cottage country, but for Geoff had always been home. And unlike the big city from which they were speeding away, everybody in the car quiet,

Michal sleeping on his shoulder, a cheque for 1,800 dollars sitting like a rock in Geoff's pocket, the history of Canada took place here, with the wood and minerals and oils and meat and fur under and beside the lakes and rivers, a history which revolved around the removal of Geoff's people in order to get at all that wood and mineral and gravel and fur and meat. A history that led to his people's rally this morning—the first of many? The first of something major?—to Adam's cheque, whether written out of guilt, charity, allyship, or something altogether more sinister.

By the time they arrived at camp, it was almost dinner. The lake was catching the sun in a giant *V* of brilliant light. Geoff hugged everybody goodbye, walked the ATV trail back to his room at his mom's house on the reserve. He didn't know if he wanted to write or play or paint, but he knew it was going to be another long night.

He didn't have to be back at the camp kitchen til tomorrow morning.

CHAPTER 30

NIGHT DUTY; PAINTING SETS; SPEAKING TO TOM

S*critch scratch.* "The boys in cabin twenty-two are going to give us a run for our money tonight. Be vigilant."

"I've got my eye out, over." Ruby released the talk button on her night-duty walkie-talkie. She was sitting on the dining hall porch in the night-duty rocking chair. It was a beautiful night, cool and breezy. Ruby and dozens of others had spent the evening watching Danielle and Orit battle it out on the tennis court; they each won a set before Danielle took the game on a nail-biting break-serve. Whoever won Brett and Yonatan's game tomorrow would play Danielle in the ladder finals. Ruby, her hood up, cinched tight against the bugs, replayed some of Danielle's more amazing shots. Around her the camp was still, quiet. As she rocked, she wondered what was happening in Temagami, on the CIT trip. What possible dramas were unfolding. She looked at her phone: eleven-thirty-five.

Regarding her own drama, Ruby had spoken to nearly enough counselors and felt like she had a pretty good sense of where everybody fell. Though plenty of staff didn't care one way or another, there was enough of a core group that Ruby felt she could make a stand. She and Etai were ready to tell Tom that if Brett had his way, the camp would be hopelessly divided. Now all she had to do was decide if she was going to do it. Not only was there Fallon's ultimatum, but, though normally not afraid of Tom, she found herself full of trepidation: she was asking him, basically, to go against his son, the anointed heir of the camp. This was Bible-level shit. Old school tragedy–level shit. Etai thought Ruby should do it; he didn't believe Fallon, thought she was bluffing, that Brett put her up to it. Ruby, who knew Fallon better, was still on the fence. Her indecision, the fact that she was thinking of not trying to stop the landgrab, gave Ruby a pulling sensation in the pit of her stomach. Even thinking about Seema, Seema's last email—which Ruby never responded to—flushed Ruby with anxiety. And now that people at the Spruce were holding marches on the road, not blocking traffic—not *yet*, as Cindy told Ruby—but making their presence felt, both in general, as part of the Summer of Sovereignty, and to remind Tom and the camp who their neighbours were, Ruby really had no excuse for not doing her part. At Rest Hour today, she had spent a hundred dollars at the tuck shop and brought over to the rally soft drinks, chocolate bars, bottles of water. It was the least she could do.

She looked at her phone; it was somehow already nearly 1:00 a.m., a half hour to go til the end of her shift. It had been an uneventful night, the staff joking over the walkies. The only action was when the girls in cabin 6 asked Ruby if she'd bring them some hot water from the showers so they could make Kraft Dinner, a request Ruby granted. Ruby was about to go return the walkie to the office when it suddenly came to squawking life, voices yelling over each other. "Hey! Get back here!" "Which way did they go?!" "There's so many of them!" "Quick—he went into the woods!"

Ruby sat straight, held the talk button. "What's going on? Over."

"We caught all of cabin twenty-two bunk-hopping. We've got them corralled outside of cabin twenty-five, their target destination." This was Michal talking.

Ruby laughed. She remembered the days an entire cadre of boys would show up flush to her cabin, the forbidden thrill of it. Ah, to be young, the biggest threat to your happiness if night duty caught the boys and scuttled your make-out plans.

"What are you going to do with them?" Ruby asked, the walkie close to her mouth, getting pulled into her role, playing along.

"Our shift is over anyways," this was Ari Dressler, tonight's head of night duty, "meet us at the basketball courts. Over."

"On my way. Over and out."

At the basketball courts, Ruby was confronted with a war-movie training montage. Dressler had flipped the court lights on, had the kids running laps around the perimeter of all four courts, the night duty staff yelling encouraging obscenities at them. Ruby joined the staff at the no-man's-land between the second and third court. The campers wheeling around her were dressed for a raid: dark clothing, hoods up, bands of green fabric covering their watch faces.

When Dressler, who was wearing a Leafs jersey over his sweatshirt, stopped the lap running, they had the campers lie down on court 2. Now it was the bunk-hoppers that were stationary, and it was the staff that circled them, raining verbal foolishness from above. It was nearing 2:00 a.m. now; the piney air was growing icy.

What Ruby would have once thought of as harmless camp fun, a real bonding experience for the cabin, she now couldn't help seeing through a more critical lens. Was it even possible to playact martiality, to enforce soft hierarchy, without the corrupting residue of organized violence—of power and all its adherent terrors—rubbing off? But still: the sky was inky black, smeared with stars, the wind was soft, the boys laughing as they stayed as still as possible on the cold court, the lights illuminating the basketball nets like the spotlit heads of strange gods.

"Alright, that's it, folks," Dressler said. The campers jumped up, dusted themselves off. Their faces were red from exertion, their breath faint fog. Their eyes aglow with adrenaline. This was a night they wouldn't forget. "I hope you have learned your lesson."

Ruby was standing next to a few of the boys when she overheard them talking about the Crown land.

"What's that?" she said.

"Oh, we're giving our profits from our oil company to Brett so he can buy more land for the camp." It was the two Jareds, the ones that had quizzed Etai all those weeks ago at Shabbat dinner. The one talking was the one with the Star of David necklace, which he had on over his black sweatshirt, the silver star catching the reflection from the court lights.

"Yeah," the other Jared concurred, "the top two oil companies struck a deal with Brett. We're getting exclusive exploratory mining rights."

Ruby scoffed. "What are you talking about? The oil companies, the car companies, none of it is real!"

The boys looked at Ruby like she was an idiot.

"Well, nothing is *real*," one of them said.

"It's a pyramid scheme for children to give up their candy!" Ruby tried.

"What isn't?!" the other one said, both of them high-fiving as they walked away.

Ruby watched them go, shaking her head.

Ruby and the rest of the night duty staff went to the river, smoked a couple bowls.

Ari yawned, stretched his arms. "Time for me to hit the hay," he said. "Big day of gaga and touch football tomorrow."

"I'm going to go see if Etai is still at the rec hall helping Andrea with the sets," Ruby said.

Walking across centre field, there was a slight, furry glow over the lake. The air was cool and wet. The night was almost over.

It was fucking late.

The rec hall was framed against a pitch blue sky, the tall white pines unfurled, metallic. A couple of staff were smoking butts at the rec hall doors, their hands covered in paint. "Here to lend a hand, Shacter?" "If you're lucky," Ruby said, pushing open the door. Inside, it was a fulsome bustle of activity, a jolt after the serenity of the sleeping camp. There were set backdrops all over the floor, cans of paint, binders with designs, tall rolls of brown kraft paper leaning against the walls. Staff were painting as they sat, stood, lay down. A stereo plugged in beside the piano belted out some kind of jam music. Andrea walked through the mayhem wearing a flowing forest green T-shirt dress, offering suggestions, making sure the different panels were going to fit together properly. The costumes had arrived that morning. A few of the actors were wearing their new outfits, including Fischer, who was wearing his Reschid costume, a rather stereotypical idea of what an Arab looked like: big beard, turban, a black thawb. It was unclear if he was actually there to help paint sets or was just fucking around, making racist jokes in a racist accent, drinking from a can of pop. Fucking prick. Ruby wondered if his hair was still spiked underneath the turban. She found Etai working alone at the back of the hall, near the stage.

"What scene is this for?" she asked, coming up behind him and putting her arms around him. Etai turned to her; he had a splotch of red paint on his left cheek. He kissed her. "It's the big debate scene between David and Rabbi Dr. Geyer, the act one closer. See this, these here are the pillars of the debate stage, and in the background are some buildings of the collective farm."

"Looks great!"

"Rabbi Dr. Geyer is a real piece of work, eh?"

Etai, like all of the Israeli staff, hadn't known the play too well upon arriving at Burntshore, but, as a member of the chorus, that had quickly changed. Ruby knew the debate song well (if not well enough to sing the whole thing from memory, well enough to sing along without missing a word), she had close read it for her class paper. It was a pivotal moment in the action of the play: the chauvinistic Rabbi Dr. Geyer, who is running for New Society president on a platform of

Jewish-only supremacy, has an impromptu debate with David, who, while emphatically not a politician (politicians not having supposed to exist in the New Society), eloquently represents the current status quo, which is that anybody, Jewish or otherwise, can become a member of the New Society. Rabbi Dr. Geyer is the clear bad guy in the play, his views anathema to both the New Society as a fictional entity and *Tel Aviv!* as a play.

Since Etai had given Ruby an opening to vent about the play—which she had been trying not to do ever since Etai joined the cast—there was no choice but to take it. "It's so hypocritical, all these diaspora Jews celebrating David's version of a non-existent Israel, memorizing his lines, while it is Rabbi Dr. Geyer's ideology that has been the Zionist position from the beginning. What else is keeping millions of Palestinians stateless in order to maintain a bogus Jewish majority but Dr. Geyer's vilified hatred of the other? The whole world is backwards!"

"It's propaganda, sure, but the music is mitzoyan," Etai said. He had put the paint brush down and was holding Ruby's hips. He danced her around the rec hall. "And the sets! Oy va voy! Priceless art!"

Ruby laughed, though she wasn't quite finished. "It's all so insidious. The Zionism of David, the Zionism that Friedrich and Kingscourt sign on to in the play's glorious climax, has never existed, can't exist. It's a beautiful lie."

Andrea was walking by. Ruby pulled herself away from Etai. "Hey, Andrea! I've been trying to talk to you for days about Brett and the Crown land!" Andrea was the only head staff Ruby hadn't spoken to yet.

Andrea kept walking, with Ruby beside her. She was a good foot and a half taller than Ruby, and with her long black hair and ghostly complexion—had she been outside once all summer?—it was like talking to some midnight apparition. "Yes, yes, I've heard all about it. I can't really think about that kind of stuff at the moment, I'm too busy with these sets. The play is in five days! Besides, it's not like Brett will just give the land to the reserve! What do you really expect to happen?"

Andrea stopped to assist some first years who had messed up their panel, bending down to listen to their explanations. Ruby walked back to Etai.

"What time are you done?"

He was back on his knees, paintbrush in hand.

"Whenever I finish this panel. Want to grab a brush?"

Ruby looked at the set, looked at Etai. She shrugged. Painting sets with your boyfriend in the middle of the night, a quintessential camp experience.

By the time Ruby got back to her cabin it was nearly five thirty. She had just over two hours to sleep.

She had made her decision.

At the cookout the next day, Ruby and Etai approached Tom. He was sitting on a picnic bench, eating a hot dog slathered in yellow mustard, Piper and Daisy lounging in the shade under the bench. He was wearing a vintage Camp Burntshore shirt, orange and tattered, the haircut he had gotten in the city last week drawing attention to his full head of black hair.

"Hi, Tom. We were, uh, wondering, if we could talk to you about something?" Ruby couldn't believe how nervous she was. Her heart was beating incredibly fast, the urge to bury her entire lower lip in her mouth a physical force she was nearly unable to resist. At least Etai next to her was a cool, calming presence.

Tom put the last half of hot dog into his mouth. Chewed. Swallowed.

"Of course, Ruby, any time."

"Uh, okay, great! Can we stop by your office tomorrow, say at Rest Hour?"

Tom wiped his mouth on his forearm, nodded. "I look forward to it."

Ruby went with Etai to join the lineup for food. She was ravenous.

After lunch the next day, they went straight to the office. Ruby was worried that Brett would be there; not that she was intimidated by him, but she felt she had a better chance to persuade Tom out of buying the land if Brett wasn't whispering in his ear (not that she necessarily thought she had a chance). Luckily, Brett was running drills with Ari Dressler all day for his finals match with Danielle, so the only other people in attendance were Debs and Jenna. Ruby, unable to shake the thought that she had come across as schleppy yesterday, had put on her fancy jeans and a black blouse.

"Now, Ruby, what can I do for you? I hear you've been bugging the staff, trying to gin up some opposition to the camp's plan to expand." Ruby couldn't have known this, but Tom was not in a good mood: that morning, he had received a rejection from a peer-reviewed journal for his article on the problems associated with seep-filled landfill methods. The second reviewer had railed against Tom's "out of left field" methodology. Government stooge, probably.

Ruby swallowed. "The camp's plan? I thought it was Brett's plan?"

"Brett's plan, yes, originally. But it is the camp's money."

This was news to Ruby, though it probably shouldn't have been. She felt woefully unprepared. She looked at Etai before turning back to her boss.

"Tom, it's just not right. We have no right to that land, and we don't need it. I don't want to badmouth Brett, but this should not be the way forward for Camp Burntshore. What will we do with ten thousand acres? The camp is a good, manageable size. Shouldn't we be trying to live in more just ways with the Black Spruce First Nation, and not continue the stealing of their land? The whole idea of Crown land is just a form of theft, not to mention the treaties we are supposed to live under, that are utterly broken, if they ever worked." Ruby didn't mention the daily rallies taking place on the road; there was no need to. "And, yes, I have been speaking to the staff, and . . . and plenty of them agree with me. At least, thirty percent, I'd say."

Tom sat behind his desk, his fingers under his chin. He was not pleased with being portrayed as the bad guy, but with Cindy and the rallies, Ruby and her strong-headedness, that was exactly what was happening. How had things gotten to this point? He exhaled slowly.

"I'm going to level with you, Ruby. If it were solely up to me, would I be buying that Crown land? No. Definitely not. But it's not up to me. Brett is my son, and he is going to take over the camp. If this is the direction Brett envisions for Burntshore, then I support him. I have to support him." What Tom didn't say was that if Brett didn't do this now, he would probably do it in five years, when Tom was retired and the camp was actually his.

"We really don't know why you're so worked up about this, Ruby," Jenna said. "This is good for camp, good for the camp community, good for camp continuity."

Ruby looked at Debs, who turned her eyes down to her clipboard. She was quite clearly staying out of it. Was this a huge mistake?

Tom cleared his throat. "Back in my pharmacist days, we'd often be visited by representatives from the major drug companies, outlining their new products, touting their amazing benefits, quietly admitting to their often brutal side effects. Was I often unhappy with the pharmaceuticals? Yes, of course I was often unhappy with the pharmaceuticals, with the direction they were taking the whole medical field. Their quick fixes, finding novel problems only to solve them with a pill, turning plants and their magical chemical properties the world over into easy-to-swallow, patentable commodities. Hoarding medical knowledge. But what were we supposed to do? We were one cog in a giant, incredibly profitable machine. If customers came in with their prescriptions for the newest miracle cure, we would fill them. That was our job. Anyways, those days have been on my mind a lot lately. What do you make about all this, Etai?"

Etai looked startled. Tom's face was serious, inquisitive. Etai glanced at Ruby, back at Tom. "Well, sir, to be honest, I've been rethinking a lot of stuff since arriving here. As Israelis, we were taught our entire lives that the land belonged to us, that we had rights to it, that anybody who tried to stop us had an irrational hatred for us. And I'm not just talking about the West Bank. I think that this is now wrong. In a situation like this, one side always has more power."

Ruby couldn't hold it in any longer. "But Tom, you did do something. You quit being a pharmacist!"

"I agree with Ruby," Debs blurted out, the first thing she had said the whole meeting. Everybody turned to her. Her red face contrasted nicely with her orange hair. "Ruby's right," she said, more composed. "We don't need that land. Tom. Jenna. You know we don't need that land."

Tom sighed. He looked out the window. Ruby noticed Etai's leg was shaking. Her own heart trying to keep pace.

"Well," Tom said, sounding resigned, "even if I wanted to stop Brett, the sale has already gone through. MNR Micky works fast. There's nothing we can do. I signed the paperwork in Toronto last week. Camp Burntshore is about to come into a whole lot of land."

Hot tears stung the back of Ruby's eyes.

"What would you suggest I do, Ruby?" Tom asked. His anger had evaporated.

"We can give the land to the Black Spruce," Ruby mumbled, barely audible, defeated.

Tom looked startled, then contemplative. Debs was staring at Ruby, a slight smile on her face. Jenna's eyes were on the floor. Etai's leg had stopped shaking. Something in the room had shifted, but what?

Tom nodded. "Okay, Ruby, thanks for this meeting. Jenna and I have a lot of thinking to do."

Outside Tom's office, Ruby and Etai fell into nervous laughter.

"That was great," Etai said, "when did you come up with the idea of giving the land to the Spruce?"

"It was something Andrea said last night. I didn't know I was going to say it until I said it though. What was with that story about the drug companies? Tom can be so odd sometimes."

Etai shrugged. "Tom thinks in stories."

They were walking past the dining hall, on the way to the ski docks.

"I hope I didn't just fuck up my time at camp for no reason," Ruby said.

"There's always a reason."

Ruby nodded.

"I imagine you'll be having words with Brett soon."

"Seems unavoidable at this point, doesn't it. This is definitely not over."

They were on the other side of the dining hall now, at the bottom of centre field. The wind was up, hot and gritty on her face.

The lake roiled, freckled with white.

CHAPTER 31

WORDS WITH BRETT; ROCKET FUEL; A JOINT IN THE RAIN WITH A FRIEND

Ruby was on her way back to her cabin when she heard Brett calling her name. She stopped. Turned.

"Whatever you're trying with my dad, it won't work." They were standing at the bottom of cabin line, where the three lines split off from the main road. Brett was in his tennis outfit, white wristbands and headband, his racquet in his hand, face sweaty.

"Okay, *Daddy* Kravitz. We'll see."

Brett shook his head. "You don't get it, do you? The sale has already gone through! The land is mine. After the thousands of years of shit we've been through, I'm building something for us that'll last."

"Don't pretend this has anything to do with the Jewish people, Brett. This is about greed. Greed, and you being an asshole."

Brett guffawed, switched the racquet from one hand to the other. "Dov keeps telling me to forget about you, that he knows plenty of girls like you in Israel, that pretend to care so much about the plight of the Palestinians, about their mistreatment, about the horrors of the occupation, but when push comes to shove, there you are, standing comfortably behind the border wall, guard towers and checkpoints keeping you safe."

Just talking to Brett filled Ruby with incoherent rage. She was at a loss as to how to respond. "Justice, justice you shall pursue!" she yelled.

Brett laughed. "Fuck you and your liberal Jewish hogwash. Being Jewish is about one thing, and that's survival. Survival at all costs."

"Go tell it to Fallon."

"Fallon? What does any of this have to do with Fallon?" Brett's eyes lit up, as if he suddenly understood what Ruby was saying. "You know I'd dump her in a second, if you have finally realized what we could have together?"

Ruby's feet and hands had turned to stone. They were pulling her to the ground. "What? What did you just say to me?"

Brett smiled, laughed silently, his chest shuddering.

"The land is mine, Ruby. The land is ours. This land belongs to you and me. And guess what? Nobody cares. Nobody will care. The world goes on. Deal with it."

He walked off.

Ruby walked to her cabin in a haze of anger. She could have walked straight into the lake and just kept going for all she was paying attention to her surroundings, but her legs, her body, knew the route. She couldn't decide what she was more furious about—Brett's assholery, that he still, somehow, thought he could get with her, what he said about Fallon's disposability (she found herself feeling strangely protective of Fallon), his flippancy and his certainty when it came to the land. She darted from red hot node to red hot node, the heat from each transferring to her like a knife on an electric stove coil.

Speaking of heat, a warm front had snuck in behind the wind. It must have gone up fifteen degrees since lunch. Ruby, in her jeans and long-sleeve blouse—black, of all colours!—was a sweaty mess. The cabin, once she got there, was stifling, empty; none of her girls were there, probably off in the shade somewhere with the unit's boys. She stomped into the staff area, tossed off her sandals, unbuttoned and threw her blouse onto the rumpled bed, and started on her jeans. It was so hot and sticky that they were glued to her legs, and with every useless yank she got angrier. They. Just. Wouldn't. Fucking. Come. Off. She was grunting with wild frustration, on the verge of a full-fledged meltdown. Finally, she managed to peel the jeans off and, the pant legs inside out—which made her even angrier—hurled them with all her strength into a corner. In her bra and underwear, she unlocked her toolbox and fumbled for her weed. She never smoked during the day, but she was feeling desperate, feeling like she had zero fucks left to give. It was her last summer anyways, right?! She grabbed the dime bag of weed she had bought from the DJ at the social last week, that she had been saving for staff banquet. "Rocket Fuel." Stuffed it and her pipe and her orange lighter into her fanny pack, finished undressing, put on her bathing suit and a beach cover up, grabbed her towel and bag, and went down to the ski docks. Etai was there, organizing the wooden rack of skis for next period.

"Take me for a ride?" Etai nodded and they got onto the boat.

"I take it you spoke to Brett then?" Etai asked as they glided away from the dock.

Ruby nodded. "We had words." They motored out to the middle of the lake, near the bigger of the two cottaged islands. "I hope . . . no, I fucking *pray* that Danielle kicks his fucking ass at the finals tomorrow." Bobbing on the water, standing with her legs planted firmly apart, she hit three full bowls in quick succession. "I'm never wearing jeans again," she said, coughing.

"I can lend you one of my sarongs."

Ruby offered the pipe to Etai. He shook his head no, turned over the engine.

"Rest Hour's over. Gotta get back."

When Ruby stepped off the boat and onto the burning hot dock, her stonedness rushed up like a litter of puppies to greet her. She swayed with the force of it before finding her footing. She walked towards the swim docks, one careful step at a time. Oh fuck. Oh shit. Oh fuck-shit. She was ripped. She was blitzed. She was way, *way* too high. (She was definitely going to get caught. Jesus fuck.) Luckily, the heat still rising unabated, Debs had called a snap beach day, the temperature on the trip shed having surpassed thirty-eight and on its way to forty degrees. Spotting Danielle and their cabin coming down from cabin line with their towels and water bottles and books, along with campers and staff converging from all directions, Ruby spread her towel out on the sand and lay down before anybody saw her.

She was stationary, stoned, the heat a weighted blanket on her chest, her head swimming. The heat was intense, an oppressive ideology that was impossible to break out of (but the lake, the lake was right there). Her eyes closed, she overheard snippets of conversation as the entire camp settled in around the lakefront, all of it melding into one übermeaningful sensation of utter understanding. "Hey, what's white and smooth and never sees the sun?" "The underside of Marula's tits?" "Close—my balls!" "I fell off a bunk bed when I was really young, but I landed on all fours." "Do you think all German shepherds are related to Hitler's?" "I think *all* dogs are related to Hitler's." "All *life* is related to Hitler's German shepherd." "What kind of bird is that?" "I think it's a thrush." "That's an amazing word." "Thrush, thrush, thrush."

Ruby, still very high, skimming closer and closer to sleep, the sun bearing down on her, daydreamed that she was on trial for betraying the camp. She was up in the docket, all alone in her beach cover up. The judge—Tom, naturally—called up witness after witness. "All she cares about are her morals. She didn't give a shit about us!" Danielle said from the stand. "She doesn't respect the chain of command!" Fallon. "Her actions are tantamount to a betrayal of the Jewish people." Dov. The last witness was Seema, wearing glittery blue eyeshadow like the one time they went clubbing together on John Street. "What can I say. I thought she was my best friend."

Ruby sat up. She was engulfed in gulping fear. She stood, walked through the pudding of the air, children frolicking all around her, to the swim docks, and, without pausing, dove into the water, only worrying for an instant that she had forgotten how to swim and would just sink to the bottom of the lake. Bye-bye, Ruby. Luckily, she had not forgotten, and the cold water did its job, cutting the bad parts of her high off with its silky, painless knife. She surfaced, treaded water as kids splashed and jumped.

Back on her towel, letting the sun and the heat dry her off, hugging her knees, June came over, sat beside her.

"I can't believe camp is almost over. I don't want to go home!"

"It's definitely bittersweet."

"Two months isn't long enough to be happy!"

"Just because something isn't permanent, continual, year-round, infinite, doesn't mean it didn't happen, isn't real, isn't meaningful."

"My mom's going to flip when she finds out I've gone vegetarian."

Ruby smiled. "People in our lives might not always understand the things we do, but that's on them, not on us."

"I love you, Ruby." June lay down, her head in Ruby's lap. Ruby played with June's hair.

"I love you too."

Later, Ruby was in the showers. Since one of the only times at camp you *prefer* ice cold shower water is during a heatwave, the showers were currently at a premium. Ruby didn't usually shower before dinner, a very popular time, but she needed to cool off, needed to *do* something. Both the girls side and the boys side were packed with campers and staff. There was a real festive air. The sound of streaming water hitting skin and tile. Everybody's shower bucket hanging off the shower handles. Danielle had brought her yellow shower radio and was blasting The Otter. The drains were a cornucopia of hair and dirt and foreign objects. Michal and Orit were showering barefoot, something a seasoned camper would never do. Ruby shampooed, lathered, conditioned, washed her face. She was beginning to feel more like herself. Rocket fuel is right. Jesus. Ruby and a few others left the shower together into the burning late afternoon, sweating again instantly. There was still a long line of campers in their towels and shower shoes, patiently waiting their turn. Heavy grey clouds were gathering. The air crackled with electricity.

"It's going to pour."

"Goddamn motherfucking hope so."

Later, after EP—cities night, a yearly occurrence where the camp celebrated all the cities the campers hailed from—Ruby and Geoff were standing under the skimpy awning of the kitchen backdoor with its flickering light, smoking a joint as it poured all around them. Smoking in the rain would always remind Ruby, who was in her rain jacket, hood up, and had borrowed Arielle's rain pants and June's gumboots, of being in high school, smoking wherever they could find a secluded spot.

"So, have you decided what you're going to do with Tyler's dad's money?" Ruby asked, raising her voice to be heard over the rain.

Geoff shrugged, sucked his cheeks in as he hit the joint. "Not yet. I can't help feeling dirty, like I've been bought. Maybe I'll just rip the cheque up."

Ruby shook her head. "You haven't been bought. Tyler's dad just loves to throw his money around. He thinks he's super benevolent or some shit."

"Maybe." Geoff seemed unsure.

"Look at it this way. Are you going to change your behaviour in any way?"

"No."

"Alter your worldview, your beliefs?"

"No."

"Talk and act differently?"

"No."

"Then nobody's bought you. Fuck it, sometimes money falls into our lap. You should buy a kick-ass guitar or something."

"I should put it towards tuition."

"Maybe so."

Ruby filled Geoff in on everything that had happened with Tom and Brett. Geoff nodded along.

"I can't stop thinking of what the Canadian government and their accomplices knowingly, passionately did. They beat, raped, murdered, and dragged your language and culture from you and your ancestors."

Geoff took a hit off the spliff. "And yet we're still here."

Ruby took a long toke. "I can't help feeling that, with this move, Brett is making Burntshore more complicit than it already is."

"Imagine how different it could have been," Geoff said. "Peoples of all kinds living along the lakes, travelling by canoe, respectful of whose territory they are on." Geoff had been thinking along these lines for days, ever since the daily rallies at the Spruce had started. He had managed to get away from the kitchen and go to a few of them—it was an amazing feeling to be marching with the people he grew up with, declaring their presence, singing and drumming to remind a country that once outlawed their singing and drumming that they were not going anywhere. He had even brought Michal yesterday. Cindy and the others were planning a drum circle in Spitsville for tomorrow.

Lightning forked over the trees, the river visible for a split second. Thunder boomed.

"I still think the world can be different, can be better," Ruby said.

"Why?"

"From what I read. From Le Guin and the Kesh. From Idle No More. From Burntshore, believe it or not. Think about the difference between how we live in the Big Wide and how we live here. Isn't that enough to prove that anything is possible?"

"I hope you're right, Ruby."

"Other times, I think that we don't deserve to be forgiven, and we never will. We're all going to realize soon enough that we can't eat money. While I was reading about the treaties and the so-called Crown land, I couldn't stop thinking that, like, if we all just stopped believing in this unjust system, it would all just go away. Why can't we just collectively let go, build something better? It seems like we never will."

Geoff released a mouthful of smoke. "Because the armies, the cops, the jails, the powerful, won't allow us to stop."

"True enough. So, in other words, we're fucked."

"Doesn't mean we shouldn't keep trying."

The smell of rain, mud, wet trees, weed smoke, the thrashing lake, all melded into a powerful, pummelling petrichor. Ruby stubbed out the joint. Well, she had put herself forward. She had tried. She had stood up for the camp. Whatever happened now was truly out of her hands. There was nothing else to do but enjoy the rest of the summer, see what came next, see what the lake brought in.

The final days were approaching.

Tomorrow, the CITs would return.

CHAPTER 32

TEMAGAMI

— DAY ONE —

Eight days ago, and three hundred kilometres north of Lake Burntshore, Raskin drove the bus of CITs, trippers, and CIT staff down a potholed logging road, enormous white pines and cedars tight to the narrow road's edge, throwing long transient shadows down the length of the bus. The canoe trailer bumped and juddered with the contours of the road. They had already been travelling for three hours and had another hour to go; though, with Tova walking up the bus aisle with a green mesh bag into which everybody begrudgingly put their watches, the CITs' sense of time was about to become a lot less precise. For the next eight days, if they wanted to know the exact time, they'd have to ask Tova, Tripper Steve, Yehouda, Polina, or Barry Blum. Either that or deduce it as best they could from the sun, the sky, the water.

Ayelet was sitting near the front of the bus with Becca. She was excited, a little nervous; she always had a good time on trip, even their unit 2 trip where it rained the *entire* time. She couldn't have been happier that Tova was leading the trip—Tova had always been Ayelet's favourite counselor. She didn't know anybody more cool or competent. Ayelet was secretly hoping to be put into Tova's canoe, but she knew there was little chance of it; Ayelet was easily the best canoeist in the CIT girls' cabin, and maybe in the boys' cabin too. Tova's canoe-mates would most likely be someone without any skill, whether paddling or social.

Yehouda was sitting in front of her. Ugh. He barely fit in the bus, kept pushing against the vinyl seat, was quaking with energy. Since changeover, they had barely spoken—thank god! Ayelet felt like an idiot for sleeping with him (though, in the subsoil beneath her conscious mind she was also proud, happy with herself for doing something so outrageous). The three weeks of being night-and-day obsessed with him seemed like a bad dream that she could barely remember. In any case, she and Martin had worked things out. She sighed. Even thinking about their illicit meetups in the TITs or on CIT Town's rocky shoreline made her shiver. Hopefully, they'll be able to find some alone time over the next eight days. Ayelet had heard some wild stories about CIT trips of the past—blow jobs performed in the tent while everybody else was sleeping, boys getting caught jacking off in the forest, steamy CSRs, games of truth-or-dare leading to wild orgies. What would future CITs remember from their trip?

"What are you thinking about?" Becca asked. "You're looking out the window and sighing."

"Oh, nothing. You ready for this?" Becca's untameable black mane was already bursting from its carefully woven braids. She made a sour face, stuck out her tongue. Being in the outdoors was not Becca's favourite part of camp.

"Freak no. I might pretend to break my ankle getting off the bus or something, ride home with Raskin."

"Haha, no, no. It's going to be great!"

"Me and Raskin, alone on a bus for five hours," Becca said, letting out an exaggerated sigh of her own, crushing after unattainable boys—even though as far as Ayelet knew she and Simon were rock solid—more familiar, comfortable terrain than the Temagami backcountry, a place of strenuous labour, bears, wolves, cold, wet. The unknown. The non-human. An eruption of male laughter cascaded from the back of the bus. Ayelet could isolate Martin's bright melodic laugh from the rest of the cackling. She homed in on it.

The boys were laughing so hard that Martin was near tears. Josh was taking big gulping breaths; Simon was cough-laughing into his fist. Christ, what a summer it had been. Martin finally fucked Ayelet; they were having sex constantly. (Yes, when he had found out Ayelet slept with Yehouda he thought he'd never be able to get over it—but, surprisingly, it quickly became something that he found he could get over. He hadn't told his boys, and he wasn't going to. If they found out, his life would become one long joke.) They were smoking tons of pot, swimming and eating and chilling in the woods at their secret spot, having a blast—he had found the perfect balance between his friends and Ayelet. After Scharfy got kicked out there was a low spot, sure, but they had come roaring back with a vengeance, smoking even more weed, giving even less fucks, living it even more up. This summer was *theirs*. Besides, the work was fun and easy; as it turned out, Martin was a natural counselor—great with the young kids, a good role model as Barry put it in his changeover evaluation. After tiring of trading their oil company stock for shoes and basketball shorts, after getting sick of the nightly poker games, and under Josh's insistent urging, they had once again started "shopping" in the other boys' cabins, teefing a few items of clothing here and there. Okay, it was more than a few: they had acquired enough for Josh to send a duffel bag full of stolen contraband home with his mom at visitors day. Sometimes, late at night, Martin felt bad about all the stealing, but it was easy enough to shake off. Just another part of a wild, unforgettable summer.

Even as they were literally embarking on it, he tried not to think of the trip they were embarking on. Eight days paddling and carrying canoes in the deep bush. Eight exhausting, uncomfortable, boring, challenging, terrifying, bug-ridden days. It would probably pour the entire time. How would they make it to the other side? It seemed unfathomable. Eight days. Thinking about all the chances of seeing some of the girls naked, their arms in the sun, their butts in the mesh canoe seats, cheered him up somewhat, but then the worries came rushing back: What if he had to portage the canoe? What if it was a headwind every time they were on a lake? Will they be able to smoke any of the weed Simon hid in a pair of his socks? Will he be able to get alone time with Ayelet?

Josh had Babka, quiet, meek Babka, pull his finger, and he farted, a long low bassoon followed by two high squeaks, and they exploded with mirth.

"You guys are *disgusting*," Natalie said, lifting the camera that she was wearing around her neck and snapping a photo of the laughing boys.

Once Tova finished collecting the watches, she stood at the front of the bus, in her standard cargo shorts and hiking boots, feet aisle-width apart, her black cherry paddle in her hands, facing the campers. The piney light swam over their adorable, apprehensive faces. This was the fourth CIT trip she had led, and she easily recognized the poorly concealed nervousness.

"Alright, everybody! Listen up! We are about to be entering the woods. The woods. It's a different place. We will be moving with the power of our own hands, our arms and cores and legs. Everything we need we'll be carrying in our canoes and on our backs. Our food, our shelter, our paddles. If we want heat, we will make it. If we want food, we will cook it. When we are done, we will pack up and move on. We will not leave a trace. Out there, we will be just one particular living element in a fused world of living elements. You may doubt me now, but by the end of this trip, I'll have you wondering why we invented cars or roads or nuclear silos at all!"

Fifteen minutes later, Raskin pulled up to a rocky beach. The CITs streamed out of the bus. It was hot hot, the air buzzing with bugs and the scent of pine. The layered, heavy atmospherics of late summer gonging and resonating all around them. Raskin and Yehouda unstrapped the twelve yellow canoes, maneuvered them off the trailer, and carried them to the lake's edge. Yehouda had a red bandana around his head, was wearing black basketball shorts, a white tank top, and his army boots, was brimming with mission and purpose. Just let him portage all the canoes, Martin thought bitterly, watching him organize the boats at the river's pebbly shore. The CITs unloaded packs, found their life jackets, their paddles, applied sunscreen, drank from one of the six four-litre jugs they'd be sharing water out of for the next eight days. Tova and Tripper Steve loaded the boats, assigned the canoes. Martin and Ayelet were in a canoe with Tori. Martin was in the stern, Ayelet started in the bow, and Tori sat on a pack midship. Once everything was ready—a surprisingly quick unload considering all the gear—and Natalie got the pre-trip picture she harangued everybody into, the fifteen boats pushed off, and the trip began.

Raskin watched them paddle away as he hacked a butt, his boots crunching on the smooth river stones. Once they were beyond view, he closed up the empty bus, put it into gear, and trundled off into the enfolding woods.

— DAY TWO —

Ayelet woke up to Tova outside their tent, gently shaking the fly, telling the girls breakfast was ready. Ayelet shivered and snuggled deeper into her bag. Her tentmates groaned and did likewise. Without her watch, Ayelet didn't know what time it was, but it couldn't have had been light for too long. Ayelet was not ready to get out of bed; she had had a fitful sleep, turning and readjusting, cold enough to be uncomfortable but not cold enough to force herself up to find extra clothes to put on. Yesterday had been a gruelling first day. After a short paddle and even shorter portage around the cement wall of a hydro dam—which, being the first portage of the trip, took an extra-long time getting the boats organized—they had paddled for hours, first along a wide river with towering canyons of jagged grey scree on either side, then across a massive, twisting lake, all before marching on two portages (Ayelet carrying a food barrel and all the paddles and life jackets she could manage, veritably bent over with the weight). And then *another* massive paddle on an angry lake. After setting up the campsite, they had spent the evening around the fire, complaining about how sore they were, giving each other massages; Yehouda, in particular, had a queue of girls waiting for his "magic hands." Ugh. Ayelet's back still felt the relentless paddling of the day before; her hands were already blistering. Maybe she was wrong to have been excited for the trip. A pang of worry pinged through her. She opened her eyes. Becca, in her lavender bag next to Ayelet, was looking at her. Their faces were inches apart; Becca looked gorgeous, her face clean and awake and alive, her brown eyes deep, clear lakes. They both laughed, which was enough of a stimulus to get Ayelet scrambling out of her bag. She put on all of the clothes she had brought, crawled over the other girls, and zippered herself out of the tent.

Ayelet was the first camper to emerge. Yehouda and Polina were down by the water smoking cigarettes with Tripper Steve. Barry Blum was still in his tent; Ayelet could hear his deep, satisfied snores. Tova was stirring a massive pot of oatmeal that was boiling away on the perfectly contained cooking fire. Ayelet stretched and yawned in the foresty chill, knelt down to absorb some of the fire's heat through her outstretched hands. Heavy mist swirled on the lake. Above her, red pines swayed. One day in and they were already deep in the wilderness.

"Did you really sleep outside?" she asked Tova, who hadn't bothered to set up her own tent last night.

"Sure did," Tova said, moving the pot off of the grill with two orange dish towels and placing it onto the dirt-and-pine-needled ground. "There's nothing like the sky for a blanket."

Sounds of fighting and groaned insults rose like woodsmoke from one of the boys' tents.

During breakfast there was further complaining about how sore everybody was. Sooner than they would have liked, they rolled up their bags, stuffed them along with their site clothes and sandals into their dry bags, pushed the air out, rolled them up, collapsed the tents, did the dishes, packed everything into the big hundred-litre packs. By the time they were ready to push off it was a hot morning, though as Ayelet had already learned, the weather out there was fickle, hormonal, surprising. They loaded the canoes, Barry Blum and Yehouda grabbing the bags being handed to them and placing them into the appropriate boats, and left the site, their first landfall of the trip. Ayelet looked back as they paddled away, took in the site one final time.

It was a sunny day of waterfalls. They spent ten hours going up one channel of the river, and then going down another, portaging around the six falls as they crashed and sprayed. There were also *many* portages around the many rapids; Ayelet lost count of how many. She had gotten accustomed to the weight of her food barrel, even though it somehow seemed heavier than it had yesterday. The loading and unloading at the portage mouths, the divvying up of packs, canoes, and paddles, was already smoother than the unorganized rigamarole of the first day. Into the canoe, paddle paddle paddle, out of the canoe, portage portage portage, into the canoe, paddle paddle paddle. Take in the waterfall, its roar and beauty and motion and stark thereness, have a snack (trail mix, apple, granola bar), chug from one of the water jugs, back into the boat. Who was lazy and who was a team player was already apparent. In general, the boys grumbled but also teased and pushed each other to go hard. Out of the girls, Becca had surprisingly taken to the tripping; it was Tori who complained, non-stop. "This is child abuse! We should be back at CIT Town! Ugh! This mud is gross! Why should we work so hard to see so many damn waterfalls, there's a river and falls literally next to camp. I wish Scharfy was here! He'd understand!" Ayelet had no idea Barry Blum was such an excellent paddler; he could stop the canoe on a dime, turn and pivot and surge forward with ease. Yehouda—ugh—was his usual fount of endless energy, a big happy smile on his big innocent face as he portaged a canoe with a food barrel on his back then returned at a run for another carry. He was all movement and strength and encouragement; Ayelet, once impressed into fixation by this, saw it now as vaguely threatening.

That night, after a dinner of rotini pasta with meat sauce, garlic bread toasted on the grill, trail mix for dessert, they sat around a crackling fire. "What do you think Tom would point out to us if he was here now?" Tova asked, tending the fire with a long, wrist-thick stick of pine.

"Uh, the rocks! Duh!" Laughter.

"Probably something about how old the land is?" Ayelet said. She herself could feel it: the age of this place was so *apparent*.

"Tom would definitely point out the age of the land. He would say that the evidence of the retreating ice is everywhere around us. He would talk about the wild waterways. Would he talk about the Teme-Augama the Anishinaabe people who call this place home? About the nastawgan, the ancient system of trails that have been traversed for thousands and thousands of years? Would he mention how we live in a blissful sliver of planetary calm? That our dumping trillions of tons of carbon dioxide in the atmosphere is threatening that calm? That the Earth is our one home? That soon, in geological time, we'll be so close to the sun that these very lakes and rivers will boil? Okay, time for s'mores!"

Fingers and mouths sticky with marshmallow, with chocolate. Hands in the cold, dark river. The nighttime forest world exhilarating and impermeable. The stars diamond dust on a frozen black lake. Tent doors zip open. Tent doors zip closed. Breath turns to smoke. The boys piss in the woods. The girls piss in the woods. The fire pissing and spluttering as Tova and Barry douse it. The waterfall pissing and roaring without cease.

— DAY THREE —

Since it was what Tova called "a short day," they were gifted with a slow morning at their waterfall site, their tents spread out on the humped rocks next to the falls. Tripper Steve and Polina cooked pancakes with chocolate chips for breakfast, made real maple syrup out of golden crystals and warm water. The boys kept a running tally of who ate the most. Martin ate six, not enough to win, but still, a respectable amount. The trip so far hadn't been as bad as Martin had feared; in fact, he was having a blast. Last night they had gone into the woods and smoked a hastily rolled joint; as usual, they talked about Scharfy, the girls and the girls' bodies, Martin momentarily worried that they'd hear them from the firepit. Simon complained about not being at the Grizzly show, hoped his weed plants were doing okay without him; Josh revealed six apples he had stolen from one of the food barrels. "Dude, what the fuck, those are for everybody!" "Relax, man, I didn't see you complaining when we were jacking people's shoes and iPods." "I should take Becca here later," Simon said. "What about you, Babka, you going to bring Tori here?" Babka looked embarrassed. "Nah, man, we're just friends. She needed somebody to talk to after Scharfy got kicked out." "Oh, she found somebody to 'talk' to alright."

Back at the morning fire, gorged on pancakes, Simon started to drum on a food barrel lid, with Martin singing an improvised chant: "It's a life of tent door zippers. Just a life of tent door zippers." Everybody joined in, laughing and singing. *It's a life of tent door zippers. Just a life of tent door zippers*. Surrounded by his best friends, by beautiful girls, by Ayelet, by the sparkly drone of the waterfall.

Martin gave the morning pack-up a little extra mustard, rolling the tent up, collecting the pegs, penguin-walking the big packs down to the boats, helping Polina douse the fire, and before they knew it, they were back on the river. It was the start of another beautiful day: warm and cool, breezy, fat, symbolic clouds cycling overhead. Two more portages and they were off the river, on a big choppy lake. Ten minutes in, a decent headwind whipped up. Other boats were having trouble staying straight, but Ayelet was sterning, and they shot ahead of the fleet. The pines swayed in the wind as Martin paddled his heart out, glancing down at the big *YES!* painted on the boat. Yes! Yes! Yes!

Sleek Kevlar sleeves of bodies and packs sliding down ancient waterways.

They arrived at a small round lake. The water was flat, a mirror, and they glided serenely through rocky hills of cedar and hemlock, the world upside-down, doubled. A long, tipping tree, green clouds speared by beer-brown branches. Tova pointed to their destination: a site atop a rocky hill. The canoes softly kissed the land. They were still setting up the tents, Ayelet and Martin returning from the backsite with armloads of firewood when bloated, heavy clouds crowded in above them like moshers rushing the stage the instant the lights go down. The air gone tingly. The hair on Martin's arms stood up. The lights had *actually* gone down: it was suddenly dark.

Tova, who had been organizing that night's dinner by the firepit, snapped into action. "Finish all the tents! Make sure the doors are closed! Yonatan, Ayelet, and Martin, help me put up the tarps. Barry, grab four CITs and bring all of the gear, especially the food barrels, under this tarp here. Steve and the rest, flip all the canoes, stash all the life jackets and paddles underneath them. Get the firewood under the tarps. Finish the tents! Move, move, move!" All the while, Tova was measuring out lines of white guy cord, tying up the corners of the tarp, standing on a food barrel to get as high as possible on the tree to tie down the cord. Everybody fell into their assigned tasks. The air was electric, alive, galvanizing. Things were happening. Adrenaline and zeal and little slugs of fear pulsed through the woods. Within five harried minutes, the work was done, and they were huddled under a sky of taut, angled tarps, all the gear stowed and piled beside them. Martin's heart was beating fast. He had never felt so engaged, so in the element, so at the world's mercy. So *exposed*.

They had barely stopped moving when the clouds burst, thick ropes of overdriven rain railing down onto the tarps, the tents, the trees, the lake pocking and bucking. And yet there they were, safe and dry under their hastily erected shelter, watching lightning rock and roar on the white-capped lake as Tova placidly cooked dinner to the sounds of thunder. Martin and Ayelet were sitting close, their rain jackets rubbing together. He found her hand.

After the storm, sitting around the spluttering fire, complaining about the ruthless mosquitoes the rain had awoken, marvelling at the hail, big diamonds of smooth ice, that were crashing all around them, the sky a scrim of glowing green. Martin couldn't believe it. He felt like he was ripped, even though they hadn't smoked since the waterfall. What was this place? Where had Tova taken them?

— DAY FOUR —

They were climbing Maple Mountain today. They left the tents up, their sleeping bags unrolled. Their wet clothes from last night hung on long clotheslines criss-crossing the site. The food barrels were hung from trees. They slipped into the boats, leaving three behind because without the barrels and packs they could fit more people in each canoe, and paddled to the trailhead, a short river and a small lake away. They could see the mountain as they approached the beach landing, a phalanx of yellow canoes with the Camp Burntshore logo on the stern moving as one: it rose above the shoreline of jack pine and spruce, covered in green with some swipes of brown rock near the top, the defunct fire tower a wilderness Eiffel stabbing the blue sky.

As soon as they finished unloading and had pulled the canoes to the side, storm clouds whipped over them for an unexpected encore. Nearly without warning, it was pouring. They huddled in the woods, getting drenched, waiting for it to pass; most of them had left their rain jackets at the site. Tori's teeth were chattering, and she was complaining bitterly; Babka had his arm around her, the rain bringing out the intoxicating floral smell of her shampoo. Tova walked among them, unperturbed, rain splashing off the hood of her blue Gore-Tex rain jacket, telling the story of the provincial government's failed attempt in the '70s to build Ontario Place North on the mountain.

"The plan was to build a giant resort with all the amenities: multiple hotels, chalets, golf courses, hot tubs, restaurants, ski lifts. It was going to accommodate six thousand visitors! Investors were banging down the door to get in on the ground floor. It was going to make a lot of rich people even richer, and the deal was as good as done." Tova was yelling to be heard over the rain. She paused. Whether upset because of the rain, cold, or, like Ayelet, simply rapt, nobody spoke. "So, do you know what happened? We rose up. We rose up to save this small part of the world from the bulldozer, from the hotel barons, from the blasphemy of asphalt and sand trap. The summer camps in the area, backcountry paddlers, and, most of all, the Teme-Augama Anishinaabe, all banded together to instigate a major protest movement. The battle lasted years: the government kept insisting that this would be the site, even after the court ruled in favour of the Anishinaabe. In the end, the province let the project quietly die, and eventually most of the area was protected as a provincial park."

As swiftly as the rain started, it stopped. The sky was an endless soundscape of curved blue once again. They emerged from the trees, shook off like a pack of wet dogs, and, Tova leading the way, Barry Blum taking up the rear, his large white shirt soaked, they started the hike. Josh was wearing jeans for some reason, which had hardened into cement; he looked unhappy, lifting his legs over downed trees and roots with strained effort.

Tori, on the other hand, was vocally unhappy. "How can they expect us to do this, we're freaking drenched! This is so hard, we should be back at camp sunning on the docks!"

Yehouda, his bandana, tank top, and basketball shorts sopping wet, threw her onto his shoulders and carried her for a hundred metres. Tori wasn't wrong: the woods were *wet*. It was hot and humid, but the leaves, thousands of cupped green palms tight on the narrow trail, continually painted them with water. It was three kilometres to the top, and they hiked single file in near silence. A scramble up a rickety steel ladder resting on a sheer rock face, and they were at the summit.

The peak was wide and flat, a taste of alpine in Northern Ontario. There were blueberry bushes everywhere. Once they all arrived, they huddled around Tova as she bent down and left under a juniper bush an offering of tobacco Cindy had packed for this purpose. "This is a sacred site," Tova said. "To the Anishinaabeg the mountain is called Chee-bay-jing. As I lay this tobacco down, I want us to think about how we are guests on this land, even though some of us have forgotten this, forgotten what this means. We have to learn how to be guests. We have to remember. Miigwetch."

Ayelet repeated the Anishinaabemowin word quietly; it felt good, proper, to speak it. After the little ceremony, the CITs and staff spread out to explore, dry off, lie down under the now-baking sun. It was blazing bright out, sunspots of purple pompoms dancing in Ayelet's vision.

Wet clothes came off, were laid on rocks. Most everybody was naked except for bras, underwear, swimsuits, boxers. A few boys tried to climb the defunct fire tower. Tripper Steve pulled a Frisbee out of his pack and tossed it with Yehouda, Simon, and Becca. Tova handed out zip-lock bags to everyone, and they filled them with blueberries, ate until their mouths and hands were purple, their stomachs pleasantly acidic. Ayelet couldn't get over the view: from up here, you could see some of the lakes they had just paddled. (Ayelet knew that if she asked Tova the names of them, she would tell her, but she sort of liked not knowing.) There was their site, there were their tents, the giant hilly rock, their clothes sagging towards the middles of the clotheslines, re-drying after the morning shower. A whole world, complex and alive. All that life emanating from the trees, the water, the soil, the horizon, even—especially—the rocks under her feet, made Ayelet dizzy. Yet she couldn't look away.

Martin and his boys emerged from the woods in their boxers—Martin's baby blue with little green martini glasses clinking each other—casting about furtive eyes as red as the blueberries were blue, slapping mosquitoes with loud thwacks. Ayelet ran up to Martin, hugged him, kissed him on the cheek. They were both nearly naked. "Isn't this amazing?! Leaving our site, climbing the tallest mountain in Ontario, and then paddling back with bags of fresh blueberries?"

"Oh yeah, babe." Martin reluctantly pulled away, ending the hug. Any longer and there would have been a problem.

"I guess it's alright," Tori said, suddenly standing next to them. Unlike everybody else, she hadn't taken off any of her clothes, was shivering with cold. "But can you *believe* we have to hike back down now and get soaked all over again?! I'm going to kill Tova! My parents are going to hear about this." She huffed off to find Babka, the only one who understood what she was going through.

Before starting the trek back to the lake, Natalie set up her camera on a log, pressed the ten-second time delay, and ran to the group for a picture of all of them under the fire tower, arms around each other, faces tanned and silly.

Martin and Ayelet ended up in a canoe alone on the paddle back to their site.

"Can you even imagine what all this looks like in the winter?" Ayelet enthused. Her mind's sluicegates were thrown wide open, everything rushing through her hefty with their proper magnitude. The canoe's canoeness, the paddle's paddleness, the river's riverness, the rocks and trees' rockness and treeness, our ourness.

"For sure, babe," Martin said absent-mindedly.

"I love A&C, but maybe I'll try to be a tripper instead next year. I don't know, I've never felt like this before."

"I think I'm going to go to CEGEP after all. Maybe teacher's college after that," Martin said.

Ayelet stretched into a long, smooth paddle, the boat responding to her every whim.

That night, there was nothing but the deep bowl of the lake, the cupped hand of the fire, the spooned stars they paddled out onto the lake to gorge on, the wind howling through the pines on Chee-bay-jing, singing otherworldly melodies, keeping everybody on edge, awake.

— DAY FIVE —

The morning opened with a chilly group swim, the lake a rug of rippling sunlight as they jumped and dove, shrieked and splashed. Thirty-odd sixteen-year-olds afloat in brisk water, surrounded by trees, rocks, sky. Barry, in a pair of tighty-whities, cannonballed into the lake, creating a momentary crater of water. Afterwards, they packed up. Everything was dry now, the rain a distant memory. They paddled back the way they came, the mountain soon lost to view, retracing their route to join up with the bigger lakes to the south. The canoes a chattering of starlings, a bale of turtles, a stand of birches.

They paddled past a snapping turtle sunning itself on a rock. They paddled past a family of baby ducks. They paddled past a ridge of sheer rock. They paddled past a lone white pine, windblown and gnarled on a small rocky puddle of an island. They paddled past long sand beaches. They paddled and paddled and paddled. They floated, a break from paddling, a rainbow hovering above them in the misty near-rain. They sang the CIT song. They sang the zipper door song. From one of the canoes came a new song: "we're going to the portage, the portage is on its way." The song quickly spread to the other boats, they sang it together, shouting, delirious. "We're going to the portage! The portage is on its way!" Ayelet was transcendent. Martin was swearing at the horse flies that wouldn't leave him alone—one of them had bitten his foot, it was bleeding all over his Teva sandal. In the canoe with Babka and Simon, Becca farted, a deck of cards being shuffled. They died.

Not until they got to their site and were unloading did they find the leech on Martin. "Dude, you're bleeding pretty hard," Simon said. Bright red blood was all over his foot, in between his toes. "I don't think that's a horsefly bite." Martin sat down on the ground. Took his Teva off. Shrieked. On the bottom of his foot was a huge leech, a grey, toonie-sized stingray. Worse, all over his foot and in his toes were dozens, if not hundreds, of tiny baby leeches, little squiggles of white, feasting on the blood. Everybody crowded around. Martin was breathing loudly. "Guys, I'm kind of freaking out a little. Will somebody, uh, do something. Please." Tova ran over with salt from the food barrel, poured it all over Martin's foot. The baby leeches curled up and died. Yehouda splashed water on the foot, to get the blood and leech and salt off. The salt, however, hadn't had any effect on the mother leech. "That thing is out of *Independence Day*!" Tova lit a stick with her lighter, jabbed the mother leech with the hot poker. Eventually it pulled its sucker out and began a hasty retreat. Tova flicked it off the sole of Martin's foot, where there was now a massive hole, an oil well spouting bright blood. Yehouda quickly bandaged him up.

Later, the excitement of the leech attack having waned, everybody lounging at the now-set-up site, beavers swimming back and forth in the water on their beaver business, Tova told Ayelet and some others about the protest encampment that took place on this lake in the '80s, to stop a logging road from being installed. Tova's parents were there, and she strongly insinuated this was where she was conceived. Tova waxed poetic about the power of group belief in change. Ayelet found herself agreeing vociferously: just being the kind of person who imagines living out here, living differently, meant she had a revolutionary spirit. When she got back to the city—the mall, her school, her friends, her family, her room, the Thornhill streets she knows like Tova knows these lakes—how could she bring this revolutionary fire with her? What could Ayelet do with her life to keep this feeling of community, this feeling of *commune*—commune as verb, as action, as outlook, as lookout—alive?

Just then, Tori, coming out of the backsite with an armful of wood, tripped on a root and fell hard, her bundle of sticks and branches clattering to the ground. (Later, Ayelet was sure she had heard the crack.) Tori screamed. Ayelet and Polina ran over to her. They helped her to lay back on the ground. Tori was crying big hot tears. She yelped with pain. Tripper Steve felt Tori's leg up and down. She howled. "I think it's broken," he said, his face grave. Tova ran to grab the sat phone, sprinting down to the shoreline to have the best angle towards the sky. By the time Tripper Steve got the first aid kit, Polina had already given Tori some Advil from her fanny pack, but she didn't have any bandages in there, so he quickly and ably splinted her leg. Tori was talking through the huffing pain. "I can't believe this. I was trying to be helpful, you know, get some wood for the fire? I was really looking forward to the tacos tonight." Ayelet held Tori's hand, tried to keep her calm. Tova came back, flushed. "Don't worry, they're coming to get you." Tori bawled harder. Babka stood beside them, stricken. "I don't want to go back to camp. I don't want to be alone there! What if I miss something?!" "Polina, will you go with her?" Tova asked. "She can't be alone." "I'll go!" Yehouda said, volunteering before Polina had a chance to respond. Ten minutes later, they heard the telltale sounds of a helicopter. A minute later it flew into view over the lake. It positioned itself above the campsite, and a long rope ladder was unfurled. Two paramedics, visitors from another planet, slid down the ladder, all purpose, emergency, focus. They took Tori's vital signs, strapped her onto a stretcher, and attached the stretcher to a grappling cable. "I'm sorry! I'm sorry!" Tori was crying. "I'll take care of your stuff," Becca said, also crying. The paramedics clipped Yehouda, still in his basketball shorts and tank top, onto the ladder. (Ugh.) Everybody stood back as the rope and Tori's stretcher were retracted back into the floating helicopter. The blades of the chopper were throwing loose clothes and leaves all around. The helicopter soared back over the lakes and trees and, just like that, was gone.

At that night's fire, everybody excitedly talking about Tori and the airlift, Ayelet thought about how far away she was from her regular life, from the Big Wide: first there was the remove of camp, already a yawning chasm, and then, within that remove, the further remove of this trip. Out here, they were at the absolute limit of Ayelet's known universe. And from this vantage, things that weren't usually obvious to Ayelet were becoming clear. An entire complete ecological system that society hadn't stuck its fumbling hands into, that, as Tova had put it, they were visiting as guests. It was as Tova had said: Everything was alive, everything had spirit. Everything had agency. What fools we were to think otherwise. Her thoughts drifted back to poor Tori, being ripped away from the group, heading back out into the Big Wide. Ayelet thought about her own double diaspora: the Jewish, the Chinese. Two endless lines of ancestors and tradition and story; two rivers flowing through the lake of herself.

The fire crackled, and Ayelet came back to the group. Tova was talking about how the Andromeda Galaxy was hurtling towards ours at 110 kilometres a second, and in a few billion years both galaxies would collide and be ripped apart, though because of gravity, no stars would ever actually touch each other. Babka looked heartbroken. Tova still had the sat phone in her lap. The lake was blue. The lake was green. The lake was blue-green.

— DAY SIX —

Ayelet woke before dawn. A pea cozy and warm in her synthetic green pod. She had had a dream so vivid she at first couldn't place where she was. Oh, right. Temagami! She had dreamt that she was in A&C, except the shelves were bare, the tables and plywood walls clean of graffiti and paint splotches. The smell of clean, fresh cedar on a summer's day. Ayelet was busily at work, transferring Shrinky Dinks from one sixty-litre Rubbermaid container to another. The hard plastic Shrinky Dinks were each of a different lake in Ontario, in Canada, in the world. All the lakes, the water blue, the islands green, haloed in white. Thousands and thousands and thousands of lakes, of all different sizes, bubbling out of the Rubbermaid, clicking and clacking. She couldn't transfer them fast enough. Friendship bracelets of rivers started falling from the ceiling, each one as unique as each river, composites of minerals and chemicals and rocks and life represented by colour patterns, stitch arrangements. Poison was seeping in through the walls, she had to transfer the lakes and the rivers, she had to save them, to protect them, but there wasn't enough time, there were too many of them. The rising smell of toxic death. She was panicking. She heard Tova's voice, clear and true: "Any of these rivers could be the main artery of the world." She was drowning in the lakes and the rivers, acetone and thread, they were up to her chest, her neck, her nose. Just before they reached her eyes, she had popped awake.

As soon as the tent started to fill with blue nylon light, Ayelet slid out of her bag as quietly as she could—a pea shelled of her shelter—found her extra socks, her toque, her sweatshirt, and stumbled out of the tent.

A life of tent door zippers, indeed. Outside, it was see-your-breath cold. Nobody else was about, except for Tripper Steve trying to get a fire going. Ayelet walked over, crouched beside him.

"Tova's not up yet?"

Tripper Steve motioned with his head towards the lake. Ayelet looked. Tova was on her way back from a dawn paddle, soloing her canoe, her black cherry paddle an extension of her arms, the pink lake covered in a thick fudge of white mist.

When she gets back here, I will tell her about my dream, Ayelet thought to herself.

Tova, I had a dream.

After a hard day of river paddling and rough portages, breaking through endless beaver dams and lifting over downed logs, they were camped on a huge outcrop overlooking a big, windy lake. The sky changed instant to instant, cascading worlds. They had enough of an early start that they still had a fair amount of the afternoon to relax and explore their surroundings.

A bunch of CITs were off swimming, a few were napping in the tents. Natalie was taking pictures of gnarled white pines, the skyline of sharp trees, interesting rocks, moose prints in the sand. Tova, Ayelet, and Becca were sitting at the firepit, watching the sky change. Barry and Polina were reorganizing the food barrels. Tripper Steve was sawing wood with Tova's red bowsaw. Martin and the boys had paddled across the bay in two canoes to collect some driftwood they had spotted on their way past. The low wind that had been a constant all day died down, the lake turned over into its glass form; the atmospheric conditions were just right for sound to travel, and suddenly, as if they were sitting next to them, everybody at the site could hear the boys across the bay talking, even though they were a good kilometre and a half away.

"Have you seen the forearms on Tova? She's ripped!"

"You know what they say about someone with big forearms . . ."

"I'd let her jack me off with those beasts!"

Ayelet and Becca giggled. They looked towards Tova—should they call out, let them know that they were being listened to? Tova held her hand up. Wait.

"Poor Babka. He was finally about to get with Tori and she had to go and break her leg!"

"I had finally thought of the perfect line to use."

"Yeah, what was it?"

"Uh, it was going to be something like, 'Tori, I'm cold, want to come into my sleeping bag and warm me up?'"

Laughter cackling and echoing off the trees.

"Yo, I can't wait to get back to camp. Lots of 'shopping' to do! Hahaha."

"Fuck, Josh, dude, I still can't believe you stole Natalie's panties."

"What's the big deal? I needed some relief!"

"You're fucking cracked, man."

When they paddled back over, their boats loaded high with smooth white driftwood, Tova and Barry Blum were waiting at the shore. Everybody else was standing behind them, the girls looking disgusted. Oh, fuck.

Busted.

They were sitting around the firepit. Everybody had calmed down some; Natalie had stopped screaming at Josh, though it looked like she could start up again any second. The caught boys were all sitting on the same log, looking terrified. Josh's head was lowered. Tova and Barry were giving a talk about responsibility, about stealing, about personal boundaries, about consent, with Polina occasionally jumping in, handing out tissues from her fanny pack to the teary-eyed girls.

"I really can't believe this, you guys," Barry said after the initial round of lecturing. Over the past six days, Barry had grown a nearly full beard, a sandy blonde shading into white near the neck, surprising under his shaggy brown hair. Disappointment and hurt were playing out on his wide, expressive face. "This is not what I expected out of any one of you. Stealing from each other? It just, it makes me really sad. We give you guys lots and lots of leeway. You must know that. Pot smoking, drinking even, if it's done discreetly and when you're not on duty, I get that. It's camp. We all went through it. That's why Scharfy was so hard for all of us. But this? I just don't understand."

Barry's earnestness, his plain hurt, was painful to witness. On the defendants' log, Martin was fighting back tears. Simon looked embarrassed. Josh's face was set in a defiant scowl.

Tova stoked the fire. Nobody spoke.

"Listen," she said eventually, laying the fire stick down, putting her hands on her knees. "There are different kinds of stealing. Stealing from big corporations, that's A-okay. Stealing from the powerful, from the corrupt, stealing as part of the redistribution of wealth, all that is great. Stealing up. Stealing from your fellow campers, from your female peers, from those less powerful than you, there's nothing freeing or radical, or cool, about that."

"What do you think Tom is going to say when he finds out about this?" Barry asked. The boys stared at him; somehow, they hadn't even thought of Tom. Martin, no longer emotional, was now petrified. He couldn't go home early! He avoided eye contact with Ayelet. He felt embarrassed, disgusted, ashamed. Tova and the CIT staff turned their heads towards each other, spoke in whispers. The fire crackled and spat.

"How about this," Barry said, once they were facing the group again. "If you give everything you stole back, if you apologize, maybe we won't have to tell Tom. But this needs to end here. Right here. Right now. What do you think about that?"

The boys nodded. Each in turn, they said they were sorry. Martin coughed his apology out with a sob, wiped his face with his sweatshirt sleeve. When it was Josh's turn, he lifted his head, meekly mumbled "I'm sorry."

"Well, I don't forgive you!" Natalie yelled.

The fire collapsed, the bigger logs stoving in the embered wood underneath. Everybody watched the fire settle into its new shape. The evening sky was every possible shade of lavender.

It was a quiet, introspective night around the fire. Everybody went to bed early. Ayelet and Becca lay in their bags, whispering. Ayelet was mad at Martin, but after what she did with Yehouda, was it really so bad? She already knew she was going to forgive him.

The loons started to sing, their metaphysical lament seeming to come from some other place, a dimension of pure, keening sound.

— DAY SEVEN —

It rained all day. Everything was soaked through. Tova yelled about human connectivity as they paddled into the driving rain. They were covered in burns, bites, scrapes, bruises. They had sore arms, legs, hands, necks, backs. Some of them hadn't slept well for a week. Ayelet didn't think it was possible to feel any closer to other human beings. If anything, yesterday had pulled them tighter together, except for Josh, who was being shunned. Ayelet was in the bow, Becca in the middle, and Barry Blum sterning. Ayelet paddled hard and purposefully, switching every twenty strokes, holding onto the new sensations as best she could; she couldn't wait to write Tara a letter explaining it all. Yes! Yes! Yes!

Every tree they passed a unique letter in the universe's own secret alphabet.

They pulled up onto the last lake of the trip. Lake Temagami. Front country. They were greeted with the alien whir of motorboats.

That night, as they sat around comparing wounds and bites and muscle stiffnesses, Tova burned the CIT bracelets onto everybody's wrist, pieces of blue cord that Tripper Steve cut with his knife. They all huddled around, fully absorbed in the ritual.

"I am, like, *never* taking this off," Becca said, holding her bracelet up to the firelight.

The rain had stopped, but the sky was still grey. It was a cool, airy night. Off in the distance, in the direction they would be heading tomorrow, a tiny peak of otherworldly sunlight, a glisk from the closing day.

— DAY EIGHT —

Their last day was a hard lake paddle in a driving headwind, the clouds a regatta of puffy sails. When their canoes touched the beach landing that marked the end of the trip, the sense of accomplishment was a drug. They were back on land! There was Raskin, smoking a cigarette! Ayelet felt the shift into the camp time zone, a physical sensation. God, she would never forget these last eight days. "Okay folks," Tova called out, "we're not out of the woods yet! Everybody help pack up."

They stopped at the first town. Everybody rushed for the washrooms. Tova bought a newspaper. The *Toronto Star*, Sunday, August 18, 2013. Back on the bus, Ayelet watched her read every page of it as they drove south, the bus mostly quiet, nearly everybody asleep. Ayelet caught some of the headlines: "Troops Raid Mosque in Heart of Cairo," "Darlin', Save the Last Trance For Me," "Man, 23, Dead in Malton Shooting," "46 Illegal Pythons Seized in B.C.," "Has T.V. Gone as Dark as It Can Go?," "Scientists Debate Monogamy Riddle," "Cowboys Beat with Six Turnovers." Tova, immersing herself back into the world. Another moment Ayelet would carry with her forever. She decided then and there that she too was going to read the newspaper cover to cover every day, both the *Star* and the *Sing Tao Daily*. She'd start once she got back to Thornhill.

Ayelet closed her eyes. She felt the lakes, the rivers, the trails, and the trees inside her.

From now on, things were going to be different.

CHAPTER 33

THE CITS RETURN; DRUM CIRCLE IN SPITSVILLE; TOM THINKS THINGS THROUGH

"The CITs are back! The CITs are back!"

The news moved through the camp like unchecked pink eye. Ruby and her cabin were sunning on centre field when they heard. They gathered their towels and ran to the gates; by the time the bus came to a stop, the whole camp was there. Tori was also there, waiting with her cast and crutches, straightened hair, and a full face of makeup. She had spent the past three days at her parents' in Toronto, had forced them to drive her back up for the last days of camp.

Out of the bus, the CITs emerged, victorious, grease-stained bags of McDonald's in their hands. The camp rushed them like they were celebrities. They were suntanned, wind tanned, their hair longer, glowing with health, marked with bites and bruises, best friends all, thrumming with secret knowledge.

"Can I see your CIT bracelet?"

"What was it like when Tori got airlifted out?"

"There was a drum circle in town this morning! We got to go—it was really fun!"

“How was it?” Ruby asked Ayelet, who was walking by. Ayelet pulled Ruby into a hug.

“I can’t even put it into words.”

“Wow.”

Tova came up to the two of them.

“You won’t believe what you’ve missed while you’ve been gone,” Ruby said.

Brett and Dov were talking and laughing with Yehouda over by the basketball courts. For the past couple of days, ever since he had beat Danielle in a surprise upset and won the tennis ladder—how could Ruby ever forget Danielle’s stricken face on that last ace, the crowd’s confused clapping, Fallon’s uncharacteristic holler of joy, Brett’s gloating little dance to celebrate yet another victory in a summer of victories big and small?—Brett had been strutting around the camp like an arrogant prick. He and Dov were always together, laughing, teasing the girls, Brett’s arm around Dov, even if Fallon was there, though she seemed to be a good sport about being a constant third wheel. After lunch yesterday, Ruby had seen the three of them come out of the Crown land together, fjord back across the river. She had boiled with hatred, rage, and hurt, but she managed to remove herself from the heat before spilling over. Let them have their plans. Nonetheless, every morning when she woke up, Ruby couldn’t get over the fact that Brett had won. And that she had failed. She was a failure. A plump boil of bad thoughts, lanced at some point in the night, spewing all over her.

For the first time in her life, she didn’t know what she’d be doing next summer.

That morning, members of the Black Spruce First Nation had held an Idle No More rally and drum circle in the centre of Spitsville. Cindy, Geoff, Tanya, and Jojo started work an hour early so they could ATV over from the camp kitchen. Ruby had Etai boat her cabin over; when Fallon had found out about the plan, she had forbidden Ruby from going. "We can't have the campers going to a political event. What will their parents think?" Debs, thankfully, happened to be walking by and overrode Fallon, much to Fallon's barely concealed annoyance. In the end, a good portion of the camp was in attendance. There were thirty or so people from the Spruce, mostly young women, as well as Elders, leading the chants and songs, some in their regalia. Cindy, who had helped organize the rally, gave a short speech, biting and hopeful and to the point. There was drumming; there was singing. Old rhythms and songs that the lake knew well. A row of OPP officers stood off to the side, silent and intimidating. The ice cream shop gave out free cones; some townspeople gave out free dirty looks. Ruby held her girls' hands, clapped, and watched. She had been to many, many protests and events throughout her life, but to be there with her campers, next to camp, on the lake she had grown up on, in allyship and solidarity and support with the nation whose land they were on, fighting back against a system and a country that had continuously tried to dispose of them, was truly a special event.

She wished Seema had been there.

Tomorrow was the staff play. Those involved had thought about near nothing else for days, practising with their scene-mates, singing under their breath on the way to the dining hall, in the shower, under the covers. The costumes that Dr. Farberman had bought for the camp were amazing, the best costumes any production at Burntshore ever had, easy. The staff had had a blast unpacking them in the rec hall after a night of rehearsals. Fischer had barely taken off his ridiculous Reschid costume, wore it to meals and everything, though he had stopped with the accents and jokes and had actually been rather quiet lately. Shortly after the CITs returned, the staff performed the dress rehearsal, which went off with barely a hitch. Andrea and her team were still working furiously on final details for the sets. The band, consisting of Stolow on guitar, Dawn on piano, and Geoff on drums, knew the songs backwards and forwards. Dawn could barely sleep for nerves. She lay in her bed, her eyes closed, hardly able to believe it.

Tel Aviv! was coming to Burntshore.

The past couple afternoons, Tom had slipped away from the office and walked through the Crown land with the dogs. He knew the deer trails and shorelines almost as well as he knew the camp itself; he had been exploring them since he was a teenager, after all. What would it mean for the camp to own this land? What does it mean for anybody to own land? He thought of the Black Spruce, of the daily rallies, of the protest in town this morning. He hadn't gone, trying to stay above the fray, but now he felt bad about missing it. The pressure from the Spruce, Ruby's agitating from within the camp, Tom felt like he was being squeezed by two plates. Something had to give. His resolve to support Brett in this endeavour had nearly completely eroded.

If he could look at it objectively, without being Brett's father, he would probably agree with Ruby. The camp was the perfect size as it was. Why should Burntshore take up any more space? Not to mention the entire mining-the-land angle. Tom knew plenty of geologists who worked for mining companies, for the Ministry of Natural Resources, for the highest bidder. That was never what drew Tom to rocks, that was not what entranced him up in the Peel Watershed all those years ago. For Tom, geology wasn't a tool of industry but a way for human knowledge to further the species. Now Brett wanted to strip-mine for profit? Ah, well. His son always did his own thing, always had his own ways and ideas. Tom could never just ground him and tell him to go to his room. Brett had to find his own way into the world. *Dig* his own way into the world, Tom thought bitterly.

He broke through the trees and came to a big rock over the water at the south side of the bigger black sand beach. From here, he could just make out the camp. Sailboats and canoes dotted the water. Kids were jumping off the high jump tower. If he listened carefully, he could almost hear the thwack of tennis balls farther from the shore, the pong of basketballs hitting backboards. Regardless of what was going on in Tom's head or out there in the Big Wide, camp went on. He could also see the reserve. He had been thinking often of the complex historical processes that had brought them to this lake, to this moment. How many thousands of years of Jewish history, of exile, of survival, of hastily packed suitcases? The ancestors of every Jewish camper and staff at Burntshore at some point crossed the ocean to come to this continent. And the people of the Black Spruce. Countless thousands of years living right here, on and with this land, only to have it taken away from them in a blink of human history—five, six generations. He knew the history, even if he rarely let himself think about it. And yet, now Tom had the ability to do something about it. A tiny grain of sand in the estuary of their histories, but still, there it was. Also on his mind lately was the future. Not the future of Brett, not the future of the next generation, but the deep future. The geologic future. When Lake Burntshore was good and gone. Will anything from these summers—infinitely meagre in the timespan of the universe—make it into the geological record? Anything that could say: we were here. We lived as best we could. We tried to do right.

Tom bent down, picked up a rock he noticed sticking out of the black sand. He studied it, worrying it with his fingers. It was basalt, dark and cratered with air bubbles. This rock was created over a billion years ago, the result of heated liquid rock bursting forth from the mantle. Oh, the majesty of this blasted planet! Our foolishness as a species! We were splitting the atom in order to kill large numbers of people before we even understood the basic mechanisms that kept Earth alive. And now, now everybody is obsessed with Iceland, with geysers and hot rivers and glaciers! As if the geology of a place like Muskoka wasn't just as meaningful, just as profound. As if what geology had revealed was anything except the primacy of the land? Which got him back to the very point he couldn't think himself out of the past few hours: that the land couldn't be owned, that he knew it couldn't be owned.

The journey this one rock had taken, from the core to the surface, iced over again and again, under water, above water, tossed this way and that, warmed in the sand, only to be picked up by Tom. This one rock, present when the last ice age receded. (Tom thinks: Recede. Cede. Unceded. Concede. Seed. Reseed.) What complicated places lakes are.

He threw the volcanic rock as hard as he could. He still had a decent arm. The rock soared through the air, reached its penumbra, began its descent, plunked into the lake, whose surface was momentarily disturbed.

And then, it was gone.

A LETTER TO SEEMA

ear Seema:

I have been putting off writing this letter, and I feel terrible about it. I don't know what to say. My mind is a mess these days. (Sorry if this all comes out in one big jumble, I think the best thing is for me to just get everything down; if I know you, you'll tease some semblance of meaning out of it.) Sometimes I feel like I don't even know who I am. I really thought camp was a place I could go to get away from the political fights I've always been passionate about, but I was wrong. Even without the Israeli soldiers, even without Brett's buying the land, without the Black Spruce declaring their presence, the political is here. It was always here. At first, I tried to ignore it, but I can't ignore it anymore. I hope you don't hate me, Seema! Of course, of course, of course, you are right: you aren't my conscience, no. But you are my best friend. And I'm sorry if I hurt you. I miss you like crazy.

I've realized that there can be two kinds of cottage mentality. The bad cottage mentality, where everything is just a resource. It's an extractive mentality. Up here, at this moment, it's all around me. I can feel it sucking up the very air we breathe. And then, then there's the good cottage mentality. Living with the world, with the lakes and the trees. But we can't have the good cottage mentality, not really, until we've abolished the current way of things, addressed the wrongs, remade this place into what human life on this planet should be: reciprocal, ecological, vital. That's the work that needs doing, the work that I can do. Will do. When Geoff called me a settler, I was upset, I was hurt. But settler isn't a bad word, it's a label in a system. It's the system that's bad. Respecting the treaties is a start; returning the land is a start; making reparations is a start. But it's a long road, and we are still at the very beginning. Maybe I'll try and write a paper about it for Prof. Zipperstein's next class; I bet he'll tear it apart.

I will not be returning to Burntshore next summer. That is a decision I made when I decided to fight back. Here are some things I will miss about camp: Living in a cabin with over a dozen eleven-year-old girls. No billboards, no cellphone reception, very little TV. Knowing everybody's name. Being able to walk the entirety of camp within thirty minutes. The stories, the myths, the rituals, the rhythms. The meals. The sense of unified purpose. The hostas Yonatan planted all over camp, their climbing purple flowers. The Saturday afternoon smell of deli meat and disinfectant in the dining hall. The balm of loon song. Hanging out with your cabin after dinner, the cool night air, anything and everything possible.

All this to say: I'm in love with Etai. I'm in love with an Israeli soldier, a soldier who tried to fight back but perhaps didn't try hard enough. He was born into his life like we all are, saw what was wrong, and tried to do something about it. I want to try too, Seema. I want to try. I don't know what else to say. We'll continue on. We dreamed of a society. The walls weren't solid, but they were there.

What do we do now that the dream is over?

I can't wait to be back in Toronto. I can't wait to be hanging out with you.

Love always,
Yours in Struggle,
Ruby

CHAPTER 34

TEL AVIV!

The whole camp was crammed into the rec hall. Staff were sitting and standing around the outer edges. It was a cool mid-August evening, jeans and sweats and flannels and hoodies broken out. The band was wrapping up their welcome music. Backstage, Jenna and Dawn were making sure everything was ready to go.

The lights went down.

The curtains opened.

Ruby was sitting in the middle of the audience, surrounded by her girls, who were, like most everybody else, beyond excited to watch the staff perform their favourite musical. Despite hating everything about this play, Ruby could not help but feel the thrill of seeing her friends performing it on the stage. The magic of the theatre was overpowering her intellectual understanding of what she was watching. David Stein was a great Friedrich, his real-life sarcasm and humour transmogrified into dramatic wit and terrific timing; the opening number, a sprawling ensemble piece introducing Friedrich, the young Jewish lawyer without prospects in thoroughly antisemitic 1902 Vienna, the chorus singing "Life is dismal here for us Jews, we might as well jump into the Danube!"

was easily the longest Ruby had seen David without his hands down his pants. At the end of the song, the lights flashed and the gates of Auschwitz appeared for an instant—a moment that will be repeated throughout the play. She had thought she knew the play quite well, but still the vision of the Holocaust took her by surprise. She was disgusted: in 1902 the Holocaust was *not* a historical inevitability! What the fuck! She wished Etai were beside her, not in costume backstage, so she could whisper her anger into his receptive ears.

The play went on. Friedrich and Kingscourt were back from their twenty-year island isolation and visiting the miraculously reborn Jewish New Society of Palestine. Three songs—"Welcome to the New Society," "David's Story," and "Meeting People"—chronicled the wonders of the Jewish commonwealth. Vlada debuted as Miriam, New Society leader David's younger sister: she looked gorgeous, was poised and assured on the stage; there was real chemistry between her and David Stein as Miriam and Friedrich flirted and sang to each other, enough that one of the CITs—Martin, Ruby thought—yelled "get a room!" Fischer came out as the Palestinian Reschid Bey, extolling the virtues of the Jewish society and all it had done to better the Arabs' lot. Fischer was stiff up there as Reschid, a little unsure of his lines—in fact, he seemed startled to be on the stage at all. A stack of sharp emotions flipped through Ruby when Brett sauntered out as Steineck, the chief engineer who sings about curing malaria so Africa could be opened to colonization. When Barry Blum burst onto stage as Sabbatai Zevi, the audience clapped and laughed through his song about his life as the infamous failed prophet, the chorus swaying and belly dancing behind him.

Ruby was relieved when she recognized "The Debate," the final song of the first act. As the musical debate swelled and began to fade, Kingscourt and Friedrich have a brief conversation: Should they themselves stay in the Jewish New Society? Neither was willing to admit yet that they wanted to, so they danced around it, talked over each other, made audience-chortling quips. They walked off the stage arm-in-arm. The curtain closed.

As soon as intermission started, Marula came up to Ruby. She had straightened her hair, was wearing eyeliner. "Tom wants to see you in his office." Good, the play was infuriating Ruby anyways.

In Tom's office, Ruby found Tom, Brett, Debs, and Cindy. Jenna, of course, was stage-managing the play. Brett was still wearing his Steineck costume: red suit, silk cravat, monocle, bejewelled cane. A miasma of bugs hugged the lamp behind Tom.

The mood was tense.

Ruby sat in the only available chair. She didn't realize the phone on Tom's desk was on speaker until Tom started introducing the people on the conference call.

"Arnold, the Chief next door at the Spruce."

"Boozhoo, everyone."

"My lawyer, Kirsten Gurfinkle."

There was a wash of choppy static.

"Kirsten, are you there?" Tom asked.

"Hello. Can you . . . me? God . . . ucking dammit."

"Kirsten?"

There was some shuffling, a clicking noise.

"Hello? Sorry about that, I was in a dead zone or something."

"Welcome aboard," Tom said, chuckling. "And, finally, Jasmine Freshwaters, from Franklin-Webber-Strathmore, who specializes in Aboriginal law."

"Happy to be on the call."

Ruby realized she had been holding her breath. She exhaled, looked around. What was going on here?

Tom interlocked his fingers on top of his desk. He began. "We all know why we're here. I won't waste any time with preamble, my thought process, the difficult decision that was before me. Though let me just say that I *have* given this a lot of thought. This might be one of the most significant decisions I've made as owner of Camp Burntshore, as a resident on Lake Burntshore's shoreline. I take the responsibility seriously." Tom paused, unlocked his fingers, put them flat on his desk. The tension was taut enough that with a cough or sneeze the office would combust.

Tom sighed, put his hands back together. Looked directly at his son, who kept his eyes on the floor for a slow instant before bringing them up to his father's. "Though I want to trust your instincts, Brett, I've decided that acquiring this land is not in the best interest of the camp. No. Wait. Since the sale has already gone through, I've decided that we are going to transfer the land over to the Black Spruce. All of it. Free of charge."

Ruby had watched Brett's face devolve from its smug smirk to surprised anger. She could only imagine what her own face had done.

Tom continued: "I, of course, didn't have much time to speak with Cindy, with Arnold, before moving forward, but speak to them I did. We wouldn't have gone ahead if they weren't interested. But since they are, the wheels are, shall we say, in motion."

Cindy cleared her throat. "This is quite the gesture, Tom."

Arnold's voice from the phone: "When Cindy told me what you were thinking of doing, I was stunned. As representative of the Band Council, of the Black Spruce people, I want to convey our deepest thanks. This is behaviour we don't normally see from white folk. No offense." Arnold gave a hearty, gruff laugh.

"None taken," Tom said. He continued speaking: "Now, it's going to take a little while to set everything up, but things are on their way. As Jasmine clarified to me earlier, it's very difficult to transfer land over to a reserve. She'll explain further."

"Yes," Jasmine Freshwaters's voice, composed, confident, friendly, with a hint of a rural Ontario accent, concurred, "it's a real byzantine system, and not by accident, may I add. To start, transfers of this kind, while not unheard of, are still pretty rare in the Canadian context. I expect this to start changing in the coming years. Also remember, this is all situationally specific. In general, First Nations do not own title to their reserves, it is the government, the Crown, that does. So, one way to add land to a reserve is through something called an Additions to Reserve process. This is very lengthy, very bureaucratic, very difficult."

"We decided right away that this was not the right way to go," Cindy interjected.

"Is that Cindy? Hello, Cindy! Yes, even if we could get it done, the land, in a way, would just revert back to the Crown. Not the route for us, especially since there are other, more innovative ways for First Nations to hold land. These usually consist of creating corporate structures that are separate from the legal entities of the reserve. Either profit or not-for-profit. In this method, property tax must be paid, revenue generated from the land is not tax free, and so on. What we settled on doing is creating a Conservation Land Trust, owned by the Black Spruce First Nations. This is in accordance with the Ontario Conservation Lands Act. Not only is this the cleanest way to return land to the Spruce under the current federal and provincial regime, but since it is being done in the name of environmental conservation, it will be eligible for tax breaks."

Ruby was having trouble following the legalese but understood one thing clearly: land was being returned.

"In any case," Tom said, "we—as in the camp—will be paying all subsequent property taxes, and any other related fees involved with the running of the land conservancy. In perpetuity."

"Kirsten here. I've drawn up paperwork to that effect," Tom's lawyer added.

"I can't believe this," Ruby said, feeling she had to say something.

Cindy laughed, shook her head in shared disbelief. "Sometimes change happens fast."

Brett, watching all this behind lidded, disbelieving eyes, had held backlong enough. "Are you serious, Pa? This is beyond fucked up." Ruby was reminded of videos of cornered wild animals. Brett glared at Ruby. "How did she get to you? She's just pissed at me because I kicked Phil out. What did she do to get you to listen to her? What did she do?!" Brett was standing, shouting, waving Steineck's cane. "We need that land! It is rightfully ours! They lost! We won! What have those Indians at the reserve ever done for us? Yeah, they've been through shit, but we went through worse shit! We were lined up at the ditch and shot. We were gassed in the showers. Our bodies were burned! We don't owe them, or anybody, shit. We, for once in our fucking existence, won! We won!" With that, Brett raged out of the office.

Ruby was in open-mouthed shock. We have been through shit, but we were here, now.

We are here.

Cindy laughed her big, comforting laugh, melting any residual tension.

"You handled that well, Tom. Don't worry, he'll calm down."

"I just want to say," Arnold said, "that ever since your father, Dan, started the camp, Tom, we have enjoyed being your neighbour. You give our youth jobs, bring renters to our cottages, keep your part of the lake healthy. This move will now cement our relationship for generations. This repatriation will help our people immensely. To be able to be out on the land can start to undo some of the damage that's been done to us."

Ruby's heart was pounding, her hands were sweaty. She was in utter disbelief.

Tom was saying goodbye to the people on the phone. Around her, everybody was standing up, shaking hands. The meeting was over.

By the time Ruby got back to the rec hall, the second act was more than half over. Ruby stood at the back for the rest of the play; it was almost too much, that not a single camper knew that the fate of the camp had just been altered. It was the middle of "The Best of Both Worlds," one of the more popular songs from the play. Friedrich, Kingscourt, David, and Reschid had arrived in Jerusalem and were learning about its wonders, the rebuilt Temple, the Jewish Academy, the peace palace, Zion University. The underlying message of the song: Jews were no longer ashamed of being Jews. Brett must not have come back, because Etai was now playing Steineck, in a hastily devised costume. He was much funnier than Brett, with a better sense of comic timing, and had everybody in stitches. Steineck, the ruthless colonialist turned into goofy comic relief (but did that make him any less ruthless?).

In the penultimate number, "The President Dies," Rabbi Dr. Geyer is defeated, and David reluctantly becomes president, singing in his acceptance speech, "Let the stranger be at home among us!" Friedrich and Miriam declare their soaring, major-key love for each other. The final song, "Tel Aviv!," sees the skyline of Tel Aviv descend behind the characters, the gates of Auschwitz flash once again, and "Hatikvah," the Israeli national anthem, plays. A banner unfurls above the skyline, with a quote from Herzl's novel: "We always live in yesterday's future."

Delirious applause. The staff came out for their bows, were greeted with standing ovations. The band took a bow. Ruby was flush with excitement, even though she knew how fucking ridiculous this play was. It was in direct opposition with what had just occurred in Tom's office, a bright, polished lie to the hard, jagged truth of what it means to be Jewish in this world, where to belong means to exclude.

All she could think about was Etai.

The afterparty for the play was held at The Patio. Raskin and Marula drove everybody there, with Raskin having to make two trips in the van. The ensemble took up the whole interior, the patio, and spilled out into the parking lot. It was a humid, buggy night. Celebration was in the air. Beer and whiskey flowed like honey, tequila and vodka like milk. The bartenders were flooded, a drawback to being a rural bar a few kilometres from a summer camp: you never knew when a horde of flush, impatient staff would descend.

Fischer shot back his fourth whiskey, chugged the last half of his third beer. He was alone at his table, still wearing his beard and turban. Some of the locals, already flummoxed by the invasion of their normally quiet

Monday night drink by excitable Jewish teenagers, were staring at him. Fischer glared back. He looked up from the table just in time to see Michal walking away from Geoff, who was standing near the jukebox, a serious, determined look on her face. Fischer's eyes flashed.

"Yo, drummer boy, Geoff!" Fischer said, walking over to him, slapping Geoff on the shoulder. "Yo, can I talk to you? Ever since I put this on, I've been rethinking so much. So much. I'm sorry for taking Dov's side. I'm sorry for everything. I don't know what I've been thinking my entire life." Fischer let out a strange sound, somewhere between a bark and a howl. "Why is everything so fucked up?!"

"Uh-huh," Geoff said.

Fischer wasn't satisfied. "I'll burn my IDF shirt. I'll burn it. I swear to you!"

Geoff looked at Fischer. "Look, dude. First of all, I don't even know you. I don't give a shit about your guilt. Second, you think because you dressed like an Arab, some racist's idea of an Arab, for a couple days, you now have some special knowledge? That you suddenly are enlightened about the plight of the Palestinian, of the Indian? It takes more than one drunken realization. Just take a step back, man. And take that costume off!" Geoff pushed past Fischer and left the bar.

Fischer stood there for a minute, his eyes dead, before stumbling back to the bar. One whiskey. One beer.

Ruby and Etai were sitting on a wooden swing in the tall grass at the far end of the dirt parking lot. The trees heaved in the night sky. "So, what did you think of my breakout role?" Etai asked.

"Are you kidding? You were great! One of the cutest chorus members I ever saw, and the way you were able to embody that unrepentant colonist Steineck?" Ruby kissed her fingers.

Etai laughed. "Jenna was none too happy when Brett didn't come back after intermission."

"You should have seen him in Tom's office. I thought he was going to burst."

"I don't imagine Brett has been told no too often in his life."

"That is such a fucked up play."

"Ah, yes, the power of the theatre."

"It's infuriating."

"So? Quit stalling. What happened with Tom?"

Ruby paused coyly, for effect.

"Tom's going to give the land back to the Spruce."

"What?! That's fantastic."

"I'm still in shock."

"Have you seen Brett?"

"Not since Tom's office. I doubt he's happy with me."

"I hope he doesn't do something stupid."

Ruby couldn't stop thinking about the play. "The craziest thing is that Geyer's version of Israel *is* Israel, is even worse. How can people not see that?"

"We see what we want to see, most often."

"It's fucking enraging. The hypocrisy. All my kids love it, what am I supposed to say to them? How can we create such beautiful art that's so harmful to humanity?"

Etai took a drink from his beer. "Maybe I should take up acting," he mused. Ruby looked at him with wet eyes. They can talk about everything. The one thing they have not talked about is what will happen after Sunday. Ruby put her hand on Etai's leg. "Let's get out of here," she whispered into his ear.

"I'll see if Marula can drive us back." Etai got up, walked carefully inside. Marula and Vlada were leaning over the bar, were deep in conversation with one of the bartenders, a townie with tattooed arms, a vest, and a hipster haircut. Etai stumbled back out. They got into the lone taxi waiting in the parking lot.

"Burntshore, b'vakasha," Ruby said.

CHAPTER 35

STAFF BANQUET; A FIRE

Andrea was pissed at whomever decided to schedule the staff play and the staff banquet back-to-back. Who would do such a thing?! After how many sleepless nights toiling over the play sets, and then, boom! No time for rest, Andrea, no "we appreciate everything you do for this camp, Andrea, enjoy your day off!" No, no, no, instead it was, "Andrea, we have to start making the decorations for the staff banquet," it was, "Andrea, we need this and we need that, what do you mean you don't have any left, can you order some," it was, "you need to spend your day off in the rec hall painting psychedelic backdrops." Her anger was more amorphous than focused—it wasn't Debs or Tom she was mad at, it was the camp. Not since her first year as staff did Andrea remember the play and banquet being back-to-back. Yet nobody knew Andrea was upset; nobody *would* know. As always, she kept it in. She was a team player, a working part of the glorious machine that is Camp Burntshore, even if she remained mostly in the shadows. She still wanted both the play and the banquet to be as successful as possible. Well, the play was a smash, and it looked like the banquet was going to be just as spectacular.

For a rare moment, she let herself bask in self-pride.

Then, back to work.

Standing in the dining hall before everybody arrived, Debs congratulated Andrea and her crew on a job well done. It really looked like the '60s in there. The walls were covered in swirling purples and oranges and greens. There was a bin of tie-dyed headbands at the door. Bubbles from the rented bubble machine floated languidly. The band, wearing shorts and bikini tops, were covered in neon paint. There was a station where staff could paint their own faces and bodies. The tables were in five long rows, set with tablecloths, plates, and cutlery for a five-course meal.

Staff banquet was one of the Burntshore traditions Debs cherished the most. The first night since pre-camp where all of the staff had the night off together: shortly, the CITs would take over from the cabin staff and the banquet would begin. A transition within the tradition, this would be the first night the CITs were fully—well, nominally, Debs would not be turning her walkie off—in charge. And it was a special night for the campers as well. Each unit had their own banquet night tradition: unit 1 all crammed into the ball hockey rink for a big outdoor sleepover; unit 2 watched *Ace Ventura*; unit 3 watched *Dazed and Confused*; unit 4 had a bonfire at the CIT Pit, which, next summer, if they were lucky enough to be asked back, would be *their* CIT Pit. After the last couple of days—she could still feel the adrenaline of standing up against Brett, putting the camp's best interests first—Debs was relieved to have something ordinary, expected, to take her mind off things. The second last night of camp was always just that: the second last night of camp.

At eight-thirty the banquet team opened the doors. Staff, most of them dressed in their best hippie clothes, entered the transformed dining hall. Cindy was at the barbecue on the porch, wearing one of the headbands Andrea had made, grilling steaks. The band was playing floaty, noodley music. As they had done the past few summers, Casey, Barry Blum, and

David Stein had gone into town and bought sports jackets at Value Village; this year, Dov, Michal, and Orit had tagged along, and they were all flaunting their discount finery. Ruby and Etai were wearing matching blue sarongs, Ruby in a low-cut black T-shirt, the white crow bead necklace she had made at the beginning of the summer.

Andrea surveyed the scene, unnoticed in the kitchen doorway: the banquet was in full swing. The staff were in the early phases of what promised to be a riotous night of revelry. More importantly, for the first time in nearly two weeks, she was free. She went into the kitchen, sat in Cindy's chair to take a breather. Before the steaks were served, she was asleep.

Stolow was on the stage, soloing in F Dorian over a slow, oceany progression being provided by Tyler's bass and Vlada's keys—because, apparently, she was also an amazing pianist. Stolow was playing an electric he had borrowed from one of the campers, a real arrogant thirteen-year-old with a mop of blonde hair who could play any Van Halen solo you requested note-for-note. The guitar was a real beauty: a green PRS with inlaid frets. He couldn't believe anybody would bring a guitar like this to camp, but it was exhilarating to be playing an electric again, after two months away. Last night he and Jojo had had their first fight; surprise, surprise, it was about Brett and the land. Jojo was upset that Stolow had told Ruby he was going to sit it out, that he didn't come to any of the rallies. Stolow realized he was in the wrong and apologized. One thing the fight crystallized for him was that their relationship was more serious than he had thought. Thinking of Jojo made him all warm and fuzzy. He leaned back and dug into his solo.

The food was served. The staff ate, they drank, they were merry (for the day after tomorrow, they would go home). The steaks were juicy, the sides were plentiful, the vibes were solid. Once Tom finished eating and bid the staff adieu, things loosened considerably. Water bottles of dark and clear liquor appeared on the tables. Blunts and pipes were lit on the balcony. Ruby—who had shared a whole bottle of Jack Daniels with Danielle, passing the bottle back and forth under the stall divider as they sat in their cabins' toilets—dropped a whole cob of butter-slathered corn on the ground just as she was about to take her first bite. She picked it up, studied it through doubled vision. It was coated in dirt and hair, but eh, fuck it. It's a party! She chomped down.

After the meal everybody recongregated at the back of the dining hall for the "summer debriefing." First, the Wall of Jewish Love was revealed. A ten-foot-high bubble chart drawn on kraft paper showing all of the summer's hookups. From serious relationships to a make-out session behind the trip shed, any coupling that was known, rumoured, or guessed at, appeared on the chart. Marula and Vlada, Ruby and Etai, Dov and Marula, Stolow and Jojo, Phil and Talia, Talia and Yehouda. Tyler's usual slew of low-key hookups. "Yehouda fooled around with that CIT Ayelet?" Ruby whispered to Marula. "I guess so! *And* Tori?! That's some serious CSR!" "And Michal and Geoff?! I'm in shock!"

Next were the staff awards, handed out by Barry Blum. Casey got hottest guy, which was a much-needed pick-me-up; ever since some of the car company workers—who had gotten the idea from Ruby when a camper overheard her talking to Etai about organizing against Brett—had tried to unionize and Casey dissolved the entire game he had been in a foul mood. Hottest girl went to Michal, the first time in years that it wasn't Talia, who smiled graciously. Biggest bitch went to Ruby—she had beaten Fallon once again, for the third year in a row.

Thus concluded the formal proceedings of the evening. Debs said goodnight, politely brushed off everybody's begging her to stay, told Raskin not to be out too late. "Don't worry, Debs, we'll take good care of him!" Casey announced. Stolow and the band started up again with "Scarlet Begonias." Most of the lights were turned off. Pretty soon the celebration would disperse to spread throughout the camp. Ruby got herself and Etai two large black coffees, "for fortification": it was going to be a long night. Marula came up to them, asked what kind of wacky shape they were going to get their molecules into tonight.

The band was just easing into the jam section of "Fire on the Mountain" when the CIT Martin exploded into the dining hall. He was panting, his hands on his knees, his shoes untied. Those near the doors turned to him.

He stood up straight. "A cabin's on fire!" he hollered. Stolow hit an ugly chord on the guitar. The music stopped. After a few seconds of chaos, someone flipped the lights on, and Barry Blum stepped onto the nearest bench. "Okay, everybody. You know the drill! Cabin staff—gather all the campers at the waterfront and do your call-offs! Speciality staff, go make sure your area is clear! Has anybody called the fire department? Where's Tom?!"

The staff rushed out of the dining hall. Within seconds, Stolow was running full bore down the gravel road towards Ropes—barefoot, topless, covered in glowing paint, a pick still gripped tightly between thumb and pointer. He couldn't remember where he left the PRS, didn't even remember putting it down, but who gave a fuck. He bent his head down and pumped his legs faster. The cold night air he was heaving into his chest scorched his lungs. He was running the fastest he had ever run; good thing he hadn't missed a morning jog all summer. When he skidded into Ropes, he turned on the lights—sudden brightness booming into the dark forest—and performed the safety checks. Shed. Clear. Climbing wall. Clear. Low ropes. Clear. High ropes. Clear. Tire swings. Clear. The surrounding forest. All clear. He took two big gulps of air, then ran, a little slower now, avoiding the rocky gravel as best he could, back to the dining hall and down to the waterfront.

When he arrived, the whole camp was already assembled. Unit heads had arranged their cabins in neat lines and were completing their counts. The staff had shaken off their drunkenness and were tending to their campers. Debs was everywhere at once. There was a frazzled, giddy excitement in the air. Some of the younger kids were crying. The CITs, huddled by themselves under the dining hall balcony, looked serious, worried, glum. Their first night of real responsibility, and a cabin had gone up in flames! The heady smell of the fire wafted over the assembled camp, thin sheets of smoke expanding over the lake, which itself was aflame from the rising full moon.

"Which cabin is on fire?" Ruby asked Andrea when she walked by, Andrea's walkie squawking incoherently. Ruby had been pretty drunk, but it had mostly flushed out of her as soon as Martin showed up. Hopefully her campers, chattering all around her in loud whispers, hadn't noticed anything off about her.

"Cabin 9," Andrea said, not breaking her long-legged stride. Did she not know that that was Ruby's own cabin?

"Where's Fallon?" Ruby shouted, realizing her unit head wasn't with them, suddenly panicked. "Danielle, watch the kids, I gotta go find Fallon!" Ruby ran off towards cabin line, Danielle calling her name, saying something that sounded like *be careful*.

Ruby stopped as she approached the cabin (which she would have gotten to a lot faster if not for the fact she was wearing a sarong and flip-flops). It was quite the scene. Half the wooden building was burning steadily, orange flames licking the black sky above, jumping up to the lower branches of the pines. Ruby could feel the heat of the fire from fifteen feet back. Yonatan and Tova were there, aiming fire extinguishers from a safe distance, their faces glowing. Tom was watching the blaze from a little farther back, yelling into his cellphone. Fallon was there too, sitting on the stoop of cabin 11, sobbing loudly, Jenna comforting her. Ruby ran over.

"Fallon! What happened?" Fallon's head shot up. She looked startled to see Ruby, started bawling again.

"I was with . . . with Brett. He had told me to meet him at your cabin, I thought we were going to, you know, fool around or something. He started, I don't know, going insane, yelling about the land, about you, about Cindy and the reserve. He was picking up stuff, throwing it, trying to break the lock on your toolbox. He grabbed a bug spray, started spraying it, I guess he must have lit a lighter, he yelled, 'This is what I'd like to do to that nosey bitch,' and suddenly there was a whoosh and your . . . your bed was on fire, he wouldn't stop spraying, and I started screaming. He, he, he . . . oh my god, Ruby, all of your kids' stuff!" Fallon blew her nose into Jenna's proffered Kleenex, started howling, Jenna there-thereing her. Fallon suddenly stopped crying, made a small sniffle. She was looking at something, her eyes big and reflecting the red of the flames. Ruby followed Fallon's gaze—there was Brett, sitting on a rock in the shadows, just out of the light of the lamp posts and fire, his knees as high as his head, his hands in his black hair. He looked up, saw Ruby.

"What the fuck, Brett? What is *wrong* with you?"

Brett jumped up. His shirt was black with ash, his eyes bloodshot and tearing. He did not look well; had he slept since she'd seen him in Tom's office last night? He glared at Fallon and his mom before turning to Ruby. "That's not what happened! She's a lying bitch. This is all your fucking fault, Ruby! I was trying to improve the camp, I was going to more than double our land base, triple, no, quadruple our income stream. I was going to finally impress you, but no, you had to go and turn my own father against me! You have no fucking idea what's good for this camp, Ruby. I know! *I* know. I'm the only one who knows. The only one!" Brett turned his spluttering rage onto Tom, who had materialized beside Ruby. "You think Ruby is so innocent, Dad? Why don't you go look in her toolbox?!"

Just then, Raskin and Dov arrived with more fire extinguishers, both of them taking huge striding leaps as they ran to assist Tova and Yonatan. Tom was staring at Brett, his phone in his hand at his side. "Now, son," he said. Ruby had never heard Tom call Brett *son* before.

Brett looked at his father. His eyes had become black mirrors, reflecting the orange flames, the pines, the moonlight. "Don't *now son* me. You're just as guilty as everybody else. Selling out the camp! I can't believe you. What would Grandpa think if he could see what you've done? He was a proud Zionist, would be disgusted at you returning land to the natives! Land for peace? More like land for the crematoriums! I try and do something good for this camp, for our people, and you spit in my face. I've had enough of your fucking bullshit! I'm out of here! You'll see—Camp Burntshore is nothing without me! Nothing! It'll fall apart within a year! Yalla, Dov." He stomped off in the direction of his cabin. Tom watched him go. Now Jenna was crying. Fallon looked stricken.

Dov looked at everybody in turn; Ruby had seen that sheepish face once before, when he was about to perform his song at coffee house. "Dude, you need to calm yourself!" Dov yelled after Brett. "Afta al atzmecha! You took this too far!"

Ruby was still not fully sober, but Brett's rampage, the hot smell of the fire—which, despite the circumstances, smelled undeniably good—had focused her. Tom was comforting Jenna and Fallon. Raskin, Yonatan, and Tova were standing in the dirt, fire extinguishers in hand. Dov was stomping out red and orange embers that had landed on the ground. The fire had more or less been contained; the flames were gone, but the roof was still smouldering.

From far off, the sound of sirens.

The fire had put a damper on the banquet, no doubt, but after the fire trucks left, and the campers were taken back to their cabins and calmed down, most of the staff were able to regroup. Ruby's girls could not return to their cabin, however, so Ruby, Danielle, and Dawn stayed with them as they got settled in the rec hall, where they were going to spend the night. Both Ruby and Danielle were beginning to feel hungover. Tova and Debs went around collecting second mattresses, sleeping bags, and pillows, brought them to the cabin 9 girls along with fresh cookies from the kitchen. They were going to have a fun sleepover! The girls were manic, telling the story of the fire again and again. At some point Etai came by to entertain them. It ended up being a fun night. Ruby hadn't felt so ensconced in her cabin in weeks.

Elsewhere, the party continued. Some old staff had driven up for the night. Phil and Margolis showed up too, well after midnight to avoid Tom and Debs. Phil had hoped to see Ruby; after hearing what happened, he settled on locating Talia. Talia, however, had other plans. She found Yehouda drinking with a bunch of other staff in the head staff lodge. Yehouda jumped up to hug her. "Shalom, babe!" Talia pushed Yehouda hard in the chest. "What the fuck is wrong with you?! Fooling around with CIT girls?!" Yehouda smiled, waved his beer bottle around. "I thought we were cool." "I'm not your fucking girlfriend, Yehouda, but those CIT girls are off fucking limits!" She slapped him, hard, and left the lodge.

News of Brett's theatrics spread through the camp. The fire beautiful against the night sky. Dov single-handedly putting out the flames. Brett's face maniacal with laughter as he told his father off. Along with astonishment, there were the questions, pondered over well past sunrise. Did Brett really start the fire on purpose? What had happened? What was he trying to prove? Was he gone from Burntshore for good? What did Tom and Jenna think? Was Ruby in the right to have convinced Tom to give the land back?

And, most importantly: What did this mean for the future of our beloved camp?

Once all the campers were asleep—which, all things considered, was a miracle to have happened at all—Ruby went to check out the damage. The wet ground in front of the cabin was covered in the large boot prints of the firemen. Ruby laughed remembering Talia and Michal flirting with them as they milled around in their bulky suits. Ruby entered the cabin. Most of the girls' stuff would be fine; it was only the staff quarters, the bathroom, and most of the roof that had burned down. Everything was soaking wet. Oh well, her girls now had a story they would never forget. And in a few years, it would just be another legend of camp, a part of Burntshore mythology. Ruby sat on Arielle's bed, the only dryish one. From the vantage point of the far end of the night, Brett's actions didn't seem that surprising. Of course he was going to lash out. Thank god nobody got hurt.

When Ruby went back to the rec hall, the moon had set and the sun was rising on the last full day of camp. A few staff were still awake; they nodded at her as she walked by. Ruby stopped to take in the lake. She was in no rush. Besides, who could sleep with all this light?

CHAPTER 36

LAST DAYS

The last full day of camp always made Debs philosophical. What better reminder that things end, what better dry run for the ending that awaits us all? Debs took a sip of her coffee (only one a day now—one of the myriad changes that awaited her and Raskin). It is not just time we are stuck in (how boring would that be?). We are trapped in a limitless series of unending orbits: our Earth orbiting the sun, the sun orbiting the heat heart of the galaxy, the galaxy orbiting the universe, the universe orbiting the ever-plunging mystery. But that's not all: we orbit our age, our friends, our place in the world, our days and nights, our meals and low moments, the luck of our birth, the certainty of our death, the patch of ground we call home. The yearly orbit around Lake Burntshore was, once again, completing its circuit. Yet, like all things, it would come back around.

Debs had thought often of trying to write thoughts like these out, getting them published; not as the dry academic writing about Jewish summer camp she read at Brandeis, but as a short story, maybe a poem. But every year it's the same: by the time she recovers from the preceding summer at camp, it's time to start planning for the next. By Labour Day she and Tom and Jenna will be discussing which staff to invite back, before moving on to CITs, the hiring process, all of it. For them, camp never really ended. When Debs, after staying up nearly all night discussing it with Raskin, decided to talk to Tom about buying the land—she had given him her swear jar, telling him she wanted to help offset the costs of cancelling the sale—she had chosen to take a side, to push back. She had had enough of being neutral. She wanted Burntshore to remain a place she could send her daughter to.

She was happy she had done her part.

Throughout that long, bittersweet day, campers lugged their duffels—retrieved from under beds, stuffed full of clothes and shoes, bookends to the beginning and end of summer—to the rec hall, portaging them like soft-shelled canoes. Some of the CIT girls were running around asking if anybody wanted to swim in a kiddie pool of mac and cheese, laughing uncontrollably. Tova and Yonatan were clearing out the burnt cabin; all of cabin line smelled charred. Last minute swim badge tests were underway at the waterfront. Andrea was handing out finished pottery to the campers who remembered to come by and claim their masterworks. It looked like she had finally gotten a bit of sun.

By lunchtime, cabin 9 were living in a fort of duffel bags. Staff and campers came by to visit, to hear the story of the fire—which had already become a story of personal and communal triumph, even though none of the girls were actually there. Cindy stopped by for a visit, had the girls in stitches telling stories of kitchen mishaps over the years. Cindy told Ruby some news of her own: she was going to chair a committee to help integrate the new land into the life of the Spruce, run the conservancy.

"What?! That's fantastic! Mazel tov! Does this mean you'll be leaving the kitchen?"

Cindy bellowed. "No way! And leave the health of three hundred campers to Geoff?"

Speaking of Geoff, he came by with three steaming platters of nachos, received Ruby's ribbing about him and Michal with stoic acceptance. Fallon visited numerous times, gave Ruby a hug, said she was sorry; Ruby accepted her apology, would joke with Danielle later about Fallon having definitely ruined her chances at a good reference letter from Tom. Ruby had recently received the undergraduate calendar in the mail and was choosing courses for next year. June sat on top of her, helping to choose between "Palestinian Speculative Fiction" and "Special Topics in Postcolonialism: Uprisings Then and Now." "I think you should take the fiction course! Haven't you done enough poco already?" Ruby took June's face in her hands. Who was this girl? She hugged her, hard.

Later, Ruby, Danielle, and Dawn were lounging on the duffel bags, their girls on their sleeping bags on the floor. "What will you remember about this summer, Ruby?"

"Hmm. Saving you girls from the inferno. The first time I was on a ski boat with Etai. Our canoe trip." What will she remember about the battle with Brett? The land? The Black Spruce rising up? Will she lose the all-encompassing feeling that had been brewing for weeks, had peaked in Tom's office two nights ago—the sensation that change was possible, that the world can be remade better, that life, that glorious explosion, was thrilling and endless?

The girls got off their bags and piled onto their counselors. "We're going to miss you so much! Will you visit us in the city?"

Arielle crawled over to Ruby, held her tight. "This was the best summer ever. Thank you so much."

After Lunch, Ruby and Etai sat on the pink rock at the river, watching the waterfall, discussing the summer.

"Can I stay with you in Toronto for a while?"

Ruby held back relieved laughter. "Well. You might have to sleep in the basement."

"I'll just post up with Otter!"

Ruby laughed. "He'd love that. So, you're not going to go back to Israel?" The one thing they had not talked about. Here it was, as plain as the water rushing past them.

Etai shrugged, bit his lip. A habit he had picked up from Ruby. "I don't know. What would I even do here if I stayed?"

"Teach Hebrew. Start a krav maga studio. Hang out at the Aroma at the Promenade with the other Israeli expats."

"All good options."

"What would happen if you went back?" Ruby asked, her voice smaller than intended.

Etai shrugged. "I'd probably refuse to serve in the territories again, get thrown in jail again. Should I give up on all that, come to Canada? Or should I stay in Israel and fight for the dismantling of the Zionist state?"

"I guess you just have to do what you feel comfortable with. There's plenty to fight for here. Just as much."

"In the sixties, before the six day war, when lots of Israelis were emigrating, there was a joke that the last person at Ben Gurion Airport should flick the country's lights off."

"Funny, but so what?"

"So, if everybody who was anti-apartheid abandoned Israel, who would be left?"

"I see." Ruby watched a branch float past them. "Well, what if, let's say, there was a clerical error, and the airport lost your booking?"

Etai looked at her, mischief on his face. His curly hair had grown a few inches since his arrival, wavy curtains to his adorable face. "Stranger things *have* happened."

"A clerical error isn't a life sentence."

"No, I guess not."

"A clerical error can be reversed."

"If it ends up being made in error, you mean?"

"Yeah. A clerical error made in error. Exactly."

"I'd be deserting, you know."

"I know."

"Worse even than being a sarvanim. The consequences could be severe."

"I guess you'll just have to decide if it's worth it or not."

They sat in silence for a while.

Etai put his hand on Ruby's knee. "You saved the camp, Ruby."

"It wasn't just me. Actually, it wasn't me at all. You think Tom would have changed his mind if it wasn't for Cindy and everybody at the Spruce? I do *not* think Tom would want to deal with roadblocks next summer. The parents would flip! And, besides, is camp really saved? I wouldn't be too sure about that. It looks like the Israeli presence is here for good."

"Did you hear those two kids, the Jareds, are planning on making aliyah, enlisting? Dov's promised to help with the paperwork."

"Well, fuck me."

"Imagine how much further we could go. Return all the land. Dismantle all this bullshit. Turn everything inside out. *Right-side* out. This one event starting a chain reaction, first Burntshore, then other camps, then entire cities, the government. The entire country flipped, the world."

"I wish. Tom happens to be a decent guy, I guess, in some respects. Not everybody in power is like Tom, though. Far from it. And we still had to convince him. But there aren't too many Toms out there, especially in our community. I'd say for every one Tom, there are ten Bretts, ten Dovs, ten Dr. Farbermans."

"A hundred Dr. Farbermans."

"A thousand!"

"Tom has as much power as anybody should ever have: in charge of four hundred kids? Anything more than that, you're fucked."

"They'll have to start all over again next year."

"They will. And they won't."

They watched the river's ceaseless tumble into the lake.

:

Cindy had the afternoon off. She spent it on the rocking chair on her porch, a pitcher of iced tea her sister had brought by and an Agatha Christie on the small table beside her. Not that she was doing any reading; she was too focused on her new role, full of possibilities for the returned land. They could open an Anishinaabemowin language immersion centre. Maybe Geoff could run it, put his gift for languages to good use. They could start hunting camps, reinvigorate the traplines. Cindy could run an intensive cooking-on-the-land seminar.

Cindy guffawed. She knew she was getting away from herself. These things take time. Time, money, intention. Did she mention money? Still, she was proud of how things worked out this summer, of her role in it. When Tom knocked on her door, a container of homemade mandelbrot in his hands, an apology on his lips, Cindy knew right away that things on Lake Burntshore were going to change. As in life, as in cooking: take what you've got, do what you can. Not that all the problems of the Spruce had been solved; far from it. Not that the world wasn't still a dark, violent place. But on the shores of Burntshore, things, for now, weren't half bad.

Which was exactly what she would say to Giiwedin when she saw him in a few weeks. The trip was all planned. Her second eldest, Ziibi, was going to drive up from Toronto a few days before Labour Day weekend to pick her up, and they'd drive down to Syracuse on the Friday. Her oldest, Freddie, was also going to fly in from Vancouver. It was going to be a little family reunion. Cindy and her boys. She took a long, cold drink from the iced tea. She couldn't wait to tell Giiwedin what had happened this summer, what the Spruce had accomplished.

Thinking of Giiwedin's surprised face, Cindy sighed, laughed. She took another sip from her iced tea, picked up her book.

The last night of the summer, and the camp quaked with energy. It would be a long, many-armed night. Since the time of Tom's father, the last night of camp started off with the camp-wide banquet and ended with a bunk night, a time for cabin and staff to reminisce, feel close, say goodbye. Once the banquet—this summer's theme: space exploration—ended, the CITs would have the run of the camp. It was their last night as campers; most of them will not return as staff, and the ones who did would be on the other side of the camper-staff divide.

It was a different kind of bunk night for Ruby and cabin 9. They had gathered all of their belongings that weren't burnt and had set up a temporary home in the rec hall. They played cards, lay on their bags. Talked about the first things they'd do once they got home. Cry! Eat! Burn myself raw in the shower! God, remember hot showers!

"Ruby, tell us a story like you used to!"

"Okay, everybody gather in. This story is about the cabin 9 kick-asses. Now, the kick-asses had lived through a lot. They had lived through thunderstorms and heat waves and even a fire. But still their search for a home did not stop. One summer, they came to a shore of a beautiful lake. There were already people living on the lake. They had lived there for so many years, they couldn't even count. The kick-asses, on the other hand, came from a long line of people who never stayed in one place for long. The people of the lake invited them to stay for a while on their land, to enjoy the bounty of the lake and the forests, and the kick-asses gratefully took them up on their offer. They lived together for many happy years."

"That's a beautiful story," June said, "even with the changes. Even though you're a meat eater."

Before turning off the rec hall lights, they played their last round of roses and thorns.

Ruby and Danielle fell asleep in each other's arms, after once again going over Danielle's defeat to Brett in excruciating point-by-point detail, the match by far the most surprising thing that had happened that summer as far as Danielle was concerned.

At six the next morning, Jojo and Geoff arrived on Jojo's ATV to start getting ready for breakfast. Geoff was down in the basement to grab some more hot chocolate mix when he heard noises in the workout room. The Black CIT with the fantastic dreadlocks was there with his girlfriend, the two of them in a single sleeping bag, their clothes strewn about. It smelled like sex and pot.

"Hey Geoff, you want to smoke some nice, clean weed?"

"Simon!" the girl exclaimed, shoving him in the bag.

Geoff laughed. "No. Thanks, though."

Geoff left them with their nice, clean weed and went to start boiling the water. It was his last day working in the camp kitchen. Geoff thought about his concept of the kitchen as a renewable resource, the land as constant change; what better proof than what had gone down this summer? The lake's allegiances shift and swell, but the land is, and always will be, the land. In a week he'd be heading down to Toronto for his second year of university. He and Ruby had promised to spend more time together this year. Geoff had his own room in a house in Parkdale, she could sleep over whenever she wanted to come down from the suburbs. Though he had yet to deposit the cheque from Tyler's dad, on his laptop back in his room he had countless tabs open: electric guitars, fancy easels and paint sets, descriptions of creative writing courses at the university. Geoff didn't know what the future held for him, and for the moment he felt totally okay with that. For now, he was going to make a massive tank of hot chocolate, with extra powder.

The last morning. The dining hall full of sad, tired, excited, dirty kids. The sadness a liquid presence, diffuse, airborne. Tom gave his farewell speech. Outside, there was lots of crying, lots of hugging, the dogs getting involved wherever they could. A bunch of girls and a few guys crowded around Dov and Michal, hugged them, cried. "Will you come back next year?" "Are you going to miss us?" "Ma, what do you think? If Tom'll have us, we'll be back."

The buses waited at main gate. Some kids were getting picked up by their parents. The Ottawa kids were being driven home by Raskin, had already left. Others will have to catch a flight from Toronto. Most of the staff will go home on the buses; those with cars will take their friends. While everyone was at breakfast, Casey had made three low-pro trips from his cabin to stuff the duffel bags of candy into his car. He stood there, staring at the bulging bags: What am I going to do with all of this? Ruby, Etai, Marula, and Vlada were going to Marula's cottage for a few days before returning to the city for the staff party at Tyler's. Ruby had never been more tired; she couldn't wait to sleep with Etai in what she had started thinking of as their bunkie. They piled into the car, drove out of camp.

Out on the road, the goldenrod was just starting to come in.

EPILOGUE

Once the campers and the staff leave, Yonatan takes a long nap. He wakes up in the late afternoon. There's a lot of work to do in the coming days. First, he will go through each cabin, to see what the state of repair is, taking notes. He will rearrange the bunkbeds, fix the ones that need fixing and are fixable, drag to the dump those that are beyond repair. He'll spend two days staining the dining hall back porch. He'll mow centre field. He'll mow new field. He and Tom have already spoken about their plans for cabin 9. It's going to get a total rebuild, and while they're at it, they're also going to rebuild cabin 20, which had been falling apart for a few summers. In his off-hours, he'll work on the pizza oven he's building at the waterfront. He had been collecting the needed materials all summer, had gotten permission from both Tom and Cindy. He fills with excitement just thinking about it—next summer, for EP, cabins could make their own pizzas on the beach! He had heard a rumour that a CIT had successfully grown twenty marijuana plants, somewhere in the forest across from CIT Town. He's going to try to find them, if they're actually there. Speaking of which, he has to plant his autumn vegetables. Once the camp is cleaned, spruced up, he'll be needed on maintenance for the month and a half of retreats Tom rents the camp out for. Yonatan will stay until the end of October, and then it will be back to the furniture warehouse for six months, living in his uncle's basement in Richmond Hill.

The bugs are pretty much gone. In a few weeks they will be gone gone. Yonatan will start sleeping outside. Before any of that, though, before the work and the pizza oven and the retreats, Yonatan takes a canoe and paddles out to Big Rock Island. It's his first time in a canoe all summer; he's out of practice, and there is a decent headwind, sending him zigzagging across the lake. Eventually, he finds his j-stroke, paddles hard until he's at the island, scrambles onto the rocks, feeling more than a little relieved, breathing deep, his muscles alive. From the island he can see the camp shoreline, the reserve (where he heard Stolow was staying with Jojo for a few days before returning to the city), the Crown land. What was once the Crown land. The land formerly known as Crown. Camp Burntshore is now sandwiched between land of the Black Spruce First Nation.

He picks up a stick, stirs the ashes of the main island firepit. It was a unique summer, that's for sure. He didn't think they'd be seeing Brett anytime soon (Yonatan had found a pile of black hair outside of the staffies this morning, where he left it for the wind, the birds). Doubtful he would ever take over the camp now. Who would? Maybe Tom would give it to everybody, to be run communally. And the whole thing with the land. Unexpected, but beautiful. One night soon he'll have to go over to the reserve, speak with Cindy, congratulate her on her new role. Yonatan had heard that once the transfer had officially gone through, the Spruce were going to hold a ceremony to commemorate the moment, probably on the black sand beaches, or maybe at the mouth of the river.

Yonatan looks out over the lake.

The sun destroys itself on the pines. It's roughly as far away from the solstice as the day he arrived was prior to it. The breeze has stopped. The water is not quite flat, but it is supremely calm; the lake's mood has changed once again. He stretches and pulls the canoe back into the water. Paddling back, each stroke thrusting him forward a good distance, the paddle feels more natural in his hands now, an extension of himself, how Stolow or Tyler or Vlada must feel holding a guitar. He can see the buildings of camp, the shoreline, the swim, ski, and paddle docks, the toothy shoreline of trees, all reflected in the shimmering water, upside down, unreal, twinned, the camp settling into its sudden emptiness in two distinct worlds. Yonatan pulls the paddle long and slow through the water, lifts it out, sets up for another stroke. The lake has smoothed to glass now; there isn't a single ripple. He's floating in a doubled world, cutting a straight liquid trail from Big Rock Island to the rocky beach beside the paddle docks. In a moment, already close enough that he can see the individual pebbles on the beach, he'll stop paddling, let the canoe glide the rest of the way before softly nudging the sand at the lip of the lake, slowing to a stop, perching on the shore, making landfall.

ACKNOWLEDGEMENTS

I've wanted to write a novel about Jewish sleepover camp since I was sixteen. The world of camp, the devotion, the problems, the land, the unique phenomenon of it all: I was, and remain, somewhat obsessed. Camp is many, many things; one of those things is a fount of endless story. Why not make my own story? Invent a camp, invent a lake, invent people with their own special relationship to that camp, that lake. From there, the world of Burntshore took shape, seemingly without much input from me, and now here we are.

Unending thanks and gratitude to Jen Sookfong Lee, my editor at ECW. I wish all writers could experience what it's like to have an editor who believes in and fights for their book as much as Jen believed in and fought for this one. Thank you to Victoria Cozza, Jess Albert, Emily Ferko, Jen Albert, Claire Pokorchak, Michael Holmes, and the entire team at ECW. *Lake Burntshore* couldn't have had a better home.

Tremendous thanks to Nathan Adler, who read the entire manuscript and gave me invaluable feedback not only on the Anishinaabe elements, but the world of Lake Burntshore as a whole. Deepest gratitude as well to Waubgeshig Rice who gave me his time and expertise as I was writing the earliest drafts. Nathan and Waub helped make the novel what it is today. Miigwetch!

Alysha Dawn, for designing the maps of the lake and the camp. Elias Hashem, for copyediting the novel's Hebrew. Lorraine Land, for discussing the legal in and outs of giving land to First Nations reserves. Dr. Ian Power, for smoothing out some of the finer points of the geology of Lake Burntshore. Dan Sadowski and Lindsay Nicholson, for crafting the list of pop songs one would hear at a camp social in summer 2013. Tyler Ball, Catriona Wright, and David Huebert, for reading early drafts of the novel and giving invaluable, insightful feedback. StichMethod Guitar, for his YouTube video tutorials, especially on the "Stash" jam.

Some of the books mentioned or quoted from in the novel are real. Others are entirely made up. The quote on page 221 is from Peggy J. Blair's *Lament for a First Nation*. The quote on page 223 is from V.P. Neimanis's article on "Crown Land" in *The Canadian Encyclopedia*. *Tel Aviv!* is a fictional play based on a very real novel. The discussion about Jewishness and the six million murdered on page 245 is inspired by Isaac Deutscher's article "Who is a Jew?"

A lot of reading went into the writing of this novel. Books that were particularly important include: *The Temagami Experience: Recreation, Resources, and Aboriginal Rights in the Northern Ontario Wilderness* by Bruce Hodgins; *Ontario Rocks: Three Billion Years of Environmental Change* by Nick Eyles; and *"How Goodly Are Thy Tents": Summer Camps as Jewish Socializing Experiences*, by Amy L. Sales and Leonard Saxe.

My friends and family are all over the pages of this novel. I'd rather not imagine what my life would be like without Cath Kreuter, David Kreuter, Ben Kreuter, Rachel Kreuter, Rebecca Garber, Sam Berns, Mark Korn, Susan Korn, Jenn Korn, Daniel Korn, Jon Geiger, Dana Bronsteter, Myra Bloom, Eric Schmaltz, Nick Kiverago, Arezou Soltani, Natasha Bastien, Brent Bellamy. Jesse and Max, my new nephews. To all the dogs, everywhere.

To my JSNTG comrades. To the LJS network. To my new academic, literary, and activist community in Peterborough, on the shores of the Otonabee.

A special shoutout to Ben Kreuter and Jeff Ebidia, for the Ben and Jeff Show, for the good times, for the endless hours in a canoe, on the hardwater, at the concert grounds. Though every time we part it's uncertain if we'll ever laugh or speak again, at least we have the memories.

This novel is dedicated to Steph Korn. There's no one else I'd rather share the music, laughter, food, friends, books, television shows, walks, ideas, mornings, nights, ups, downs, sideways, struggles, and joys of this life with.

Finally, for Noa. May the better world that is just around the corner arrive in time for you to partake and thrive in.

Entertainment. Writing. Culture.

ECW is a proudly independent, Canadian-owned book publisher. We know great writing can improve people's lives, and we're passionate about sharing original, exciting, and insightful writing across genres.

Thanks for reading along!

We want our books not just to sustain our imaginations, but to help construct a healthier, more just world, and so we've become a certified B Corporation, meaning we meet a high standard of social and environmental responsibility — and we're going to keep aiming higher. We believe books can drive change, but the way we make them can too.

Being a B Corp means that the act of publishing this book should be a force for good — for the planet, for our communities, and for the people that worked to make this book. For example, everyone who worked on this book was paid at least a living wage. You can learn more at the Ontario Living Wage Network.

This book is also available as a Global Certified Accessible™ (GCA) ebook. ECW Press's ebooks are screen reader friendly and are built to meet the needs of those who are unable to read standard print due to blindness, low vision, dyslexia, or a physical disability.

This book is printed on FSC®-certified paper. It contains recycled materials, and other controlled sources, is processed chlorine free, and is manufactured using biogas energy.

ECW's office is situated on land that was the traditional territory of many nations, including the Wendat, the Anishinaabeg, Haudenosaunee, Chippewa, Métis, and current treaty holders the Mississaugas of the Credit. In the 1880s, the land was developed as part of a growing community around St. Matthew's Anglican and other churches. Starting in the 1950s, our neighbourhood was transformed by immigrants fleeing the Vietnam War and Chinese Canadians dispossessed by the building of Nathan Phillips Square and the subsequent rise in real estate value in other Chinatowns. We are grateful to those who cared for the land before us and are proud to be working amidst this mix of cultures.

ecwpress.com